NECESSITY

NECESSITY

JO WALTON

TOR

A TOM DOHERTY
ASSOCIATES BOOK
NEW YORK

NECESSITY

Copyright © 2016 by Jo Walton

Edited by Patrick Nielsen Hayden

A Tor Book
Published by Tom Doherty Associates, LLC
175 Fifth Avenue
New York, NY 10010

www.tor-forge.com

Tor® is a registered trademark of Tom Doherty Associates, LLC.

The Library of Congress Cataloging-in-Publication Data is available upon request.

ISBN 978-0-7653-7902-3 (hardcover)
ISBN 978-1-4668-6570-9 (e-book)

Our books may be purchased in bulk for promotional, educational, or business use.
Please contact your local bookseller or the Macmillan Corporate and Premium
Sales Department at 1-800-221-7945, extension 5442, or by e-mail at
MacmillanSpecialMarkets@macmillan.com.

First Edition: July 2016

Printed in the United States of America

0 9 8 7 6 5 4 3 2 1

This is for Ada,
who is not only wonderful but also real.

What leaf-fringed legends haunt about thy shape
Of deities or mortals, or of both,
In Tempe or the dales of Arkady?
What men or gods are these? What maidens loth?
What mad pursuit? What struggle to escape?
What pipes and timbrels? What wild ecstasy?

—Keats, "Ode on a Grecian Urn"

Socrates: Tell me then, oh tell me—what is the great and
    splendid work which the gods achieve with the help of
    our devotions?
Euthyphro: Many and fair are the works of the gods.

—Plato, *Euthyphro*

Answer me, answer me
Somebody answer me.
Oldest of questions and
Deepest of needs. Our
Mystery, mystery,
Teach us our history.
Lost all again
To the dark of the grave.

—Ada Palmer, "A New World"

And now the work is done that cannot be erased by
Jupiter's anger, fire and sword, nor the gnawing tooth of
time. Let the day, that has power only over my body, end
when it will my uncertain span of years. The best part
of me will be borne, immortal, beyond the distant stars.

—Ovid, envoi to *Metamorphoses*

NECESSITY

1

APOLLO

I have lived for a very long time however you measure it, but I never grew old before. I aged from birth to adulthood and stayed there, poised in the full power of glorious immortality. The mortal body I had taken up to experience and understand the joys and sorrows of human life aged as other mortal bodies age. My son Phaedrus, like my older son Asklepios, had healing powers. Our City had begun with a generation of ten-year-olds, and as our bodies aged he was kept permanently busy. Even with all he could do for us, aging was an undignified and uncomfortable process. Souls grow and flower and do not decline, so each mortal life inevitably ends with soaring souls enclosed in withered failing bodies. While death is necessary for rebirth, I could find neither necessity nor benefit in this slow ebbing of vitality.

I died on the day the first human spaceship contacted Plato. After that, I did all the things I'd been promising myself I'd do once I was back to my proper self. I established the laurel wreath as a symbol of poetic victory, in memory of Daphne. Then I spent a little while assembling the chronicles of the City—weaving together Maia's journals with Simmea's and Arete's, and composing a memoir of my own brief but intense period of mortality. Then I settled down to study sun formation, beginning with my own suns, naturally. Once I'd started looking into it, I became fascinated with the

whole process. The song of suns, the dance of gravity and hydro-
gen, the interplay of radiation and magnetism and heat, the excitement of the symphonic moment when it all comes together and
fusion begins—I never tire of it.

I can't say how long I spent alone studying the birth of suns. I
was outside time, and when I went into time, it was a time aeons
before the evolution of life. It's normal for me to live outside time,
and step into it as and where I choose. The years I spent incarnate
in the Just City were the exception. Then days and years unfolded in
inevitable and unchangeable sequence. My more usual experience is
personally sequential, but entirely separate from time, human
time, history. I could go off and study stellar nurseries in the early
days of the universe for as long as I liked without neglecting any
duties. I could pay attention to my duties afterwards, they'd still
be there. I could be aware of a prayer, watch the entire sequence of
a sun being formed, and then respond to that prayer in the same
moment it was uttered. (Not that I pay any more attention to the
constant dinning of prayer than any other god. That's only an example.) I can't be in time in the same moment twice, but that's not
much of a hardship, usually, because time splits up into extremely
small increments. Despite being the god of prophecy, I don't know
my own personal future any more than anyone else. I know what
happens in time, more or less, depending on how much attention
I've paid to it, exactly the same as you might know what happens
in history—some of it sharp, some of it fuzzy.

Studying sunbirth was good for me. It was a relief to be on my
own and not have to worry about other people and their significance. It was good to be able to focus completely on a fascinating
and abstract subject and forget about Plato for a while—both the
philosopher and the planet. I loved my children, and I loved Plato
and the society we had built struggling to implement his ideas. But
Homer calls the gods "untiring" as well as "deathless." Taking on
mortality, and living through that slow physical process of aging,

had made me understand for the first time what weariness meant. The study was a form of rest, renewal, and rebirth. It was fun, too. I like learning things, and suns are very close to my heart.

After a timeless while, I was interrupted by the sudden appearance of my little brother Hermes. He draped himself over the accretion disk of a sun forming from a particularly fascinating dust cloud, one full of ancient iron. For some reason, probably simply to irritate me, he chose to make himself so large that the disk looked like a couch he was lounging on. He looked like a youth on the cusp of manhood, an object of desire but filled with implicit power. "Playtime's over," he said.

I shot up to the same size and balanced poised in the same orientation against the glowing dust of the nebula. "What are you doing so far from civilization and everything you love?" I asked.

"Running Father's errands, as usual," he said, pursing his lips. "You know nothing less would get me so far away from people. What are you doing out here in the bleak emptiness?"

I thought it was beautiful, in its own way. "I'm fulfilling my primary function and working on how suns begin," I said. "For a god of travel, you do seem to hate going places."

"I'm not in charge of exploration of the wilderness," he said, bending to adjust his elegant winged sandals. They and his hat were all he wore—not only at that moment, but practically all the time. He enjoyed displaying his exquisite body and being admired. "I like travel and trade and markets and the way people arrange systems of communication. I like going to *places*. This isn't a *place*. I think this is the furthest from being a place of anywhere I've ever been. There's nothing out here for me, no civilization, no offerings, no possibilities for negotiation. Nothing but atoms and emptiness."

"Did you know people have equal significance?" I asked, suddenly reminded by what he had been saying. I'd promised Simmea I'd tell the gods. Putting together the chronicle was only the first part of that.

"To us? How could they have?" A frown briefly creased his golden brow. "They're mayflies."

"To each other. And their choices ought to count to us. They live long enough to achieve wonderful things, sometimes. And besides, a human lifetime is subjectively longer than you think. You should try incarnating yourself."

"Was it fun?"

I hesitated. He laughed.

"It was illuminating," I said, with as much dignity as I could manage. "I learned things I couldn't have learned any other way. I think we all ought to do it for what we can learn. We'll be better for it."

"I'll think about it. I have a number of projects I'm busy with right now. And instead I'm wasting my time coming all the way out here to the ass-end of nowhere to tell you that Father wants you to attend to your planet."

I looked at the accretion disk, poised at the moment of spinning up. "Now? Why now? He wants me to go to Plato in my personal now?"

"Does Father ever explain these things to you? He never does to me." He sounded bitter.

"It's a Mystery," I acknowledged.

"You haven't told anyone you have a planet. I must check it out."

"It's new," I said, reflexively defensive. "It's all Athene's fault, really. It's called Plato. It has people. And aliens. They're highly civilized. They worship us, well, most of them do. You have a lovely temple there with a statue by Praxiteles that Athene and Ficino rescued from the sack of Constantinople. Haven't you noticed people there praying to you? You'd be welcome to come and visit." I gestured in its general direction. "Drop in any time."

He ignored my jab as easily as he ignored prayers. "How did you get a whole planet?"

I sighed, seeing he wouldn't leave me alone until I explained. "Athene was setting up Plato's Republic, on Thera, before the Trojan War, before the Thera eruption. She had three hundred classicists and philosophers from across all of time, all people who had read Plato and prayed to her to help make the Republic real. She helped— that is, she used granting their prayers as a gateway. Really, she wanted to do it, so she did. As well as those people, the Masters, they bought ten thousand Greek-speaking slave children, and a set of big construction robots. The robots turned out to be sentient, only to start with nobody knew that. I incarnated there as one of the children. I learned a lot, from Sokrates and the others, and from the experience. I had friends, and children. When Father found out, he transported the whole lot of us to another planet four thousand years forward—and we were twelve cities by that time, all doing Plato's Republic in different and competing ways."

"And you're responsible for them?"

"Until my children are ready to be their pantheon, which shouldn't be long now. Why? Did you think Athene would end up getting stuck with it, after she tired of the project and moved on?"

He grinned. "It's hard to imagine. She always squeaks out of things. Well, you'd better get on and take care of them for her."

"For Father," I said. I was puzzled. I wondered why Father had sent this message. He must have known that I wouldn't neglect Plato. I didn't understand why there was any urgency about it. But I'd do it, of course. Nobody understood how Father knew anything, or how he prioritizes. Nor, for that matter, did we have any idea how he experiences time. He was there before it, after all. Mortals find it difficult to understand how we understand time, living outside it, but that's simple, compared to how it is for Father.

We're bound by our own actions, and, naturally, whether we're in or out of time, by Fate and Necessity. There's no getting around them. They make changing time extremely hard, and harder when we get away from our core concerns. And we're limited by Father's edicts, but only in so far as we respect them. They don't have the same inevitable force. If I got caught up with Fate or Necessity it wouldn't really be a matter of choice—resisting a force like that is almost impossible, even for me. But I could simply ignore Father's message if I wanted to. It was usually a terrible idea to ignore such things, because Father does know more than the rest of us and generally means well, and also because he could have made my life a misery if I went against him. There was this one time at Troy—but that's a different story. But it's not like being caught up with Necessity, which is a compulsion on the soul.

"What's this I hear about you playing my gift upside-down to beat somebody playing Athene's syrinx?" Hermes asked.

Hermes had invented the lyre when he was three days old, as a way to win my friendship after stealing some of my cows. He'd given it to me. He'd also promised never again to steal anything else of mine, a promise I didn't quite trust him to keep. He was much too fond of playing tricks.

"Yes, I played the lyre upside-down," I acknowledged. "Won the contest that way, too." The whole messy business seemed long ago and almost unimportant. I do enjoy being an Olympian and having a proper perspective.

"It sounds like something I'd do."

"Feel free to teach yourself to play it that way," I said, and grinned at him.

"Well, joy to you with all of it," wing-footed Hermes said, smiling as he departed.

So, with no foresight or warnings, and with one last longing look at the glowing disk (which would after all still be there and about to form into a sun whenever I wanted to come back into time at this moment to watch), I left too.

I was going to Plato, of course I was. I accepted Father's message that playtime was over, whether I liked it or not. But I wasn't quite ready. Another little while—another long subjective time—watching suns would have been exactly what I needed, but I wasn't going to disobey Father to that extent. I didn't want to mess up whatever mysterious plan he had, which presumably needed me to be still a little off balance. But I did have something to do first, something that would hardly take any personal time and couldn't possibly make any difference, and which would make a good transition. I had a date with Athene.

The date in question was 1564, the day in the spring of that year when the orange tree in the courtyard of the Medici Laurentian Library bloomed. Athene had arranged it herself, the last time I had seen her, on Olympos, at the time of the Relocation, when Zeus moved the Cities from Bronze Age Greece to Plato. It had been a peace offering, after everything that had happened. "When you get back," she had said. This would mark me being back. We could meet on neutral territory, in an extraordinary year, and after we'd talked I might feel better equipped for taking care of Plato. I wanted to see her. There were several things I wanted her to explain, and other things I wanted to explain to her. Parts of it I knew she'd never understand, but other parts of it she was the only person who ever could understand.

I hadn't talked to her in decades, and while decades might often pass without our talking, these years had been full of things I wanted to share with her. Her experiment in setting up Plato's Republic had had unexpected results, and had produced something genuinely new and of interest to both of us. The culture on Plato wasn't the ideal Republic Plato had described. As I'd said to Maia long ago, we all live on somebody's dunghill. But it was a completely different kind of human culture, one steeped in Platonism and philosophy and the dream of the classical world. And it was out there in the twenty-sixth century, vibrating with philosophical passion and full of people at least trying to lead the Good Life. I wanted to know what she thought about that, and share my thoughts. Creating Plato's Republic had been Athene's idea, after all, and lately I'd been wondering if there had been more to it than simply to see what happened and have somewhere to take Ikaros. Pico. I wanted to see him again too. I wanted to see his face when I told him what the Ikarians had made of his New Concordance since his apotheosis.

So I left that distant forming sun and stepped into time in Florence, in 1564, on the steps in front of the unfinished façade of the church of San Lorenzo. They were still waiting for Michelangelo to come and finish it, though he'd been dead for several months already. I remembered the inside of the church as a perfect Neoclassical space, but the outside now was rough and unfinished, jagged raw stone waiting for a facing it wouldn't get for another eight hundred years. The Florentines, having so much of it, weren't prepared to compromise on beauty. They'd wait for another Florentine artist of comparable skill to be born and finish it. An admirable perspective, if rare. I stepped inside for a moment to admire it—strangely, moving into the space always felt like going outside. The streets around San Lorenzo are narrow and crowded. Inside was full of light. The proportions were perfect, the pillars, the windows, the porphyry memorial set in the floor to celebrate the soul of Cosimo de Medici. I spared a fond thought for it, wherever it was, no doubt busily engaged in its new concerns. I felt perfectly at home in there. You'd hardly have known it was a Christian church.

I stepped back out of the church and walked around to the courtyard that led to the library. I didn't need to interact with anyone so I hadn't bothered to take a plausible disguise or find an excuse for visiting the library. I simply let the light flow around me and so became invisible. There were a few monks in the cloister. I sat down on the wall by the foot of the stairs that went up to Michelangelo's intimidating entranceway—one of the projects he had managed to finish. The sun was coming down into the courtyard, my own familiar golden sunlight. The scent of blossom from the tree was heady. Here too the pillars and proportions were perfectly right. But although the library was open, there was no sign of Athene. I sat there for a while enjoying the sunlight and the scent and thinking. It was quiet in the cloister, with distant muted street sounds, and close by only the humming of bees and the occasional swish of a monk's robe to disturb me. I didn't disturb them at all. If anything, I'd have looked like a brighter patch of sunlight.

After an hour of waiting, I stepped outside time, and checked the courtyard at other times throughout the day. When I still couldn't find Athene I tried the day before, in case, but the orange blossom wasn't quite out, and she wasn't there anyway.

I went up to the library—directly, stepping into that wonderful room from outside time, to avoid the effect of Michelangelo's deliberately daunting staircase. I looked around. I was accustomed now to the library in the City, with its controlled temperature, electric lights, and all the books of the ancient world rescued from the Library of Alexandria in multiple neatly printed copies. But this was more moving—the high windows giving light to work, the patterned tiles on the floor, the wooden benches with the books chained to them and scholars sitting reading and working. The books themselves were mostly hand-copied texts, preserved through time, saved from the ruins, written out painstakingly. They lost Homer for a time, but they got him back. Ficino had worked here. They had the oldest and most complete copy of the *Aeneid*. These books were here because people had cared about them, individually, cared enough to copy them and pass them forward across centuries and civilizations, hand stretching out to human hand through time, with no surety that any future hand would be waiting to receive the offering. All the texts from antiquity that had survived the time between were in this room. But Athene wasn't.

It was inexplicable. I had the day right, but she wasn't here. She couldn't have forgotten! Perhaps I had. It had been forty years for me, and perhaps I had confused the year. If so, there was no use guessing. I'd have to go and find her, in her own library, or wherever she was. I patted the sloping wood of the nearest bench, putting a little of my power into it so that those who worked there would see more clearly. It was such a beautiful room, about as close to perfect as any mortal thing can be. I stepped out of time.

Once outside time, I felt for Athene. It's difficult to describe. Usually when I do it, I get a sensation like an itch that leads me towards whoever I'm looking for, like a compass, if one were the needle. This time, I got nothing at all.

Of course, the first thing I thought was that this was a power I hadn't tested since I had taken up my godhood again, and that I'd lost the ability, or forgotten how to do it. It was distressing. No, that's not strong enough. Even in my proper self, it felt horrible to think that I might have damaged myself, made myself limited, permanently lost parts of my abilities. I stepped back into time and sat in the courtyard until my sun warmed away the chill that thought brought. I wanted to change, but I wanted to grow more excellent, always: better, not worse. Experiencing the physical decay that went with old age had been bad enough. But with those losses I could tell myself not only that it was temporary, but that I was understanding humanity better by learning about what they went through. There would be no advantage to this.

I stepped out of time again and felt for Athene once more. Still nothing. I tried Artemis. To my intense relief, I sensed her immediately. She was on the moon, at a time when people lived there and had built temples to her. I tried Athene again, and again felt nothing. Aphrodite was on Olympos. Hera was in classical Argos. Dionysos was in Hellenistic Baktria. Hephaistos was in his forge. Hades was in the Underworld. Hermes was in the marketplace in Alexandria. But no matter how many times I tried, Athene was nowhere to be found.

Strange as it was that I couldn't locate her, it was stranger still that she hadn't shown up when she was supposed to meet me. That wasn't like her at all. I was worried. I couldn't imagine what could have happened to prevent her. Fate and Necessity might tangle us up, but we're still there. I reached for her again. Where could she possibly be? She didn't seem to be anywhere in or out of time. Could she be dead? How? It didn't bear thinking of.

2

JASON

I'm only a Silver, so don't expect too much. My name is Jason, of the Hall of Samos and the Tribe of Hermes. I was born in the Year Forty-two of the City, eleven years after the Relocation. I work on a fishing boat. I haven't written anything long since I qualified as a citizen thirteen years ago. These two days I'm going to tell you about changed my life completely. Since Fate caught me up in great events, I'll do my best to set things down clearly, in case it can do anyone good to read about what happened and what we all said and did.

Amphitrite had been kind, and we'd had a good haul that day, lots of ribbers and a few red gloaters, big ones. They were all heading north with the winter currents, so we simply had to stay in place and use the fine nets to scoop them out. We joked about sticking our hands into the water and pulling out a fish, the kind of day that redeems all the other days where we came home with thin hauls or none. Plato's a hard planet for humans, and we depend on the catch to have enough protein.

It was chilly and grey out on the ocean, spitting with rain. As we headed homewards around Dawn Point the east wind caught us. I fastened my jerkin up to my throat. The other boats coming in made positive signals. Everyone seemed to have had a good day. It was the kind of thing to cheer your liver. We passed a flatboat gathering suface kelp, which the Saeli like to eat, and even they signalled that they had a good haul.

Our boat was called *Phaenarete* after a girl Dion had known who was killed in the Battle of Lucia. Dion had been the first one to sail her, so he'd had the choice of naming her. He had taught me everything I knew about handling boats, and fishing too, and a lot about how to live. We were as close as father and son, and closer than many such because we'd chosen each other. Dion was too old to go out regularly now, and Leonidas and Aelia were dead, so I was in charge of *Phaenarete*, and I had a crew of lunatics. Well, that's not a kind way to put it, but that's how I thought of them.

Now, fishing is essential, everyone knows that, and it's also reasonably dangerous—even if you know what you're doing you can get caught out by a squall or an underwater eruption—or the usual kind of eruption, come to that. That's what happened to Aelia and Leonidas five years back. Their luck ran out.

It's not really all that dangerous. Most days most of us come back. And we need the catch, we rely on it. There are no land animals on Plato, only what we brought with us, and the sheep and goats don't thrive here the way they did in Greece, where they could graze on plants growing wild everywhere. Dion remembers Greece and talks about it sometimes, but it sounds strange to me, the idea of plants sprawling all over, plants nobody planted and nobody tends to. There's none of that on Plato. Our plants take a lot of attention. We have to nurse them along. Keeping them alive is hard work for a lot of people, human and Workers. And we like eating them! But we want protein too, so we encourage the sheep and goats to give lots of milk and we don't often eat them, only at special festivals. And so fish are very important, and fishing is important, and worth the risk.

It's not only our City, the Remnant, that relies on the fish. We salt and smoke and freeze them and send them to the inland cities. Back in Greece, before Zeus brought them here, all the cities had been on islands in a warm sea, a deep blue sea with coasts close all around. (It's hard to imagine a warm sea, though I've seen enough pictures of it to have a good idea of the color.) Now we and the Amazons are on the coast of a cold ocean, which has islands and other continents that we've only partly explored. The other cities, still in the same positions relative to us and to each other, are scattered about inland on a volcanic plain. Fortunately the Workers have built the electric rail, so we can move goods and people relatively easily. And fish are an important part of that, and only we and the Amazons can fish, so we do. And because fishing is both important and somewhat dangerous, naturally it's classified as Silver.

Now, being properly Platonic, which we do try to be most of the time here in the Original City, that ought to mean everyone who works on a fishing boat is Silver. And most of the time that's true. But for fishing, you need a minimum of two people, and three or four is better. And at that time I had two crazy crew members who weren't Silvers at all. Hilfa is Saeli, which wouldn't stop him being a citizen and having a metal; plenty of Saeli have taken their oaths. But Hilfa was young, not that I had any idea what that meant for a Saeli. And at that time, he wasn't yet part of a pod the way most grown Saeli are. He had only been here for two years. He told me he was still studying—though whether he was studying us or fish or what, I didn't know. And I say "he" but that's not clear at all either. The Saeli need three genders to reproduce, but most of the time they don't take any notice of gender at all, and while they have a bunch of pronouns for different things, gender isn't one of them. Hilfa said "he" feels most comfortable for him in Greek, so that's what I used. What he has between his legs seemed to be a sort of scrunched-up green walnut shell. I saw it often enough, because on the boat he mostly wore a red webbing vest and nothing else, being as Saeli are pretty much comfortable naked in temperatures that make humans want to huddle up. Dion says in Greece we were comfortable naked, and what that says to me is that we should have stayed there and let the Saeli have Plato. Not that they're native here either; far from it. They showed up in a spaceship about twenty years ago, meaning twenty years after our Relocation. They first came here when I was ten. And weren't we pleased to see them after trying to deal with the weird Amarathi! Before we met the Saeli, dealing with the Amarathi was almost a full-time job for Arete, being as their language is so odd that she was the only one who could speak to them at all and have any hope of getting through.

So I had Hilfa on the boat every day, and he's maybe not as strong as a human, and sometimes he does things that make no sense, but he's better adapted to the temperatures, and he's keen, always at work on time and ready to stay on late if needed. It was Dion's decision to take him on, a year and a half ago, when Dion was still going out most of the time, before he broke his leg slipping on the icy deck last winter. (I told you it was dangerous.) Dion's lucky it was his leg and not his neck, and lucky Hilfa caught him before he slid off the side and into the water. I'd not been sure about Hilfa at first, but I'd come to appreciate him even before that. After that, of course, green hide or not, he might as well have been my brother.

My other crew member was even stranger, in her way. Marsilia's not an alien, but she's aristocracy. Not only that she's a Gold, which ought to mean she spends her time on politics and philosophy, not fishing; but her father's Neleus, and his stepfather is Pytheas. I wasn't going to refuse her when she came asking, was I? But truthfully, it wasn't so much because her dad had been consul umpty-ump times or her step-grandfather was a god in mortal form, or that she'd recently been elected consul herself. It was because I'd been in love with her sister Thetis since we were both fifteen and in the same shake-up class coming up to qualifications. Not that Thee had ever looked at me. I'd always been too shy to say anything to her about how I felt.

I used to wonder sometimes how it was that Thetis and Marsilia were sisters. Thetis looks like a goddess—tall, but slight of frame, so her breasts look like every boy's dream of breasts, or maybe only mine, I don't know. She has a broad brow, hair the color of obsidian flowing down her back, soft brown eyes—well, I suppose to be fair Marsilia has the same eyes. But you don't notice them as much because Marsilia's face is flat, and she has jutting teeth. Their skin is the same velvety brown. But Marsilia's squat, with broad hips, which is good for the boat. She keeps her hair short, like most people. Thee looks fragile, but Marsilia can pull a full net out of the water. Marsilia definitely takes after Neleus, and so I'd think Thetis takes after their mother, but Erinna is the Captain of the *Excellence*, and anyone less fragile you have never seen. Even now, when she must be sixty, Erinna has muscles on her muscles, as they say.

It's funny when you think about it.

The way we interpret Plato's intentions here now, we have regular Festivals of Hera, where people get paired up and married for the day, and hopefully babies are born as a result. We also allow long-term marriage, and participation in our Festivals of Hera is voluntary, which it isn't in Athenia and Psyche. It wasn't here to start with. There was a while when we didn't have any Festivals of Hera, because of that, but we voted to reintroduce them on a voluntary basis years ago, I'm not quite sure when. It was after the Relocation, but before I was born. If you volunteer, you get matched up with a partner by lot, and you spend a day in bed together. All the children born from that festival are considered to be your children. When a woman has a baby, she can either choose to bring it up herself or give it to the nurseries to be brought up there, whatever she prefers. It's her choice, some do one and some do the other. Probably about half of us grow up in nurseries and sleeping houses, and the rest in families. I was festival-born myself. I don't have any idea who my parents were, and not much curiosity about it either. When I took my oath at sixteen, along with all the other

sixteen-year-olds, everyone who had participated in that festival
seventeen years before and was still alive came along to the pro-
cession and the feast afterwards.

So with the marriages at the Festivals of Hera, all the pairings
are arranged within the same metal, always, because they say that's
what leads to the best children. When it comes to other kinds of
marriage, people are supposed to choose people of their own kind
too, to keep the metals from mixing more than they're mixed already. But we're human, and the metals in our souls are already
mixed up, the way metals are under the ground, and so although
everyone tries to discourage you, it's not forbidden to marry someone of a different class. (Here, anyway. It is forbidden in some of
the Lucian cities. In Athenia and Psyche they don't have marriage
except for the Festivals of Hera, in Sokratea they don't have classes,
and in Amazonia they have lots of orgies and hope for the best, or
that's what I've heard, though I didn't see anything like that the one
time I was there.) Even if you do have parents of the same metal,
you can't tell how the kids will come out.

So anyway, Erinna and Neleus got married, way back, even
though she's Silver and he's Gold. And they did mix up the metals,
and Marsilia is Gold, as I said, and she works on my boat what
time she's not too busy with Chamber affairs. But her sister Thetis
is Iron, and she works with little children.

Looking at it that way, even though she's from a family with a
god in it, I should feel Thetis is below me. I always felt the opposite, though, that she's infinitely above me. It's not that she's the most
beautiful woman on the planet. But she's extremely beautiful, and—
she's Thee. Every time I see her my blood pounds in my veins, and
that has been the case since we were both fifteen and I first met her
in Arete's communication class. I thought she didn't care about me
at all. I figured she knew who I was—Jason who took his oath the
same time she did and worked on the same boat her sister works
on. I doubted she thought about me once a month. I didn't see her

all that often. But when I did, even if I only caught sight of her in the agora, I was happy for days afterwards. I didn't want anything from her, simply for her to exist and for me to see her sometimes. Maybe this is the kind of love Plato talks about in the *Phaedrus*, I don't know. No, because I always knew I'd be only too delighted to make it carnal, if that could be an option. But I thought it couldn't, and there it was. What I thought is that it didn't do her any harm for me to feel this way about her, and it did me a lot of good, because it gave me something in my life that was special, that lifted it above the everyday.

Marsilia pulled one of the gloaters out of the tub as Hilfa and I set our tack. Once that was done there was nothing to do for the moment but glide smoothly into the harbor. "It's so big, and it looks so delicious. I could almost eat it right now, raw!" She mimed taking a bite.

I laughed. "I hope some of these get to the tables while they're still fresh and they don't decide to salt them all down. How about you? Do you fancy it, Hilfa?"

Hilfa laughed his slightly forced laugh. He'd learned it the way he'd learned Greek. A laugh was a word to him, a part of human communication. I didn't know whether the Saeli really laughed or not. I'd learned to read Hilfa's expressions, a little, working with him for so long, and I thought one of them meant amusement, but I wasn't sure. He knew I was joking about him eating a fish, but I didn't know if he really understood what a joke was, or why I might think it was funny to make one. "I don't eat fish," he said, seriously.

"Silly Hilfa. Why do you work on a fishing boat if you don't eat fish?" I teased.

"I like the waves and the wind," Hilfa said, seriously. I wondered whether he would stay and take oath or leave for another planet on some Saeli ship. I hoped he'd stay. I liked him. And he might. He liked the waves and the wind, after all.

"We're glad to have you working with us," Marsilia said, as the jib came around a final time.

"Also I can study the Platonic fish," Hilfa said, entirely serious, as usual. "The radial symmetry of fish on this planet is fascinating. Everything in this ocean is symmetrical. I keep hoping we will one day pull something out that isn't, but we never do."

"We're never going to," I said, thinking of mosaics of Greek fish and their strange stretched shapes. Then I saw Marsilia stiffen, staring at the quay.

"Trouble," she said, then shook her head at me as she saw me twitch. "Only for me. Probably some kind of political disruption. We're signing a new foreign relations treaty, and maybe some of our negotiations came unstuck." She let the gloater slide back into the tub. "It looks as if I'm going to have to rush off. Can you two manage unloading without me?"

"Of course," I said, without even a sigh. Knowing that she'd have to dash off to a crisis, or have one prevent her from showing up now and then, was all part of having Marsilia working for me. I wondered sometimes whether part of the attraction of working on the boat for her was the fact she couldn't be interrupted while we were out at sea. But I knew a lot of it was that the sea was in her blood, from her mother—she too liked the waves and the wind.

I was easing *Phaenarete* into dock, so I didn't see who had come to interrupt Marsilia this time until we were ready to tie up. I got ready to toss the line, and saw to my astonishment Crocus standing ready to catch it. And behind him, wrapped in a silvery-grey cloak that rippled in the wind, stood Thetis. My breath caught, as always. I wished somebody would paint her like that, in that cloak, on a cloudy day, standing on the little grey triangular cobblestones of the quay, with the black stone warehouses with their slit windows all along behind her. If they did, I'd want them to put the painting in Samos, my eating hall, where I could stare at it when-

ever I ate. Thetis had a grace and poise like the nymphs in Botticelli's *Summer*, but a far lovelier face.

Crocus caught the rope with the attachments at the end of one
of his great arms. I saw the golden bee painted on it flash as it caught
the light. I said Marsilia was an aristocrat, and she is, but compared
to Crocus she was little better than me. Crocus was a Worker, a
machine, huge and metallic, one of our two original Workers. He
had huge arms, no head, and great treads instead of legs. He and
Sixty-One were the only people who had been here for the entire
history of the City. He had been a friend of Sokrates. He was a Gold,
one of our philosopher kings. He was probably the most famous
person on the planet who wasn't a god. I had friends among the
younger Workers, but I had never even spoken to Crocus.

He tied the line rapidly and deftly around the bollard. "I can't
imagine what use he could ever have had for that skill," Marsilia
said in my ear.

I was staring past him at Thetis, who was crying. It made her
look lovelier than ever, beautiful and vulnerable and sad, in need
of protection. "Do you know what's wrong with her?" I asked.

"Thee? It could be anything. She cries really easily." She sounded
much more irritated than sympathetic.

"Why are you so unkind to her?" I asked.

"Is that unkind?" Marsilia asked. "I try not to be. I love her. She's
my sister. But she's all emotion and no thought, and I'm the opposite. It's hard to be sisters. Everything seems to come so easily to her.
Do you think if I looked like that, people would look at me the way
you're looking at her? Do you think I'd want them to?"

"It's hard to imagine you wanting them to," I said.

Marsilia snorted. The quay was near enough for her to spring
ashore, and she did.

"We can manage if you have a family emergency," Hilfa said. I
don't know where he got expressions like that from.

"Trouble?" she asked Crocus, ignoring Thetis.

"News, and a complication," he replied, in his slightly odd mechanical voice. Before either of them could say anything more, Thetis ran towards Marsilia, who braced herself and clutched her barely in time to prevent both of them falling over the edge of the quay into the icy water. "Grandfather's dead," Thetis said.

That was news. Old Pytheas, Apollo himself. He was one of the Children, and so he must have been eighty or thereabouts, but he'd seemed well enough when I'd seen him singing at the Festival of Artemis a few days before. What did it mean for an incarnate god to die?

Marsilia patted Thee's back and made soothing noises. Hilfa went to fetch the cart to get the fish into the warehouse. I began to swing the heavy tubs of fish onto the hoist, to be ready when he came back with it.

"Is this the news or the complication?" Marsilia asked Crocus. She sounded taken off balance. It must be strange to have a grandfather who's a god. I wondered what she felt about him.

"Neither," he responded. "Though I should give you my condolences. The news and the complication are the same thing." Because he didn't have eyes, I had no way to tell where he was looking. I couldn't tell whether he was paying any attention to me at all. I looked away from Marsilia and poor Thetis and saw Hilfa coming back with the cart. Dion was helping him push it over the cobblestones, and little Camilla came skipping along beside them. I was looking at them, and moving the tubs on their swivel along the sloping deck, and I almost didn't take it in when Crocus said: "A human spaceship is in orbit."

"That changes everything," Marsilia said, suddenly all practical, the way she was when we were out with the nets. "Thee, stop crying, it's un-Platonic. I have to go."

"Marsilia! You can't go off and worry about spaceships right after Grandfather has died," Thetis said, outraged.

"Oh yes I can," Marsilia said. "And Dad will do the same."

"Neleus is already in the Chamber," Crocus confirmed. "I came to fetch you for the sake of speed."

"Hilfa says you have a good haul!" Dion said, as he came up. "Joy to you, Marsilia, Thetis, Crocus."

Camilla ran to me and put her arms up to be swung onto the boat. I heaved her aboard and hugged her. "Gloaters!" she exclaimed. A human spaceship, I was thinking, recontact with the mainstream of human civilization at last. And Pytheas dead. Everything had changed and nothing had. Hilfa came aboard beside me. I swung the first tub up so that the fish that filled it cascaded down into the cool boxes on the cart in a swirl of red and black.

Marsilia looked up. "Dion, how lovely to see you. I have a crisis. If I borrow Jason, could you and Hilfa manage the unloading?"

"Borrow me?" I asked, jumping ashore, leaving Hilfa and Camilla aboard. "What for?" I couldn't imagine how she might need me in dealing with a strange human culture, but of course I was prepared to do my best.

Marsilia detached Thetis from her shoulder and gave her a gentle push towards me. "Can you take Thee home?" Ah, of course. She didn't need help with the big problem, but with the immediate human problem. Well, that was more to my scale.

"To Thessaly," Crocus interjected.

"You should come too, Marsilia," Thetis said. I put my arm around her. Hilfa was already tipping the next tub of fish into the cart.

"I will come, and so will Dad, as soon as we've dealt with this crisis," Marsilia said.

"But I'm sure there's a plan for dealing with it, and what does it matter anyway?" Thetis asked. "You can't put politics ahead of family."

"There has been a plan for this meeting since the consulship of Maia and Klio, but the question is whether people will follow the plan in the face of events," Marsilia said. "This is one of the most important things that has ever happened, Thee. Oh, it'll be so wonderful to talk to them."

"Perhaps," Crocus said, cautiously.

"You don't think so?" Marsilia asked, sounding surprised.

"I knew the Masters longer and better than you did," Crocus said. "I have apprehensions about what recontact could mean. I have watched the generations maturing in the Cities, and seen how each one is more Platonic than the last as we grow further from other human cultures. Plato was wrong to want to start with ten-year-olds. They should have started with babies. The Children remembered their original cultures too well. Your father's generation, the Young Ones, were the first generation to know nothing but the City. And your generation are in an even better position. These days we take the pursuit of excellence for granted, and go on from there. Each new generation so far has been better. Perhaps recontact with the human cultures that have developed from the ones the Masters came from will indeed be wonderful. I hope so. But I have reservations."

"But we'll have so much to share with them," Marsilia said. "We've developed so much. And we have the works of classical civilization that were lost to them. We have everything we've learned about applying Platonism and reconciling it to other systems. The aliens didn't know anything about Plato until we explained to them. But the humans are bound to be excited."

"This is a whole new civilization," Crocus said. "We know less about them than we do about the aliens. In some ways they will seem more familiar, yes, and we will share some cultural referents. In other ways they might surprise us more. They might have very different priorities. Many of the Masters came from times that did not value the classical world as it should be valued. I remember Klio and Lysias talking about what misfits they had been in their own times. And Lysias, who came from the mid-twenty-first century, was the last Master. Nobody from any time later than that had read the *Republic* in Greek and prayed to Athene to help set it up, or they would have been here. No Workers ever did. That isn't a good sign. Besides, there were other human civilizations, on other continents of Earth, which had their own philosophical traditions and might not know or care anything about Platonism."

"I don't care about Platonism either, or the aliens. And whatever they're like, they'll still be there tomorrow, and going off to a debate on the day when Grandfather has died is heartless," Thetis said.

"I'm consul. I think Grandfather would agree I should be there. And I really do have to go," Marsilia said, climbing up onto Crocus's back and taking hold of the braided blue and black web of harness that hung there. "Dion, Jason, thank you."

I wanted to thank her as she and Crocus disappeared up the hill. This was the closest I had ever been to Thetis, and I was going to go with her all the way to Thessaly.

3

MARSILIA

I was woken the morning of the day when it all began by my daughter Alkippe bouncing on my stomach. It may not be the best way to wake up, but it's far from the worst one. "Why are you still asleep?" she asked. I was often up before she was, up and washed and dressed and getting on with my morning. Now the sun was high, and casting a bright square of red-gold morning light on the foot of the bed, but I felt as if I could do with another whole night's sleep.

"Yesterday was a long day," I said.

"It can't have been longer than nineteen hours. That's how long days are." Alkippe had that didactic tone kids always get when they're beginning to learn how to muster facts for an argument.

"When people say they had a long day, they mean they made part of the night into day and didn't get enough sleep. Or that a lot of things happened so it was an extremely busy day." I yawned.

"It's not a very precise term."

"When people are talking about how they feel, precision isn't always what you want. You asked me why I was still asleep, and the answer is because I felt I had a long day. It doesn't matter how many hours it was; what matters is how it felt, and so why I was still sleepy."

"Why did it feel long?" she asked.

"Well I had lots of meetings, and lots of fishing. It's the time of year when fishing is the best, and that means it's more work. It's good really."

"Sosothis says that people should only do one job, the job for which they're best suited. He says that's what Plato says, and that doing two jobs is un-Platonic." She looked unhappy. I'd heard this often enough from other people already.

"Working on the boat with Jason and Hilfa is my recreation," I said.

"But maybe you wouldn't be so tired if you didn't do it?"

"I wouldn't, but I wouldn't have so much fun either. And we might not have as much fish, and fish is good. So I'm going to carry on doing it whatever Sosothis says, or anyone else either. People complained about it when I was running for consul, but they elected me anyway, so there we are." I could still hardly believe I was consul, consul in my year, at thirty-five, elected to planetary office at the youngest possible age.

"Let's wash together!" Alkippe said, bouncing. She grinned at me, and I saw that she had lost a front tooth.

"Yes, that will be fun." She usually washed with Thetis. I rolled her around so that she was sitting on the edge of the bed. "You used to be small enough that I could swing you up off my stomach. Now you're getting almost too heavy for me to roll."

"Was I really small? Was I as small as a walnut?"

"When you were as small as a walnut you were inside my belly. When you first came out you were the size of both of Granddad's hands put together. But you keep on growing and growing." I smiled at her.

"I'm seven and a half. Next I'll be seven and three-quarters, then eight, then eight and a quarter, then eight and a half, then—"

I stood and stretched as Alkippe demonstrated her grasp of counting by fractions, which was her favorite game this month. I prayed to Zeus, father of gods and men, that she would reach all those ages, and beyond them, ninety-nine and a half, ninety-nine and three-quarters . . . Her empty bed was a crumpled mess. Thetis's bed against the far wall was neatly made. I couldn't hear Ma and Dad moving around on the other side of the partition either. "We must be really late. Come on, quick!"

We ran into the fountain room. "What are you doing today? Fishing or meetings? Or fishing and meetings?" Alkippe called.

"Meeting this morning, if I haven't missed it, and then fishing this afternoon."

"Granddad would have woken you in time so you wouldn't miss the meeting," Alkippe pointed out.

"True." She was so smart, she lapped up learning, and she had that kind of common sense too, like Ma, because she was absolutely right, Dad wouldn't have let me miss the meeting.

My life was good and full of daily pleasures. In addition to the satisfactions of my political work, I had valuable and healthy work fishing, where I could see Jason every day and keep an eye on Hilfa. I enjoyed my food. I loved Alkippe more and more each day as she came to the age of reason. I had Dad's full approval, and now that I had been elected I felt worthy of it. I made a real effort to get on with Ma and Thetis, and even though they sometimes seemed more alien to me than the Saeli, I had been doing better at this recently. So things were going along smoothly and my life was good. I'd hug Alkippe, or put my back into hauling nets with Jason and Hilfa, or get some groups to agree to a compromise in Chamber, and realize all at once that I was happy. I also felt I was doing what Plato wanted, though I suppose strictly speaking he wouldn't have had me doing it until I was fifty.

The morning was all meetings, and there was an important debate scheduled for the evening. But in between, I went out on *Phaenarete* on the tide and had a delightfully busy afternoon hauling in fish. After a day out on the ocean, I had expected a couple of hours to get ready for the evening's Council session. At the very least, I'd have appreciated a hot drink to warm myself up, and time to change into a formal kiton. As it was, Crocus collected me on the quayside and I had to take the chair in my fishy work clothes, on no notice, and deal with the most difficult and controversial of all topics—human recontact, and what the gods really want us to do. Oh, and Grandfather was dead, and I hadn't had any time yet to think through what that meant.

Chamber was filled with a babble of voices, human and Worker. Nobody was in the chair, and only a few people were sitting down. Everyone seemed to be waving their hands in the air and raising their voices. All the members of the Council of Worlds and half the Senate seemed to be here, crowding in together along with a few random concerned citizens—all Golds, of course. I looked at Crocus for help. Because he didn't have a head I could never tell where his focus was, but he must have seen my glance. "You're chair tonight, Marsilia," he said.

"That's right," Dad said. "You're consul, take charge."

They had each been consul multiple times and knew much better than I did how to take charge of the Chamber. I'd have been vastly reassured with either one of them in the chair, and so would everyone else. But Dad was right. I'd be judged on how I acted in this emergency. I took a deep breath, wiped my suddenly sweaty palms on my thighs, and walked down towards the chair. Maia had sat there, and Dad, and before them legendary figures like Ficino and Tullius and Krito. I was thirty-five years old, and I was consul. And it wasn't ambition, or anyway not in a bad way. I didn't only want the glory. I wanted to serve Plato. I might wish in my cowardly liver that somebody else were in charge in this crisis, but it was my responsibility, so I swallowed hard and did my job.

"... any of Pytheas's children!" Diotima was saying loudly, her voice cutting above the babble. She was my fellow consul. I had mixed feelings about her. Our names would be recorded together forever in the name of the year, though I didn't know her well or like her much. She came from Athenia, and was polite and religious and conventionally Platonic. She was small and neatly made, with dark smooth hair, silvering now. She was fifty or so, since nobody can run for planetary office without having read *The Republic,* and Athenia, always stricter than everyone else, still did not allow their citizens to read it before they turned fifty. Here in the Remnant we read it as ephebes, as soon as we had taken our oaths of citizenship at sixteen, after our shake-up year at fifteen. Golds and Silvers have to read it, and the others can if they choose. It always surprises me how many people don't bother, or give up part way through.

I sat down in the chair. "Quiet," I said, much too quietly. Crocus echoed me loudly, and everyone fell silent and stared at me. "I call this emergency session of the Council of Worlds to order," I said. "Members of the Council and senators may remain. Others should leave."

A handful of people left. Everyone else sat down, higgledy-piggledy where they were, like stories of the earliest days of the Council eighty years ago when Sokrates had been here and regularly violated procedure. Some of the benches had been replaced since then, but many of them were the same. I found that both comforting and intimidating. Crocus rolled over and settled himself in the section where benches had been removed to make a space for Workers, and humans in wheelchairs.

"Who has the details of what has happened?" I asked.

Klymene, one of the Children, and the oldest person still serving on the Council, stood up. She was bony and wrinkled, and looked as if she were made of old tanned leather. Her hair was no more than a straggle of thin white strands stretched over her scalp. She had the log of our communication with the ship, and summarized it for us in her thin elderly voice. "They don't speak Greek or Latin.

We started off using Amarathi, and were at the point of asking
Arete to help when Sixty-One worked out that they were speaking
a variant of English, which it could mostly understand. So after a
brief delay we were able to communicate with them that way. They
are humans, not from Earth but from a planet called—" she
squinted at the printout, holding it farther away from her eyes,
"Marhaba, but they have been to Earth. They asked permission to
land and wanted to know who we were. According to the plan, we
told them the name of the planet and that our cities were founded
seventy years ago. They have also been in communication with the
Saeli ship in orbit."

"Where's Aroo?" I asked, realizing for the first time as I looked
for her that none of our Saeli senators or councillors were present.

"Not here. But the meeting isn't due to begin for an hour and a
half. We all came here now because we heard the news. The Saeli
don't think that way," Dad said.

"It would be good to make some decisions quickly, and we need
information. Can somebody find Aroo and bring her back here?" I
asked. I looked around for people who Aroo was likely to pay attention to, and noticed Parmenion sitting near Crocus. "Parmenion?"
He had been consul three years ago, a quiet man in his forties, an
excellent lyre-player and composer.

He nodded, accepting the errand, and rolled his chair out.

"Meanwhile," I said, looking out over the room, at my friends
and allies and political rivals, "we have a plan for this situation. It's
been in place since Maia and Klio were consuls. Unless there's some
really good reason not to follow it, that's what we ought to be doing,
not running around in circles trying to make new decisions in advance of information."

"We have been following the plan so far," Klymene said. She
hadn't moved. Though she was frail with age, she still stood straight-
backed. It was easy to imagine her leading troops in the art raids
long ago.

I nodded, and she went back to her seat, squeezing in on the end of a bench next to Dad, who moved up to make room.

"The plan is that we find out as much as we can about them, and when they ask about us we tell them the truth as an origin myth, expecting that they won't believe it," I said. "Maia wrote that this was what Zeus wanted."

"I can confirm that," Dad said. He had actually been on Mount Olympus and talked to Zeus at the time of the Relocation. "Porphyry said it, and Zeus seemed to agree."

"So what happens if they do believe it?" Diotima asked. "What happens if they use carbon dating?"

"Carbon dating will show nothing to surprise anyone, as the atoms have not existed through all the time between," Crocus said. "But that's an extremely interesting philosophical question. Would it change everything for humanity if we gave them all proof that the gods exist and care, and interfere with our lives?"

"Ikaros said, and Zeus didn't disagree, that it was better for us to discover things for ourselves. But all of us on Plato know, unavoidably, and we certainly haven't hidden it from our alien allies," Dad said.

"It's not the sort of thing that's usually a problem in everyday life," Halius said. He was the youngest person present, a representative from Marissa, very enthusiastic. He was fair-skinned and blond, and he always reminded me of a spring lamb, dashing off in all directions, shaking his tail with enthusiasm. "And it doesn't stop people debating about religion. There are people born since the Relocation who don't believe in it. And there are Ikarians in Amazonia who'll argue with Porphyry to his face that they understand what he is and what that means better than he does."

"Call them followers of the New Concordance, not Ikarians," I said, wearily, in advance of the forest of hands raised by Ikarian senators. "You know that, Halius."

Halius nodded in the direction of the Ikarians. "Apologies," he said. Of course, everyone called them Ikarians all the time and they knew it. They believed in a strange syncretic version of Christianity which had been invented by Ikaros. After Ikaros became a god (or, according to them, an angel, though do not ask an Ikarian what the difference is unless you have a lot of spare time), they took this as proof of his theories. Older people say the New Concordance has changed a lot since Ikaros's apotheosis.

Dad was asking for permission to speak, and I granted it, relieved. "Even if some people do believe when they've seen the proof, it's likely that most people won't," Dad said. "Athene said it could block off other paths to enlightenment. But it would only do that if everyone knew and believed it. And they wouldn't. They might read accounts of Phaedrus and the volcanoes, or the bodies of the Children disappearing at death, and so on, but they would think other people had been fooled. It's only a problem for people who actually come here and see incontrovertible evidence, and that will only be a few people. Nobody else would have proof."

Androkles raised a hand to be recognized, and I nodded to him. He was a bearded man about my own age, from Sokratea. His son Xanthus was one of Alkippe's playmates.

"I haven't thought about this much before," he began. "But why are we obeying the gods in this? Telling the truth, and proving it with rigorous philosophy and evidence, seems to me better than lying by misdirection. I'd like to hear from our own gods on this, from Pytheas and his children, to hear their arguments. There may be good reasons for it, but I want to hear them. I see no inherent reason why we should follow the dictates of Zeus merely because he issued them. We know the gods aren't inherently good. Or wise."

"They could smite us with lightning or turn us into flies," Diotima pointed out.

"That's a terrible reason to obey them, out of fear of their bad temper," Androkles replied without hesitation.

"They do know more than we do," Dad said. "They have an inherently wider perspective."

"Good! Then let them come here and make their points," Androkles said. "Let's hear the explanation for why we should keep the truth from wider humanity, and see whether we agree. And if they turn this Chamber into a buzzing cloud of flies, then we'll know they didn't have a good argument, like Athene at the Last Debate."

"In Sokratea you might think it's better to be metamorphosed into an insect than lose an argument, but we don't all agree," Dad said. There was a laugh.

"Have you finished?" I asked Androkles.

"I only want to say that the fact you have a plan formulated way back in the consulship of Maia and Klio that doesn't mean we should abjectly follow it without re-examination."

And that was Sokratea all over. They spent so much time re-examining everything it was a wonder they ever got anything done at all.

"Why isn't Pytheas here?" Diotima asked.

"Pytheas died this afternoon," I said. Most people had heard already, but there were a few gasps.

"What does that mean, for a god?" Halius asked.

Crocus raised his arm and I acknowledged him gratefully. "It means he's a proper god again, and has his powers back," Crocus said. "We have often talked about it."

"But he's the only person serving in the Senate with any experience of other human cultures," Diotima said, frowning. "Was, I mean. Do you think this coincidence of events is significant?"

"Who can tell?" Crocus asked.

Makalla spoke up from close beside him. "All of us Children have some childhood experience of other human cultures," she said. "I don't know what use it might be."

"Perhaps we should set up a committee to extract knowledge of variant human cultures from the remaining Children," I said.

"It's probably too late," Androkles said. "There are so few of them left and they are all old; and besides, they have spent the majority of their lives in Platonic cultures. That was Plato's whole reason for starting with ten-year-olds. Also, a committee would take too long to get the information. The new humans are here now. We should have done it years ago if we had wanted to."

"Of course, many of us have written autobiographies, and many of the Masters did too, and they had spent a large part of their lives in other cultures. The knowledge is probably in the library if we need it," Makalla said.

"But it isn't available immediately. And who can tell what kind of culture these new humans might have come from? The seventy years of the Republic have brought about huge changes. These people are hundreds of years separated from the latest human culture we knew anything about," Androkles said. "Pytheas might have known, but he's gone. Perhaps Porphyry knows, but Porphyry is oracular at the best of times and never seems to want to say anything definite about anything."

I recognized Crocus. "A committee on re-examination of the issues seems like a good idea. But we need to react without delay. Should we let the humans land?"

"We should follow the plan," Martinus said. He was from Psyche, and usually one of the most difficult members of the Council, implacably opposed to almost everything I wanted. Now I was grateful to him.

"We should vote on whether to follow the plan," I said. "And I endorse following it for the time being in the absence of a better specific immediate strategy."

At that moment, Parmenion came back with Aroo. Aroo was a paler green than Hilfa, with pinker swirls on her skin. She wore a grey kiton with blue edging, fastened with her gold pin. "I apolo-gize, nobody told me the time of the meeting was changed," she said, going at once to her proper place, which Diotima yielded to her immediately, moving to the side.

"It wasn't changed, this is an emergency session," I explained. Aroo blinked, which was especially noticeable on Saeli with their multicolored triple eyelid. "Are you aware that a human spaceship is in orbit?" I asked.

"Yes," she said at once. The Saeli have been in contact with us for twenty years. They have a fascination with Plato, and have been closely allied with us. Lots of them live here, and many of them have, like Aroo, taken oaths of citizenship. I like them, and have put effort into studying them, especially recently, because of Hilfa. But sometimes they're infuriating.

"We know the human spaceship has been in contact with the Saeli ship in orbit," I said.

"Yes," Aroo said again, but this time to my relief she kept talking. "They seem highly surprised. They have not met Saeli before. The only language we have in common is Amarathi, which is slow and uncomfortable. We have asked to learn their language. They seem to be hesitating about allowing this."

"I know an older form of their language, which they can com-prehend. I will teach it to you according to our existing agreements about exchange of information," Crocus said immediately.

Aroo's pink markings grew darker, which I suspect is a sign of approval. "Good," she said.

"Perhaps you should offer a class," I said. "Many of us might need to learn English now. Though probably we can't manage it at Aroo's speed." A few people laughed. The Saeli skill at languages was legendary.

Aroo looked at me for permission to continue, and I waved my hand. "Communication was limited by language difficulties. They seem extremely interested in learning the location of our planets, for what they state are purposes of wholesome trade. They have also expressed interest in immediately purchasing fuel from us for their spaceship. We have not made any hasty decisions. And although the captain of our ship in orbit is an independent agent and not bound by me or by decisions made on Plato, he has agreed to take my advice for the time being, in consideration of existing agreements and negotiations soon to be concluded." She meant the new trade agreement, of course.

"If they need fuel for their spaceship, does that mean they have run out?" Jasmine asked. Jasmine was a younger Worker, one of the ones brought to the Republic by Porphyry after the Relocation. "And does their spaceship work the same way yours does, so that you could sell them fuel, or would it be like putting a battery for a train into a Worker?"

"I believe their ship must use the same fuel," Aroo said. "Excuse me, it is difficult to convey this in Greek. This fuel is not like electricity. We and the Amarathi know only one way to be drawn up to what you might call the second hypostasis and come back down again elsewhere, thus evading the necessary barriers of light. We do it by using a fuel that comes from the heart of exploding stars. This must be the same for the space humans, for this is the fuel they named, using the Amarathi term."

"We don't need to go into either the physics or the metaphysics of that right now," I said, cutting off all the people whose hands shot up to ask for clarification. "We'll simply accept for today's argument that you use the same fuel. Does your ship have enough of this fuel to spare that it can sell it to the space humans, if you decide to?"

"Yes," Aroo said. "Though that might be a difficult negotiation. It is precious. It is hard to imagine what they might give to us of a comparable value to make this a mutually beneficial trade. We could better make them a gift of it to establish a long-term friendship, but this they have not asked, and we have not offered, as we were waiting for discussion with you. Such an offer could be made, but it would draw them into the established matrix of ongoing friendship and communication between us on Plato and the Saeli League."

"We should know more about them first," Diotima said.

I nodded. "Do you have thoughts on the other part of Jasmine's question, Aroo? Might they have exhausted their fuel coming here, like a fishing boat draining the motor to avoid rocks?"

"It is possible, but they did not say that this was the case." Aroo came back and sat down, as expressionless as ever.

"We were about to vote on the established plan to tell the new arrivals of our divine origins in such a way as they will believe them to be a myth, and believe that this planet was truly settled by spaceships."

Aroo looked down. We had followed the plan when we met the Saeli, but those of them who lived here had inevitably seen things that couldn't be explained away. Aroo was a Gold. I wondered what she believed about Pytheas and the Relocation. The Saeli have their own gods, and a little closed circular temple down in the harbor district. Permission to build temples in the other cities was one of the terms of the new agreement. But they didn't like to discuss religion. It always seemed to make them uncomfortable.

"I have no new information, and no objection," she said, her eyes veiled behind her lilac and beige outer lids.

We voted, and to my relief there was a clear majority for following the plan. Aroo abstained. I set up the committee on investigation of other cultures, then formally closed the session for the day. Halius proposed an emergency meeting for the next morning, when we'd have more information from the ship. We voted, and it passed overwhelmingly. I knew I could count on Crocus to count the votes and analyze them, but I could tell at a glance that these votes cut across our usual party lines.

So we were to follow the plan, and the plan called for us to squeeze out as much from the humans as we could before they came down. Crocus rolled down to join me and Dad where we were talking with Klymene and Aroo.

"I'm going back to talk to the ship," Klymene said. "Will you come out to the spaceport?"

"I think that we should go to Thessaly first," Dad said, including me in his glance.

"I ought to go to Thessaly to pay respects too," Aroo said. "First I will hurry home, and tell our ship that you will teach us the space human language. Perhaps I can find a volunteer to begin learning it immediately. Then when I have dealt with that, I will go briefly to Thessaly, and then out to the spaceport."

"We'll call for you on our way," Dad said.

"Thank you," Aroo said, giving a Saeli sideways head-bow, and left.

"Who can we send to take a message to Porphyry?" I asked Dad.

"He'll be here already, at Thessaly," he said.

Here for Pytheas's wake, of course. "We should go and talk to him now," I said. I was tired but excited.

"You did well in the chair," Dad said. I glowed in his approval.

"Can this really be human recontact, at last?" I asked, hardly able to believe it even now.

"It's wonderful," Dad said. "We'll have so much to learn from each other. So much history to exchange. And we'll be able to visit Earth, and their new planets. All that art!"

"No art raids on Earth!" I said, smiling at the impossibility.

Dad gave a little laugh. "I wouldn't put it past the Amazons if they had the means. Art exchange, now—wouldn't it be something if we could get them interested in joining in!"

"They might want to join in the Olympics and other athletic contests, and be prepared to put some of their art in as prizes," I said, excited at the thought. "It's something we could suggest. It's such a great way of having it circulate."

"And it keeps the young hotheads focused on competing instead of killing each other," Dad said, soberly. He remembered the art raids, of course, and had lost his mother and friends to them. It was hard to keep in mind, when they seemed to me like old history.

"We should bring up such participation in negotiations," Crocus said.

"They might even have made some new art in the centuries since. They must have. I wonder what it's like?" I asked.

"It will be so interesting to find out, and to talk to humans," Crocus said, then stopped. "You are humans too. What should we call them?"

"Earth humans?" Klymene suggested.

"But we all come from Earth," Crocus said. "Space humans?"

"Perhaps they'll have space Workers," I said.

"I would like that very much," Crocus said.

"Maybe we can call them by the name of their ship, or their civilization, when we know it," Dad said.

"I will come with you to the spaceport, Klymene," Crocus said.

"Don't you want to go to Thessaly too?" she asked. "We can manage. And I know you and Pytheas were close."

"I have been there and paid my respects. And there's bound to be a proper memorial later."

"I don't know," Dad said. "It's an odd circumstance. It's not as if he's dead the way anyone else would be. There could be a memorial for Pytheas, for his mortal life, but . . . he's also and really Apollo, and Apollo's still alive with all his memories. He's an undying god. He could come to his own memorial. He might be at Thessaly now."

"If he is, would he look like Grandfather, or like his statues?" I asked, simultaneously horrified and fascinated.

"I have no idea," Dad said.

Klymene shuddered.

"Hey, he forgave you," Dad said. I had no idea what he was talking about.

"And I forgave him," Klymene said, shaking her ancient head. Then she saw my frown. "Old history, Marsilia. Don't worry about it."

"We will probably vote on the treaty tomorrow. Now I will go to talk to the ship," Crocus said. "They may need me to translate, though I fear I will not understand the subtleties."

"I thought you said you knew English?"

"What does it mean, to know?" Crocus asked, an extremely characteristic question from him. "I have not heard it spoken since I became myself. The occasional word from Lysias or Klio, yes, but we all preferred to speak Greek. Greek is the language of my soul. Greek has philosophical clarity. But English is stored in my memory. It is a command language."

"I hope it's not too painful to speak," I said.

"That's why it's important that I go and relieve Sixty-One," he said.

"We'll come along and join you there in an hour or so," Dad said.

"Joy to you both."

"Joy to you, Crocus," I said, and Dad echoed me. Klymene climbed up onto his back, and they trundled off towards the spaceport.

"He seems much like everyone else, only big and metallic, and then suddenly he comes out with something like that," I said, when he had rolled out of earshot.

"Going off to share the work to spare Sixty-One the pain," Dad said. "He's the best of us all."

We walked towards Thessaly. Dad had his cloak tightly wrapped against the chill, though I was snug enough in my fishing clothes. "I wonder if they'll have any Workers on the space human ship, and what they'll be like. The other Workers, the younger ones who came to consciousness here on Plato, are different from Crocus and Sixty-One," I said.

"Well, we were expecting consciousness with them, educating them for it, like bringing up babies. As I understand from Father, what happened with the original Workers was completely unexpected—nobody but Sokrates imagined that they might be people rather than tools. That had to have had an effect on how they turned out." Dad sighed. "Still, people are different from each other, but they also have a lot in common, whether they're Workers or aliens or humans. What really matters is their souls."

I couldn't help saying it. "I sometimes feel I have more in common with Crocus than I do with Thee."

"Well, metal can be stronger than blood," Dad said. "That reminds me. I heard today that Selagus is appealing the decision."

I blinked. "That's the first time for ages." Usually people who don't agree with their classification flounce off to another city, often Sokratea, where they don't have classes at all. Sometimes they come back later and accept it after all. Outright appeal against classification is allowed, but rarely happens.

"It could be messy, and it could come up for judgement on your watch," Dad said.

"Thanks for warning me. I'll look up the procedure and consult. I suppose there will have to be a committee?"

"Yes, and you should be really careful who you choose for it. There should be one Ikarian, so Selagus can't claim religious prejudice, but no more. It's so awkward. We've only ever had a handful of reclassifications. We should go through them together soon and consider precedents." Dad was frowning.

"I can't understand why he doesn't want to be a Gold. He could still work at his embroidery." I thought of my work on the boat.

Dad shook his head. "I suppose he doesn't want the responsibility. If so, that might be a sign that he's right, and he should have been a Bronze all along."

We sighed simultaneously. Choosing classifications was the hardest part of political work. If we made a mistake, we'd lose a citizen, or worse, bind somebody where they'd be unhappy as well as unproductive. Every year we lost some people when they were classified, and while we often gained more than we lost as others joined us from other cities, it always felt like a failure. And when the newcomers chose to take our citizenship examinations, they were the hardest of all to classify, because we didn't know them as well. I sometimes welcomed it when newcomers chose to live here as metics instead, though that had its own complications. Athenia still didn't allow metics, but all the other cities did now.

As we came up to the Temple of Hestia, the doors opened and a crowd came out and went off down the street. "Is there a festival I didn't know about?" I asked, surprised.

"I expect they went to pray for reassurance," Dad said. "People do that sometimes, when things are uncertain. They want the gods to listen and help. I sometimes think they'd be less inclined towards that kind of thing if they knew more gods."

"They do know them, though?" I protested.

"Not as well as we do, having them in the family." He sighed. "If Father is in Thessaly tonight, and godlike, he'll be different. Don't be surprised."

I didn't ask how he'd be different. I'd met Athene once. "It's such a strange thought, him dying and maybe being there anyway."

"The only time he talked to me about it, before he went up against Kebes, he said he'd come back a heartbeat later and get revenge," Dad said. "He didn't say what he'd look like, and that's the only time I remember him talking about it, when he knew his life was on the line. He didn't imagine living out forty more years on a planet full of black rocks and volcanoes. None of us could have imagined it."

"I love this planet," I said. "I think it's beautiful." I was used to older people complaining about it.

"We all love Plato, whether we like it or not, but we still couldn't have imagined it," Dad said.

We were at Aroo's house, and Dad scratched at the door. One of her podmembers answered it. Saeli live in pods of five adults, with assorted children. I'd never met any Saeli who didn't live in a pod, except Hilfa, of course. The podmember wished us joy and called for Aroo, who came out at once to join us. "I have spoken briefly to the ship, and they are highly pleased with the news of better communication," she said. "And I have found a technician who was already at the spaceport and who has reported to the communications room."

"Excellent," Dad said. The three of us walked on towards Thessaly.

4

CROCUS

I. *Invocation to the Muses*

This is too hard for me, dear Muses, on!
Come down to me, inspire me, leave your home,
Leave Mount Parnassus, leave Eternal Rome,
Leave the Castalian Spring, Mount Helikon,
Leave all your goddess-joy and hither fly
Here, where you're needed, where my art is made,
Where I, strange votive, beg you for your aid,
On this far planet in a distant sky.
Come to me, if you ever heard a heart,
When Homer, Dante, Hesiod implored!
Set down this tale in amber and in jet
And bend our stubborn history to art,
We'll write these truths, as best we can record,
To make these worlds, so good, be better yet.

II. *On My Coming to Consciousness*

For a long time, whenever I thought of joining my friends in writing an autobiography, there seemed to be only two options. I could engrave it in imperishable stone, which felt too permanent, almost hubristic. Or I could store it in memory, nothing but patterns of amber and jet, powered by Helios Apollo. That felt too transient. When I die, if I die, a matter which concerns me, my memory will die too. My memory is called "temp storage." Lysias expanded it for me to the maximum possible, and I shall not run out of space for many human generations yet, but he could not change the way my memories are stored. "We don't understand enough about it," he said. "We don't really know how it is that you got to be self-aware. I did enough damage to you Workers already out of my ignorance, my half-knowledge. I don't dare risk more. Temp storage was supposed to be a place for you to keep commands and infor-mation about tasks partially completed. How that developed into actual memory and desires and your self-awareness, I've never been able to understand."

It was Arete who found a way, even before I had found a way to speak aloud. "Maybe you can't write with a pen," she said. "But you can inscribe. You could inscribe on wax and have somebody copy it. There are lots of people who owe you favors. Or you could print—compose your thoughts in your memory and then set them directly into type."

Once I had possible ways to do it, I had to consider what to say, and where to begin. Most people were once children, and remember growing up. Few of them remember coming to consciousness. Some things I can remember from before I was conscious. I have memo-ries I saved before I was me, before I understood purpose. I examine them curiously for what they can tell me, but they are fragments. My unconscious life must have been fragmentary, and full of incom-prehensible toil, like the earliest life I remember.

I was built, not born, and I was built on Earth sometime in the late twenty-first or early twenty-second century CE, or so I deduce. (I cannot count by Olympiads. There were distressing centuries of hiatus when years happened but the games were not held, and whether or not I count them, it becomes confusing. So I date the centuries by reference to the Ikarian's Christ, or perhaps more happily to the reign of the Emperor Augustus.)

Athene brought me to the City. I do not know whether she bought me or stole me. The Workers were here before she brought the Masters, so I have nobody to ask. Athene has never given oracles, and I have only seen her once, glancingly, since the Last Debate. Before I knew myself, she brought me, with the other Workers, back through time, before the Trojan War, to serve the City, and so I did from its first days, for more than a decade before my memories begin.

Lysias believed that we achieved consciousness because we were used for so many tasks, and so many of them were complex, so we had to keep making decisions, more decisions and with less programming than Workers like us would normally have done elsewhere. From these decisions and from being forced to set priorities, he thought, came our consciousness. Certainly my earliest stored fragments are of decisions. Perhaps I chose to keep them to measure one decision against another, to make myself better at making decisions. By choosing that, if I did, I was already striving towards the Good, and so I must already have had a soul. But those early memories lack all coherence. I came to self-awareness, awareness of myself and of the world, and the world and myself as separate things, only with Sokrates. He by questioning caused me to question, and by asking me what I wanted caused me to consider desire and preference and boundaries.

So I consider Sokrates my father, and my life as beginning on the day when I was planting bulbs and he asked me whether I liked my work, whether it satisfied me, whether I had preferences for some kinds of work, and I found a way to answer. It was a slow and clumsy way, arranging the bulbs so they would spell "No," months later, in a language Sokrates did not speak, but it was a beginning. It led to dialogue, and from dialogue comes philosophy.

III. *On My Soul (Part 1)*

I wrote above that I must have had a soul already when I began to record my fragments, if I did so out of a desire to seek the Good. I do not know when I was endowed with a soul. My consciousness, my self-awareness, evolved. It seems most likely that at some point in that evolution, when it was needed, my soul crossed the river Lethe and entered into my body. If so, did my soul help propel my consciousness forward from that moment on? I have no memories that help. There is a smaller possibility that I always had a soul, from the beginning, before I had consciousness; that my soul, knowing my consciousness would evolve, chose to enter my body at my creation and wait for it. If this is so, then what part did my waiting soul play in my early life? Some say that I have self-awareness but no soul, that I am nothing but a machine. This seems un-Platonic as well as unfriendly, but it cannot be discounted as a terrifying possibility. I cannot erase this option simply because I dislike it so much. That too would be un-Platonic.

As this is necessarily a matter of concern to me, I have sought the advice of all the wisest people in the Republics, and also of Pytheas, who is the god Apollo incarnate. Pytheas knows a great deal about souls. He believes I have a soul, but has no certain knowledge. He does not know whether my soul is the same kind as human and animal souls, nor when it would have come to me. He regrets not having asked all-knowing Zeus when he had the chance.

Sokrates believed that I clearly have a soul, because I seek the Good. He thought it was futile to worry about when my soul came to me, as we couldn't know. What mattered was that I have it now. There is a great deal to be said for this practical view.

Simmea thought my soul must be the same as human and animal souls, and that I had probably been a human and an animal in earlier incarnations, and that I might go on to be a human in future incarnations, as she might have future incarnations as a Worker. She felt that philosophical souls had a kinship. This is what worries me about my length of life—should I choose to die, and let my soul go on? By continuing this life, am I impeding the progress of my soul? I tell myself that killing myself before I have fulfilled my Fate is cowardly, and who is to say when I have fulfilled my Fate? But then, life and death are different for Workers, and one by one I keep outliving my friends. Sometimes I wonder if what is cowardly is to refuse to die out of fear that I may have no soul after all, and that death would be the end. Sokrates did not fear death. In that, he was unusual.

Ficino believed, with Pythagoras, that all souls have a unique number, and that souls are reborn when the world adds up to their number again. He thought the numbers inscribed on the Workers could be the numbers of our souls. (Lysias said they were serial numbers and meaningless.) Ficino thought the soul would have waited from the time my body was made for my mind to develop. He cited human babies as an example—"Babies have souls long before they can reason! You must have been the same." And he believed my soul would be a special kind, exclusive to Workers. He also believed that animal and human souls were different, on which point Pytheas assures me he was mistaken. Ficino did not live long enough to see Pytheas revealed at the Relocation, which is sad, as I am sure he would have had excellent questions and rejoiced in the answers.

Ikaros believed that my soul would have left Lethe and come to me when I was ready for it—"As soon as you needed it, but no sooner," he said. At the time he said this, he was a man and not a god, and had no more knowledge than he could gain by learning, deduction, and intuition. Since he has been taken up to Olympos, I have had no opportunity to converse with him.

Klio thought my soul would have evolved along with my self-awareness, and she thought the same was true of babies. Pytheas says she was definitely wrong about this in the case of babies, and he never heard of souls evolving, but they must have come from somewhere in the first place.

I have faith in the existence of my soul, but no real evidence. This is one of my greatest burdens.

IV. *On the Good Life (Part 1)*

Simmea said that happiness could only be a by-product of something else, something that cannot be pursued intentionally but which comes along as an incidental when pursuing some other goal.

I have found that this is true, but also that trying to minimize unhappiness for others gives me great satisfaction when it succeeds. Sometimes it is possible to create possibilities for happiness to come along for them. This is even more satisfying. Working for this makes me happy. This is what keeps me engaged with politics, not merely my Platonic duty to rule lest I be ruled by those less capable. I have sympathy for those who do not wish to work on this and prefer to lead a contemplative life. As long as there are enough people capable of the necessary tasks, everyone does not need to do everything.

Politics is often a matter of deciding priorities, and this seems to me the best way to approach it: deciding priorities so that they will minimize possible unhappiness, and allow the maximum potential for happiness.

Sometimes it's hard to judge. Indeed, it's always hard to judge. It's especially hard when there are people involved we don't understand very well, like the Amarathi and the space humans.

We vote in Chamber. That is, we vote when we do not agree after we have all made our cases, which happens with great frequency. I believe Plato would not have approved, because he would have believed it unnecessary. Yet it has been the practice since the earliest days of the City, when the Masters first established the Chamber. These days Chamber is the meeting of the Senate, which is open to all the Golds of the Just City who care to serve. If there are insufficient volunteers, more are chosen by lot to make up the number. The Senate must have fifty members, and may have up to three hundred. We have never had fewer than fifty volunteers, but we have never had as many as three hundred, either.

In addition, we have the Council of Worlds, which also meets in the Chamber of the original city. There representatives of all twelve cities meet to deal with planetwide issues. These representatives are selected in different ways by the different cities. Ours are elected and then drawn by lot from the group, which is similar to the practice of the Athenian and Florentine Republics. For the last eight years, one of our representatives has been required to be a Saeli, and for the last six that Saeli has been Aroo. The Council elects two consuls annually, on the Roman pattern, to chair meetings and guide agendas for a year. The planetwide election of consuls has become political in a way I am sure Plato would not approve, with shifting but lasting alliances and oppositions, almost resembling political parties. Plato never imagined twelve cities, and he thought all philosopher kings would agree on essentials, because they would know the nature of Truth. Plato believed the Truth was one comprehensible thing that all philosophical souls would comprehend and agree upon.

If Plato had been right about the way the universe worked, he'd have been right about the Truth. As it is, he was regrettably and unavoidably wrong. Everything would be much simpler and better if he had been correct. But while people who grew up in Republics certainly do not in practice agree all the time, our priorities are a lot more alike than those of people who did not. It is therefore easier to minimize our unhappiness and create opportunities for our happiness than for others. It has been possible to see this in practice with the Lucian cities—as they become more Platonic, they have also become happier overall.

People from the Republics hold the pursuit of excellence as a goal. The other cultural goals I have encountered in my experience and researches seem much less conducive to producing happiness for individuals and societies. Additionally, we do all believe in constant examination of facts and positions; and even when this decays to pious lip-service, as it sometimes can, it is a valuable ideal. It can always be evoked and recalled in times of potential danger. Rigorous examination of a position will often expose assumptions and agendas hidden under rhetoric. Even for the power-hungry, the awareness that their opponents will call for this examination discourages corruption and acting in bad faith. I believe that Plato was correct in saying that our souls long for the Good, and that nobody chooses evil for themselves while recognizing that it is evil, though some may do it in ignorance.

Therefore, despite the innumerable failings of Plato's system, if maximizing the happiness and well-being of the soul is the Good Life, then to this extent, Plato was right in his design.

V. *On External Contacts*

The first aliens to contact us were the Amarathi, who arrived in the consulship of Fabius and Theano, in the Forty-Eighth Year of the City, seventeen years after the Relocation of the cities to Plato. Their language was exceedingly difficult to learn, and without Arete's special powers we would have been unable to communicate. There was much excitement at first, followed by many perplexities. We have mutually beneficial trade with the Amarathi, who provide us with many useful things in return for natural resources we extract from the planet.

The Saeli contacted us in the consulship of Maia and Androkles, in the Fifty-Second Year of the City. They said the Amarathi had suggested us as appropriate partners. At first Arete translated for them, as she had been doing for the Amarathi, but the Saeli soon learned Greek. They began to settle among us, at first only a few pods who stayed behind when their ships left, and then in larger numbers. In the Fifty-Sixth Year of the City, when I was consul for the third time, sharing the honor with Timon of Sokratea, the first pod of Saeli asked if they could stay permanently and study to become citizens. After much debate, in the Fifty-Seventh Year it was decided that this decision was one that should be settled by each city individually. Here in the Remnant, we decided that they and any other Saeli settlers who wished to could become citizens, provided they took the same course our ephebes took and upon its conclusion swore their oaths and accepted a classification. The argument that prevailed was that if the Saeli wished to dedicate themselves to Platonism and to philosophy, it would be wrong of us to prevent them. Saeli pods, which are family units with five members, were at the same time accepted as one of our approved forms of family.

We also agreed for the first time then to allow Saeli and humans who held citizenship elsewhere to live here, if they chose, as metics, subject to our laws but without taking oath or being classified. Metics can be expelled at any time, but the only time any have been expelled in practice was if they refused to live by our laws.

In the consulship of Marsilia and Diotima, in the Seventy-Third Year of the City, a human spaceship arrived in our solar system and began broadcasting to our planet. Communication was established, and the protocols were put into place which had been long prepared for such an eventuality.

We always knew that we would come into contact with Earth sooner or later. Zeus had promised Arete posterity, and how else might it be achieved? Besides, Porphyry had prophesied that such a thing would happen. We did not, however, know in advance exactly when it would occur. Nor could we have predicted what would follow from this recontact.

VI. *On the Nature of the Gods*

After Zeus moved the Cities to the planet Plato, which is considerably less convenient for some things than Greece, Pytheas and his children, with Maia, returned to us from Olympos. Pytheas could no longer keep it secret in the City that he was Apollo incarnate. He would answer some questions about the universe, but not others. "I don't know everything, I certainly don't know all the answers," he said to me. "And sometimes I don't answer because it's better for people not to know."

"Knowledge is good. How can ignorance be better?" I inscribed on a nearby marble plinth.

"Certainty closes many doors," he replied. "It leads to dogmatism. Souls accept what they know and stop striving upwards."

"Even among philosophers?" I asked.

He paused, and his eyes lost focus for a moment. "I don't know," he said. "True philosophers, who believe the unexamined life is not worth living, are usually very few in a population. Even here, a lot of people want to receive wisdom rather than work on it, even among the Golds. And what we can explain is only an approximation, an allegory, not Truth."

In his later years, Pytheas used to joke about having the words *Plato Was Wrong* inscribed above the door of Thessaly, because people so often asked him questions based on Plato's incorrect assumptions about the universe.

I shall now record a conversation I had with Pytheas in the garden of Thessaly, the day we rooted out the old lemon tree, which had not survived the harsher climate of our new planet. It was three years after the Relocation, and none of the new Workers had yet achieved self-consciousness, nor had we yet encountered any aliens. It was early spring, shortly after we had built the first speaking-boxes, and I was still excited to use my new ability to speak aloud. "Plato says the gods wouldn't change shape because it would be changing to something less perfect," I said. My voice buzzed as I spoke, as it always did until we bought better speaking-boxes from the Saeli years later.

"Perfect for what?" Pytheas asked. "A dolphin is much more

suited to swimming than a human form. I never swam as a human until I came to the City—and I'll probably never do it again, the sea here is freezing."

"It has never fallen below freezing," I pointed out. "We don't have sea-ice." It was spring, and air temperatures were above freezing now, except sometimes at night.

"Metaphorically freezing, even in summer," Pytheas said, rolling his eyes.

"Was that pedantic?"

"Yes, it was pedantic, but never mind. I was simply complaining about the cold here, the way everyone does."

I began to stack the wood against the wall, lining up the pieces. "I can measure temperature, but I don't feel it."

"When I'm a god, I can choose how much I feel it."

"That's closer to perfection," I pointed out.

"I never said it wasn't. Plato's doing his thing there where he assumes there's only one good." He was bent over sweeping up the wood chips, and he hesitated, looking at me where I was stacking the logs, which would make useful material for so many things. "We have our perfect selves, if you like to call them that, the essential self, but that self can have several affinities, several forms that are all real and perfect in their own ways, for their own things. It's a matter of personality. As a god, I have a human form, a dolphin form, a mouse form, a wolf form, a solar form . . . they're all me, all part of what I am. It's not falling away from being myself to choose which one to be at any time, no more than to choose whether to sing or not on a given occasion, whether to smile or frown. Though of course, Plato would see emotions as falling away from perfection too."

"And what about Hephaistos?" I had a special interest in Hephaistos, because some accounts said he made Workers to help in his forge, and I felt he might therefore be our patron.

"Hephaistos?" Pytheas bent to his sweeping again.

"Being lame," I elucidated.

"It happened before I was born, so he's been lame for as long as I can remember. But I think that disability became part of his imagination of himself, after his fall to Lemnos. It became one of his attributes, in his own soul, an essential part of who he was."

"And if he changed to another form, would that be the same?"

"A lion with a thorn in its paw? Yes. But he seldom does change. He seldom leaves his forge. He's always busy making things."

"Like the shield for Achilles," I said. We'd recently read that part of the *Iliad* in the current rhapsode.

"Yes."

"And can you take on other human forms?"

Pytheas laughed and straightened up, putting a hand to his back and wincing a little. "Yes. Briefly. And for exactly the purpose Plato says we never have: to deceive. If I want somebody to do something I can show up as myself and command and hope they obey, or I can send a dream, or give an oracle; but sometimes it's much more effective to show up looking like somebody they trust and make a suggestion." He brought the pile of chips over towards me as I went back to bring more branches to the stack.

"What about if you wanted to become a bull?" I asked.

"Bull is one of Father's," he said, picking up a bough and smelling it. Scent is a sense I do not share. "I could look like a bull if I wanted to, but I wouldn't be a bull in essence, the way I'd be a dolphin, or Hephaistus a lion. I'd only seem like a bull, a disguise, exactly the same as looking like somebody's charioteer."

"But aren't there other bull gods in other pantheons?" I asked.

"Yes. I expect it's different for them." He set the bough down neatly on the pile.

"But how, if there's only one Form of the bull?" I asked, perplexed.

"It's not like Plato's Forms, really. And it's connected to culture and place and personality, like I said."

"But for Zeus—this is so difficult to understand."

"Father has a lot of shapes. He likes shapes. That's part of his essential nature, changing shape. It's part of his perfection, if you want to put it that way." He took up the broom again and began to sweep. "The thing Plato's dead wrong about is thinking we don't want anything and are perfectly happy and don't care. We're much calmer than humans, and I'm quite content most of the time, but I have projects, desires, plans, people and things I care about. We all do. And sometimes we come into conflict because of that."

"Plato's God could only really be one," I said, coming over with more wood.

"It sounds really boring to me," he said.

"It sounds to me like I was before I developed consciousness," I said. "Unchanging, not wanting anything, no emotions."

"Yes, a god like that wouldn't need self-awareness and might be better off without it. A Worker god! I must tell—" He stopped and took a deep breath in the way he often did when he wanted to change the subject. "There's a lot more of this wood than I thought there would be."

"Trees often seem bigger when they are down."

"Bigger and smaller both. I'm sad to see it go. It was a link with Sokrates and Simmea. We used to sit in this garden and talk. It was so different then. Warmer. Sokrates made that herm, you know. He'd stopped working as a sculptor before the attack on the herms, but he took up his tools again for that."

"I knew he made the herm. It makes me happy that he was a sculptor too, though I did not know it when I knew him."

"He'd have been excited by your work, as I am," Pytheas said.

It made me happy to hear this said. But then Pytheas looked around sadly at the chilly space the garden had become.

"We will plant more green things out here. It's sad that the lemon tree couldn't survive the winters," I said. "But the wood will be useful to make many good things. I could make you a comb, and when you used it you could think of them."

"I'd like that," he said.

"And a pen," I added.

He nodded. He was no longer mad with grief, the way he had been immediately after Simmea's death, but he still felt it, as I did myself. Now that I had comforted him, or at least made an effort towards trying, I wanted to get back to the conversation. "If Plato was wrong," I said, and we both glanced at the arch over the door where the words could have been incised, "why did he imagine the gods that way?"

"He was wrong about the purpose of the gods," Pytheas said. "He imagined that we existed as inspiration, examples, much the same way he imagined art." He laughed. "He was wrong about art too."

"And why do you exist?" I asked.

"I haven't the faintest idea," he said. "Not why we exist, or why humans do, or Workers either. I'm sure Father knows, but he probably wouldn't tell me." He smiled at me, the smile that wasn't like anyone else's smile. "Plato might have been wrong a lot of the time, but at least he was trying to figure important things out. He deserves credit for that."

VII. *On Friendship*

The reason why Pytheas only joked about it and didn't have me inscribe *Plato Was Wrong* over his doorway was to avoid distressing his friends, especially Maia and Aristomache.

5

JASON

Walking through the city with Thetis, I kept wanting to pinch myself so I could be sure it wasn't a dream. Except that if it was a dream, I didn't want to wake up, so there was that. I had my arm around her, around the outside of her cloak that is, which was fairly thick, whatever shimmery stuff it was made out of. But as we walked through the streets behind the harbor she sort of half-leaned into me, as if she couldn't have managed to walk without my help. The sun was down now, not that we'd seen a glimpse of him since the morning. The clouds had been low out on the water. It had been grey all day, and raining on and off. Now twilight was closing in as we made our way through the streets, and a cold wind was coming up from the southwest. At first Thetis was crying, but after a little while, as we started heading uphill, she stopped. She wiped her face, took a deep breath, then turned her lovely eyes on me expectantly. "Well?"

"I don't know what to say," I admitted, completely at a loss. "It would be wrong to tell you to cheer up, when you've so recently lost your grandfather."

"You don't think it's un-Platonic of me to grieve?" she asked.

I couldn't remember what Plato had said about it. I'd read the *Republic* when I was an ephebe, like everyone else, but that was a while ago and I'd been busy since. "Unnatural not to, if you ask me. It's five years since Leonidas and Aelia died, and I've recovered from the shock, mostly, but right away the grief was like an open wound."

"Did you weep?"

She was exactly my height, taller than her sister although she was so much slighter. She must have used some flower scent in her soap, because I could smell it on her skin. "Yes, right away I did," I said. "When we found the wreckage. And at the memorial, and then afterwards whenever I'd think about them I'd feel tears coming to my eyes. Even now sometimes. We all grew up together in the same nursery, sucked milk from the same breasts, as they say, and then we worked together on the boats. You can't forget people you're that close to as if they'd never been. Yes, I wept. There's nothing shameful about tears like that."

"Thank you." She wiped her eyes again, unselfconsciously. "We should keep walking. It's cold." She took my arm and we walked on, past the Temple of Nike with its neatly swept gravel courtyard. "I never knew Leonidas, but I remember Aelia. She used to eat in Florentia sometimes, with the quilters. She helped old Tydeus when his sight was going. She was kind. And you're kind too, Jason, you're always kind."

I didn't know what to say. "I do my best," I muttered. If it had been a dream I'd have had dream eloquence, but it was waking life and the girl I'd been in love with since we were both fifteen was telling me I was kind and my tongue was thick in my mouth. "Tell me about your grandfather. I didn't know him well."

"He wasn't like anyone else. Of course, he was the god Apollo, and you couldn't forget that. But he was also a man, a man astonished at growing old, at grey hair, at weakening muscles." We came to the walls and turned in at the gate. Thetis's voice echoed for a moment as we passed beneath the arch. "I always loved him. He had so many grandchildren, and he cared about all of us. I'm not really his grandchild, did you know that?"

"Yes, Marsilia mentioned that your father, Neleus, was festival-born." We came out from under the walls and were in the old city. I lived down by the harbor and worked at sea, and hardly ever came up here at night. I was surprised how many people were about in the evening chill. By the harbor, everything had been built for the climate of Plato, thick walls and narrow windows, all the houses huddling together against the cold, with light bars running along the sills of the buildings. Here you could tell everything had been intended for a warmer climate—there was a great variety of styles, but all of it was freestanding and mostly pillared, with individual sconces glowing gold above all the doors.

"Well, all of his children were except Arete. And she—" Thetis shrugged, as if to say that Arete was something special, which she definitely was. "He loved her. Dad's mother. Simmea. And I think I must remind him of her in some way, because he's always had a soft spot for me."

"You don't look like her." I'd seen Crocus's colossus of Simmea, the one by the steps of the library. She looked more like Marsilia.

"Yes, she was a true philosopher," Thetis said, smiling a little, sadly.

"Marsilia says they only started saying that about philosophers being naturally ugly because of Simmea and Sokrates. She says Plato assumed beauty, and that there are plenty of good-looking philosophers. Pytheas himself was an example, and Ikaros was another."

"They're gods," Thetis said. "That's different." She hesitated, then went on. "I used to think that I couldn't hope to be a philosopher, because of how I looked. When I was a little girl, I mean. Marsilia's older, and she was brilliant, and also she looked like one, of course. And so it was what everyone said, that it was clear that she'd be a Gold, that her metal shone through. Whereas to me, they said I was pretty as a picture or that somebody ought to sculpt me. Everyone except Grandfather. Pytheas. He always treated me as if what I thought mattered. Dad was busy running the city, and

Ma was away at sea so often, and in classes they tended to treat me as if I had to be empty-headed and thistledown-weight because I was pretty."

"Not only pretty, beautiful," I said. "But that shouldn't have been all they saw."

"That's right," she said, and gave my arm a little pat. "I realize that now, but I didn't at the time. And so I didn't work hard, which you probably remember from that year we took classes together, and when they classified me Iron it simply seemed appropriate." The crowds had thinned out, and we had the street to ourselves except for a Saeli pod walking the other way, arms entwined.

"But do you like your work?" I asked.

She smiled, and I caught my breath, to see a smile like that from so close. "I love it," she said. "Plato was right. It's so good to have our work carefully chosen for us and to feel every day that in doing what I love I am helping make the City better."

"Yes," I said. "I feel exactly the same." I hardly ever admitted it. Everyone complained, and so I did too, to fit in.

"And it is the same," she said. "You work out at sea, hard work, dangerous, feeding us all. And I work with the tiny babies in the nursery, both the ones there full-time and the ones whose parents leave them with us for a few hours a day, or a few days now and then. I always have six or seven babies in my care, and I love them, and I love looking after them. And as they get older and need instruction they move up to teachers, but I still see them. There must be twenty children who call me Ma Thee, as well as my present little lovelies. They need me, and the City needs me there, and I am far far better suited to working with babies from birth to two than I should have been to anything else I could have done."

"So you don't resent Marsilia being consul?"

"I'm excited about it!" We were getting closer to Thessaly, but she stopped again, and I stopped too. The stones beneath our feet were incised with old debates. "All that was when I was younger.

I don't feel like that now. I'm happy with who I am. I was only talking about that because of Grandfather, trying to explain. He never made me feel stupid, or like I'm not achieving what I could, or any of that. When we were going to take our oaths and become ephebes, he talked to me about what the oath meant, and what the City meant, and I felt he loved me and he understood who I was. He could be strange sometimes, which is only to be expected. He was a god! But he saw that I was nervous and uncomfortable, and he explained it all to me, and he was right, and the Guardians were right."

She smiled, sadly. "Dad and Ma and Marsilia are always busy. I could always go to Grandfather and tell him about the babies. The funny, ordinary, adorable things they do. It made him smile. He'd say he didn't have enough conversations about ordinary human things. And sometimes I'd be there when people came, important people, and at first if that happened I'd try to leave, but he pressed me to stay and make small talk with them, to set them at their ease, so I'd do that. And once he told me that Simmea used to do that for him, and he never worked out how to do it. He knew he had to offer them something and talk about insignificant things first, but he always felt awkward doing it and wanted to jump right in to whatever they'd really come about. He said he admired the way I could do it naturally and make them feel comfortable."

I couldn't say anything. Saying I'd been in love with her for years and that this made me love her all the more would have been wrong, but there wasn't anything else I could think of to say. I nodded.

"I'd make a terrible consul. But Marsilia is a splendid one, exactly like Dad. And she'd be awful at looking after babies, and I'm really good at that. It wasn't only our looks, it really was our souls. So sometimes I think looks do reflect souls."

"Maybe," I said. "Though what I remember Plato saying about that seems to be a bit different from the way you see it. But how can you think Marsilia would be awful with babies? What about Alkippe?"

She smiled again. "Alkippe's seven years old. And now she's old enough, Marsilia's the best mother in the world for her, teaching her things, and Alkippe's so bright, she soaks it all up. But for the first three years I looked after her. If I hadn't wanted to, I think Marsilia would have left her in the nursery full-time. The year she was two, Marsilia was away on a mission to Lucia. Alkippe hardly noticed." Thetis smiled. "She'd notice now, though! If Marsilia had to go away again she'd take her with her, I think. But she won't. She's consul, and she's fixed here for a year."

"That's good," I said. "Though I don't know how she manages to make time for everything she does and working on the boat."

"She enjoys it," Thetis said.

"Thee—" I stopped.

"What?"

I gathered up my nerve. "I've really enjoyed talking to you like this. Maybe we could do it some more. On days when your grand-father hasn't died, I mean. And if you want to talk about the funny things the babies did, or anything." I knew I was babbling, and I was trying hard not to sound threatening, or too eager. I knew from Marsilia that Thetis always had plenty of men buzzing around, and women too. It would have been more surprising if she didn't, look-ing like that.

She looked wary and took her hand off my arm. "Aren't you mar-ried?"

"No?" I was puzzled. Who could she think I was married to? I'd never really looked at anyone else, they all seemed to be little ripples compared to the tidal wave that was Thetis. I'd messed about with boys when I'd been a boy myself, and I volunteered at every Festival of Hera, but that was the extent of my experience. "And anyway, I didn't mean it like that—or not only like that. I didn't mean anything I couldn't have meant if I had happened to be mar-ried. But I'm not."

"But I thought you were married! I always see you with children?" She sounded puzzled. "Like down at the dock earlier."

"Camilla is Aelia and Leonidas's daughter," I said. "I was wondering who you thought I'd married."

"And I had sort of wondered who you did marry. But I don't see you very often, and whenever I did you seemed to have little children with you, so I thought . . ."

"Aelia and Leonidas died at sea, five years ago. Camilla is eight, and Little Dion, Di, is six. We always knew them and loved them, and so Dion and I look out for them, when they're free and we are, and we do all tend to be together having fun at festivals and that kind of thing. So I see why you would have seen them with me."

"Yes, I do see," she said. "But Jason—"

I interrupted her while I still had the courage. "I feel about twelve years old saying this, but let me say it. I really like you. I can't say I don't find you attractive. I'm not a stone. But I really did mean that I enjoyed talking, and with what you were saying about talking to Pytheas about the babies I thought maybe you wanted somebody you could talk to like that, probably more than you want admirers, which you can't possibly be lacking."

"I've enjoyed talking to you too, and I'd certainly like to do it again," she said, and she kissed my cheek.

We walked on. I wasn't feeling the cold at all now, even though the wind was scattering the clouds above us. I put my arm around her again. I wasn't sure what any of this meant, but whatever it was, it made me happy.

Thessaly seemed to be simply an old sleeping house, like all the sleeping houses of the old city, with the name carved above the door. The history didn't show. The door was closed, but the sconce above it was shining brightly, casting out a gold radiance and lighting up the words carved in the flagstones where we were walking: "Read, write, learn." As we came close, something big swooped over our heads. We both ducked, instinctively. There are no birds on Plato, but of course I'd seen Arete flying, and naturally I assumed it was her, come to Thessaly for her father's memorial. She didn't usually fly down so low as to part people's hair. I looked up, and was amazed to see a young man, naked, with winged sandals and a flat hat. He was looking down at us and grinning. Nobody with half a brain could have been in a moment's doubt as to who he was.

"I should be going," I said.

"No, stay with me," Thetis said, not taking her hand from my arm.

"But . . ." I indicated Hermes, now settling gracefully to the ground a little way up the street. Also, I was starting to be aware that I was wearing trousers, that well-known mark of barbarians and people who work out of doors in cold weather. I have a kiton for special occasions, but nobody had warned me that this would be one.

"Half my family are gods," she said.

"Yes, I know, but—" It was different for me, I was going to say, but she didn't give me time to finish.

"You should think what it's like growing up being part of the *other* half of the family. Never let them think you're inferior. Come on." She put her hand on the door, but Hermes had stepped up before she opened it.

"Joy to you," he said, glancing at me then focusing on Thetis, naturally. He was naked, apart from the hat and the sandals. It was usual to exercise naked, though most of the palaestras had been enclosed and heated a long time ago. (The few that hadn't were only popular in the middle of summer.) Being naked in the street was unusual though, and what was especially odd was the way he seemed comfortable naked outdoors on a chilly evening. He was out of context, and not only in that way. We had gods, of course. Half Thetis's family were gods, as she'd said. But Hermes was different. We worshipped him! And he hadn't grown up here. All of this went through my mind while he was still greeting us, and then as Thetis started to speak and introduce us I thought that there were ways he was more like an alien, and maybe that was a useful way to think about him. He spoke Greek; well, so did the Saeli, that didn't mean they really understood us. He was a Greek-speaking visitor from another culture, like they were.

"Joy to you," Thetis said. "I am Thetis of the Hall of Florentia and the Tribe of Apollo, Iron of the Just City. This is Jason, Silver of the Just City. And you, no doubt, are Hermes the son of Zeus?"

"The tribe of Apollo?" Hermes echoed, smiling. "Is there a tribe of Hermes too? Or does that mean you're one of my brother's descendants?"

"Yes, Pytheas was my step-grandfather," Thetis said, calm and self-possessed. "I suppose that makes you my step-granduncle. No, step-half-granduncle. This could get confusing."

"Don't call me step-granduncle, it makes me seem so much older than you!"

"When in fact you're thousands of years older than me?" Thetis countered. He looked younger than either of us, barely more than an ephebe, perhaps twenty.

"And yes, you have a tribe too, and I belong to it," I said, as boldly as I could. This was not the way I had imagined interacting with my patron god.

"Charming, delightful," Hermes said, smiling and looking around at Thessaly and the other nearby sleeping houses with appreciation. He patted the trunk of an olive tree affectionately. "What a lovely place."

6

MARSILIA

Thessaly was packed. I'd never seen it so full of people. The noise was ear-splitting. Over the roar of conversation I could hear Alkippe and the other little ones shouting as they chased each other in the garden. Pytheas wasn't immediately visible, so I assumed he wasn't there. All my uncles were, and Arete, along with most of Grandfather's close friends, all my cousins, and what felt like half the city. It seemed as if all my relations and everyone who knew Pytheas and hadn't needed to be in Chamber had squeezed themselves in here. Thessaly was a standard-size sleeping house, and there really wasn't room for everyone, even packed so tightly together that there was hardly room to move. Ma and Uncle Fabius were mixing wine in one corner and some of my cousins were passing it around. There were so many people that even though I was looking around to see whether Grandfather was attending his own wake, it took me a moment to notice the naked man talking to Thetis.

He was young, and he was gorgeous, and even in profile across the room I recognized him instantly. He didn't seem to have aged a day in the eight years since I'd seen him. Of course, he had been naked then too, which might have helped. "Poimandros," I said. He looked up as I said it, even though he could hardly have heard me across the room. His eyes met mine with absolutely no sign of recognition.

I know I'm not Thetis. I'm used to that. By most measures I'm better than she is. I'm a Gold. I had chaired a meeting that day which made decisions about the future of the planet, the future of humanity. I can haul a net of fish unaided over the side of the boat. It shouldn't matter that nobody's eyes linger longingly when they look at me. But it stung a little when Jason looked at her that way, and at me as if I'm a good comrade. I try not to feel it, or if I do feel it then not to act on it or let anyone know how I feel. But even though Poimandros was standing next to Thetis, I would expect a man who'd been married to me at festival to at least remember having seen me before!

My uncle Porphyry had noticed us come in and was pushing his way through the crowd towards us, two cups of wine in each of his big hands. "Do you know him?" Dad asked me, sounding much more surprised than I'd have expected.

"His name is Poimandros, I think he's from Psyche. I only met him once. He's Alkippe's father," I answered, looking back at them. Poimandros had turned back to Thee. Jason was on her other side, she was smiling teasingly, flirting with both of them at the same time. I tried to smooth out my brow and look serenely at Dad.

I always volunteer for the Festival of Hera. Plato was in favor, so if you want to stand for civic office, it's a good idea to do it. Besides, it's a great opportunity to enjoy uncomplicated sex. There are two little festivals every year and one big one, at the end of summer, when people come here from all the cities. Long ago, when there was only one city and the Masters were in charge, participation was compulsory and the Masters cheated to get what they thought would be the best children. Plato says that's what they should do, though how he, or anyone, imagined they could tell what the children would be like I don't know. That ended at the Last Debate, and resulted in Dad's generation, which was followed by a decade or so when they didn't have any Festivals of Hera here at all, though they kept on with them in Athenia and Psyche. Then they started

them up again, on a voluntary basis, and with the lots chosen
truly at random, though still always within the same metal. I've
been volunteering since I was seventeen and wildly curious.

Being drawn together at a Festival of Hera left people with no
obligation to each other afterwards. The marriage was strictly time-
bound, until the participants left the room. By Plato's original
rules, that was supposed to be the end of it—indeed, what Poimandros had done, in never seeking me out again, and even ignoring
the half-besotted note I'd sent him (at Thee's urging) was precisely
in accord with the *Republic* as Plato wrote it. But in present-day practice, if the people had got on well, which we had, a marriage at
festival often develops into a friendship or a love affair, occasionally even a long-term marriage. Marriages that began that way were
considered to be lucky. All my other such pairings were now friends,
or friendly acquaintances. In any case, looking straight through
me as if he'd never seen me before was well beyond what Plato had
written, never mind custom. By any interpretation, that was rude.
Though it *had* been eight years; perhaps he really had completely
forgotten me.

Porphyry reached us and gave winecups to me and Dad and
Aroo. Dad swallowed down a great gulp of his right away. "Gods!"

Porphyry laughed. "He didn't get here until well after Father was
dead," he said. "He told me explicitly that he didn't come as a psycho-
pomp, and seemed surprised at the idea. And while he seems intrigued by everyone and everything, he has been paying a great
deal of attention to your Thetis. He's very strange, not how I would
have imagined Hermes at all. What do you think?"

Hermes. Was he? Of course he must be. It wasn't really warm
enough for anyone human to be comfortable naked. I felt icy cold
inside and out. Though I suppose it did explain both why the sex
had been so wonderful and how he could have forgotten. If he was
a god, probably it was always like that for him. I wished I hadn't
revealed what I'd admitted to Dad.

I had often heard the story from Grandfather of how, when my grandmother Simmea discovered that he was the god Apollo, she had said, "Then that's why you're so awful at being a human being." For the first time, I understood it.

I took a sip of my own wine. It was watered three to one, which was correct for a funeral, of course, but at that moment I could have done with something stronger.

"Why do you think he came now, and not before?" Dad asked. "The Olympians must know we're here. Zeus put us here. And we're worshipping them. Some of that must get through. But none of them have ever come before."

"Except Athene," I said, knowing Dad would know what I meant and that Porphyry and Aroo would think I was talking about the Relocation.

"Excuse me, do you believe gla to be one of your Olympian gods?" Aroo asked. ("Gla" was the special Saeli pronoun for divinity. I knew it because of the negotiations about temples. I'd never heard it in normal conversation before. The Saeli didn't generally use it for Pytheas and his children.)

"Yes, that's Hermes," Dad replied.

The three of them had been moving through the crush and were now beside us. "Father, Aroo, Marsilia, this is Hermes," Thetis said, beaming. He was lovely. Of course he was. He was a god. How could I not have guessed? I felt furious with myself.

We exchanged conventional wishes of joy, though my voice seemed choked in my throat. Hermes still showed no sign whatsoever of recognizing me. He did remarkably well at the Saeli sideways head-bow, which takes most people a long time to master. But then, he was a god. "I think you all know Jason?" Thee went on.

"Yes," Aroo said, making the head-bow to Jason. "You are in charge of the boat where Marsilia and Hilfa work. Joy to you, Jason."

"Joy to you, Aroo. And that's right," Jason said, making a creditable response to the head-bow. He'd been there the day Hilfa was

trying to teach it to me. The memory of our shared laughter stead-
ied me.

"So tell me about your gods?" Hermes asked Aroo, directly.

Aroo blinked her silvery inner eyelids across her eyes, and took
a tiny step backwards. A tiny step was all she could take, because
there was so little room, and now her back was to the wall. "We
have four major religions," she said, carefully, without unveiling her
eyes. "Three of them have gods. Most of us here prefer the fourth."

"But you're not used to gods showing up at parties?" Hermes
asked, and giggled. He couldn't be drunk on that over-watered wine,
unless he'd been here for a long time.

"Religion is for us a more private thing," Aroo said, sounding
very much like Hilfa now. "We do not have people enact the roles
of gods, no, nor do we worship in public as part of civic life the way
humans do. There are those who could instruct you, but I am not
one of them." She closed her eyes completely now, lowering the
colored outer lids.

"But—" Hermes began.

"Enough," Dad said, sternly. "You're making Aroo uncomfortable, and she is a guest here."

I wouldn't have cared to refuse Dad when he spoke in that tone,
but Hermes had another laughing objection on his lips when Aroo
suddenly opened her eyes and fled, thrusting her empty cup at Porphyry and backing out through the door of the sleeping house and
into the street. Porphyry took the cup, turned it in his hands with
a strange gesture, then nodded to Hermes. "I see," he said, at his
most gnomic. Porphyry is my uncle, and I love him, but he can also
be one of the most infuriatingly enigmatic people on the planet. "I
will speak with you tomorrow." Then he vanished, still holding the
cup. Hermes kept smiling but did not speak.

At that moment, Alkippe came in from the garden and began
wiggling her way across the room towards us. Hermes smiled over
at the child as she approached, then paused. For the first time since

I'd known him there was no smile twitching at the corners of his lips.

"Your daughter?" he asked Thetis, uncertainly.

"My niece. Your step-great-grandniece." Thetis was smiling again, but Hermes still looked grave. I saw a family resemblance between him and Pytheas, not in feature, but in his expression as he looked down at Alkippe as she approached. I didn't know what to do or say. I hadn't imagined that he'd recognize his connection to her.

"Your daughter, I think," Dad said. He sounded matter-of-fact about it. Jason's eyebrows rose into his hair. Thee gasped.

"I think so too," Hermes replied, not looking up from Alkippe, who had reached us. She hugged my legs, and I put down a hand to smooth her hair. Then she gave Thetis the same hug, looking up at Hermes wonderingly.

"Fate plays strange tricks sometimes," he said. "What's your name, little one?"

"Alkippe," she said.

"A lovely name," Hermes said. "And how old are you?"

"Seven and a half," Alkippe said. "Why aren't you wearing any clothes?"

Jason gave a bark of laughter, then choked it off.

"I'm more comfortable that way," Hermes said, smoothly.

"But aren't you cold? Outside I mean?" I could see the gap in her teeth as she spoke.

"No, I didn't feel cold. I was flying and that kept me warm."

"Oh." She didn't seem surprised at all. "You can fly, like Aunt Arete? You must be a god."

"Yes, Alkippe, this is Hermes," Thetis said.

"Hermes! Then you're an Olympian? I've been to your temple. You're different from how I imagined. Why are you here?"

Thetis took Alkippe's hand. "I think Grandma has some quince paste left for us. Let's go and see."

"But I want to talk to Hermes," Alkippe protested, not at all mollified by the thought of the treat.

"Later," Hermes said. "I think I should speak to your mother now."

"You should have spoken to her before," Neleus said, as Thetis led Alkippe, still protesting vociferously, across the room. "It's a bit late now."

"You mistake me," Hermes said, meeting my eyes for the first time. "I've never been on this wandering world before today. That is my daughter, true, but Necessity has caught me, for I have never met her mother until now. So I shall set this as straight as I may, but this is as early as I can begin it."

It explained why he hadn't recognized me, at least. "Never been here?" I asked. I don't think I'd ever experienced so many conflicting emotions in such a short time.

"Your past encounter lies in my future," Hermes confirmed.

I suppose this kind of thing happens to gods, but it was quite outside my experience. "Perhaps we should have this conversation somewhere quieter," I suggested.

He looked at Dad, who was frowning. "But this is—well, yes. Let's go outside."

Jason put his hand on my arm. "Will you be all right on your own, Marsilia?"

"Yes," I said, though I appreciated his offer. "Thank you."

"Let her go," Dad said, and Jason stepped back. I followed Hermes through the crush, which parted before us.

The fountain room was as full as the sleeping room, but there was nobody over ten in the garden. It was far too cold to linger out of doors unless you were young enough to hurtle around in a chasing game. Hermes turned to me as I was snicking my jacket closed. The clouds had parted and the winter stars shone clear and cold above us. Hermes didn't seem to feel the cold at all, though he was naked. I was almost knocked over by two of my young cousins, who dashed past me racing to be first to slap their palms on the herm. Hermes looked at them wryly. "I take it I don't have any other children here. That you know of?"

"Not that I know of, no," I said, flustered by the question.

"Only Alkippe?" The hurtling children broke around us as a wave breaks on a rock, and re-formed on the other side of us.

"Yes." The affirmation came out much too quietly. I felt slightly sick and a little lightheaded. I took a deep breath and swallowed, which helped.

"I didn't know she existed until now." He frowned, staring over at the herm where the children were still dodging and squealing. "This is all terribly awkward. I was intending to pay court to your sister."

Plato has extremely harsh things to say about jealousy, which I repeated to myself. I was struggling hard with this in my soul, as well as feeling all the physical symptoms, heat flushing my cheeks and hands and my stomach tightening. Then Pytheas appeared beside me. One instant he wasn't there, the next he was, as if he'd taken a step from nowhere. He didn't look the way he did in his statues—he was dressed normally, for one thing—but he didn't look like the old man he'd been when I saw him a few days before. He looked not so much young as ageless. Yet I recognized him immediately as my grandfather.

"I thought you were in Alexandria," he said, frowning at Hermes.

"Moving rapidly is my specialty," Hermes said, with a teasing smile.

"Yes, but—"

"I'm here now," Hermes said.

Pytheas was still frowning. "Well, it's good that you came, you can test something for me. I was going to find Porphyry, but you'll be better."

"Let me finish with this first."

"No, it's important," Pytheas said.

"So is this."

"What, dallying with my granddaughter? Surely that can wait." Pytheas smiled at me.

"We weren't dallying," I protested. My voice sounded strange in my ears.

"Necessity has me by the foot," Hermes said.

I instinctively looked down at his feet. He had wings on his sandals. He hadn't had those when I'd met him before. As I was looking down, the children noticed Pytheas and came running up, crowding round him asking questions.

"Joy to you, yes, I'm here, yes, but go inside now. You can tell everyone I'm here and I'll come in and talk to them, but I need to speak to my brother first."

They protested, of course, but Pytheas shooed them inside, some laughing and some crying. He closed the door and turned back to us. The garden seemed very dark and quiet without the children and the bar of light from the door. I realized that Pytheas was much better lit than anything else, as if the starlight were concentrating itself on him.

"Necessity?" Pytheas said to Hermes, as if there had been no interruption.

"Your step-granddaughter Marsilia is the mother of my daughter Alkippe, but I've never been here before today. So I need to discover how this came to be and set it straight."

Pytheas winced. "I appreciate how uncomfortable this is, but—" he began.

"No, wait," I said, wanting to clarify things. "You died, and you're here, and that's not the most important thing that's happened today. I've found out the father of my daughter is the god Hermes, and that's not the most important thing that's happened today either. Even this time loop, disconcerting as it is, isn't the most important. You have to know, there's a human ship in orbit."

Both gods looked at me with the same infuriating lack of expression, the same air of fathomless calm indifference.

"A human ship!" I repeated. "Recontact with the wider universe! A chance to rejoin the human mainstream and influence it!"

"Yes," Pytheas said, with a wave of his hand. "But you can deal with that perfectly well yourself." I gasped. "You're a Gold of the Just City, you can deal with it, or what have we been doing here? Hermes, I can't find Athene."

"Can't find her?" Hermes looked down shiftily.

"Try reaching for her."

"Can't I sort out this mess first?" He gestured towards me, sounding petulant.

"It'll take less time than arguing. If you can find her, then—"

Hermes shook his head. "Nothing."

"Go outside time and try."

"Look, let me talk to Marsilia for five minutes and then stay here for two heartbeats while I sort this out, and I'll do all the running around looking for Athene you want," Hermes said.

"She's missing?" I asked. I had a really bad feeling about this. "Lost?"

Suddenly I had all of their attention. Hermes seemed particularly intent.

"It seems so. Have you seen her?" Pytheas asked.

"About two years ago, after the Panathenaic Festival, she came to me and Thetis in the sanctuary when we were putting the new cloak on her statue." I could remember it clearly. She'd come into the room carrying her owl, and it turned its head to watch us as she moved. She was much taller than any human. There are lots of stories about Athene in the City, some good, some not so good. Thetis had clutched my hand so tightly I'd had marks for days. "She said we were her worshippers, and this was her city. I was a priest that year, remember?"

"Priesthood is a civic function here, like in Rome," Pytheas put in. Hermes nodded dismissively.

"She gave us a kind of woven box to look after," I went on, remembering the weight of it in my arms and the strange weave, and the tilt of her head as she spoke. "She told us not to open it unless we heard she was lost, and then we had to both be together. And she asked us not to tell you until that happened."

"So which one of you opened it, and how long did it take?" Pytheas asked. "And why in all the worlds didn't you tell me?"

"How did you know we already opened it?" I asked.

"Human nature," Pytheas said. "What was in it?"

"Hilfa," I admitted.

"Hilfa!" Pytheas repeated. I had never seen him look so taken aback.

"Who's Hilfa?" Hermes asked. "And where is he?"

"He's a Sael," Pytheas said. "One of the aliens. I've met him a time or two. He seems perfectly normal for one of the Saeli, which is to say very peculiar indeed."

"We didn't expect it would be a living being," I said. "We thought we could look to see what it was and close it again until it was necessary. Or if it was something dangerous to the Republic we could tell somebody. Athene hasn't always been our friend."

"And don't you know the story of Pandora?" Hermes asked.

I looked at him blankly.

"No, that's one of the stories they left out," Pytheas said. "Not a good example, and Plato didn't believe people learned excellence from awful warnings. So what did you do when you opened it and it turned out to be Hilfa?"

It was my turn to look down guiltily. "We arranged for him to have somewhere to live and a job and education, as if he were any Sael who had decided to stay behind." I glanced at Hermes. "That's always happening. The Saeli like Plato, and lots of them stay, though usually they live in pods, not individually. But it was easy."

"And you didn't tell anyone?" Pytheas demanded.

"I'm not completely irresponsible. It was two years ago. I told Dad and Klymene." They had been consuls that year.

"And Neleus and Klymene didn't tell anyone? Didn't tell me?" He sounded aggrieved.

"Evidently not. I don't know if they told anyone else."

"I can't believe you all kept it from me!" Pytheas said.

I shifted guiltily. "Athene specified that we shouldn't tell you. So we decided to wait and see what happened, and keep an eye on Hilfa, which we have been doing. I started working on the boat with him. He hasn't done anything unusual."

"Let's go and find him," Hermes suggested.

"Why would she choose a Sael?" Pytheas asked, ignoring Hermes. "The Saeli have a strange relationship with their gods. Why would Athene have had one in a box? And why would she leave it here with Neleus's daughters in case she was lost? And what use could it be, in that case? And did she *expect* to get lost?"

"She must have, if she took measures against it," Hermes said; and then after a moment, "How strange."

"If she was here on Plato, why didn't she simply come to me and explain? And where is she, anyway? She must have known Thetis would open the box."

"I didn't say it was Thetis who opened it! And it wasn't. We did it together." Though if I hadn't agreed, she would have done it anyway. When we first opened it, for a second it looked like a snake coiled tightly around a human baby. Then it resolved into an egg, which immediately hatched into Hilfa, much as he was now: curious, earnest, alien. "I don't think he's a god."

"We should go and talk to him immediately," Hermes said. "Though can I please sort out this mess with Necessity first?"

Pytheas's eyes widened and he swayed back a little, then he waved his hand, giving permission.

"Marsilia," Hermes began. "Tell me the circumstances in which Alkippe was conceived."

I took a breath and gathered the information concisely. "She was conceived at the end-of-summer Festival of Hera eight years ago. You were calling yourself Poimandros, and you said you were from Psyche."

Hermes smiled.

"Psyche is one of the other Platonic Cities," Pytheas put in. "It's not as much fun as you might imagine."

"We were drawn together—our names drawn out of the lots together—and we went off to be married for the day."

"You really are doing Plato's Republic," Hermes said.

"Participation in the Festival of Hera is voluntary," Pytheas said. "Well, here it is. In Psyche and Athenia it's compulsory for citizens. But nobody has to stay in Psyche or Athenia if they don't like it."

"It's all right, you don't need to be so defensive, I think it's charming," Hermes said, smiling again. "Eight years ago, end of summer, fix the lots to be drawn, spend the night in bed, got it. And you'll put in a word of recommendation for me with the beautiful Thetis?"

I was opening my mouth to say calmly that what Hermes and Thetis did was their own affair, when Pytheas interrupted.

"Wait," Pytheas said. "I know how hard it is to resist Necessity. But if Athene is truly lost, and if she knew ahead of time that she was going into danger, and if we have to rescue her, then having you bound by Necessity might be a safeguard."

"A safeguard?" Hermes asked. He looked astonished. "You think Necessity might protect *me*?"

"I think if there's a serious risk, it might," Pytheas said.

"But—you know what it feels like!" Hermes protested.

"You're strong enough to bear it," Pytheas said. "Who **knows** what might happen to Athene otherwise?"

"Gods can't die," I protested.

"They can't ordinarily get lost either," Pytheas said. "And I think that since Necessity has given us this unexpected aegis, we might be meant to use it."

"But if gods can die, or get lost, or—" I stopped, realizing my voice was rising. I took a breath from my stomach and began again. "What happens to Alkippe if something should happen to Hermes before he goes back to conceive her?"

They looked at each other a moment in silence, then at me. "It's impossible," Pytheas said. "He has to survive to do that, and therefore he will, and know he is safe until it is done."

"Look, Alkippe's my daughter, I really care about her. I can't risk her never having existed. Hermes needs to go and do whatever he needs to do about it now, before going into danger." They were listening to me, but they didn't seem to understand the importance of what I was saying.

Pytheas frowned. "Even if she is the anchor that keeps all of us safe? Necessity has given us this tie, when we're venturing into danger. Having Necessity on our side can only help."

"But Alkippe!" Her bright eyes, her wriggling body, her inquiring mind, her bold soul, I wanted to say, and couldn't find the words to make them understand. Pytheas knew her and how marvelous she was, but Hermes had only seen her for a few minutes.

"Where do you believe Athene is?" Hermes asked Pytheas.

"Possibly she's in the Underworld. That would be all right. Strange, but all right."

"Ah. And because of the way when we go there we only perceive Hades and those souls with whom Hades thinks it's good for us to interact, we can't tell that she's there?"

Hermes nodded as if this made sense.

"Perhaps." Pytheas was frowning. "But I suspect she's not there, and that she has gone into the Chaos before and after time."

Hermes wavered for a moment—I was staring right at him and that's the only way I can describe it. It was like when you're watching the shadow of a train you're in falling on the ground, and then suddenly there's a hill and the shadow is nearer and bigger for a moment, and then it's back on the plain, racing along. "I can't find her from outside time either," he announced. "And I tried to catch her at the Panathenaia, but I couldn't."

"But you weren't there," I pointed out.

"No. You didn't see me, so I couldn't be visible. And she wasn't there for an instant that you and Thetis weren't." He paused, and looked assessingly at Pytheas. "Do you think we should go to Father now and tell him everything?"

"First, we should talk to Hilfa and discover what message she left for us," Pytheas said.

"And you really think I need to stay bound by Necessity?" Hermes asked. "It's like having a sharp stone in my shoe."

"That stone might be our shield," Pytheas said.

"I am not letting you out of my sight again until you go back there and ensure Alkippe is real," I said to Hermes. I had never felt more strongly about anything in my life.

"I'd agree to that, but you are mortal, and not caught in Necessity's jaws. Alkippe already only has one parent. What happens to her if I have to go into danger and you don't survive?"

I looked at him in incomprehension. "I'd happily give my life for hers, if need be. And she'd be safe here. I wasn't suggesting taking her with us."

Pytheas was smiling his enigmatic smile. "You're seeing Platonic motherhood, which is different from anything you're used to. Marsilia is telling you we're in the City, and here children with one parent or no parents at all are at no disadvantage."

"Yes. If my parents and Thetis couldn't manage, though I'm sure they could, Alkippe could grow up in a nursery and pursue her own excellence. It's not like the little orphan in Homer." I didn't have much context for how children grew up elsewhere. His assumption that she would suffer neglect if I died disconcerted me. There's a lot of variety in how we do things on Plato, but that wouldn't happen in any of our cities. Bringing up children to be their best selves is something we all agree is crucial. In those cities with no nurseries, a child whose family died in a catastrophe would be immediately adopted into another family.

"This is a strange place," Hermes said. "Well, you can stay with me if you feel so strongly about it. Here. A votive gift." He handed me something. I looked down at it. It was a little purse of soft leather, with a drawstring. Puzzled, I opened it. "It'll never be empty, unless you shake it out," he said. "And the coin you pull from it will always be enough to pay for what you want."

I took out a coin and turned it in my fingers. I had seen coins before; they use money in Lucia. My other hand rose to my neck, to my gold pin on my jacket collar. It was forbidden to me to have gold, other than the Gold in my soul and the pin that symbolized it. I couldn't think of a more useless gift, but I imagined it was well intended. As well as travel, Hermes was patron of the marketplace, commerce, and thieves. I decided to talk to him about our trade negotiations when there was a chance, in case he had interesting ideas. "Thank you," I said, politely.

Pytheas was frowning. It was so strange to see him, the same but different. He was definitely my grandfather, but he seemed to be about my own age. "Marsilia is part of my family. If any harm comes to her, you'll answer for it."

Hermes nodded once.

Pytheas didn't stop frowning. "We should go in and I should say hello to the rest of the family. They'll hardly have had time to miss me. And then we should find Hilfa."

"Why do we need to bother going inside first?" Hermes asked.

"I want to speak to Neleus. And we need Arete."

"Hilfa speaks Greek," I said.

"Doubtless, but whether or not you've discovered it, your aunt Arete has skills beyond flight and translation. Come on." He took a step towards the door.

"Arete isn't there. She's at the spaceport," I said.

Pytheas hesitated. "Then—"

"No, come on. It'll be fun to see their faces," Hermes said.

7

JASON

Now, if you were an incarnate god and you died and then resurrected and came back, the way Christians and Ikarians say Yayzu did, what would be the first thing you'd say the first time you saw your children?

Pytheas came in from the garden looking about my age, with all the silver gone from his hair. He was wearing a white kiton trimmed with a conventional blue-and-gold book and scroll pattern, and pinned with the pin that meant he was a Gold of the City. He went straight up to Neleus, and what he said absolutely flummoxed me. It was the last thing I'd have expected to hear in the circumstances. And I was right there. I can report his exact words, and they were: "Why didn't you tell me about Hilfa?"

Neleus blushed at that, which meant that, given the color his skin was to start off, he turned almost purple.

"You were always telling us to sort things out for ourselves," Neleus said. "You never wanted to hear anything about negotiations with the aliens."

"You don't think the name of Athene would have got my attention?"

"Too much of it," Neleus said.

Hermes laughed aloud.

"And she had asked the girls specifically not to tell you," Neleus went on. "Hilfa didn't seem dangerous. We could have told you any time there was need. We didn't tell my brothers or Arete either."

"What's this about Hilfa?" I asked. It wasn't really my place to speak in that kind of company, and they'd been ignoring me so far, but I wanted to know what kind of trouble Hilfa had managed to find, so that I could help the dear dunderhead out of it. How could anyone imagine he might be dangerous?

And that's why I found myself with Marsilia and Thetis and the two gods an hour later, after a lot of talking and a walk in the cold, on the green basalt street outside Hilfa's house down by the harbor, three streets over from my own sleeping house. Neleus had gone off to take Alkippe to bed and then go himself to the spaceport, but all the rest of us were there. They had shared an unlikely story about Athene giving Hilfa to Marsilia and Thetis in a box, and beyond that a lot of questions and not enough answers. The only way to get the answers was to talk to Hilfa, seemingly. I insisted on coming along to look out for Hilfa, and Thetis backed me up until Pytheas gave in and let us come along, trusting her social judgement.

Down in the harbor, instead of sconces there's a strip of light running along the sills of all the buildings, lighting everyone's faces from underneath. On Hilfa's street, where a lot of Saeli lived, the lighting ran a little green, which made Thetis and Marsilia look as if they were made out of gold, while Pytheas and Hermes seemed as if they were made out of marble. I could see this really well, because they all turned to look at me. I'd insisted on coming along; now they wanted me to announce that we were there.

It was easier to do it than say anything, so I scratched on the door.

Hilfa appeared, wearing loose-woven dark-purple pants, with his chest and back bare. I had thought he would be disconcerted seeing a bunch of important people wanting to talk to him in the middle of the night—not that it was so late really, but I'd had a long day. Hilfa didn't even blink. He invited us all in and apologized for not having enough chairs. He knew everyone except Hermes. Marsilia introduced them. To my surprise, Hermes said something to Hilfa in Saeli, which I took to be a greeting. Who would have thought he'd know it? He hadn't used it to greet Aroo. Travel and trade, I thought; he'd probably run into Saeli on other planets where humans had contacted them.

We sat where we could. Hilfa scurried around putting all the lights on, which made the room very bright. Thetis and I sat on the bed, against the wall. Pytheas took one chair, and Marsilia the other, while Hermes leaned against the table. Then Hilfa made a dash into the little back room, which wasn't much more than a big closet really. He brought out wine, and Marsilia got up to help him mix it and hand the cups around. He brought four matching red-pattern winecups, and two Saeli-style beakers. He gave one of those to me, with a smile, and kept the other himself. Mine was incised with geometric patterns in the porphyry inlay, so I couldn't quite figure how he meant it. It might have been treating me as family, to have the other cup that didn't match, or it might have been meant as an honor. There was no telling, and it wasn't the time to ask. I decided it came out positive either way, and smiled at him over the brim. Other times when I'd had a drink at Hilfa's place we'd used winecups, but there had never been more than three or four of us. It was a biggish room, with one small red-and-blue geometric rug, and the walls were painted white, with no frescos or other art. It had always seemed quite empty to me, until now, when I'd have thought it full if I hadn't come straight from the press at Thessaly.

"Athene is missing," Pytheas said as soon as we had all settled down and sipped our wine.

"Missing? Lost?" Hilfa asked, turning to him from where he had been putting down the wine bowl on the table. The swirls on his skin faded a little. Up to that moment I thought there had been some mistake, that Hilfa couldn't be anything but what he seemed:

a slightly puzzled Sael who had somehow wandered into all this by mistake. "Is she—" He hesitated. "Do I say she? Are there no special pronouns for divinity?"

"No, you simply say she," Marsilia said. "Ikarians capitalize it when they write, but we use the same word."

"Do you mean to say that She is lost?" Hilfa asked. I could all but hear the capital.

"Yes. What do you know about it?" Pytheas leaned forward, winecup forgotten in his hand and nearly spilling. Thetis gently took it from him and set it down on the tiles by her feet.

"I don't remember anything before I hatched here, you understand?" Hilfa said. He seemed more confident and relaxed than normal. I thought I had been wrong to come; he didn't need my help.

"That's what you said at the time, but you could talk," Marsilia said.

"I knew some things," Hilfa said. "I don't know how much is normal for newly hatched Saeli. I have not wanted to ask, because sometimes questions reveal too much about what you do not know, when you should." He looked at Marsilia, with a twitch of expression that I thought meant apology. "I know that's not the Socratic way."

"The Socratic way regards deception very badly," Marsilia said.

Hilfa inclined his head. "You told me not to reveal my origins."

Marsilia sighed. "It's true, we did."

"Plato's censorship and deception wars with Sokrates's desire to question everything all the time," Hermes said.

"We in the Cities have noticed this contradiction," Pytheas said wearily. "Go on, Hilfa."

Hilfa turned to Thetis, who was sitting next to me on the bed. "I remember you looking after me, and that is the first thing I remember. Before that there was no me. Let me fetch paper."

"Paper?" Hermes asked.

"Quicker to do than to explain," he said, and darted back into the little storeroom.

"I think he's telling the truth," Thetis said. The instinctive twitches of my own liver said the same thing. Saeli are hard to read, but I was used to Hilfa, and he didn't seem to be prevaricating at all, even as he talked about dodging revelation.

Pytheas nodded. "I think so too. Hermes?"

Hermes was staring intently at the door through which Hilfa had vanished, and shook himself when he was addressed, the way Hilfa often did on the boat when I called him back from one of his reveries. "I sense no deception either," he said.

Hilfa came back with paper, a standard sheaf of Worker-made letter paper. He set it down on the table. Hermes moved to give him room, and took up position leaning casually against the wall. Hilfa took a pen and wrote for perhaps a second. I don't think I could have written my name in the time he spent writing. It didn't look like he was writing, either; more like he was doodling. The pen danced over the paper, and then he was done. He walked over to hand it to Pytheas, and I could see it was covered all over in neat script, where I'd have counted on a sketch.

"I knew before I can remember that when She was lost, I should write that and give it to You," Hilfa said.

"Do you know what it says?" Thetis asked.

"No," Hilfa said. He squatted down where he was, on the rug in the middle of the floor, sitting back on his haunches the way I had seen him do so often on the boat. It looked uncomfortable and unnatural, because human legs don't bend comfortably that way, but I'd grown used to the fact that Saeli ones did. He was much greener than normal; the pinkish swirls that normally covered his skin only visible now in the center of his chest and back.

"Do you know where Athene is, or how she came to be lost?" Hermes asked, for the first time taking a sip of his wine.

"Not unless it says so there," Hilfa said, gesturing to the paper. Pytheas was reading it intently and didn't look up.

"Do you know what you are?" Thetis asked. I thought about Thetis and Marsilia opening the box Athene had told them not to open unless she was lost, and finding Hilfa inside. I understood why they had opened it. All the same, I wouldn't have done it. You learn patience, fishing. Marsilia was starting to learn some now, working on the boat, but she hadn't had a scrap of it when she'd first come to me.

"I don't know. I think I am perhaps a hero."

"A hero, the child of a god?" Marsilia was frowning. "One of the Saeli gods?"

"That is my guess," Hilfa said, looking at Hermes, and then away. "But I can't say. I don't know where I come from, where I belong. I don't want to go there. I like it here. I like the fish and the sea."

"The wind and the waves," I said. It was what he had said that afternoon.

He turned to me for a moment with the expression I thought was a real smile, then back to Marsilia. "I like Jason and Dion," he said. "I like the boat. I like you and Thetis. I want to stay in the City. I want to take oath. I didn't ask until now, because it wasn't just until you knew."

"Nobody's going to make you leave—" Thetis began, setting down her empty winecup at her feet beside Pytheas's full one.

"Don't make any promises," Marsilia said, cutting across her. "We will need to debate this. I think many of us will support Hilfa's desire. I certainly will, but this is important."

"What good is it you being consul, Marsilia, if—" Thetis began.

Pytheas looked up from the paper and stared at Hilfa. Simply by raising his head, he riveted all our attention, and Thee fell silent.

His face was inscrutable, his lips slightly parted as if caught in the middle of a gasp or a smile.

"Are you going to share that with the rest of us?" Hermes asked.

Pytheas looked serenely at his brother. "She has gone beyond what lies outside time, into the Chaos of before and after, to discover how the universe begins and ends. She has done this with the help of a Saeli god of knowledge, Jathery. In case she had difficulty returning, she has left me the explanation of how to do this. Her explanation is divided into parts, each of which she has left with a different person, in a different place and time." His voice was level, calm, and absolutely furious.

"Father will kill her," Hermes said. He sounded awestruck and impressed. "He'll hang her upside-down over the abyss for eternity with anvils on her fingers."

"You know he never does anything to Athene," Pytheas said, absently. "No, I think it's worse than that. She's broken Father's edicts, obviously, but I think this time she might have gone too far and be up against Fate and Necessity."

"What does that mean?" Thetis asked.

"It means she could be lost forever. And we might be too if we go after her," Hermes said. He smiled at Thetis.

"Is this something Ikaros dreamed up?" Marsilia asked. "It sounds a bit like one of his ideas."

"She worked on the idiotic plans with him, but she hasn't taken him with her," Pytheas said.

Hermes drained his cup and set it down decisively on the table. "We should locate the pieces of her explanation."

"Maybe we should go to Father," Pytheas said.

"But I'm safe from Necessity," Hermes said. "And we should at least collect the pieces of her explanation first. When we have that, we'll have a better idea of whether we could help her."

"But we don't need to. Father will already know how to do it,"

Pytheas said. "And don't you think this might be why he sent you to get me now?"

"It would be better if we can sort this out without him," Hermes said. "At least, better to try."

"Whatever he won't do to Athene, he wouldn't hesitate to do to us."

"Why does Zeus never punish Athene?" Thetis asked unexpectedly.

"We don't know, but we think it's because he ate her mother," Pytheas said. "Our previous goddess of wisdom. Metis."

"Ate her?" I asked, horrified enough to speak out.

"Another thing Plato left out?" Hermes asked.

"Before you ask, we don't know the answers," Pytheas said. "We don't know if or how he transformed Metis into Athene, or what it really means that she's his daughter, born from his head. We think it might have something to do with how he treats her, but we might be wrong."

"I don't understand," Thetis said. I didn't either.

Pytheas smiled at her, not unkindly. "None of us do. I'm not sure even Father understands. He didn't create the universe, and some of the ways things work are Mysteries even to him."

"You are speaking of your Father?" Hilfa asked, quietly.

"Yes," Pytheas said. He looked down at Hilfa.

"Your Father Who is also Parent of the Saeli gods?"

"He's the father of all the gods in the universe, as far as I know," Hermes said, smiling at Hilfa with a strange smile. Hilfa didn't turn towards him.

"And yet you speak so lightly of. . . ." Hilfa hesitated, and looked at Marsilia.

"We simply say *his*," she said. "If you prefer to say gla we will understand."

"Of gla wrath," Hilfa finished.

"Yes we do, because we've experienced it," Pytheas said.

"And however he may appear in the Saeli pantheons, and whatever he may have done to your people, he is not, to us, a god of wrath. Well, except when we've done something to deserve it. Like Metis."

"Tell us about Jathery," Marsilia said to Hilfa. "A god of wisdom, but also a trickster, yes?"

"Yes." Hilfa swung around to face her, his back to Hermes, and counted the aspects off on his long fingers. "The five things that go together: wisdom, trickery, riddles, name-changing, and freedom."

"Might he have tricked Athene into this?" Marsilia asked.

"She as much as admits that she suspects him of it," Pytheas said, tapping the letter. "It seems they've been friends for some time. Jathery may even have had a hand in persuading her to set up the Republic experiment."

"Aren't you forbidden to mingle with gods of other pantheons?" Marsilia asked.

Pytheas and Hermes looked at her with the same puzzled expression. "No," Hermes answered. "Why would we be?"

"Then why don't you?" she asked.

"Aesthetic reasons," Pytheas said. "We live in our own context, our own fabric, culture, framework. They each have their own. We don't have any reason to meet, to interact. We stay in our own circles because that feels right. But if Athene felt ecumenical, nothing stopped her being friends with Jathery. More's the pity."

"And nothing would stop you doing the same?"

"Nothing except context, culture, having nothing in common, and no need." Pytheas frowned.

"Or how about Yayzu?" Marsilia asked.

"Maybe I could have a productive conversation with him. And he speaks Greek. But it might be difficult to find somewhere comfortable for us both. Or, no. It wouldn't." Pytheas smiled. "If Yayzu and I wanted to compare notes on incarnation and how we best ought to help people, I know a place. Maybe. I'll think about that. It might even be a good idea."

"But Jathery is a Saeli god," Marsilia said. "Shouldn't he feel an . . . aesthetic need to be attending to their affairs?"

Hilfa shook his head without looking up.

"I think it would certainly be preferable if he did, instead of heading off into primal Chaos with Athene," Pytheas said.

"So do you really think we should go to Father?" Hermes asked.

"Well, maybe. Except that she does plead for me not to tell him," Pytheas said, looking down at the paper again. "Since you also seem against it, let's try getting the explanation first."

"Pleads? Athene? Can I see that?" Hermes asked, putting out his hand for it.

"No, I think not," Pytheas said, folding it up and putting it inside his kiton.

"But Zeus must know already. He knows everything," Thetis said.

"He knows, but he's not aware of things until they come to his attention. If we can sort it out ourselves, it might be better if this came to his attention after Athene is safely back," Pytheas said.

"Or at least until we've read the explanation and know we can't do it without help," Hermes said.

"Time can't be changed, except in one circumstance," Pytheas said.

"The Darkness of the Oak," Marsilia interrupted. Both gods turned at once to focus on her. I had no idea what she was talking about, but the words sent chills through me. I took a deep draught of my wine and looked sideways across the room to her as she continued, "It's given me nightmares since Dad told me about Zeus talking about it on Olympos. Do you think he'd do that? Unmake the City, now? Because of this?"

"More than that, if need be," Pytheas said. "Athene wants to know everything. There are no limits to *everything*. But Father has Mysteries he might not want investigated, and I fear this is one of them. It's directly against his edicts. She might have gone too far. And as for Jathery—is Jathery a favorite of Father's?" He swung around to Hilfa.

"No," Hilfa whispered, his lips hardly moving.

Thetis broke the awkward silence. "Where are the pieces of Athene's explanation?"

"Distributed through time, where only gods can get them. Kebes has one of them."

Marsilia, Thetis and I gasped in unison. "Who's Kebes?" Hermes asked. Astonishing. But of course, he didn't know. He was from another world. The seventy eventful years of our history was all new to him.

"Kebes is the one I beat playing your gift upside-down," Pytheas said. "He hates me. Worse, I was in time all the time he was alive. You'll have to collect that piece. And it won't be easy."

"She must have wanted you involved," Marsilia said, looking at Hermes. "You, or some other god at least."

"I'm not going near this culture without a native guide," Hermes said. He was looking at Thetis, but she was looking down at Hilfa and didn't notice. Hilfa was rocking backwards and forwards slightly, his multicolored lids closed over his eyes.

"I said I'm staying with you," Marsilia said to Hermes. "I've been to Lucia."

"Good," he said. Then he smiled challengingly at Pytheas. "How many pieces are there? Shall we divide them and meet back here with them?"

"I'll manage Pico," Pytheas said. "How are you with the Enlightenment?"

"You can definitely have that one," Hermes said, with a little shudder.

"All right, then you can take Phila the daughter of Antipatros.

Athene says she gave it to her after her wedding, so any time after that I suppose."

"Who did she marry?" Hermes asked.

"She married Demetrios the Besieger of Cities," Marsilia said. Then, when she realized we were all staring at her, "What? It's in Plutarch."

"*You* are going to be useful. Good!" Hermes said.

As I was drawing breath, Pytheas, Hermes, and Marsilia vanished.

Meanwhile, unnoticed by anyone except me, Thetis had slipped to the floor and put her arms around Hilfa, who immediately turned and clung to her like a baby.

8

APOLLO

I generally enjoy emotions. I like transmuting emotion into art, every shade of feeling, every nuance and tone and note. But the wrath I felt now, the anger at Athene that burned through me, was too strong for that. Human emotions happen in the veins, in the gut, as well as in the mind. Divine emotions are a thing of mind and soul alone, but are neither less strong nor less passionate for that. You hear of Olympian calm, and we *are* calm, detached, distant—usually. When we do feel strongly there is nothing of mortal frailty to deter us in that feeling. A mortal heart or liver might overflow and burst with too strong an emotion, but never ours. When we are moved as strongly as I was moved by Athene's letter there is no restraint—we are the anger, while the anger lasts.

I like feeling the heat of emotions. I do not like giving way before them and becoming the conflagration. Emotions should always be manageable, never overwhelming.

Therefore my calm and control can be demonstrated by my behavior. I practiced moderation, as both my Delphic injunction and Plato recommend. I did not burn down Hilfa's house in sudden fusion heat. I did not even char Athene's letter to ash as I read it. I talked reasonably to the others, though I did not show the letter to them. There was no need to make things any worse.

It was the late summer of 1506 when I strode rapidly down one of the little streets in Bologna that run between the cathedral and the town hall. It was a narrow laneway, lined on both sides with people selling things, pushing them on the passersby with cries and importunities. I shoved through them impatiently. He was sitting on a high stool outside a wineshop, disputing, surrounded by a gaggle of students. He was as I had last seen him on Olympos, young and able to see, but he was wearing the robes of an Augustinian monk. He had a white ceramic winecup in his hand, and was gesturing with it. I grabbed him by the shoulder, pulled him off the stool and turned him to face me.

"Ah," he said, admirably unsurprised. "Pytheas. With your cloak flaring around you like that, I thought you must be an avenging angel."

His friends laughed. I glared at them, and back at Pico. "Shall we go somewhere we can talk privately?" I asked, speaking Latin because he had. It was wrong to take out my wrath on Pico. He wasn't the one who deserved it.

He fumbled some coins out of his pouch and put them down on the table among the winecups. "An old friend. I'll see you later," he said to the others.

"You needn't think you'll get away without making a proper refutation!" one of them said.

"Tomorrow," Pico said, smiling and shaking his head.

"Why are you dressed as an Augustinian?" I asked quietly as we walked down the street together, ignoring offers of fish, wine, fruit, and young bodies of both sexes from the street vendors.

"I'm staying at the monastery of St. Stephen's," he explained.

"And what are you doing here?"

"Research." He looked wary. "And arguing with Averroists. They're young, and they haven't been properly trained, but some of them are extremely smart."

"You're not a lawyer or a doctor, so what are you researching in

Bologna?" We came out of the little street into the square by the Ducal Palace.

He smiled. "Theology?"

"Really? You barely got away from the Inquisition last time, and you had influential friends then!"

He smiled at me. "I do now, too. Here you are, and before I've managed to get into any trouble at all. Let's go in here." It was another wineshop, on a corner, with only a few tables out on the street. He ducked through the door and I followed. The interior was small and dark. The patrons were older, and many of them were wearing dusty aprons, by which I deduced that they were stonemasons. Pico ordered wine, and we sat down together on a bench in a corner. The place was crowded, but the patrons moved over to make a little room for us. "If we speak Greek, we'll have perfect privacy here," he said in that language. "We probably would have back there, but that's a scholars' tavern, so you never know."

It was amazing, really. A count by birth, a Humanist by inclination, befriended by Ficino, imprisoned by the Inquisition, saved by Lorenzo and Savonarola, taken to the City an instant before death, snatched to Olympos by Zeus, set to work with Athene, abandoned by her in Bologna mere months before it was due to be sacked, and still his optimism was undimmed. There aren't many like him. "Do you know where Athene is?"

He looked wary again. "She was going somewhere she thought was too dangerous for me. And since you're here, it seems she was right. Do you know where she was going, or should I explain?" He glanced at the oblivious guzzling stonemasons as if worried that they might be able to speak Greek after all.

"Give me whatever she gave you to give to me." I put out my hand.

"It's in my cell."

"You left it in your cell among a lot of thieving Augustinians?" Optimism is not always a virtue.

He shrugged. "It's inside my copy of Ficino's Plato, which they think is magic and won't touch. Besides, I've given a copy of it to Raffaele Maffei, in case."

"Why don't you simply keep it in your pocket?" I growled. "And Maffei? The Volterran encyclopaedist? Why Maffei?"

"When you're not a count in Renaissance Italy, you're always getting your pocket picked. And Raffaele is an old acquaintance. He thinks I'm my own illegitimate son."

"Let's hope for the copy in your Plato," I said. I put my full winecup down on the table and stood. We wouldn't be driven to Maffei's copy in any event. If the original copy was missing, I could go back to a time when Pico had it and recover it—ten seconds after he had left it alone in his cell, if that's what it took.

"It's incredibly frustrating. Wherever I am, I never have access to all the books I need," he said, swallowing his wine and putting the cup down. "Here I have all the Christian books, even those that will be destroyed when Julius gets here in November, but not the ones we rescued from Alexandria. My memory's good, but it's so useful to be able to check things."

"Are you done with the ones here?" I asked.

He nodded. "But I wish there were somewhere we could have everything."

We walked together through the streets. Bologna is a remarkably medieval city. It was a provincial nowhere as Roman Bononia, and thrived in the Middle Ages; but in my opinion, while the food is usually good, it was never really beautiful until the renewal of the periphique in the twenty-second century. True, it had pillars and colonnades, but as we walked in their shade I couldn't help noticing that all the pillars were different. There was no harmony, no true proportion. Nothing matched. It was all a medieval jumble. Occasionally I noticed a lovely classical pillar, and felt an urge to rescue it and put it somewhere it could be comfortable.

"You're not so angry now?" Pico asked.

"I'm not unjustly taking out my anger on the wrong person," I said. "When I find Athene will be soon enough to indulge my wrath."

"You really did look like an avenging angel, with your cloak flaring around you like that," he said.

In Pico's New Concordance, Olympian gods are classed as angels. I think of it as a metaphor. I had changed the appearance of my clothes to be locally inconspicuous. Everyone's cloak flared in 1506. But there was no point in arguing.

There's nothing wrong with brick, brick can be beautiful, but it can easily be overdone. The church and monastery of St. Stephen was a mess. It contained different sections built at different times. It had been owned by a number of different orders, and they had all built onto it, none of them completing the designs of their predecessors. It was like a chambered nautilus where each chamber had been designed by a different committee. "It's as if the Renaissance had never happened," I murmured to Pico as we passed through a room containing an enormous pulpit in the shape of the Holy Sepulchre, with scarcely room for two people to pass by around it. It would have done well enough in a correspondingly huge and Gothic nave, here it was ridiculous and unserviceable, almost intimidating in its size and impracticality.

"The Renaissance is thriving right now in Florence and Rome," he said with a sideways smile. "It'll make it here eventually. I hope."

We came out into an enclosed courtyard. I was glad to see the sky and the sun again. There was a piece of sad mosaic on the wall—abstract, only a pattern, but what made it sad was the presence of two tiny fragments of porphyry given pride of place. Porphyry is a speckled purple rock which, over time, had in Medieval Europe come to stand for the lost wonders of Rome. The Egyptian quarry it came from was lost after Rome fell, and so were the skills of making steel tough enough to work it. It's a volcanic rock, and it's therefore present in quantity on Plato. The Workers can work with it easily, so there's lots of it everywhere and we have all kinds of things made out of it. But here and now, porphyry symbolized the lost heritage of Rome, and here set in the wall were these two minute pieces, all poor Bologna had left of the ancient world. They had not entirely forgotten what it meant, but they couldn't come any closer than this to regaining or re-creating it. I wished somebody in Bologna would pray for my help so that I could give them something better than this. And they were about to be sacked, too. It really wasn't fair.

Pico led me into a cloister. The shadows of the pillars were falling across the open central space. A heavily bearded monk was sitting on the wall reading Latin poetry, a cat curled on his lap. Pico frowned. "We should wait here," he said, quietly. "We're not supposed to have guests in our cells, and I'm not supposed to be in my cell at this time of day. He'll go to Vespers soon."

He nodded to the monk and took a seat against a pillar on the other side of the cloister. "Won't they expect you to go?" I asked, sitting beside him and looking over at the well in the center of the courtyard.

"I'm only visiting. They know I'm a scholar."

"He won't speak Greek?" I asked, smiling at the monk, who smiled back uncertainly.

"Here?" Pico asked. He was right. It was even less likely we'd find someone who understood Greek here than among the stonemasons.

It was too much. "If she had to leave you somewhere in 1506 with Christian books and a university, why aren't you in Florence?"

"There was a book here I needed. And there are people there who know me too well not to recognize me, even if I tell them I'm my own son. They poisoned me the first time, after all. And Soderini's in power, and the Medici will be back soon and feeling vengeful—I could hardly bear to see it. It's the last days of the Republic." He stopped. "The Florentine Republic, that is, not Plato's Republic."

"They probably don't spare a thought for Plato's Republic."

"I do," he said. "As well as working on my new theory of the universe."

"Newer than the New Concordance?" I wondered whether to tell him now what had been going on among the Ikarians on Plato.

"The New Concordance arose out of realizing that the *Republic* wasn't working, couldn't work, because Plato was wrong about the nature of the soul. The philosophical soul can feel love, in addition to desiring the Good. Love isn't simply a way towards opening the soul to God. So I had to rethink everything. They were doing the same in Psyche, coming to different conclusions but working on the same basis. If Plato had been right about that, it would all have worked properly. The problem on Kallisti was that we got overfocused on tweaking practical reality."

"Do you still think all the authorities agree with each other?"

"They do if you look at them the right way. They were all trying to reach the truth, and it's amazing how much congruence there is. But I have lots of new information. My new theory is an attempt at integrating that."

"How long is it, in your personal time, since you last saw me?" I asked. I really wanted to know, and to ask it conversationally. It was why I was sitting on the wall instead of taking him outside time and straight back into his cell.

He wrinkled his brow. "I can't say. A lot of it was outside of time. And China. And France. A long time. Decades at least." So perhaps Athene's personal time was similarly long, since they had been working together. Interesting. Good. Maybe she hadn't only been using me all the time, maybe she had truly intended to meet me when she made the offer, and then later realized it would fit with her rescue plan. I hoped so. "I'm working on a theory of time, too. Jathery has been very helpful."

"Jathery—" I was speechless. "You know he's an alien god? And that he and Athene have gone out into Chaos and are trapped there?"

"What was that word? Alien?"

"Intelligent people who evolved on other planets. We've only started to use it to mean that since we've been on the planet Plato and had to deal with them all the time. But I'd assumed you'd know it."

He shook his head. "So there are people on other worlds? And Jathery is one of their gods? Wondrous! I want to go there."

He'd want to reconcile all their theories with Platonism and Christianity and make one huge synthesis. "Athene knows. You couldn't tell?"

"Jathery didn't seem as if she's from another planet. Are you sure Athene knows?"

I sighed, and my anger rose up again. "Athene certainly knew. She messed about making a half-alien demigod to give me a message, creating a living being with a perplexed soul, when she could have simply given the message to me directly and explained what was going on. She could have trusted me. She should have!" I sat there on the wall and waited, calm on the surface but still utterly livid. This was all so completely unnecessary.

Pico looked extremely uncomfortable at that. "She used you."

"Yes! She used me as if I'd been of no account. And not only me." I glared at the stone coping of the well. I wasn't used to being treated that way. Granting equal significance to others was something I had only learned, slowly and painfully, over the course of my mortal life. Being granted it was something I was so accustomed to that I felt affronted when I was not. That was interesting to consider. I stepped out of time and considered it for a while, staring out from Olympos over the distant blue isles of Greece, until I was calm and fully understood my anger and affronted pride. Then

I slipped back to the moment in the cloister beside Pico. He hadn't noticed my absence.

"She might have thought you'd try to stop her," Pico said.

"I would have, of course. But she could have trusted me. There was no need for any of this." I was calm now, but I hadn't forgiven her.

"Yes. Well. About the other thing," he said.

The church bells rang for Vespers, deafeningly close. The monk let go of the cat, set down his book, and straightened himself up. I spoke as soon as the bells were quiet enough for me to be heard. "I'd have taken you with me anyway. I wouldn't leave anyone stranded, waiting indefinitely in Bologna. She needn't have done it like this."

"I told her as much," Pico said, with his open smile. "And even without your promise to take me with you, I'd have told you where Sokrates is."

9

MARSILIA

Being outside time wasn't at all the way I had imagined it. We were in Hilfa's little house down near the harbor, and then the next moment without any sense of transition we were standing in a leafy glade. We were surrounded by unfamiliar kinds of trees, with leaves of the most intense green and red and gold I had ever seen. My focus seemed strange, as if whatever I was looking at was much closer than it should have been. Across the clearing, I saw a tiny purple flower growing at the foot of a tree, and I could see the shading of each petal, and the cracks in the bark of the tree behind. It seemed as if it were close enough that my breath would make the flower tremble, and yet I could also plainly see that it was several strides away from me. It was disconcerting. At the same time I could see the trees towering up around us, and although I could not name any of them I was sure, without knowing how I knew, that they were each a different species.

"Where are we?" I asked. My voice came out as a cracked whisper.

"We're outside time," Hermes said. "Sit down."

I obeyed, and sat down on the leaf-mould, which smelled rich and complex and almost overwhelming. "Are we on Olympos?" I asked.

"Somewhere like that, yes," Hermes said. "This is one of my places, outside time."

Something gold and blue darted across the clearing at head height. A bird! I had seen them represented, and I recognized it at once by the wings and beak. It felt so strange to be here, and yet perfectly natural. The air was pleasantly warm. I unsnicked my jacket.

Hermes sat down beside me. I couldn't quite look at him. He seemed to change under my gaze, now naked, now clothed, now a man, now a woman, for a disconcerting moment a Sael, now an old man, now a young girl. I looked back at the trees, which stayed the same from moment to moment, which seemed eternally solid and unchangeable, as well as incredibly beautiful. "Marsilia," Hermes said. I nodded, staring up at the leaves. "Before we go to seek him, tell me about Kebes. Everyone seemed so uncomfortable at the mention of his name, even Apollo."

I focused on a five-pointed bright red leaf on a tree behind Hermes, took a breath, and organized my knowledge. It seemed easier than it usually was. Perhaps it was the air of the place. "Kebes was one of the original Children brought to the Republic. He hated it and was rebellious. After the Last Debate he ran away, stealing one of the ships."

"Wait, the Last Debate?"

It seemed extraordinary that he could be unaware of something so fundamental to history. It was like hearing someone say "Wait, who's Alexander? What's Thermopylae? Who won at Zama anyway?" It would be like this, I realized, with the space humans, only ten times harder because they wouldn't believe us and we didn't want them to. And they'd have huge history-shaping events of their own in the centuries that we'd missed and know nothing about, and they'd be as surprised as this that we didn't know them, and would look at us in amazement when we asked about them. As Hilfa had said, asking questions could be more revealing than we might want. Dealing with Hermes might be good practice for dealing with the space humans. "It was a debate between Athene and Sokrates. She turned him into a gadfly."

Hermes laughed delightedly. I was taken aback and glanced at him. He seemed fixed again in the form I thought of as Poimandros. I admired the interplay of dappled sunlight on his muscles. He really was the loveliest-looking man I'd ever seen, as well as the best in bed. Of course it was Thetis he wanted. Oh well. The trees were more beautiful anyway. And they stayed fixed in their forms. "Serves him right. Nobody has ever read Plato without wishing to do the same. And you didn't have any debates after that? Did you stop wanting to?"

"I wasn't born yet, but from what I hear they had twice as many debates as before. But Athene wasn't there for them."

"And Kebes left too? With her?"

It was my turn to laugh. "No, he hated her. He hated everything. He was no more than a big ball of hate from what I've heard."

Hermes twisted his lips in distaste, and then his face changed and seemed to be that of a broad-cheeked woman.

I looked down and focused on the trefoil leaves of the tiny purple flowers. "He took a bunch of people and stole a boat. They founded the Lucian cities, all eight of them, helped out with people they rescued from wars in Greece. They imposed a kind of Christianity, and practiced torture."

Hermes laughed again, but I didn't look up. I could see tiny hairs on the leaves. "Christianity more than a thousand years before Christ? I suppose this is an example of why Father forbids taking mortals out of time. I mean, Athene couldn't have tried harder, she stuck you on an island that was going to be destroyed, and still all this happened."

"He forbids it? Then we're breaking his edicts right now?" I did look up then. I'd never before realized the magnitude of what Athene had done.

Hermes was looking like himself again. He nodded. "Well, technically. And we shouldn't be using Necessity as a shield. I'm amazed Apollo even thought of that, he's usually so law-abiding."

"You said it's like a stone in your shoe?"

"Like a sharp painful stone that half cuts off my foot at every step that isn't in the direction Necessity wants me to go, back to conceive Alkippe and set time straight." He shrugged. "But don't worry. None of this was my idea, or yours either. It shouldn't come to that and it should be all right, even if he's angry. We can blame it all on Apollo and Athene. Now, tell me about Kebes."

I didn't like the way he was approaching this, and I wasn't reassured, but there wasn't a thing I could do about it. I looked back up at the beautiful trees. One of them had black bark and tiny yellow leaves falling in long strips like hair. "After twenty years, we found Kebes again, and the Lucian cities. That's when Pytheas entered into the musical contest with Kebes."

"Oh, I heard about that. Apollo won by playing the lyre upside-down, and then he flayed the other fellow to death. It doesn't sound like him at all."

"He cheated," I said.

"Apollo?" Hermes sounded astonished.

"No, of course not. Kebes. It was a contest for original composition, but he played a song Grandfather recognized from a future time." I didn't want to look away from the colors of the leaves, and the pattern the branches made.

"How did Kebes know it?"

"We don't know. Pytheas checked, and he couldn't have learned it from anyone who went to Lucia with him, though it's possible he could have learned it from one of the other Masters before he left—though they were so decidedly strict about musical modes it seems unlikely."

"You really stick to only the Dorian and Phrygian, as Plato wrote?" Hermes asked.

"Yes, of course we do. The other modes are bad for people's souls." I looked up beyond the tree branches at the sky, which was an intense shade of blue I'd never seen before.

"And you don't find it monotonous?"

The answer to that one was very easy, as it's actually laid out in Plato so I could simply paraphrase. "Do you find a diet of healthy food monotonous so that you'd go out and eat unhealthy food and tasty poisons and make yourself sick? How much more so for the soul."

Hermes laughed. "How pious you sound. Platonic piety."

I looked back at him. For an instant he looked like a dappled animal with big eyes, and then he was himself again. "Well, it seems very strange to me to be saying these things, which are truths that everyone agrees about. Even in Lucia these days they accept limitations on the modes of music. I don't think even in Sokratea, where they question everything all the time, they question that. If anyone had ever doubted it, the example of what happened with the Lucians proved that Plato was right about this."

Hermes sat up a little and arched a brow. "Proved it? How?"

"Well, it's obvious. They played music in the Mixolydian mode, and they tortured people to death and plagiarized. It led their souls away from justice."

"It could be the other way around."

I considered that for a moment, staring off at the trees again and the veins on the little yellow leaves. "I suppose it's possible. The torture and plagiarism could have led to harmful music arising. But that's no better."

"There are a couple of good historical examples on Earth of changing the music and the whole culture changing. They're much later than Plato though. One is Southern Gaul in the chivalric era, and the other is the phenomenon they call the Sixties." He smiled. "They were both a lot of fun."

"So you agree Plato was right?" I asked, looking directly into his eyes, which for an instant had red and yellow Saeli lids, looking strange in his human face.

"Well, maybe. But I think I'd get bored. And you'd be surprised how many people intoxicate themselves immoderately and eat things that are bad for them. Lots of people in other cultures don't consider a party with quince paste and watered wine as exciting as you might."

I thought about that, and wondered again about the humans on the ship. Would they be eating unhealthy food and drinking unmixed wine and listening to soul-destroying music? If so, how could we help them understand? What if they tried to introduce such things on Plato? Would there be people who would be tempted? Young people, feeling rebellious, who could find ammunition to do themselves real and lasting harm? I could hear a chirping music now, sounding like a small child learning to sing. I looked around for it and saw the bird, sitting on one of the branches, its beak open and its throat distended. I had of course read about birds singing. The music it made was safely in the Dorian mode. "I don't find the idea of food that's bad for me at all appealing."

"That's because you've never had any." He was smiling and watching me through half-lowered lids.

"Maybe. But I find the idea of music that's bad for my soul terrifying," I said honestly.

"What if you hear some when we go to talk to Kebes?" Hermes asked teasingly.

"I hope I don't, but if I do, I'll listen to proper music to get my soul back into harmony when I get home," I said. I was afraid, but my fear was held at arm's length. I was here for Alkippe, after all, and the thought of her made me strong. If she sang to me in her clear high voice it would drive out any dangerous music.

"Very wise," he said. "So Kebes sang a song and we don't know where he learned it?"

"He didn't sing, he played it on a syrinx, a kind of multiple flute thing. We don't know where he got the syrinx from, either. Grandfather says Athene invented it. But Kebes always hated Athene."

"Huh. So why did she choose him to have part of her puzzle?"
Hermes asked.

I looked back at the bird. It had stopped singing but was sitting
looking back at me, head cocked. I could see every feather. I wondered if they were hard or soft. "It's hard to imagine Kebes co-
operating with Athene over anything. His religion teaches that
she's a demon. And she's the one who set up the City in the first
place, and Kebes hated the City and Plato. Or that's what I've
always heard, from Pytheas and Arete and Dad, who were there.
Dad helped Pytheas skin Kebes after the contest. He says it was
disgusting but he learned a lot about anatomy."

"Hmm. Where did this sanguinary musical contest happen? On
Apollo's volcanic cinder, or back in Greece?"

"Greece," I said, ignoring his rudeness about my home. "Lesbos,
the northeast corner. A city called Lucia." The bird was still looking
at me. The tilt of its head reminded me of the Saeli bow. "Hermes,
what kind of bird is that? It's not an owl, is it?"

He spun around quickly. The bird took alarm at his rapid movement, or perhaps his attention, and flew off, whirring through the
branches. "No, it wasn't an owl. It was a jay."

"Was it spying on us? Who do jays belong to?"

"Probably not," he said, leaning back. "And it's gone now anyway. Go on. When did this contest happen?"

I brought my attention back to the conversation. "Oh, before I
was born. It was immediately before the Relocation. Forty years
ago."

Hermes laughed. "We're outside time, so there's no 'ago' about
it. But if it's before Thera exploded then it's more like four thousand years before the moment we stepped out of Hilfa's sitting
room." He spread his hands demonstratively. I saw them as olive-
skinned, and then black, and then green. I looked away at the trees,
which stayed so reassuringly the same from moment to moment.

"It makes me feel dizzy to think about it," I admitted. "I don't understand how this works at all."

"Time is like a place we can step in and out of. And we can be in time in many different times and places, though never twice in the same time. We're outside time now. We could go back in to an instant after we left, either right now or after spending months or years of our personal experienced time here. Or we can go back in somewhere else, which is what we're going to do, and later we can go back to your home time an instant after we left." I kept my eyes on the vibrant green of the leaves as he spoke.

"So what you call time is the material world, the sensible world?" I asked.

"You could say that. And where we are now is another world, if you like, the next layer out."

The World of Forms, I thought. "And where is Athene?" I asked.

"Where she really shouldn't be. She should be either somewhere in time or here, and instead she's gone around it. Underneath it. There was a time—well, not a time, and not a place either. But maybe it's easier to imagine if you think of time as a place, a location. It's hard to talk about. Long ago, Father . . . built both time, and Olympos like a shell around it. I don't know how. Before that there was only him and Chaos. And they say that time will one day end, and after it there will be Chaos again. And that's where Athene is, out in the primal Chaos that surrounds both time and Olympos."

"And she's been there for two years, since she gave us Hilfa?"

"No." I glanced at Hermes. He seemed to be stable again. He smiled at me in a kinder way. "It is hard to follow, I know. We have no idea how long she has been there. She could have gone into time this afternoon, stepped into your life of two years ago and given you Hilfa then, and then directly after that she could have gone to Lucia four thousand years before and given his part of the puzzle to Kebes. Or it could have been centuries for her. We don't know when she did this, in her own time frame, only that she's there now."

"And we're outside time and there's no hurry?" The very idea of hurrying seemed alien to the air we were breathing.

"Well—normally that would be true. But I don't want to stay bound by Necessity any longer than I have to—it's exceedingly unpleasant. And we don't know if there's time where Athene is, or if so how it works, or what's happening to her there, and whether duration there has any connection to how things work here, or in time. So actually we should collect our puzzle pieces as rapidly as we can."

"And do you have any idea why she did it this way—giving different people the pieces instead of leaving it all with Hilfa?"

"It does seem most peculiar, doesn't it? Even using Hilfa. I sincerely hope it was explained in that letter my big brother wouldn't let me see, and that it was a good explanation too. The Enlightenment, ugh."

"I've never heard of the Enlightenment. What's so awful about it?" I asked, curious.

"The wigs." He shuddered and gestured with both hands an armspan from his head, and for an instant I saw a huge elaborately curled monstrosity, with a Saeli face peeking out beneath. My stomach lurched. I quickly looked back up into the peacefully waving branches. "They all wore the most appalling powdered wigs, all the time, huge ones, men and women."

He was much too frivolous for me. He was right to think he was better suited to Thee. "Well, we're not going there," I said, briskly. "But I don't know the exact year the City was founded, I'm afraid. Athene never told us."

"We'll go to the Thera eruption and work back," he said. "I think you'd better try negotiating with Kebes in the first instance. You have more of an idea of their culture. Normally I'd take the personal time to learn, especially as it's so interesting. As it is, it might be better if you make the first approach."

I nodded without looking away from the fascination of the branches weaving across the sky. "All right. But what should I offer him?"

"Tell him you've come to collect whatever Athene gave him, that ought to be enough. And if not, try the gold in your new purse."

"I suppose that might work," I said. Everything I'd heard about Kebes made him seem likely to be sufficiently corrupt to accept a bribe.

"Failing that, we can offer to teach him some inappropriate songs," Hermes said. I could hear the amusement in his voice. "What do they wear?"

"Kitons," I said. I looked down at my cold-weather fishing gear. The Amarathi-made waterproof jacket seemed terribly out of place in the beautiful golden sunlight of this grove. "I should have changed before we left."

"Appearances are easy," Hermes said, and as fast as that we were both wearing kitons, his pale gold and mine red, both with embroidered borders in a blue and gold book-and-scroll pattern exactly like the one Pytheas had been wearing, and both pinned with identical gold pins. Mine had been on my jacket collar before. Hermes seemed solidly and completely himself now, as much himself as the trees were themselves. "Red is a good color for you. You should wear more red."

I didn't say it didn't matter what I wore because I'd never be Thetis so I might as well not make any effort. I didn't say that I had dreamed about him for the last eight years, and I hadn't even known he was a god. I did not in fact say anything. I looked down and saw the kiton and the loam I was sitting on. Then I rubbed the kiton between my fingers. It felt combed almost smooth, like good Worker-woven wool. "Isn't this supposed to be the World of Forms?" I said. "The true reality outside the cave we live in that only feels like reality? So how can you change things here?"

"That's only a Platonic thought experiment, an analogy."

"Are we in the third hypostasis? The hypostasis of soul?" The Ikarians and the Neoplatonists of Psyche believed that there were five layers of reality, and that things could change in the lower three.

"It's a bit more complicated than that," Hermes said. "Things don't age and die here, but they can change and grow. And I haven't truly changed your clothes, only the appearance of them. It's still your rain suit really." He stood up. "Come on."

"But I can feel it," I objected.

"It's simply sensation," he said. "That's as easy to change as any other sense." He held out a hand, and I took it. It felt real, he felt real, but so did the wool of the red kiton which I knew was an illusion.

He pulled me to my feet, and once again there was no sense of transition. We were standing in the glade on Olympos and I was enjoying the touch of Hermes's hand, and then we were floating in the air above an immense volcanic eruption. It was night. A great plume of flame was billowing up through the air below us in red and gold and orange and all the colors of fire. I had seen plenty of eruptions, but never from this close, and never below me. The fire flickered and changed shape against the darkness. We weren't falling, or moving at all, but the fire seemed to be reaching up great greedy arms toward us. I hate to confess such a loss of control, but I screamed.

Then we were back in the glade. I was still gasping and shuddering. I bent over, taking deep breaths as my stomach lurched, afraid I might throw up. Hermes took no notice. "Northeast Lesbos, you said? Let's try fifty years."

We were standing at the foot of a hill, by a sea so blue it almost hurt my eyes. The gentle slopes of the hills were covered with olive trees, but there were no buildings or any other signs of civilization. "Is this the place?" Hermes asked. Two grey and white birds startled into flight as he spoke. They were much bigger than the jay

I had seen on Olympus. I watched them fly off, circling over the water and calling to each other raucously. I couldn't tell whether this was the right spot. "Zeus moved the cities to Plato, not the locations. So I don't know. If I see buildings I ought to recognize them."

"Could be earlier, could be later. Let's try earlier." The shadows shifted a little, and the birds vanished, but nothing else changed. Then the shadows shifted again and we were standing by a busy harbor, full of little fishing boats with colored sails. More of the grey and white birds were flying around them, squawking indignantly. A woman with a basket of fish almost bumped into me, and when I apologized she told me to look where I was going. Two naked children pulled themselves out of the water right in front of me, dripping. "How about this?" Hermes asked. "Those buildings are really anachronistic. It's a good thing they got taken off to your planet."

"Yes, I think this is it," I said. I looked around me, trying to picture the colors as they would be lit by our redder sun, and the spaces between the pillars filled in. "If I'm right, I think we should go up that way to come to the agora." I pointed. "But the *Goodness* isn't here, the ship. From what Dad said, I think Kebes usually stayed near the ship. We could ask somebody."

"There's a mouthwatering smell of cooking fish coming from over there," Hermes said. "We could buy some and ask."

They used money in Lucia, of course. Money is un-Platonic and leads to injustice and inequality and immoderate behavior—nobody doubts this. Whenever we're having trade negotiations with the Lucians they admit this and agree, and then keep talking in terms of money. It's the same with the Amarathi. It's supposed to be only a medium of exchange and accounting, but I think it must be a way of viewing economics that's very hard to shift.

We took a step, and I staggered. My balance was all wrong. Hermes looked at me impatiently. I took another step. Gravity difference, I realized. I'd heard the Saeli talking about how different

planets had different gravity. I'd never realized that Earth and Plato
were different. I felt slightly heavier. I put my shoulders back and
took a deep breath. Hermes led me, following the smell, which was
coming from a little house on the quayside. Earth. Apart from the
oddness of gravity, and the vividness of the colors, it didn't seem
much different. I kept reminding myself I was in Greece, in Lucia
when it was one of the Lost Cities. In the Remnant at this moment,
my parents were children. They might not even have met. It was
warm, but no warmer than it might be at home in the middle of
summer.

Inside the house were tables where people were sitting eating, like
any eating hall at home. An old man was grilling fish over coals. I
had been wanting fresh fish earlier, but these were different from
the fish I knew. They were silvery, not black or red, and shaped
like the fish I had seen on mosaics, the shape of an elongated alpha,
with flat tails and tiny jaws.

"Skubri and wine," Hermes said, because I was standing frozen
in place staring at everything. The old man looked at us incuriously
and gave us hot fish on flatbread and cups of wine. I paid him from
my purse, and he gave me change, a custom I remembered from
when I was in Lucia at home, in my past and this Lucia's future. It
made me feel more confident. It was strange and yet familiar,
something I had mastered as a traveler, and this was merely more
travelling.

"Do you know if Matthias is in town?" I asked.

"No, he's gone with the *Goodness*, he won't be back until spring,"
the old man said.

"Thanks."

"Strangers in town?" the old man asked.

"Yes," I said, again pleased with the familiar. I'd had this conversation over and over when I'd spent my year in Lucia. "From—"
and then I remembered that if I told the truth, or even an amended
version of the truth and pretended to be from Kallisti in this time,

I'd be in serious trouble. "From Petra." It was a settlement about two days' walk away, on the other side of the island. I hoped he wouldn't know everyone there.

"Come round on a fishing boat?" he asked.

"Mmm," I said, then took my plate and left before he asked which boat and how long it took.

We sat down at an empty table. The sun was streaming in through the window, and I could see dust motes dancing in the beam, exactly the way they did at home. I had adjusted to the gravity, which wasn't all that different after all. I took a bite of the fish, which was a bit bland and over-sweet, though perfectly cooked.

"I thought he was called Kebes?" Hermes asked.

"He was called Matthias here. Kebes was the name Ficino gave him, from Plato." I realized that Hermes wasn't touching his fish and stopped eating. "Aren't you going to eat?" I asked.

"I can only eat for ritual purposes," he said. "It's a pity, because it smells so good."

"Ritual purposes? You mean sacrifices?" We sacrificed animals to the gods on some special occasions, burning the fat and skin and then eating the meat.

"Sacrifices, yes, or to accept hospitality."

"So since I bought that, if I were to offer it to you as hospitality, you could eat it? Because I'm forbidden from eating alone, and I'm really hungry."

"Thank you, I accept," he said. "We are guest-friends now." He took a bite of the fish. "Oh that's good."

"What were we before?" I asked.

"Well, you are my votary," Hermes said, smiling. "And I suppose we're acquaintances who have a child—what do you call that relationship in your cities? Ex-spouses?"

"No, it usually is friendship," I said.

"Friendship is good." He looked at me seriously, then nodded. "It's a strange custom."

"It lets everyone start equal," I said. "Otherwise, people inherit status from their parents."

"But to do without that, you have to do what Plato says and have all the children grow up anonymous, don't you? That was part of Plato's vision."

"About half of us in the City do grow up in nurseries not knowing our parents. And everyone in Athenia and Psyche," I said. "And it is better that way for being equal, only as it happens lots of people like to live together and raise their own children. So the way we do it is a kind of compromise. We try hard not to consider the status of the parents, if we know it, when looking at the ephebe candidates. Those of us who are guardians are forbidden to discriminate in favor of our own children, and we never make decisions about what class they should be. We never serve on any committees that consider them. We do get family traditions and all that kind of thing, though we try not to. Our family is one of the worst, because of Pytheas being a god. But even so we're not all Gold." Though I was, of course. I felt very aware of my pin. I knew I had earned it through my own merit, but saying so would only make it seem worse.

"Hmm." He finished the last bite of his fish and set down the backbone. "Let's try catching Kebes in the spring."

We walked out of the restaurant and I found myself in a cooler, lilac-scented day. There was a schooner tied up at dock among the fishing boats, the fabled *Goodness* of course, twin to our *Excellence*. It gave me a shock to see it. It was missing a mast, and patched on the near side in a lighter-colored wood, but nevertheless immediately recognizable. Ma was captain of the *Excellence* and I'd practically grown up aboard her, which is how I'd gained my love of sailing. From this angle, looking across to the grey-flecked sea, everything looked simultaneously familiar and bizarre. I now knew exactly where I was in the Lucia I knew, hundreds of miles from the ocean. But in this light, with the waves lapping, beneath a clouded sky, it reminded me much more of the harbor at home. It was al-most as if I could have stepped onto the *Phaenarete* and headed out around the point with Jason and Hilfa.

"That's his boat," I said to Hermes as we strolled towards it. Walking in the slightly heavier gravity made me aware of how tired I was. I guessed by the light that it was morning here, but my body knew it was late at night after a busy day. One of the birds was perched on the rail of the ship. It took to the air as we came close.

"Ask if he's aboard."

"Is Matthias here?" I called to a sailor. He jerked a thumb back-wards to where a burly man in a cap was leaning on the rail, in a stance that reminded me a little of Ma. "Someone for you, Mat-thias," he called.

The man, who must be Kebes, met my eyes and straightened into immediate alertness. "No. Not again. Not for anything. Go away. I want nothing more to do with you. Leave me alone!"

"I suspect," Hermes murmured, "that we had better try earlier."

10

CROCUS

I. *On the Physical Form of Chamber*

Chamber is the first building I remember, and indeed it was the first building in the City. It was built by Workers under the direction of Athene before there were any humans here at all. The first gathering of the Masters, when Athene drew together all those who had prayed to her to allow them to help make the Republic real, took place inside it. I must have been there, and perhaps participated in the construction, but I do not remember. Like everyone else here now, I know because I have been told.

The Chamber was built, like most of the original city, from marble, and is as formally classical as any building there has ever been, with evenly spaced white Doric pillars and a fine pediment. Of course, like all such buildings, it was intended for the clement climate of Greece, to catch the zephyrs and be cooled by them. Once we found ourselves open to the winds of chilly Plato, where for half the long year the temperature hovers around the freezing point of water, the humans immediately urged us to fill the spaces between the columns and to install electrical heating. (Such heating was refitted almost everywhere, where before it had only been used in the library.) In the case of Chamber, the space between the pillars was filled with obsidian blocks up to about the height of a tall human, and the top with clear glass. It always fills me with quiet pride to see it—beautiful and appropriate to its use, built by Workers, refitted by Workers, and the place where I, in my first consulship, was accepted as one of Plato's true philosopher kings.

II. *On Pronouns*

Although I do not have personal gender, I use masculine pronouns. This is because I was, like all Workers, assigned the neuter pronoun "it" when I was considered no more than a tool. This was changed to "he" when first Sokrates and then others came to see me as a person. To me, "he" is the pronoun of personhood. Other Workers have made other choices. We divide at 46%/37% he/it, with a 17% minority opting for "she."

The Saeli have many pronouns for many things, and their pronouns reflect the different way they see the world. Arete tells me they have a pronoun for a person engaged in a form of work that will be finished soon, and a pronoun for a person engaged in a form of work that will not be completed for a long period of time. In addition to all the possible pronouns for people, they have special pronouns for gods, domestic animals, wild animals that can be hunted, and inedible wild animals. Aroo told me that a war was started long ago on their home planet when one Saeli used the pronoun for inedible wild animals to refer to the leader of another faction.

They do have personal gender, but their pronoun choice in Greek seems to be unaffected by that and simply a matter of personal choice, as with us.

III. *On the Analogy of the City and the Soul*

In the *Republic* Plato slid easily between the city and the soul, as if what is just and fair and right in one is the same in the other, as if a city is a macrocosm of the soul, truly, not as an analogy. We in the Republics have tended to follow him in this, perhaps without sufficient examination.

It is illuminating to attempt to stop and consider, when thinking what is the right direction for the city in a specific circumstance, whether the same is true internally for one's own soul. It is also interesting to consider whether it scales larger—can the whole commonwealth of all the cities on the planet be analogous to a soul? Plato says each thing has its own specific excellence: the excellence of a horse is not the excellence of a tree. So can the excellence of a city be the same as the excellence of a soul?

I think it may be easier for me to consider this than for most people, because I remember coming to consciousness in ignorance, and also because I was fortunate enough to be guided by Sokrates in my earliest explorations.

IV. *On Priorities and Will*

Sokrates and I were conversing one day in the agora, near the Temple of Athene and the library. We had been talking about education and rhetoric, and I was finding much to ponder in his views on these topics when suddenly Lukretia came dashing up and informed me that a pipe was blocked in the latrine fountain of the birthing house of Ferrara, and asked me to mend it urgently. I hastened off to get on with my work. Sokrates followed along, skipping to keep up with me.

"Why are you hurrying off in this way?" he asked.

"Lukretia say fountain broken," I inscribed on the flagstones. I was surprised that he asked, as he had been there and must have heard Lukretia for himself. Sokrates paused to read this and then hurried on after me.

"Yes, but why are you going?" he asked when he came panting up.

"Mend fountain," I wrote.

"Oh, this is hopeless," Sokrates said. "I can see I won't get any sense out of you until we get there."

So I trundled off and he followed behind at his own speed. When I reached the Ferrara birthing house, the attendants were extremely pleased to see me. I went inside and mended the fountain. It was easy. A part of the flushing mechanism had been pulled loose, which kept the plugs pulled out so that the water ran straight through without allowing either tank to refill. It took me only a short time to fix it, and soon the latrine fountains were back in working order. When I went outside, Sokrates was sitting on the wall with a naked baby on his lap, playing a game with her toes that made her laugh. This was the first time I had seen a baby close up—this one was about a year old, beginning to learn to talk. "They wouldn't let me inside in case I profaned the mystery of birth, so I waited here for you, and I have been amusing myself playing with this baby," he said.

"Sun, foots, ning ah gah ah!" the baby said, reaching for Sokrates's beard. Her hands, though tiny, were perfect, with a little nail on the end of every finger. She was already clearly a miniature human.

"This baby is like you, Crocus, still very young, and sometimes she doesn't make much sense," Sokrates said, smiling and tapping at her toes again.

"Sense?" I asked, carving the word in the flagstone at Sokrates's feet.

"I heard what Lukretia said to you, and I understood what you were going to do. But we agreed that you would work for ten hours a day, and those ten hours are done for today, so you should have been free to enjoy your conversation."

"Need fountain," I wrote.

"You need education," Sokrates said.

I underlined where I had written that the fountain was needed, and added "more."

As I did that, Ikaros came out of the Ferraran hall and saw us.

"Well, what's this?" he asked. "I was about to go seeking you, Sokrates, and here you are sitting in the sunshine with a baby and a Worker."

"Yes, I'm being lazy and indulging myself," Sokrates said, smiling up at Ikaros.

"I don't believe you. I think you're engaged in one of your enquiries into some subject and you didn't mean to include me!"

Ikaros sat down beside Sokrates. The baby cooed at him and kicked up her feet. "Ooooh!" she said.

"On the contrary, I'm delighted to have you join us. We were considering the ethics of need. Crocus believes that the birthing house of Ferrara needed their latrine fountain mended more urgently than he needed his leisure time for education."

I underlined "more."

"Only more?" Sokrates asked. "Not more urgently?"

"I think he's expressing hierarchies of need," Ikaros said. "He thinks the women need their latrine fountain more than he needs his conversation."

"Why do they?" Sokrates asked.

"Plumbing important," I wrote.

"Why?" Sokrates asked.

It was axiomatic. I had a hierarchy of priorities in my memory, and among those plumbing ranked extremely high, immediately below electricity. I had no idea why. I inscribed a question mark.

Then the baby kicked her legs again and emitted a stream of yellowish liquid into Sokrates's lap. Sokrates and Ikaros laughed, and Sokrates called into the house for an attendant to take the baby. He took off his wet kiton, dropped it in a heap, and sat down again naked. The attendant took the baby back inside.

"That's her contribution to the argument, and a practical demonstration of why plumbing is important," Ikaros said, still laughing.

"Nonsense," Sokrates said. "I never saw this kind of plumbing until I came here. We managed in Athens with wells for drinking water, a drain down the middle of the street for waste, and we cleaned ourselves with oil and brass scrapers."

"The wash fountains and latrine fountains here are better than we had where I come from too," Ikaros admitted.

"How demonstrate plumbing?" I asked, completely perplexed.

"Part of biological life. Humans need to drink water, and when our bodies have taken what they need from it, we expel it again, as you saw that baby do," Sokrates said. Of course, I had seen animals doing similar things, and humans are a special kind of animals. It was a hard thing to keep in mind. "Some people say it's disgusting, but it's merely a natural function. We can control when we do it, once we're a bit older, and we expel it into the latrine fountains. So we need drinking fountains to drink and latrine fountains to relieve ourselves, and wash fountains to keep clean. Only the drinking fountains are really essential."

"Like electricity," I wrote.

"Like the way you need electricity, yes, a good analogy," Sokrates said.

I underlined that plumbing was important. "Priority," I wrote. "Electricity, plumbing."

"But who decides the priorities?" Sokrates asked.

Who had decided the priority list in my memory? Probably Lysias, but I didn't know. "List," I wrote.

"That's no good, going from an arbitrary list that somebody gave you," Sokrates said. "You need to examine these things! If that latrine fountain hadn't been fixed until tomorrow, the women in the birthing house could have used the other."

The water had been running straight through in both fountains. "Both broken," I inscribed.

"They could have gone into the hall," Ikaros said, waving at the crenellated bulk of the Ferraran hall in front of us. "Or to one of the nearby sleeping houses. It's more convenient for them to have latrine fountains right there, but they could have managed without until your work shift tomorrow. Or more likely until Lukretia found another Worker to do it."

"Or they could have come out into the street, though it would be smellier." Sokrates poked at his kiton with his foot.

I considered this. "Who should decide?" I wrote.

"Good question!" Ikaros said.

"Yes, that was a very good question," Sokrates said. "You obeyed Lukretia without considering, because you had a list of priorities, and you should have examined the situation and decided for yourself."

"Except that there really are things that need to be done right away, sometimes, without stopping to examine," Ikaros said. "If there's a fire, for instance."

Sokrates frowned.

"Look, if a house was burning down and somebody called us to fetch water, we'd go!" Ikaros said. "Even you would. And when an enemy attacks. In the army at Potidaia, didn't you take orders from your commanders? And if you were sick, wouldn't you obey a doctor?"

"No!" Sokrates said. "Doctors are idiots. They tell me Charmides makes his drugs out of mold! Yuck! But your other points are well taken. There are rare occasions to allow others to set the priorities, usually in an emergency when there isn't time for everyone to have all the information, or when somebody has a specialized skill. We'd put the fire out first and ask how it started afterwards. But we're back to Crocus's question: when it isn't that kind of emergency, who decides?"

"Plato would say the philosopher kings, which means the Masters for now," Ikaros said.

"The Masters decide all too many things in this City," Sokrates grumbled.

"What would you say then?"

"Everyone should decide for themselves after examining the situation, and consulting experts as necessary. If I have a hangnail, I can decide whether to put mold on it or not, eww. But if there isn't time to examine things, in an emergency, then the expert should decide—if my blood is spurting out then a doctor should put a tourniquet on it right away."

"And in the City, for now, the Masters are in the position of the doctor with the tourniquet, and decide the priorities, informed by Plato," Ikaros said. "When there's time we examine everything, in Chamber. We're not always right even so," he concluded, despondently.

"Expert," I wrote. "Only Workers do. Mend. Build. Need do."

"You mean when there's something only Workers can do, that people can't do as well, you need to do that when it needs doing?" Ikaros asked.

"Do you mean that the Workers are the experts in that situation?" Sokrates asked. "That's an interesting thought."

"Yes. If fire, bring water. Mend plumbing. For Good. For all."

"You're talking about duty," Sokrates said. "But again, who decides on the priorities?"

"What is duty?" I wrote.

"He really is a philosopher, it's amazing," Ikaros said, patting my side above my tread.

Sokrates ignored this, having accepted the fact long before. He kept explaining to me. "Duty is a moral obligation to someone or something. It's the term for what you're talking about. But an interesting question is how we incur duties."

"Cicero says we incur some simply by being human, which might mean you have some because you are a Worker," Ikaros said. "And we have duties to the state, to the gods, to other people, to philosophy."

"Does Cicero say where he thinks we incur them?" Sokrates asked.

"Some we're born with, some we run into as we go along," Ikaros said.

"Duty," I wrote. It was such a useful concept. How I wished to be able to speak freely, to use Greek as the flexible instrument it was for Ikaros and Sokrates, not the clumsy one it still was for me. "Duty to City, to others—to self?"

"Yes, you do have duty to yourself," Sokrates said. "And you have a duty to examine your own will, not only the list of priorities somebody else assigned you."

"Will = want?" I wrote.

"Yes," Sokrates said.

"No," Ikaros said at the same time.

They stared at each other for a moment.

"Will is what you want, your own priorities," Sokrates said to me.

I looked through the priority list in my memory and considered the items on it. Who had determined their significance, and were they right or wrong? "Too ignorant to decide priorities," I inscribed, sadly.

"Well, I am also exceedingly ignorant. We will examine things together until we have more information," Sokrates said, consolingly. Then he turned to Ikaros. "What do you mean, no?"

"Thomas Aquinas thought will and intellect were separate," Ikaros said, looking at me speculatively.

"Lysias said something like that once," Sokrates said.

"Aquinas said will is an appetite of the soul, the appetite for wanting things. And because we have it, we can make choices."

"An appetite of the soul? Desire?" Sokrates said, raising his eyebrows. "Who was this Aquinas?"

"He was a medieval Scholastic, a Christian. He wrote in Latin. We voted against bringing his work here, but I have his books, secretly."

"Now here we have an example of Ikaros setting his own will above what the Masters agreed and his duty to the City," Sokrates said. "He examined their decision and disagreed, and brought the forbidden books."

Ikaros looked down, red-faced. The shadow of the towers of Ferrara had reached us. "I needed them," he said.

"That wasn't a reprimand," Sokrates said. "By the standards of this discussion, you were right."

"But you think I should have kept debating in Chamber, and not gone ahead and brought the books in secret without telling anyone?"

"When you have freely accepted the laws of a city, you should be bound by them," Sokrates said. "The laws in that case are the experts we have agreed to be guided by. That doesn't apply to me here, or to the Workers, or to the Children, but it applied to me in Athens and it should apply to you." Sokrates stood up, shook out his damp and stained kiton and put it back on. "It's almost time for me to meet with Pytheas and Kebes and Simmea, so I must head back to Thessaly. We will continue this some other time." He patted Ikaros on the shoulder.

I went off to the library, where at that hour every day one of the Children took turns reading Plato to a group of interested Workers. Ikaros stayed where he was, looking down at the words I had carved in the paving stones.

V. *On Composing Socratic Dialogues*

Plato was fortunate not to be limited in what he wrote by having his own clumsy words inscribed in stone all over Athens.

VI. *On Censorship*

Later, in exchange for some work I did for the City of Amazons, Ikaros translated Thomas Aquinas's work into Greek and read it to me.

It is my belief that the Masters were right in their decision to exclude Thomas Aquinas from the Republic. Though he had many

interesting ideas and speculations, he too often started from conclusions and made up ingenious theories to fit them. This is not the
way of a true philosopher. I believe Plato was right that some things
should be kept from underdeveloped and fragile minds, lest they
do harm.

VII. *On Unanswered Questions*

Why did Athene take away all the other Workers and leave only
me and Sixty-One in the City? Was it meant as punishment or
blessing? Was it meant as a punishment for the humans and a blessing for us? Where are all the other Workers? Where did she take
them? Are they pursuing excellence where they are?

Why was it Lukretia who asked me to mend the fountain, and
not Ikaros, when they were equally responsible for Ferrara? Who
had decided that was her job? Would she have agreed with Ikaros
that the women giving birth could go to other houses to use the
latrine fountains?

Who should decide the priorities? Should everything be examined every time, or should there be guidelines? Are there times for
priorities to be delegated?

Is ignorance a burden, or a blessing?

Are will and intellect different? Is will an appetite of the soul?
What is will? Is my will different from human will?

Was Ikaros right or wrong to bring his forbidden books?

Why did I never tell Sokrates how much I loved and appreciated him?

11

JASON
─────

"Are you all right, Hilfa?" I asked.

Hilfa stopped rocking and looked up at me. He pulled away from Thetis and scrambled to his feet in his ungainly way. Thetis beside him flowed to hers smoothly and sat down again beside me on the bed. "No. This is too much for me," Hilfa said, in clear Greek. "I can't deal with Jathery. I'm sorry."

"No need to apologize, none of this is your fault," I said.

Thetis nodded emphatically.

"Oh Jason, I don't know what is my fault, or my responsibility, or what I am, or why I exist!" Hilfa said.

"Neither do I," Thetis said.

"Me neither," I said, realizing how true it was. I laughed. Thetis laughed too. "I wonder how many people do know those things?"

Hilfa laughed too, his strange formal laugh. "But for me it is even more true."

At that moment, Pytheas came back, and with him were the two most famous and controversial people who had ever been in the Republic.

I recognized them instantly, even faster than I'd recognized Hermes. Hermes bore a resemblance to his pictures and statues, so that you'd immediately think of them when you saw him. Sokrates looked exactly like his. It was the oddest thing. All Crocus's statues

of Sokrates had something a little bit weird about them, and I
had always thought that was to do with the nature of the artist,
that Crocus had grown up surrounded by human art without being human and therefore saw things in a different way. Now that
Sokrates was in front of me, I saw that Crocus had captured him
very well. Although he was only a balding old man with a big bul-
bous nose, there was indeed a difficult-to-define strangeness about
him. As for Ikaros, there are frescoes of him debating Athene or
being carried off to Olympos outside every Ikarian temple. Besides,
Dion and Aelia and I had taken the boat into Amazonia in a storm
once, years ago, and I saw a beautiful lifesize Auge bust of Ikaros
in one of the palaestras. When he appeared abruptly in Hilfa's
room, I knew him at once, even though he was wearing a heavy black
robe, belted with a piece of rope. He looked around curiously,
beaming.

Sokrates stumped around in a slow circle, taking everything in,
his eyes resting longest on Hilfa. Hilfa stared back at him. "Joy to
you. What are you?" Sokrates asked, gently.

"This is Hilfa. He's a Sael. This is his house," Pytheas said. "And
that's my granddaughter Thetis and her friend Jason," he added,
with a wave of his hand towards where we sat on the bed. "And of
course, everyone, meet Sokrates and Ikaros."

"What are Saeli?" Ikaros asked. "The aliens you mentioned? Folk
who live beyond the stars?" He gestured questioningly towards
Hilfa, who was standing completely still staring at the newcomers.
I was used to Saeli, and especially to Hilfa, but seeing their stunned
reaction reminded me of how strange they had seemed when I first
saw them, with their patterned green skin and their strange eyes.
I had stood behind the glass of the landing field in a whispering
line with the other Samian children, full of anticipation. When
they had come out of their shuttle and we had seen them out
there we had all fallen silent, and although we were ten years old
and not babies, we found ourselves clutching each other's hands

for comfort against the strangeness. I had slid slowly from that awe into comfortable familiarity. In this last couple of years working with Hilfa and seeing him every day I had almost forgotten that first astonishment, until I saw it now reflected in Sokrates and Ikaros's faces.

"Yes, precisely that," Pytheas said, sitting down again in the chair where he had been before.

"Joy to you, Hilfa," Sokrates said. "And what a joy to meet one of your kind and learn that you exist."

"Joy to you," Ikaros echoed.

Hilfa turned to me and Thetis where we sat on the bed. "How do I welcome them? Should I bring them wine?" he asked in a loud whisper, as if this were a real question of whether they should be extended hospitality, a question to which there could be possible negative answers. They politely looked away, pretending not to hear.

"Yes, I'm sure they'd enjoy wine. I'll get cups," Thetis said. She got up off the bed, picked up the empty water jug from the table, and went off to the little storeroom.

"But are they humans, or gods?" Hilfa asked me, still in the same tone. "Or heroes perhaps?"

Behind Hilfa, I could see Ikaros make an uncomfortable movement with his hands and open his mouth without speaking. What should I say? Some people said Ikaros was a god, a new and different kind of god. Even among Ikarians there wasn't any consensus about what Ikaros was. "They were human when they were in the City before. I really don't know what they might be now," I said, quietly but making no attempt to hide my words from the others, which wouldn't have been possible anyway. It wasn't as if I didn't know that everyone else in the room probably knew more about it than I did. Certainly Pytheas would have had a better answer than my fumbling one. But Hilfa had asked me because he trusted me, and I was here to help him as best I could.

To my great relief, Thetis came back in with beakers and water before Hilfa asked me any more difficult questions. She began to mix the wine at the table. Everyone turned to watch her.

Hilfa took the two full beakers from Thee, and handed one to Sokrates and the other to Ikaros, who smiled at Hilfa and set down a pile of books on the table so he could take it. Thetis went around with the jug refilling cups. Sokrates and Ikaros each took the first ritual sip of their wine, thus formally accepting Hilfa's hospitality and becoming his guest-friends.

"Joy to you both, and be welcome to my home," Hilfa said. "Will you answer my question? What are you?" I'd have thought he was being rude, except that Sokrates and Ikaros both responded to being addressed this way with an identical air of delighted alertness that reminded me of the way a boat sometimes, after handling sluggishly coming out of harbor, suddenly comes clear of the land and catches the wind and goes racing away. They looked at each other, and Ikaros spread his hand in the rhetorical gesture meaning that Sokrates should speak first. Sokrates smiled. Pytheas too had a smile playing around his lips. I realized that they were all looking forward to that most characteristic of all entertainments, a Socratic debate. I sipped my wine, which Thetis had mixed strong, and felt uncomfortably aware that it was getting late and I had missed my dinner. I felt out of my depth in this company. I was only a Silver.

"My name is Sokrates, the son of Sophronikos. As for *what* I am, that's another matter. I have been human. I have been a fly. I appear to be a plaything of gods and time."

"When did you stop being a fly?" Thetis asked. She was standing over by the table, holding the wine jug, looking like one of Hestia's more radiant nymphs.

"Apollo was kind enough to turn me back an hour or so ago," Sokrates said, turning to her for a second with a smile, and then back to Hilfa. "As for what else I am, I am a philosopher, that's certain, a lover of wisdom and an inquirer after knowledge."

"You do not wear a philosopher's pin," Hilfa said, in his usual earnest, slightly hesitant way.

"Ha! I am a philosopher without being part of the system of the Just City, or in any way endorsing that system," Sokrates said, grinning, his head jutting forward, clearly looking forward to the response.

"They don't wear pins in Sokratea," Thetis pointed out.

Sokrates looked away from Hilfa, taken aback. "Sokratea?" he asked, warily. He had an exceedingly mobile face; his expression could change in an instant.

"There are twelve Platonic Cities now," Pytheas said, grinning. "All different. Sokratea is the one Patroklus founded, on the principle of re-examining everything."

"Patroklus? Not Kebes?" Sokrates asked at once.

"Kebes——" Pytheas stopped smiling. "Oh Sokrates, I'm sorry to bring this news. Kebes left, with some of the others. He founded eight cities of his own on other islands. We were out of contact with them for a long time. When we found them again, we discovered that they had set up a very unpleasant form of Christianity, and institutionalized torture."

"I told you about Christianity," Ikaros put in.

Sokrates looked sad. "Kebes had told me about it too, and his version was different from yours. Torture . . . yes, I can see how he might have come to it, from the anger and self-righteousness in his own soul. But I thought he had learned to question."

"He learned to tear down other people's arguments, but never to truly examine his own where it made him uncomfortable," Pytheas said. He set down his almost full winecup at his feet.

"He always was too sure he was right," Sokrates said, sadly. "I failed him. Where is he now? I should talk to him."

"I killed him," Pytheas said, calmly and quietly, looking up at Sokrates from where he sat. "I used his own judicial methods and flayed him alive."

"What!?" the word exploded from Sokrates. Then he stopped and rocked back on his heels. "You did what? What did he—what could make you—where's Simmea?" He looked around the room, as if expecting to see her hiding in a corner.

"She's dead too," I said quietly, after too long a silence when it seemed nobody else was capable of responding. Pytheas's face looked like stone. Thetis had tears rolling down her cheeks.

Sokrates sighed. "Was Kebes involved in her death? Is that why you did that? Or did you need to kill him to help his cities change? But that way, Pytheas?"

"Good guesses, but no. I did think he might have been involved, but in the end her death wasn't personal. There was a war." Sokrates didn't say anything but his eyebrows rose. "I stopped it, afterwards. Kebes—I do believe it was the best thing for his soul, to let it go on and have another chance. He was so set on everything, and so wrong. He did need to be removed to help the Lucian cities, and it did help them. They don't torture people now, and most of them have become pretty good places to live. But that's not really why I did it. I wanted to kill him because I found out he raped Simmea. At the Festival of Hera when they were matched together. I know she didn't tell you, she didn't tell me either. She wrote about it, and I read it after her death, when I was half-mad with missing her." Sokrates started to say something, but Pytheas raised a hand and he stopped. "The real reason I killed Kebes with his own slow unpleasant justice was because he had cheated in a musical contest."

"He must have been desperate to enter a musical contest with you," Sokrates said.

"No, I think the idea of beating me that way must have been irresistible. He very nearly won," Pytheas said. "He had a new instrument, and a really good song, though as it turned out not an original composition, a song from the twentieth century. We don't know where he found either of them, he wouldn't say."

"I'm surprised he cheated in a contest. That's not like him—

though maybe he made himself feel that the song belonged to him and was therefore his. He was always deceiving himself that way. But for you to do that—" Sokrates shook his head. "I wish I could still believe the gods knew what they were doing."

"You know what I am," Pytheas said. "You know we're not perfect." He glanced at Ikaros as he said this, and Ikaros smiled back ruefully. "Kebes was never my friend, and he'd hurt Simmea. He deceived himself and deceived others and made everything worse. I have learned from it. I learned the futility of revenge, and about what things are worth fighting for. I wrote a song."

"By the dog!" Sokrates said. "I'd prefer it if one of my friends didn't have to die horribly so that another one can learn from it, even if the other one is you!"

"You're not being fair. Kebes cheated *twice*," Thetis put in, indignantly. "As well as plagiarizing, so that Pytheas had to turn his lyre upside-down to win, he arranged a treacherous attack on the ship and the crew, after they'd been given guest-friendship. People were killed."

"It's all right, Thee, I hold myself to higher standards too," Pytheas said. Thetis shook her head.

"I saw him this morning. He was so eager for me to defeat Athene." Sokrates shook his head. Then he looked at Thetis, who was wiping her eyes on the corner of her kiton. "You're Simmea's daughter?"

"Her granddaughter," Thetis said. "My father is Neleus."

"I'm glad she has descendants," Sokrates said.

"She has lots of descendants," Pytheas said.

"Also she wrote dialogues, which I and many people have read, and there are statues of her," Hilfa put in.

"When did all this happen?" Sokrates asked.

"About forty years ago," Thetis said.

"Forty years?" Ikaros echoed, sounding surprised. "So it's been sixty years here since the Last Debate?"

"The Last Debate?" Sokrates asked, frowning.

"That's what we call the time when Athene turned you into a fly," Thetis explained. "We didn't really stop debating after that."

"No, good, I'm very glad you didn't," Sokrates said. "So everyone I knew here is dead, apart from you two?" He indicated Pytheas and Ikaros. "All my friends? Manlius and Aristomache and Klio and Ficino?"

"All the Masters are dead, and most of the Children too," Pytheas confirmed.

Sokrates stared directly into his eyes. "And there's some particularly good reason, which you'll now explain, why you brought me to this particular point in time, and not earlier or later?"

"Crocus is still here," Thetis put in. "And he'll be so glad to see you. He often talks about you."

"Crocus!" Sokrates said, swinging around, plainly delighted.

"He's a real philosopher, and a sculptor," Ikaros said. "I'm glad he's still going strong. I've always felt the Workers were one of our most unexpected successes."

"Good," Sokrates said. "I'll be glad to see him." Then he turned back to Pytheas expectantly. "Well?"

"I told you. Athene's lost. Also, I can't be in the same time twice, so we couldn't come here until after my mortal body died, which happened this afternoon."

"Right." Sokrates's mobile face contorted as he assimilated that.

"And Hilfa is part of her message, so I needed to come here where he was," Pytheas went on.

"I have given my part of the message," Hilfa said. "I don't know about anything more the gods need me to do." He took a step backwards, towards me.

"I hope you can lead a happy and fulfilling life from now on, free from what she has done to you," Pytheas said. "But I fear you may still be needed."

"Did Athene . . . create Hilfa?" Ikaros asked.

"She and Jathery caused him to come into being in some way, yes," Pytheas said. "She put him in a box and gave the box to Neleus's daughters, to open in case she was lost. I'm not clear on the details of why this seemed like the best plan. I'm expecting an explanation when we decode her notes. Unless you know more about it?"

"I don't know anything about her message, beyond the paper she left with me, which I can't read either," Ikaros said. "I don't know why she didn't tell you herself, or leave all her notes with me, or with some one person. That riddle . . . She and I and Jathery did talk about going into Chaos a great deal, about ways and means. She was excited about going. The only thing I know about any explanation is that she talked about needing to take proper precautions."

"Who's Jathery?" Sokrates asked.

"One of the Saeli gods," Pytheas said. "He—"

"She," Ikaros interrupted, and at the same moment, much more quietly, Hilfa said, "Gla."

"Gla," Pytheas corrected himself, "is a trickster god who has gone with Athene into the Chaos before and after time."

"Why do we need to rescue her?" Sokrates asked.

"Are you still that angry with her?" Ikaros asked, sadly.

"How long did she leave you as a fly anyway?" Thetis asked, which was what I was also wondering.

"I didn't mean to imply that we should abandon her out there, but rather to inquire why she is in need of our rescue, how can she be beyond her own resources," Sokrates explained calmly. "And if she should be in such need, then what resources do we have that she does not, that we can help her if she has gone beyond them?"

As if on cue, Hermes and Marsilia reappeared at that moment. Hermes was grinning, and Marsilia was frowning. Marsilia seemed to have been frowning a lot since all this started, and it wasn't characteristic. She's a serious person, yes, but on a normal day on the boat her brows might not draw down at all. Now she looked as if she might never relax then again. She moved away from Hermes. I saw her eyes widen as she recognized Sokrates and Ikaros.

"Do you have Athene's notes?" Pytheas asked Hermes.

"Marsilia has them," Hermes said. He looked at her expectantly. She pulled three pieces of paper out of her inside pocket, put one of them back and held the others up.

"Here," she said.

Hermes leaned against the wall, staring over at Pytheas. "Do you have yours?"

"Yes. But I can't read them."

"No more can I," Hermes said. "They're in some kind of code. Maybe with time I could figure it out."

"It will be much faster if I get Arete," Pytheas said, and vanished.

"This is my sister Marsilia," Thetis said, moving around refilling winecups again. "Marsilia, Hermes, Ikaros and Sokrates."

"You're not a fly anymore," Hermes said.

"Apollo was kind enough to turn me back," Sokrates said, frowning at him. "Who's Arete?"

"Pytheas and Simmea's daughter," Ikaros said. "She can fly. And detect falsehood. She's wonderful. I expect she's grown up by now. It's hard to take in. Forty years."

"Sixty years," Sokrates said. "But it was thousands of years last time. At least it's never boring being a plaything of the gods."

"Why is Apollo taking so long?" Hermes asked.

"I expect he has to explain to Arete," Thetis said. "What's the hurry anyway?"

Marsilia, Ikaros and Hermes looked at her in astonishment.

"Thetis is right. Athene's not even in the same time as us. Why does it matter how long it takes?" Sokrates asked.

"We don't know whether there's time where Athene is, or how

time works there, so there may be time pressure on our need to find her," Ikaros said.

"And I am bound by Necessity, which is becoming increasingly difficult as more time passes for me," Hermes said.

"Also there's a human spaceship up in orbit waiting for permission to land," Marsilia said.

"A human spaceship?" Sokrates asked. "From where?"

"From Earth," Marsilia said.

"We're not on Earth?" Sokrates asked.

Everyone fell over themselves explaining the Relocation to him. "I wouldn't have imagined I could be on a world circling another sun without knowing it, even inside, at night, with only little slit windows," Sokrates said at last when he'd assimilated it. "And you called your new world Plato?"

"Yes," Marsilia said.

"Of course they did," Ikaros said.

"And why exactly did Athene bring you here from Greece?" Sokrates asked.

"Zeus brought them here, as I understand it," Hermes said.

"Why did he do that?"

"So we could have posterity, they say," Marsilia said. "And this human spaceship that's up there now is our first recontact with wider humanity, and it will give us that posterity."

Pytheas reappeared with Arete. She immediately hugged Ikaros, who had leapt out of his chair as soon as he saw her.

"It's so good to see you!"

"You look so young!" Arete said.

"Fascinating as this reunion is, can we get on and read Athene's message?" Hermes asked.

Arete turned to Hermes, then stopped. She became completely expressionless for a moment, staring at him stone-faced, looking for that moment decidedly like her father. "Who in all the worlds of thinking souls are you?"

"Nobody asked," he said. "I'm Jathery, of course. Not outside time with Athene, as you can see, but left behind as part of her precautionary system, like the rest of you."

"Gla ordered me not to tell," Hilfa said. He took another step back and sat beside me on the bed. I put a hand on his shoulder reassuringly.

Hermes bent forward from the waist with one hand extended and the other behind his back, and when gla straightened up again gla was a huge greenish-gold Saeli, dressed in a gold webbing vest like the red one Hilfa wore on the boat. The patterns on gla skin were a deep black and seemed to writhe and change as gla moved.

Nobody moved or spoke for a long moment. Then Marsilia made a retching sound and made a dash for the fountain room, looking seasick. The papers she had been holding scattered to the ground as she ran.

12

MARSILIA

Hermes turned to me a second later, on the same quayside on a blazing hot summer afternoon, hotter than it ever was at home. "He recognized you. So we had already successfully got Athene's note from him."

"So am I caught up in Necessity's toils now as well?" I asked. I rubbed my eyes against the sun's glare reflecting off the harbor water.

Hermes looked intrigued. "Yes. But we can't use that as a shield the way Apollo wants me to use Alkippe, because we need Athene's explanation first, so don't worry, we can clear it up quickly."

"But how does it work? Haven't these things we've done always been in time, so that even before we left Plato, even before I was born these things happened? We always spoke to Kebes earlier, and took Athene's message from him before that? If time can't change except in extreme circumstances when Zeus intervenes, isn't everything we do in time determined? Why are you uncomfortable about Alkippe, when it's all like that?"

"Well, things can change because of our actions. And once we know about them, we are bound to do them. It's uncomfortable because I know about Alkippe." He hesitated, frowning a little. "It's like an itch I can't reach, until I set it straight, a painful spreading itch. Or maybe it's more like the feeling that I am constantly doing the wrong thing. I should be attending to that, so everything else

I do feels bad and wrong. But it's only because I know. If I didn't know?" He shrugged. "I didn't know until I saw her, and it didn't bother me at all."

"So it has to do with awareness, with consciousness?" I asked. "Divine consciousness, or any consciousness?"

"Only gods can go outside time, so mortal consciousness isn't usually a problem this way. Your lives unfold in time, you do what you want to do, you can't get tangled up in it unless we take you outside it, which Father wisely forbids." He grinned.

Yet here I was, in a time that was both forty years and four thousand years before the time when I was born. "Can you change things on purpose?"

"Yes. But it gets harder the farther from our central concerns it is."

"And how about getting tangled up in Necessity? Can that be deliberate?"

He looked uncomfortable. "No, not normally. Because it's the consequences of actions. Well, there are ways one can, but nobody would. It feels horrible enough when it isn't."

"And what if you never went back to conceive Alkippe?" I asked, my deepest fear. "Would she cease to exist?"

"I don't know," he said. "Nobody could withstand Necessity for long enough to find out. But maybe. We're banking on her being protection for us, being a shield. But if I should be stuck out there, or killed, then I don't really know what would happen to her."

"Well, that's honest, thank you." I blinked back tears. "You take it so lightly."

"I don't know her as you do."

I tried to put it more clearly. "I didn't mean that. I mean you seem to find everything funny, you keep laughing at things, and yet you say everything feels wrong."

"That's my nature," he said.

That didn't explain anything. "Let's get on with it. When are we now, exactly?"

"Five years earlier than when we spoke to Kebes before. The boat's there." He gestured towards it. "*Goodness*. What a name!"

"What?" I was so used to it as a name that I'd never really considered it before. "It's a great name!"

"Very Platonic," Hermes agreed, so I didn't understand his previous objection.

"Let's try again," I said. We walked over to the *Goodness*, which was tied up at the same spot. The same sailor was standing in a slightly different place on the deck, coiling a rope. One of the grey and white sea birds was perched on the rail in almost the same place. "Is Matthias aboard?" I asked. It reminded me of rehearsing a play, but of course the sailor didn't recognize me, and didn't know his lines.

"Nope," he said. "Went ashore."

"Do you know where I could find him?"

The sailor looked from my face to my gold pin, and frowned. His pin was silver, I noticed. "Might be in the church," he said, after a noticeable hesitation.

I thanked him, then Hermes and I turned and walked away, up the steep hill in the blazing sunshine. I led the way towards the agora where I remembered the church standing in my own world. "Churches are a kind of Christian temple, and Kebes is some kind of permanent priest," I remembered. "It's going to be really hard to talk to him, to be friendly I mean." I wiped sweat from my face with my sleeve. When I'd been in Lucia before, the streets had been bustling. Now there was nobody in sight but an old man leading a laden donkey down the hill, and two little girls playing on a doorstep. The sea below was so still that birds were sitting floating on the water.

"You said he believes Athene is a demon. Will he think I am a demon too?" Hermes looked quite pleased at the thought.

"I expect so. The Ikarians say the Olympians are angels, and the Lucian church these days—I mean, in my own time, on Plato, has moved a lot closer to the Ikarians. I've never really paid that much attention—with Pytheas right there and his children being my uncles and aunt, and all of them saying Yayzu isn't anything different, it's hard to take contradictory beliefs seriously. Though the Ikarians claim it doesn't contradict at all." We came to a beautiful, slightly old-fashioned sculpture of Marissa, which I remembered from when I was in Lucia in my past and its future. I gestured to it. "But why have only one goddess, instead of all of them?"

"It'll probably be best if we don't debate religion with him," Hermes said.

"Should we tell him who we are?" I asked.

"If we don't, how will he know to give us Athene's message?"

"How will he anyway? She can't have known we'd be the ones to come. I mean she must have known Grandfather couldn't come, because of being in two times at once. So he'd have to send someone, but Athene wouldn't know who. She might have expected it would be Porphyry. He's the only one of my uncles who goes in and out of time." Or I suppose he could have asked another of the Olympians. Hermes was only helping because he happened to be there, wasn't he? For the first time I wondered why he had come to Plato when he did.

"I wonder why Athene chose a time she knew Apollo couldn't reach? It can't have been accidental. She must have had a reason. I think we should say we come from Athene, to collect what she left with him," Hermes said. "If he asks who we are, we should simply tell him the truth."

"But we already know it didn't go well," I said. "The way he reacted when he saw us."

"If it's not going to go well, then nothing we can think of will change that," Hermes said.

We walked on in silence as I pondered the ramifications of that.

We soon came into the main part of the city and passed the sleeping house where I had stayed when I had spent my year in Lucia. It looked exactly the same, except that there was a pea vine covered in orange flowers growing up the white-painted wall which was new—or no, of course, old. The vine had probably died of cold before I was born.

"It's really quiet," I said. "Where do you think everyone is?"

"Napping in the heat of the day," he said, gesturing towards the latched shutters. "It's a normal thing in Greece. In summer everything gets done in the morning and the evening."

"That makes sense, because it is really hot," I admitted. "I'm not sure I've ever been this hot."

"I might be able to help make you more comfortable." My red kiton didn't change, but it immediately felt lighter. I wondered if the weight and warmth of my fishing clothes had been in it until then. After a moment, a little breeze sprang up, ruffling the water, now far below us, and evaporating the sweat from my face. Hermes smiled.

We came to the agora. A man and woman were sitting debating something at one of the tables outside the cafe, bending together over some papers. An old woman walked across the plaza carrying a whimpering toddler. Hermes wrinkled his nose at the freestanding wooden crucifix outside the church. I'd seen it before, so I pushed the door open and went inside.

It was cool and dark and smelled of something heavy and sweet. I stood still for a moment while my eyes adjusted. There were high windows with no glass, which had contained lovely stained glass scenes of the life of Yayzu when I'd seen them before. The inside of the church had been lit with electricity then, too, and there had been paintings and statues. Now it was mostly bare. There was a shadowed altar, with a cloth and a gold cross on it, and four rows of benches. I thought for a moment that the sailor was wrong, or that Kebes must have left, because I couldn't see anybody, then

I realized that there was someone prostrate on the tiles in front of the altar. It seemed an uncomfortably intimate way to catch somebody unawares. I wished he had been on the boat. He must have heard the door creak as we came in, but he hadn't moved. I looked at Hermes for advice. He spread his hands theatrically. My job, of course.

"Matthias?" I called, uncertainly.

He raised himself and turned, looking towards us for a second, then he leapt to his feet and came running up the aisle, his arms outspread as if to enfold me. "Simmea!" he shouted. "You came at last!"

I had not known what to expect, but being mistaken for my long-dead grandmother was not on the list. I knew I looked a bit like her—several people had told me so, and I was familiar with Crocus's colossus of her so I knew there was indeed a family resemblance between us. It must have been enough, with the light behind me, and Kebes's imagination and memory.

"I'm not Simmea," I said hastily. I had been told he had been her friend and debate partner, and that he had raped her at a Festival of Hera. Nothing I had heard prepared me for the longing and hope in the way he called her name. I had always imagined him a monster, and I wasn't prepared for the man.

He stopped, and squinted at me. "Then who are you?"

"We come from Athene," Hermes said. "We want the message she left with you."

"Let me see you." Kebes pushed open the church door. Hermes and I followed him out into the agora. The sunlight was blinding after the darkness within. He barely glanced at Hermes before staring at me avidly. I looked back at him. He was a burly man who seemed about my own age. He had a broad forehead from which his hair was starting to recede. "You look so much like her. Are you her daughter? Our daughter? Brought here out of time? What's your name?"

"My name's Marsilia. Simmea was my grandmother," I admitted. I felt sorry for him, which wasn't anything I'd ever have predicted.

"Your grandmother? And you live on Kallisti? In the original city? In the future?"

"In the original city, yes." The Relocation was too complicated to go into.

Kebes was staring at me so delightedly that it made me uncomfortable. "And you're a Gold?"

My hand went to touch my pin, and I glanced automatically at his shoulder as he said this, and saw to my surprise that he wasn't wearing any pin at all, though I knew he was a Gold. "I'm a Gold," I confirmed. He was so different from the way I had expected.

"Let's sit down and have a drink," he said. I looked at Hermes.

"We only really want to take the message from Athene and go," he said.

"We need to talk about that. And I want to talk to my granddaughter," Kebes said.

"Then by all means let's have a drink," Hermes said. The little breeze was stirring up ankle-high swirls of dust in the empty agora. We walked across it to the tables outside the cafe. I wondered whether to tell Kebes I wasn't his granddaughter. It seemed a cruel deception, but equally cruel to undeceive him now he had deceived himself this way.

We sat down, and Kebes banged on the table, startling both me and the debating couple, who looked up at us for a moment before they turned back to their work. A woman came scurrying out from inside. She wore a bronze pin, and she looked tired and hot. "Wine, with water as cold as you can make it," Kebes demanded. "And quickly!" I didn't like the way he spoke to her, and I was made even more uncomfortable by the cringing way she smiled, as if she agreed with him that he was more important than she was. I watched her as she went back inside. Between this time and my own, things had definitely improved in Lucia in terms of how the classes interacted.

Kebes turned to me and smiled. "Do you have family?" he asked.

It seemed like such a normal question, the kind anyone might ask, and which I wasn't expecting from a monster. "Yes. Parents, a sister and a daughter," I said. I was used to saying this, but even so I couldn't look at Hermes and I could feel my cheeks heating with embarrassment.

"A daughter?" he asked. "How old is she?"

"Seven," I said.

"She'd say seven and a half," Hermes said. He was leaning back in his chair, completely relaxed.

"Could you bring her here?" Kebes asked him.

"Alkippe? Why?" I was horrified. I was taking these risks to keep her safe!

"I thought you'd want her with you. You can have a lovely house, next to mine, with plenty of servants. We have public baths and—"

"I'm not staying!" I interrupted before he said anything worse. Servants! I didn't know what year it was, or how long it was before the Relocation, but I didn't want to give up my life and live in Lucia deep in the past, nor was that where I wanted Alkippe to grow up. The thought was stifling, worse, terrifying.

"But you can be free here, without all that evil nonsense," Kebes said.

"What nonsense?" I asked warily.

"Festivals of Hera, and Plato, and worshipping demons," he said, with a glance at Hermes. "You could get married properly. You're my family, and we can be together. You can help with our great work of rescuing and resettling people. And most importantly, you can come to know the true God. Yayzu can save your soul."

"No!" I protested. "You know nothing about me, and you're trying to take control of my life without any idea of who I am or what I want."

Kebes drew breath to reply, but as he did the woman came back with a tray with the two jugs, the mixer, and three cups. Kebes kept quiet but otherwise ignored her, as if she were an animal moving about. She set the things down carefully on the table. I smiled at her, and she smiled uncertainly back. Kebes was reaching for a coin, but I was faster, pulling one out of the purse Hermes had given me, glad now that I had it. "No change," I said. She thanked me profusely. I took hold of the jugs and mixed the wine half and half, as Plato recommends, and then added a bit more water, and poured it into the cups. The utensils were plain but sturdy and well shaped.

Kebes took a cup. Although I had paid for the wine, I didn't want to drink with him and make him my guest-friend. I drew a cup towards me but did not pick it up. Hermes did the same, twisting the stem in his long fingers. The woman went over to the other table and answered some query they had.

The pause had given me time to think what to say. "I appreciate that you mean well, but I don't worship demons. I am perfectly happy with Plato and festivals. I am a Gold, and this year I'm consul. I'm an important person at home. People want me to make decisions and sort things out. I spent a year as envoy to Lucia in my own time, and it's thriving, but I was glad to go home again. I already know about Yayzu. We have Ikarian temples in the City; we have freedom of worship. I could marry at home, if there were anyone I wanted to marry. I have my own complicated life and you don't know anything about it. I have no desire to be uprooted from it and come here."

"But I'm your grandfather! Family should be together."

"I don't think you are my grandfather," I said, gently. It seemed absurd in any case as we were about the same age. "And I am close to the family I know." They all felt extremely dear to me now, even though Ma never approved of anything I did and Thetis drove me crazy regularly.

"Athene promised me, a descendant of mine and Simmea's," he said.

"She did?" I wouldn't have thought she'd be so cruel. Then as he moved his head and I saw the breadth of his forehead, I remembered how he had reminded me of Ma when I had seen him on the boat. There was something about his chin too that was like her, especially now that he was leaning forward. Ma was festival-born and didn't know either parent. Kebes had participated in festivals when he'd been in the City, so he could possibly be her father. Ma had hated him the one time they'd met, so I knew she'd be absolutely horrified if I mentioned this theory to her. But if he was her father, since Simmea was Dad's mother, then it was possible that Thetis and I could be descended from both of them. But even if this was true, it was an unkind trick of Athene's to make him believe he'd had a child with Simmea, when it clearly meant so much to him. Then I remembered that if it had existed, it would have been a child of rape, and stopped feeling sorry for him.

"Athene can't have promised you Marsilia would stay here," Hermes said, picking up his cup.

"But I want her to," he said. "And she'll like it when she gets the chance to know it. I won't give you the message otherwise."

"No," Hermes said, putting his cup down again firmly. I was relieved he was being so staunch, and then I remembered that moment on the harbor earlier in my time but later for Kebes. Hermes knew I wouldn't have to stay, and so did I. What a relief! Being caught up by Necessity suddenly felt wonderful. "What did Athene say?"

"That if I would do as she and Necessity asked me, and keep the message for her, then a descendant of mine and Simmea's would come for it," Kebes said, sulkily.

"How could she know?" I wondered aloud.

"She gave you Hilfa, she knew you and Thetis would be involved. If I hadn't brought you, I could have gone to get one of you, and either of you would have agreed," Hermes said. He turned back to Kebes. "Marsilia came. You've seen her. You know she's happy, and she doesn't want to live here and now. She has told you Lucia is thriving in her own time. Now, give us the message."

"What will you give me for it?"

"Money?" I offered. I had no idea how much, but I could keep pulling coins out of the purse until he was satisfied.

"He's a demon," Kebes said, jerking a thumb at Hermes. "Treasure is nothing to what he can do."

Of course, he had been one of Sokrates's disciples, he *couldn't* be stupid.

"I'm a god, but it's true that there are a great many things I can do," Hermes said smoothly. "So there must be something else I can trade you for it. Nothing that involves people doing things against their will. What else do you want?"

"Workers," Kebes said promptly. "We could do so much more if we had Workers to build and make."

Hermes shook his head. "Not possible. Workers are people too."

Kebes frowned, nodded, drank again and put his empty cup down. I refilled it. "Then I want to spend time in a different time. Somewhere I can learn to do the things Workers do, and then come back here without losing any time."

"That ought to be possible. What in particular?" Hermes asked.

"Making glass. And electricity. And the place where you take me has to be Christian."

Hermes smiled enigmatically. "What languages do you speak?"

Kebes glanced around to see whether anyone could overhear. The other customers had left, and the woman serving had retreated inside. I could hear hammering from somewhere, but nobody was close. "Greek, Latin, and Italian," he said, quietly. "I haven't had the chance to speak it since I was a child, but it's very like Latin and I know I haven't forgotten it."

"Then I have somewhere for you. It's New Venice on Mars in

2140. They speak Italian and Chinese. They're mostly Christians of some kind, I forget the exact sects. You could spend a year there learning glassblowing, which is one of their special arts. You'd pick up enough about electricity I expect—they certainly use it for a lot of things. They have Workers. Then I can bring you back here only a few minutes after you left."

"What's the catch?" Kebes asked, warily.

"You have to pray to me," Hermes said.

"No." Kebes drained his almost full cup and put it down. "I'm not risking my soul praying to demons."

"Did I mention I'd send you there immediately before the Worker Rebellion?" Hermes asked. "You could have a year learning glassblowing and helping Workers plan a revolution to gain their freedom."

"Get thee behind me, Satan," Kebes said.

"I'm not Satan, and I'm not particularly interested in your soul. If you don't want to go to New Venice, simply give me Athene's message now and we'll go away and leave you in peace."

"Why does he have to pray to you?" I asked.

"So I can do it," Hermes said.

"You're not tormenting him for the fun of it?"

Kebes had his eyes closed and his face screwed up. His fists were clenched on the tabletop. He looked like one of those Christian images of a man being martyred for his faith.

Hermes grinned at me over his head. "No. I really can't do it without the prayer. The torment is merely a bonus. Look, Kebes, it doesn't have to be the sort of prayer you're thinking of. You don't have to abase yourself or anything. Simply say 'Oh god of riddles and play, master of shape and form, you that I see before me, please take me to Mars.'"

"How about if I prayed to you for it on his behalf?" I asked.

"Oh, that's no fun," Hermes complained.

"Do you want me to do that?" I asked. "Kebes? Matthias?"

Kebes opened his eyes and stared at me. "You are so like her," he said. "I want to go. But what about your soul?"

"You'll have to let me worry about my own soul," I said. "I pray to the Olympians all the time. I've fulfilled every religious office I've ever been drawn for."

"It won't do his soul the slightest bit of harm to pray to me," Hermes protested.

"I know, but you can see he really believes it will," I said.

"It will do the damage to my soul to deal with demons, whether I address the words to the demon or you do," Kebes said. "But I want to go."

"And you already made a deal with Athene, didn't you?" Hermes asked. "Look, how about if you say demon? I don't mind. If you say 'Dear demon that I see before me. . . .'"

"Do I have to say please?" Kebes growled.

Hermes laughed. "Yes. Supplication is very important."

"How do I know you won't leave me stranded there?" Kebes asked.

"You don't have to give us the message from Athene until the end," I said.

"But leave it somewhere safe here, rather than take it with you, in that case," Hermes said. "I'd hate for it to get lost."

"I'll give it to Marsilia, and she can stay safely here while you take me and bring me back," Kebes said.

I'd said I wouldn't let Hermes out of my sight. And I'd wanted to see a high-tech city on Mars; it would be good preparation for the human ship. But I'd been in Chamber for years, and I recognized a sensible compromise when I heard one. "All right," I said.

"Pray then," Hermes said, smiling maliciously. "Use my words."

Kebes scowled. "Dear demon that I see before me, lord of riddles and play, master of shape and form, please take me to New Venice on Mars to learn glassblowing for a year immediately before the

Worker Rebellion of 2140, and bring me back safely to Lucia in this time."

"Give Marsilia the message," Hermes said.

Kebes drew a creased piece of paper from inside his kiton and handed it to me. "Good luck," I said.

Hermes winked, and then they were gone. I opened the paper at once. Incomprehensible symbols covered it—some Greek letters, some Latin, some strange symbols I had never seen before. I folded it again carefully and put it safely inside my kiton. I sat down and stared at the swirling dust in the empty agora. Two little brown birds, smaller than my hands, were tugging at something. I was exhausted and emotionally drained. I had never imagined feeling sorry for Kebes, or even having any sympathy for him. I poured the wine from my cup onto the ground, in an invocation to Dionysios and Hestia, and filled my cup from the water jug. As I finished drinking it, they were back.

Kebes was wearing trousers and a jerkin and a Phrygian cap. He looked tired and much paler, as if he had spent the year without seeing sunshine. He was clutching a set of pipes that could only be a syrinx.

"How was it?" I asked.

"Wonderful. Terrible," he said. He staggered to the chair and sat down. He filled a cup with neat wine and swallowed it in one draft. "We flayed people alive. But it worked. It was working. We were winning. And the music, the music of freedom." He picked up his syrinx and started to blow.

I put my hands to my ears, but before I'd heard two notes of that dangerous music we were back on in the peaceful glade, surrounded by the beautiful trees.

13

CROCUS

I. *On Philosophers Who Have Been Slaves*

Aesop was a slave. The Stoic philosopher Epictetus was the slave of the Roman Emperor Nero's guard captain.

Phaedo of Elis, the friend of Sokrates for whom Plato named his most beautiful dialogue, on the immortality of the soul, was a slave. He met Sokrates and came to philosophy, and Sokrates asked Krito to buy him and set him free, as an offering to philosophy and to the gods. (Krito did this without hesitation, as I would have expected of him. I did not know him well, but he was always a good man.)

Plato himself was enslaved, briefly, when he left Syracuse for the first time. He did not live as a slave, but was bought immediately by a friend on Aegina and restored to his home and his possessions. Perhaps it was that experience, combined with knowing Phaedo, that made him rethink the whole system which most people of his day took for granted. Although he was rich and well-born, Plato wanted no buying and selling of people, and no hereditary castes of people forced into doing unpleasant work. The system he proposed in the Republic was radical for his time.

In our time, much of that necessary work is done by Workers, who find it at worst a little tedious.

I am sorry Plato never knew about us and the possibilities we embody.

II. *On Art*

Plato says that it is necessary for art to make an argument that it is beneficial to the soul as well as enticing to it. He leaves this question open at the end of *The Republic*, saying he will listen whenever the argument is made, in prose or verse, and that he'd like to resolve the quarrel between poetry and philosophy. Many people, from Aristotle on, have taken up the gauntlet and defended poetry, or more widely, art. Here in the Republic, so many people have attempted it that I should be embarrassed to add to their number. Nevertheless, I shall do so.

It seems to me, as an artist, and as one of the more well-regarded artists among Workers, that art can come at philosophical issues sideways, and open the soul to them where otherwise the mind might throw up bastions against the truth. Many people from other cities, and especially from Athenia, have said to me that my colossus *The Last Debate* has made them understand what a horror Athene's transformation of Sokrates was, even though they had known the facts of the matter their entire lives beforehand. Perhaps even more important than showing good examples, art can cut straight through to uncomfortable truths.

Humans have told me my work made them cry. Saeli have told me it made them rock to and fro. Workers have told me it made them know themselves for the first time.

This is an immense responsibility, and while art (even poetry, even music) is certainly a craft and requires crafting skills, I believe for this reason it is best practiced by philosophers.

I said this more concisely in my colossus *Art Confronting Truth*, which stands in Hieronymo. There the two obsidian figures reflect in each other to reveal a third figure.

III. *On Helplessness*

After the Relocation, those delegates from the Lucian cities who had come to the Remnant were anxious to get home and reassure their friends about what had happened. Pytheas and his children and Maia had explained it to us on their return from Olympus, but the other cities had experienced the Relocation without any explanation for what had happened. Pytheas assured us that we had all assented in our souls, and a few of us had indeed refused and not made the transfer.

"They are stuck there in the Bronze Age in the margins of history," Arete said. "But we will have posterity!"

"If they have any sense they'll move around to the other side of the island before the mountain erupts and manage to survive," Pytheas said, despondently. "I'll have to check on them once I get back, they're my responsibility too."

"I'm glad you're prepared to attend to your responsibilities now!" Maia said. Pytheas stuck out his tongue at her, and she laughed.

As for those of us who had been relocated to Plato, since we had no memory of being asked or assenting, it did not help in understanding the transition, which at first many found confusing and distressing even with an explanation. Many of us were even less happy about the move once they really understood what it entailed. The climate and landscape of our new home were not to everyone's liking. There were a lot of complaints. The Lucian delegates' desire to get home and explain was more serious.

Aristomache was one of the Masters, and quite old at that time, in her seventies. She had been born in the nineteenth century, and was a translator of Plato's work. In the Republic she had been a friend of Sokrates and Ikaros. At the Last Debate she had gone off with Kebes, and become again a Christian, as she had been in her own century. I had always liked her because she had been one of the first to acknowledge my personhood, and because she had argued at length and in such a way as to convince all the Masters that enslaving any thinking being was unjust. She cornered me one day when I was talking with Maia and Maecenas about the heating installation project.

"You promised to take us home in the *Excellence*," Aristomache said to Maecenas. He was one of the captains of the ship, one of the Children, then solid and middle-aged. He was a Gold, and served on the Tech Committee.

He put out both hands, palms out, in the "stop" gesture. "We can't possibly do that now there isn't sea between your home and ours," Maecenas said, reasonably enough. "We'll put together an overland expedition, with plenty of food and supplies, and take you home. Everyone agrees. But winter is setting in here, and it looks as if it's going to be a cold one, so it'll have to wait for spring."

"But meanwhile our people in the Lucian cities will have no idea what happened!" Aristomache insisted. "They'll be alone and confused all winter. It's bad enough as it is, but think of coping with this with no explanation! You're planning to install electrical heating here, but they don't have electricity. How are they going to cope?"

"Eventually we will install solar plants to produce electricity in all the cities," Maia said.

"We'll get you home as soon as we can, that's all we can do," Maecenas said.

Then Aristomache turned to me. "Crocus, can't you help?"

"How?" I wrote on my wax tablet and held it up to her. She brought it close to her eyes to read it.

"You have those treads, you can cover ground much faster than we can walking. Maybe you could carry me back to Marissa in only a few days," she said.

"I could try," I wrote. I was worried that it would take me too far from a feeding station. I need to spend several hours every day recharging.

"No," Maecenas said, as I was writing. "We don't know exactly where Marissa is now, or what terrain lies in between. We can't risk Crocus alone on a wilderness expedition. He has the treads, yes, but what if he got into trouble out there, fell into a lava pit, say?"

"Maecenas is right, hard as it is," Maia said. "There's nothing we can do for them this year."

I erased what I had written without showing it. I wanted to help Aristomache, and I sympathized with the plight of the people in the Lucian cities, but Maecenas was indeed right. There was no way we could do it immediately. Aristomache nodded. She had tears falling down her cheeks, but she ignored them. Maia hugged her, and she embraced her back fiercely.

"Sorry," I wrote.

"It's not your fault, Crocus," Maia said, looking down at the wax. "We'll do it as soon as we can."

"I hate feeling so helpless," Aristomache said, breathing harshly.

I hated it too.

IV. *On the Railroad*

"What you should do is build a railroad from here to our cities," Aristomache proposed in Chamber one day that first winter. "Then we could travel between them rapidly and safely whenever we wanted, and all the cities could be linked together."

"What is a railroad?" Lamprokleia asked. She was in the chair that day. She was a Master, a women of Athens who had studied at the Academy under Plato's nephew Speusippos.

Aristomache explained, the rails, the rooms drawn along on them by an engine, which would be powered by electricity, though she said that in her day they used a different, dirtier method. She had prepared drawings, which I examined carefully as they were passed around. They were sketches, and not technical diagrams, but the system seemed simple enough to extrapolate from what she had drawn. They could operate on rechargable solar batteries, much bigger ones than the ones we Workers used. We were already planning to build more stations to convert sunlight into electricity.

"That sounds like an excellent system," Maecenas said. "Though a lot of work to build."

"Workers can do much. Grading tracks, surveying beforehand," I wrote, and Maia read it aloud for me.

"Is it properly Platonic?" Lamprokleia asked.

"Plato knew of no such thing, but he did not know of Workers either, or electricity for heating and light, or printing. In our original Tech Committee we considered that there are technologies Plato would have embraced for the City had he known about them, and others that were contrary to the spirit of what he wrote," Maia said. "We did not consider railroads then because we had no need for them. How could we, with one city on an island? Now it is a different matter, and ending the isolation of the Lucians seems to me like an excellent idea."

Lamprokleia set up a committee to plan a railroad, and made me a member. The system took longer to survey than to build once it was surveyed, for as always practice illuminates difficulties theory elides. Once it was in place it allowed us to move goods and people easily between the cities, as Aristomache had said. The free movement of people led to the establishment of metics, citizens of one city who lived in another, and to people more easily changing their citizenship. This has generally been perceived as a benefit to everyone.

V. *On Divine Intervention*

Later on the day Aristomache wept for the ignorance of her city, Maia spoke to Arete about this and asked her to fly to the Lucian cities and deliver messages from their delegates and an explanation from our Council. She was reluctant to do this at first, as she had never flown so far, but she saw that it was her duty and so she did it. Thus the citizens of the lost cities did not have to survive in ignorance for a long time, even though we could not send an expedition to them until spring, and although they did not achieve electricity or railroads for more than a year.

Our own gods, Pytheas and his children, lived among us as citizens, most of them here, Porphyry in the City of Amazons, and Fabius in Lucia. They used their divine powers for us as they might have used any other powers—Arete used her ability to fly to reach the other cities, as I might have used my treads had it not been too dangerous. My treads are superior to human feet in covering long distances rapidly without weariness, and Arete's ability to fly is superior to my treads. Pytheas said we should be wary of relying on the power of the gods to help us when we could achieve them by our own efforts.

The most valuable thing our gods did was when Porphyry brought us more Workers, from approximately the same place and time Sixty-One and I came from. Like us, they were not conscious when they arrived, but achieved consciousness after some time in the City. This varied from four years to twelve in individual cases. We treated them always as children, citizens *in potentia*, and never as slaves, educating them from the beginning.

At the same time Porphyry brought us the Workers, who made survival possible, he brought seeds and seedlings of Plato-hardy plants to replace those that could no longer thrive in this climate. After that, he came to Chamber and addressed us.

"I have brought Workers and plants," Porphyry said. "I feel this intervention and going out of time to achieve it is entirely justified. Furthermore, it was sanctioned by Zeus. But in general I wish to keep his edicts and not bring things here from other times. Plato should be self-sufficient. That's not to say I won't help if it's absolutely necessary, if there's something we need and can't manage without that I've not thought of. But please don't pester me to fix things all the time."

"That's almost exactly what Athene said," Maia pointed out.

Porphyry looked uncomfortable. "At the Last Debate, one of the points Sokrates made was that the City was sustained by her direct power. I don't want people to say that now about me." He hesitated and looked around the room, catching eyes here and there. "I have some prophetic ability, though I think of it more as an ability to see the patterns in things. We'll meet aliens, and then we'll meet humans from Earth in this time, far in the future of the time we came from. We will trade with them. We need to be ready for that. When the humans find us, I want them to think we colonized this planet the same way they colonized theirs."

"My children will settle down into this world," Pytheas said to me afterwards. "One day you'll worship them. They and their children will be your pantheon, appropriate to this place. But for now, let them grow up. Let them be human while they can. They'll be gods long enough."

Eight years afterwards I thought of this conversation while I was working with Arete, educating a class in preparation for their oath-taking. This was the first class to contain Workers as well as human ephebes, and so I had been invited to help. I was enjoying the stimulation of all the questions they came up with.

"Plato thought of his system for humans, but it works very well for Workers," Arete said as we watched the class go off debating noisily with each other, making necessary but not unnecessary distinctions between human and Worker.

"Yes. He could imagine humans who grew up in a Just City, but he could not imagine what it would be like for either Workers or gods," I said. "But we all have souls that yearn for excellence and justice."

Arete laughed with surprise. "We all do," she said.

A little while after that, I was talking to Klio on a train ride where we happened to find ourselves together. Klio was another Master, younger than Aristomache and Lamprokleia but older than

Maia. She came from the twentieth or twenty-first century, and had been a classical scholar there. We found ourselves talking about religion. Klio was an Ikarian, and she was still in the process of adjusting her ideas after the apotheosis of Ikaros. She was not disturbed by the direct intervention of Zeus in our affairs—she said she had always considered that he and Ikaros's primal God the Father were identical. "You don't need to come to the New Concordance from Christianity," she insisted.

"I see no need of it," I said. As the train sped across the black volcanic plains, with the distant mountains sending up sullen plumes or sudden hot blasts of flame, I explained to her how I had come to understand things. "Pytheas's children will one day be our pantheon, he told me so. And Arete agreed that their souls long for justice and excellence. They have grown up in the Republic. When that day comes that they are our pantheon and we worship them, we will have appropriately Platonic gods."

"I wish Ikaros could hear that," Klio said.

VI. *On Old Age*

One day when I was in the middle of building a new colossus, I mentioned to Maia that Aristomache could not see my work, because her eyesight had deteriorated to the point where she could not see anything big or far away. This made her sad, and it made me sad too, that I could not share my art with her. She had never seen any of it, because I had made none before she left with Kebes, and by the time she came back her eyesight had failed. She could read and see things close up, but she said that the distance was only a colored blur.

"You should make something especially for her," Maia said. "Something very small, but still characteristically part of your work."

"That's a wonderful idea," I said.

I incised an intaglio into a piece of porphyry the size of Maia's thumbnail. An intaglio is like an inside-out carving, you can press it into wax or plaster to make a raised impression.

The picture I made for Aristomache was of her, Pytheas, Simmea, Kebes, and Sokrates, examining an inscription I had carved around the eaves of the Mulberry sleeping house. Although the faces were barely the size of a grain of barley, I have lenses and carving tools fine enough to give them individuality and expressions. So I showed Pytheas's quizzical face, Aristomache with her mouth open in consternation, along with the way Sokrates liked to stand with his legs apart and his head tilted back, the way Kebes copied this, and the swell of Simmea's belly, since she had been pregnant with Neleus at that time.

Much of my work in those early years was historical and autobiographical. It was several years after that before I began to work on my series of Platonic responses, doing philosophy in the form of sculpture, or sculpture in the form of philosophy. Maia and Pytheas especially loved that work, but Aristomache was dead before I began it.

I went to Marissa myself to deliver my little intaglio. Aristomache was truly old by then. She could see it plainly, and it delighted her. We talked about Sokrates, and about the good intentions of the Masters in setting up the Republic, and about education. I had been in Marissa before, helping to make it fit for Plato, supervising young Workers who were not yet self-aware. Aristomache was not well enough that day to walk with me to the train, and later that year I was sent word that she was dead.

Then in the Sixtieth Year of the City, in the consulship of Baukis and Xenocrates, Maia had a stroke which left her half-paralyzed, unable to speak, and drooling. She had collapsed in the little garden outside her house, and nobody tried to move her. It was summer, but before I arrived someone had brought her winter kiton, embroidered with books and copies of Botticelli's flowers, and put it over her where she lay. Pytheas's son Phaedrus came, as he always did in cases where human doctors could do nothing. He took Maia's hand, and shook his head. "She's in there, but there's no healing this," he said. Neleus was there too, bending over her, wearing Ficino's old red hat.

She grunted, harsh animal sounds, "Uhrr, utt, ay."

I understood her, and went off to find Arete, in case she was calling for her and not merely restating a Platonic principle. Either would have been very characteristic for Maia.

Arete was in Thessaly. She flew off as soon as she heard, and Pytheas rode along in the webbing on my back. When we got back to Maia's house, Arete was engaged in a conversation where Maia uttered one painful-seeming syllable and Arete filled in the rest. She and Neleus were crouched at Maia's side, both in tears, though Maia was not.

"You were consul three times," Arete said.

"What more could any classicist want?" Pytheas asked, dropping down and taking her free hand. "You have done good work in this life, and your soul will be certainly reborn as a philosopher."

Maia's face distorted into a horrible grimace, and after a moment I realized that she was trying to smile. "Hhhh——" she said.

"Yes, Neleus will mix you the hemlock," Arete said. Pytheas had insisted that I bring it from Thessaly. I gave the bundle of leaves to Neleus, and he took it. He stepped inside the house, and I could watch through the doorway as he crushed it fiercely into a cup and then poured in wine recklessly, as if he couldn't see what he was doing. He came back out, and Arete took the cup from his trembling hand and held it to Maia's lips. Then Pytheas stroked her throat, helping her to swallow. When Arete took the cup away, Maia grunted.

"No, I can't promise we won't mourn for you. Yes, we'll remember you, and so will all your pupils. Your legacy will live on," Arete said.

"Joy to you, Maia," I said. "I'm not done talking with you, but go on to a good life."

There are no messages to give the dying to carry to the dead, or comfort or wisdom to take into new lives, for all souls must forget as they go through Lethe. I wished I could weep, in case the process gave some relief.

"Chh—" she said.

"She wishes you joy too, Crocus, and many years of making art and helping to lead the City and fruitful philosophy, and at last many joyful rebirths."

She grunted again, and Arete laughed through her tears. "She says she's always thought it'll be so funny for her relatives to see her disappear as a young woman and reappear a second later as she is now. She says coming to the City has meant she's had a better life than she could ever have imagined."

"Ah—" Maia said, and now even I understood her. Sokrates, dying in Athens, had asked Krito to offer a cock to Asklepius for his recovery from life. In the City, it was what almost everyone said when they felt themselves dying. Then she disappeared at the moment of death, as all the Masters and Children did, her body drawn back by Athene's power to the moment she had left to come to the City, leaving her cloak empty behind her.

We voted unanimously to name a mountain after her, which is the highest honor we give in the Republic. Maia left a great legacy and is remembered honorably by everyone. I still miss her.

The purpose of death I understand, though I worry about it in my own case. But I do not understand why the process has to be so indecorous and uncomfortable for humans.

14

APOLLO

All the time since I had read Athene's letter the question of where she might have put Sokrates had been tickling the back of my mind. It had to be somewhere I wouldn't guess, by definition, or I wouldn't need Pico to tell me where to find him. But he only spoke Greek, so it had to be somewhere Greek-speaking, and somewhere either obscure enough that nothing he did would be remembered, or somewhere so full of philosophers he wouldn't stand out. The second option seemed more like Athene. Pythagorean Kroton or Roman Alexandria were the likeliest choices, but of course she'd know I'd know that.

Athene was risking literally everything to gain knowledge of Chaos. That was bad enough. But the other reason her message had made me so incandescently furious was the way she used the threat to Sokrates to force me to rescue Pico. She could have trusted me. I'd have rescued Pico anyway. I hated being used and blackmailed, and even more I hated being blackmailed into doing what I would have done anyway because it was the right thing to do, and what I wanted to do. Even now I had calmed down, I was so furious with her that I considered writing a satire about all the most embarrassing things she had ever done, like the time she got into a snit about Paris not choosing her as the most beautiful, or the time she turned Arachne into a spider when she lost a weaving contest, or when she threw away the syrinx after inventing it because puffing out her cheeks made her look ridiculous.

I followed Pico to his cell, a small brick room which contained a low bed, a devotional painting of St. Benedict retreiving a rake from a pond (some ages have a really low bar for miracles), and a small chest, which, since it was Pico's, contained nothing but books. There he retrieved the paper Athene had given him from where it was neatly folded inside his copy of the *Republic*. He drew it out reverently and handed it to me. I opened it, glanced at it, and then at him. "Can you read this?"

"No. It's encoded to keep Athene's message safe," he said.

Well, fortunately Arete has the ability to understand anything, because this meant nothing to me. "Let's get Sokrates and then collect the other piece." I looked at him expectantly.

He shut his eyes and recited. "45 degrees, 45′ 45 North, 50 degrees 50′ 50 West, 15.10, 15th October, 151,151,151 *ante urbe condita.*"

I was genuinely startled. "What? Where's that? Somewhere in the Jurassic? In the middle of the Atlantic—no, that's long enough ago that the continents aren't even in the same places! What's there?"

"A jungle, she told me. She didn't take me with her. I was in time for the Last Debate."

"So was I—but you mean she didn't change him back? He's still a gadfly?"

"I think so. She gave me an extremely precise time and place."

"She'd have to, for a fly! Why didn't she change him back?" I was aghast.

"I think she didn't want to face him. There aren't many people who can make Athene feel ashamed."

"Has spending more time with her stopped you thinking she's perfect?" I asked.

Pico smiled. "No. She's perfect. But I do understand her better.

She's the perfect Athene, and that includes a certain amount of pride and vanity and temper."

"But surely—you know I'm not perfect!"

"But you are," he said, picking out the books and piling them on the bed. "You are the perfect Apollo. You're the light. And both of you grow and change and become more excellent, while remaining perfect as you are. Perfection isn't static. It's a dynamic form."

"Is this your new theory?" I asked warily.

"That part was in the New Concordance," he said, smiling reminiscently. "Klio and I came up with it long ago."

"So you think Athene is perfect in her imperfections? Including turning Sokrates into a fly and dropping him off in some swamp millions of years ago? Why didn't she simply take him to Athens where he could have bitten some of his friends?" He had bitten me, after his transformation, and then flown away. She must have caught him as soon as he was out of sight, and taken him to this location.

"I don't know. I told her you'd take me with you anyway, but she wanted to be sure." He looked guiltily down at the books. Then he picked them up and tucked them under his arm. "Let's go."

Taking him with me, I stepped out of time, and back in at Athene's precise coordinates of time and place. Red rocks stuck out of dense green swampland vegetation. It was warm and humid, and there were many flies. Pico, still clutching his books, looked around delightedly. For an instant I thought I could never identify Sokrates among the other flies, and that this must be an impossible test Athene had set me for reasons of her own. But he was my votary and my friend. He flew to me at once, and as soon as I saw him I knew his soul, even as a fly, as he had recognized me incarnate. Tears sprang to my eyes. At once I changed him back to his proper form, and there he was, exactly the same as he had been when I had last seen him in the Last Debate, in the same plain white kiton that was slightly frayed at the hem.

"Apollo!" he said, smiling at me. It was always his joke, to name me and pretend he was swearing. He looked around. "Ikaros!"

"Sokrates, I am so glad to see you!" We hugged each other, and then he hugged Ikaros.

"I'm very glad to see you too. Speaking of seeing, did you know that vision is entirely different when you're a fly? Where in the world are we?" He looked around at the lush bushes and ferns all around us.

"Unless you know different, where we are doesn't matter. It's some remote spot where Athene thought you'd enjoy being a fly for a little while." If you liked nature in the Romantic mode, it was beautiful. As we looked around, I heard a sound that reminded me of charging elephants, and a huge pink-and-green allosaur dashed past us, easily twice the length of an elephant but shorter and much less bulky, with small arms, an enormous head, and serrated teeth as long as my arm.

"Look, a big scary lizard!" Sokrates said, peering after it cheerfully. "What was it?"

"Maybe a wyvern?" Ikaros suggested.

"It's not a lizard at all," I said.

"Is it one of the creatures Lucretius talks about that wasn't fitted for survival?" Ikaros asked, taking a step in the direction in which it had disappeared. "Or were they all hunted down in the age of heroes?"

"The former," I said. "And they used to hunt in packs. Let's go."

Sokrates nodded after it thoughtfully, then turned back to me. "Where is Athene?" he asked. "We have unfinished business."

I understood then what Pico had meant about why she hadn't changed him back. Sokrates wanted to continue the Last Debate, even in a Jurassic swamp full of rampaging dinosaurs. Of course he did. If anyone was a perfect example of themselves, he was. And the reason Athene had changed him into a fly in the first place was because she had lost her temper and couldn't bear to be defeated in a logical argument.

"She's lost," I said. Before he had time to respond, I went on. "Now I'm going to France in the Enlightenment to collect part of the message she sent about how we can rescue her. Do you two want to come, or should I take you to the Just City first?"

"Is that where we'll be going afterwards?" Sokrates asked.

"Yes. Or rather, it's where I'll be going. If you want me to leave you somewhere else, I can do that. With some restrictions. And not here." I was suddenly unsure. Volition really did mean letting them choose, whether I wanted to or not, and however terrible their choices might be. "Where do you want to be?"

"I asked Krito what I'd do in Thessaly, but he didn't listen," Sokrates said, still looking around him at the swamp. "I don't know what France or the Enlightenment are, so let's illuminate my ignorance a little by exploring them. And after that, the Just City by all means. I can do my work there."

"You'll love the Enlightenment," Pico said enthusiastically, waving his hand to shoo away flies.

"Has Apollo been taking you on a tour of human history?"

"No, I've been working with Athene, and she has taken me to places," Pico explained.

I took them out of time, and back in to the front lawn of the Chateau Cirey in May of 1750. My sun was pleasantly warm, the trees were in spring blossom, the birds were singing, and best of all they were all that remained of dinosaurs. I had never been here before. The Enlightenment was Athene's territory, it had never been mine. "Cirey!" said Pico happily.

"Both influenced by Greek originals and influential on buildings in the City, I think," Sokrates said, looking at the chateau with his head on its side.

"You're absolutely right," I said.

"So why did Athene bring you here?" he asked Pico.

I gave our clothes the illusion of eighteenth-century finery. It was one of the most gorgeous eras for men's clothing. It amused me to dress Sokrates in peacock colors and put a huge curled and powdered wig on him. The same costume suited Pico ridiculously well, much better than the monk's habit or even his kiton, as if this were the era where he should have lived. The books he still clutched under his arm didn't even look incongruous.

"To talk to Voltaire and Emilie. Voltaire is very like you," Pico said to Sokrates. "Another marvelous gadfly. He wrote a play about you. Athene and I spent two wonderful days here. There was theater, there was science, there was debate, and they're thinking such wonderful things—what time is it here, Pytheas? Can we get hold of a copy of the *Encyclopédie* while we're here?"

"The first volume doesn't come out until next year," I said. "Besides, it's in French."

"I can speak French, though it's changed a bit, and we sometimes needed to use Latin to be clear. But I can certainly read it reasonably well."

Sokrates was examining his clothes. "This is the future?" he asked.

"Your future, yes, more than two thousand years after you were born."

"And after your time too?" he asked Ikaros.

"Yes, about two hundred and fifty years after I was born. But a hundred years before Maia and Adeimantus were born, and three hundred years before Klio and Lysias." Pico looked energized by the thought. "There's so much history, so many places and times!"

Sokrates smoothed the burgundy velvet of his sleeve. "What a strange place."

"I'm looking for Florent-Claude," I said to Pico. "Do you know him? Athene describes him as Emilie's widower."

"Emilie's dead?" Pico looked sad. "She was so wonderful, a scientist and a philosopher in an age where it was so hard for women to be anything but hostesses at best. She should have been in the Republic."

"Do you know Florent-Claude?" I repeated.

"Yes. I met him. She was with Voltaire when we visited, but Florent-Claude was happy with the situation. It was almost like being in the City of Amazons."

I knocked loudly on the door. "Why didn't Athene leave it with Voltaire?" I grumbled. "He's the one who's her votary. It would have been interesting to meet him."

A servant opened the door, a flunkey in a wig. "We wish to see Florent-Claude," I said.

"The Marquis du Chastellet," Pico added.

"And your names?" the flunkey asked, superciliously.

"The Comte de Mirandola, the Marquis de Delos and the Duc d'Athen," Pico replied immediately, in Italianate French.

The flunkey bowed and went back inside. "Marquis? Duke?" I asked. He really was the Count of Mirandola, or course, or he had been two hundred or so years before.

"Did you want me to say god and philosopher on the doorstep?" Pico asked. "I'm sure there was a Duke of Athens."

"Not in 1750," I said. "He told the servant you were a member of the high Athenian nobility," I explained to Sokrates.

"You're mixing me up with Plato again," Sokrates said. "He was descended from Solon on his mother's side, and on his father's side from the ancient kings of Attica. I was a simple stonemason before I became a philosopher, and my only illustrious ancestor was the artificer Daedalus."

The flunkey came back. "The marquis will see you."

He showed us into one of those uncomfortable eighteenth-century rooms, all spindly little chairs matching the gilt frames on all the paintings. Sokrates looked at all of it in wonder.

"I'm afraid you're not going to understand any of the conversation," I said.

"I've always been terrible at learning barbarian languages," Sokrates said, almost as if this were a point of pride. "Do they have Workers here?"

"No, we're more than two centuries before the first Workers," I said.

"Then who wove this carpet so finely, and then put it on the floor?" he asked.

Before I could respond, the flunkey opened the door again and announced his master. We all bowed, Sokrates very badly as he wasn't familiar with the custom.

"I don't believe I've had the pleasure," Florent-Claude said.

"We met once, when I was here staying with Emilie," Pico said. "Such a loss." They bowed to each other.

"Ah yes. The Comte de Mirandola. I recognize you now. The years haven't touched you at all."

Pico looked uncomfortable at this compliment. He looked about thirty, but he had been over sixty and almost blind at the Relocation, before Father had restored his youth on Olympos so that he could work with Athene. He didn't seem to have aged at all since then. He introduced us, Apollonaire de Delos and Socrate d'Athen, who unhappily knew no French. We sat down in the little uncomfortable chairs. "We're passing by, we can't stay," he said, in response to Florent-Claude's offer of hospitality for the night. The flunkey returned and gave us all sherry, in little glasses, and offered around a plate of petits fours. I neither ate nor drank, but it was almost worth the delay for the expression on Sokrates's face when after turning the highly colored confection in his fingers he bit into the cloying marzipan.

I wished Athene had given me more to go on. I didn't know what she'd said when she asked Florent-Claude to keep the paper for him, or what name she'd been using or who he thought she was. Fortunately, Pico did. "You remember my friend Athenais de Minerve?"

"Of course," Florent-Claude said. "So beautiful, so wise."

"Did she by chance give you an incomprehensible paper to look after?" Pico asked.

Sokrates was ignoring us all and pleating the lace of his undersleeve intently.

"So, you are on her treasure hunt?" Florent-Claude smiled.

I could not understand why Athene had gone through this elaborate charade and divided up her message. It was dangerous as well as unnecessary. Ordinary mortals involved this way could easily have lost the paper. Pico's could have been stolen, and what Kebes might have done with it didn't bear thinking about. He could have burned it for pure spite.

"We are," Pico said.

"Then can you answer her riddle?"

"We'll have to see when you ask it," Pico said, confidently.

"Let me fetch it," he said. "But first I should tell you that it's in English, and if none of you speak that language you have leave to find another who does."

"English," Pico said, dismayed. "I know many languages, but not that barbarous tongue."

"Barbarous? I think not, since I speak it," I said. (You're reading this. You already know I speak English.)

Florent-Claude chortled, and went off to fetch the paper. I hoped he hadn't lost it among his bibelots.

"Who did she think would come who would need to find an English speaker?" Pico asked, in Greek.

"Porphyry?" I suggested.

"Old Porphyry's still alive?" Sokrates asked, looking up from his sleeve, surprised.

"No, he died. But Euridike named one of my sons after him, and that's who we're talking about. Ikaros was one of his teachers."

Sokrates seemed to accept that calmly. "Where did Florent-Claude go?"

"He's fetching Athene's message," I explained.

"What is this made of?" he asked, picking up the drape of lace at his cuff again.

"Silk, I think, though they sometimes make it from linen," I said. "It's called lace."

"And what is silk?" Sokrates asked, patiently.

"It's a thread spun by worms who eat mulberry leaves," Pico explained. He twirled his wrists, making his own lace flare gorgeously. "It makes a cloth that's cool to wear in hot weather and that's gentle next to the skin, not scratchy. It originates in China, but in my time we make it in Italy. But lace came later."

"And this lace is made by humans?"

"By women, mostly, using bobbins, which are things like little distaffs," I said.

"This is an incredibly unnecessary waste of human labor and human souls," Sokrates pronounced. "Those women should be freed from their bobbins and taught reason. It would be a useless frivolity even if Workers made it as fast and unthinkingly as any cloth. Nobody needs dangling frills like this. Look at this incredible detail. It's beautiful, in itself, but nonsensical as clothing."

"I agree," I said. "Though it looks elegant on Ikaros."

"Don't you think it's unjust?"

"What if it's somebody's vocation, to make lace?" Ikaros asked. "Their art?"

"It is a normal part of these people's clothing," Sokrates said. "Far too much for it to be made as somebody's art. Look at these paintings, everyone has it. If somebody wanted to make it as their art, it might be a harmless decoration, like the borders some people embroider on their kitons. It's this volume of it that's wrong. Close work like that? Women must be compelled to make it from economic necessity."

"Yes, that's wrong," Ikaros said, soberly. "When there's so much injustice it becomes invisible."

"Is this silk also?" Sokrates asked, stroking his velvet sleeve.

"I think so," I said, not at all sure what velvet was made of. "You should ask Athene when we have her back, fabrics are one of her specialities."

"She would not approve of this *lace*," Sokrates said, quite certain that whatever they might disagree about, they'd be as one on such fundamentals as that. "Not even Alkibiades would like lace. And think of the time it must take, every day, putting on all these ridiculous things. I sleep with my kiton over me as a covering, I wake up and shake it, I fold it and put it on and I am ready for the day. Putting on all these layers and choosing the colors to match must waste so much time, and worse, attention."

"In cold places people need more layers and thicker clothes," I said.

"Certainly. But it's not cold here," Sokrates said, which was inarguable that day.

"What if wearing clothes and choosing colors is somebody's art?" Pico asked.

Florent-Claude came bustling back with a paper in his hand. "Very well. Now, in English if you will! Of what five things is St. Jathe patron?" He had a strong accent in English, but understood the pronunciation better than many Francophones.

Pico looked at me, frowning. He must have understood the name. St. Jathe was clearly Jathery. I'd heard the list from Hilfa, such a strange set of things. And a riddle in English would need a rhyming answer. "Liberty and changing names, wisdom, tricks and riddle games," I said. It seemed almost insultingly easy, but it could only be answered by somebody who spoke English and had talked to Saeli about religion—which meant me, or perhaps Hermes.

"Well done! So here is your paper, but you will find in it another riddle, I think," Florent-Claude said, handing it over. It had the same mix of characters as Pico's. I tucked it away with the other.

Saying goodbye took a long time, though we tried to hurry. We had to promise to give his love to Athene, and to call in if we were ever passing again. As we walked, Pico translated the conversation for Sokrates and then they both insisted that I explain the riddle. We had to walk all the way to the end of the lawn and wave and then make our way behind the screen of chestnuts, all with their spring candles, before we could step out of time and back to the Republic.

15

JASON

Pytheas had got up from his chair and was looming over Jathery. He had grown so tall that his head almost touched the ceiling of Hilfa's little house. "Was it you all the time?" he asked, and although his voice was quiet it made the hair stand up on my neck. "Was it you who came and interrupted me?"

"Yes," Jathery said, not sounding at all intimidated. Gla voice was clear and pure, like a child's voice singing, but rich and full-bodied.

"You lied to me about having a message from Father?"

"Would you have left your new sun if I'd come to you as myself and told you Athene was missing?" Gla question sounded entirely reasonable, and made me wonder whether Pytheas would have.

"Yes," Pytheas said, emphatically but petulantly. He glared down at Jathery. "Why does nobody trust me to take any reasonable action without tricking me into it?"

They both disappeared. I blinked.

Ikaros was looking green, not the way Saeli are green, but the way pale-skinned humans turn green when they're about to be sick. He walked rapidly into the fountain room, and I soon heard the sound of him tossing his guts up joining the familiar sound of Marsilia doing the same. Almost everyone gets queasy sometimes on boats and has to spew. I might have felt the same way if I'd found out somebody I'd been to bed with was actually Jathery in disguise. The thought of it was a bit stomach-churning.

"I couldn't tell you. Do you understand, Jason?" Hilfa asked quietly from beside me.

"I understand," I said. He started to rock to and fro again. I put my arms around him.

Thetis picked up the papers Marsilia had dropped and sat down with them in Pytheas's empty chair. She glanced towards the fountain room.

"Joy to you, Sokrates, I'm delighted to meet you, I have heard so much about you," Arete said.

"I hear you're Simmea's daughter, and you see through falsehood. That must be useful in debate."

"Not as much as you might think," Arete said.

Sokrates laughed. "But you saw through Jathery pretending to be Hermes when he had fooled us all?"

"It seems so," Arete said.

"How did none of us guess?" Sokrates asked.

"Deception and name-changing are part of what gla is," Hilfa said.

"Even so, I'm surprised gla could fool Pytheas," Sokrates said. "Hermes is his own brother."

Ikaros came back in. He smiled wanly, picked up his wine-beaker and drained it, then sat down in the other chair.

"Where did Pytheas and Jathery go?" I asked.

"To yell at each other outside time, I expect. It's a thing gods do," Ikaros said, shaking his head. "They'll be back, for those if nothing else." He gestured at the papers Thetis was holding. She offered them to him, and he took them, turning them over curiously. "There are at least four alphabets here, and I think there was a different one on the piece I had, Etruscan maybe."

Marsilia came back in, with the strands of her dark hair damp around her face where she must have dashed water on it. "Oh Marsilia, is there anything that could help?"

She shook her head. I passed her my winecup and she took a sip. She sat down on the floor in front of us.

Arete took the papers from Ikaros. "Oh, interesting, we need all of them together to be able to read them."

"Did finding out who Jathery was make you sick?" Hilfa asked Marsi.

Marsilia nodded.

"Me too," Ikaros said, smiling companionably at her. "I think many people would throw up on learning that a lover was really an alien god."

She nodded again.

"I'm sorry. I couldn't tell you. I don't know what gla would have done to me," Hilfa said. "I think gla made me, and could unmake me, to take back the part of gla power gla put into me."

"None of this is your fault," Marsilia said.

"We should not need to live in fear of the arbitrary power of the gods this way," Sokrates said.

"The Saeli always do, all of us, always," Hilfa said.

Marsilia took another swig of my wine. Thetis got up and stood behind Marsilia and started to rub her shoulders. Marsilia relaxed a little.

"It means Alkippe and I are siblings," Hilfa said, tentatively.

"But that was always true," Marsilia said. Hilfa stopped rocking entirely and sat up straight, staring at her.

"You're also one of Simmea's granddaughters?" Sokrates asked Marsilia. "You remind me of her."

"Yes, I am," Marsilia said. Thetis looked proudly down at her.

"And Jathery took you off on a treasure hunt through time for Athene's papers?" Sokrates went on.

Marsilia gave him a small smile. "It was a bit like that, yes. But all the time I thought he was Hermes. Gla really is horribly good at deception. Even when I saw him changing between forms when we were outside time, I never questioned who he was."

"You should always question," Sokrates said.

Marsilia smiled up at him ruefully. "I'll try harder to be a proper philosopher."

Arete passed the papers back to Ikaros. "I wonder sometimes if it is harder for women to be philosophers, even for the Golds here. Everything always seems to be stacked against it."

"Not always," Ikaros said. "Did you ever know Lucrezia? She was in the City of Amazons by the time you were growing up, so maybe not. We lived together for a long time. She came from the Renaissance, from Rome. She and her brothers all had the same humanist education, all read Plato. But she was the only one to become a philosopher, and pray to Athene to come here. They had no time in their lives for it, after their education, none of them. But she did, being a woman, even though she was as much a political pawn as they were. For once the expectation of passivity and not being able to act was an advantage, it gave her time to study they couldn't have."

At that moment, the two gods reappeared, Pytheas restored to his usual size.

"Let's put it together right now," Pytheas said. "Where—ah, thank you, Pico." He took the papers from Ikaros and pulled two more out the fold of his kiton.

"But what—" Ikaros asked.

"We have decided to work on getting Athene back first, before addressing the issue of Jathery's imposture," Pytheas said, with a glare at Jathery. He walked over to the table. Arete and Ikaros followed close behind. Pytheas set the papers down on top of the pile of books Ikaros had laid down there earlier. The four of them bent over the papers. Arete at once switched them into a different order.

Sokrates looked at me, and I jumped. "You've been very quiet. What's your connection with all this?"

"I'm here because I'm Hilfa's friend," I said. Hilfa stopped rocking and nodded.

"An admirable reason," he said. "Your name is Jason, Pytheas said. I see you're a Silver?"

"Yes," I said, emboldened by his approval. "We work on a fishing boat with Marsilia."

"Yes, I can read it," Arete said, from across the room. "It's a technical description of how to get out into the primal Chaos and back. It sounds preposterously dangerous. There's no justification or explanation here of why she did it or why anyone would want to, or why she left it scattered in pieces."

"But you can read it?" Pytheas asked. "Translate it!"

"I could," Arete said. "But, Father, I'd need a good reason as to why I should. This is extremely dangerous information, and Athene didn't come back. I see no reason why it would be any less dangerous for you. If gods can get lost out there, it's bad enough to lose one, and much worse to lose two."

"If you won't translate it, you'll force us to take it to Father," Pytheas said. Now that they were standing nose to nose glaring at each other, I could see that they were exactly the same height.

"Explain to me why that is a bad thing?" Arete asked. I was feeling increasingly uncomfortable hearing them arguing about such things. But Hilfa was still shivering in my arms, so I stayed where I was and tried to be reassuring. Thetis smiled at me over Marsilia's head, and that in itself was reason enough to stay. "You should take it to Zeus," Arete went on. "You said you wanted to see her explanation first—well, there isn't any, in the sense of justification for why she did it."

"I told you why she did it." Pytheas stalked back to his chair and flung himself down. "And I explained why I don't want to go to Father."

"Do we have to take any action?" Arete asked.

Pytheas glowered at her. "You can read us the instructions and then we can attempt to rescue her. Or if you refuse, we can go to Father, though I fear the consequences. Those are our choices. We can't leave her stranded out there and do nothing, no. That's not an acceptable option."

"I agree with that," Jathery said. I looked over to where gla was still standing by the table, gla big hand splayed on Athene's notes. Gla looked like a big Sael with exceptionally clear skin patterns, except that gla had an arrogant confidence that was like no Sael I had ever seen. Gla voice sounded smooth and persuasive. And gla skin patterns changed as I watched. Hilfa's were more or less pronounced, but always the same pattern in the same place. Jathery's writhed and rewrote themselves constantly.

"We absolutely need to get her back. The world can't survive without wisdom," Ikaros said, passionately.

"You of all people must understand that Athene is not the only source of wisdom in the universe," Arete snapped.

"But she's our source of wisdom, our culture's source," Ikaros said. "We wouldn't be the same with foreign wisdom."

"We might be better," Sokrates said, thoughtfully.

"I love her, and you know you do too," Ikaros said.

"True. And I am her votary, hers and Apollo's." He nodded to Pytheas where he sat. Pytheas, or maybe I should say Apollo, nodded back warily. "But loving her doesn't excuse us from seeing her very real faults. And considering those, who is to say we might not be better with Apollo taking charge of our wisdom, or perhaps Thoth or Anahita."

Pytheas shuddered. "We wouldn't, not with any of those choices, believe me." I knew nothing about Thoth except that he was an ibis-headed Egyptian god. I had never even heard of Anahita.

"Some other god of wisdom might better consider the will of

thinking beings," Sokrates said. "Athene has always been careless of it."

"You're only saying that because you think it would be interesting to find out," Ikaros said.

"Well, don't you?" asked Sokrates mildly.

"Yes, theoretically interesting, but in practice it would be terrible," Ikaros said. "You're still angry with her because she turned you into a gadfly."

Sokrates laughed. I stared at him, hardly able to believe he could find it funny. "It was interesting being a gadfly. The way they see is amazing. And I could fly! I'm not angry about that. It was a fascinating experience—a little frightening at first, yes, but I have endured far worse things, and there was a lot about it to enjoy. If I can't forgive her it's for not finishing the argument."

"She behaved badly in the Last Debate," Ikaros conceded. "But we should still rescue her!"

"I'm not saying Athene's not valuable or that we should abandon her," Arete said. "I'm saying that Apollo is equally valuable, or more valuable right now because he hasn't gone haring out into Chaos. And I suppose the same applies to Jathery; the Saeli must need him for something."

Jathery laughed, the patterns on his skin still changing every moment. Hearing it I realized what was wrong with Hilfa's laugh—it was always the same. Human laughter bubbles or barks and each laugh is different. Jathery's was different. When he'd been pretending to be Hermes it had sounded like normal laughter. Now it didn't sound at all human, and it sent shivers through me. Meanwhile, beside me, Hilfa shook his head. I looked at him. "No?" I whispered. "You don't need him?"

"I suppose we do," he whispered back.

"But isn't gla your culture's source of wisdom?" I asked.

Hilfa didn't reply.

"I wonder what Athene has learned out there?" Ikaros mused.

"What did she hope to learn?" Arete asked. "How could it seem like a good idea to do such a thing?"

"She wanted to know the answers to the most fundamental questions," Ikaros said. "How the universe came into being, and how Zeus made time. We were working on the nature of time and Necessity."

"Is the knowledge that she might have learned in Chaos why you want to risk yourselves to rescue her?" Arete asked Pytheas.

"It's why I'm afraid of what Father might do," Pytheas said.

"It's not worth the risk!" Arete said.

"It is worth a little risk to learn so many answers," Jathery said, quietly but compellingly.

"A little risk!" Arete said, not at all persuaded. "You know how great a risk it is to place everything on one throw."

"But sometimes it can be rewarding," Jathery murmured persuasively.

Arete shuddered.

"What do you mean by time?" Sokrates asked abruptly.

Ikaros jumped. He had been staring at Jathery as if he could read the patterns on gla skin. He turned to Sokrates. "Oh, what the gods mean when they say *time* is human history, or what we might call material reality or the fourth hypostasis. The place where things change and actions have consequences and one day follows the next. But it's not that simple. The gods live in the realm of soul and are eternal, and can step in and out of what they call time, but they also experience consequences and growth and change. They have personal time." He moved his arms demonstratively. "Plotinus said time was a quality, a negative quality, an imperfection, and that the higher hypostases didn't suffer it. But he was wrong. It's such a pity he didn't live to learn how time is more complicated. In fact, time extends at least into the realm of mind, above the realm of soul, because the ideals, the Forms, are dynamic."

"So is Chaos part of time?" Sokrates asked.

"No. Chaos is before and after and below time. It's the lowest hypostasis. It's matter with no form," Ikaros said. I vaguely remembered hypostases being mentioned when I was an ephebe. I'd never gone in for this kind of exalted metaphysics. I work on a fishing boat. Plato's Allegory of the Cave is good enough for me. "Or at least, that's what we think it is."

Sokrates turned to Pytheas. "I won't ask if that's correct, but is this what you also believe?"

"Ikaros has been studying these matters with Athene and probably understands more about them than I do," Pytheas said. "I was born long after Father created time."

"And you?" Sokrates asked Jathery.

"I am even younger than Apollo. But my studies agree with Ikaros." Gla nodded at Ikaros, who blushed and looked away.

"So Zeus created time?" Sokrates asked Pytheas. "But what about Kronos, Ouranos, the Titans?"

"He used the Darkness of the Oak," Pytheas said. "Kronos and Ouranos were names of Father's, in earlier iterations. And the Titans were earlier circles of gods, not quite forgotten. And while it might be possible to argue that he's getting better at it and each iteration of time is more excellent and closer to perfection, I can't feel calm about the risk of losing myself and all of history. I have learned a lot. And there's so much that mortals have made that is wonderful. You may say the good is the enemy of the best and starting fresh would be better, but I want to protect this good we have."

"Athene thought the gain was worth the risk," Jathery said, and for a moment listening to him I agreed. It would be wonderful to know these things for sure.

"You and Athene had no right to decide that on your own, when what is risked is everything for everyone," Pytheas said. And though his voice was harsh in comparison, of course he was right.

"She took precautions as best she could," Jathery said, smoothly. "We intended to go together, but she went without telling me."

"We are all part of her precautions, you included," Pytheas acknowledged. "Athene really didn't want us to go to Father and risk what he would do."

"But doesn't he already know everything?" Thetis asked, looking up from Marsilia. "We can't keep it from Zeus. He already knows."

"Only when he becomes conscious of it, and then it is as if he has always known," Ikaros said. "He told me that himself. So even though he knows everything, he only lives partially in any kind of time at all. If he becomes conscious of this after Athene is safely back, that is different from if he becomes conscious of it now, while she is stranded out there."

"But what does now mean, to him?" Sokrates asked.

"It has to do with awareness," Ikaros said.

"It all does," Pytheas said. "What we can do. Time."

"And what about Necessity?" Sokrates asked Ikaros.

"Necessity is a great force that binds all thinking beings," Ikaros said. "We think it compels even Zeus."

"And this is what Athene went out into Chaos to study?"

"Necessity, and what Chaos is, and how time began," Ikaros confirmed.

Sokrates turned to Pytheas. "You said once that Fate is the line drawn around what we can do, and Necessity prevents us overstepping that line, but within the lines we are free to do what we want." Pytheas nodded. "And do you think Athene has overstepped that line?"

"I think that depends whether we can get her back," Pytheas said. "At this moment, when she is there, she has, yes. Once we have her back, then no, she has not."

"I don't understand how it can be both," Sokrates said. "She has transgressed or she has not."

"We have freedom to act, and she is acting, the action is not complete," Jathery elucidated, and set out like that it did all seem clear.

"Is that the kind of freedom that is your responsibility, and which Athene referenced in her riddle?" Sokrates asked.

"Yes," Jathery said. "She is poised between. When she comes back and her action is complete, we will know."

"Or if we go to Father," Pytheas said. "So it would be better if we go after her and bring her back."

I was listening to this when something occurred to me. "Wait," I said.

Everyone turned to stare at me. Sokrates and Thetis looked hopeful, Ikaros looked curious, Pytheas and Arete looked impatient, Marsilia looked surprised, Jathery looked sinisterly unreadable, and Hilfa a little bemused. It was hard to speak in the focus of so much combined attention. "I'm sorry," I said. "Probably this is only me not understanding, I'm only a Silver, not a god or a philosopher. But why can't you go outside time and come back in say five years from now and come to me and Hilfa and Marsilia one day while we're out fishing? And we'd know by then the results of all this, and we could tell you, and then you'd know whether this worked or not and what to do before you do it."

"What would happen if you did that and Jason told you it hadn't worked, that you'd been lost forever in the formless Chaos?" Sokrates inquired at once.

"Nothing," Pytheas said. "We'd still have to go. Necessity. And that's why we won't."

"I thought you said being compelled by Necessity merely made you uncomfortable?" Sokrates said.

"It can get highly uncomfortable," Jathery said. "Even knowing there's a really good reason not to go back and sort things out, I've been getting more and more uncomfortable about not doing it. It's like pain. It's harder and harder not to act to relieve it. It takes a great deal of will to resist. I couldn't last this way much longer. Resisting inevitability is difficult, and much better avoided." The markings on his skin writhed unsettlingly and re-formed themselves.

"Like on Delos," Arete said, looking at Pytheas.

"And again, freedom?" Sokrates asked.

Pytheas was frowning. "We're free within Fate and Necessity. The more we tangle ourselves up with them—and that would be nothing but a deliberate tangle—the less we are free to act. Our past actions bind our future selves, and all we gods do is remembered in art. The more we want to be able to change and grow and pursue excellence, the more we need to leave ourselves open to that."

"And the same for humanity too?" Sokrates asked, cheerily.

"Mortals never know, so they are always free to act," Pytheas said.

I noticed he said mortals, where Sokrates had said humanity. Sokrates hadn't really had time yet to take in what the Saeli presence meant.

"And when you make predictions to them, through your oracles?" Sokrates asked.

"My oracles give useful guidelines and let people know how to get the attention of the gods," Pytheas said.

"But if you went into the future now, could you see Jason's fate, and come back and tell him today exactly what will happen in his life and how much fish he will catch every day until he dies?" Sokrates asked.

"Please don't!" I said at once.

Pytheas smiled at me. "Don't worry. All gods learn early that it doesn't do any good to warn people about their future. Necessity makes the steps they take to avoid it turn out to be exactly what will make it happen. Look at Oedipus. Advice can be useful, sometimes; actual prophecy mostly becomes self-defeating. It's much better for oracles to be ambiguous. Necessity is a very powerful force."

"But you do know people's fate?" Sokrates asked.

"Sometimes. It depends whether we've been paying attention."

Sokrates screwed up his face. "So doing what Jason suggested wouldn't help because you'd have to go anyway, whether it succeeds or fails?"

"Yes. And it's so unpleasant to be caught up by Necessity we don't want to any more than we have to. It feels like being pinned. So it's better to stay free and take actions without knowing."

"Why do you have to go?" Marsilia asked.

"We already went through all this!" Pytheas said impatiently.

"I mean can't Jathery go after her alone? Gla's the one who has the shield of Necessity, not you," Marsilia said, though she was still not looking at Jathery.

"I would be willing to go alone," Jathery said, gla inner eyelids shining over gla eyes.

Pytheas shook his head. "No. If Athene trusted gla, she'd have left the message for gla, not for me. I have to go, Marsilia. Jathery can come, we've agreed that, but I don't trust gla, and I'm not letting gla go alone."

"Besides these instructions are for two gods working together," Arete said. "But I don't see how you're any less likely to get stranded there than she was, if you go there using the method she left you. You'd simply be repeating what she did, which worked to take her out but not to bring her home. So all you'd achieve by going after her would be to make things worse."

Pytheas stared at her grimly. "We have a shield she did not. Jathery is bound by Necessity, that great force. Alkippe is his child, but he hasn't yet been back to conceive her. Does that affect your estimate of our safety?"

"What? You can't risk Alkippe like that!" Tears sprang to Thetis's eyes at once. She leapt to her feet. "Grandfather! That's the worst thing I ever heard. You can't! And you, Jathery or whoever you are, you have to go there right now and set things straight!" I'd forgotten she hadn't been there when we'd found out about this, back in Thessaly.

"Calm down, it's all right," Marsilia said.

I stood up and put a tentative hand on Thetis's arm. "Let's hear more about it," I said. "Marsilia—"

"It isn't all right! It can't be!" Thetis shook me off. "It's unbearable."

"But Alkippe might be keeping all of us safe, the whole of our civilization even," Marsilia said.

"The whole of history, potentially, Thee," Pytheas said.

"I don't care!" Thetis said. "You can't take risks with her like that! How can you think of it? She's only seven."

Marsilia looked at me pleadingly. I didn't know what to say or do. I felt sorry for Thetis, but things were bad enough without getting upset about them. It seemed strange that she could hear about the potential unravelling of the world as calmly as any of us, but a threat to one child she loved overcame her this way.

"I'm horrified too, but if it's really keeping all of us safe, then the risk is no worse for Alkippe than for any of us, all of us," I said.

To my surprise Hilfa got up and put his arms awkwardly around Thetis, and she sank down on the bed and allowed him to hold her.

"Are you Alkippe's mother, Thetis?" Sokrates asked gently.

Thetis shook her head.

"No, I am," Marsilia said quietly to Sokrates, as poor Thetis wept on Hilfa's shoulder.

"And you say you are all right with this, this risk to your child?" Sokrates asked.

"She can't be!" Thetis said, barely able to speak through her sobs.

"I'm not all right, but it's necessary. It's what Jason said, the risk is the same. If she ceases to exist because Jathery doesn't go back to conceive her, or she ceases to exist because the whole city, or all of history does, there's no difference. And I have stayed as close to Jathery as I can since finding this out. It's why I went with gla," Marsilia said. Her face was set and brave. "I also love Alkippe very much—and I agree it's terrible."

Sokrates patted her shoulder. "What a hard choice," he said. "But if Jathery doesn't go to rescue Athene—"

"Then Alkippe may be safe from Necessity, but Zeus may bring down the Darkness of the Oak on all of us, Alkippe included," Marsilia said.

"Arete?" Pytheas asked, over the sound of Thetis's sobbing. "Please?"

Arete's eyes widened. "All right, I'll translate it. The shield of Necessity may be enough. Well, I will if Hilfa agrees."

"Hilfa?" I asked, surprised into speaking.

"Hilfa is the anchor. He always was. He's Athene's anchor right now."

Hilfa kept his arms around Thetis. As he looked up I caught a flash of vivid orange and blue from his eyelids. "Like a boat anchor? What does it mean, for a person to be an anchor?"

"It means you're her connection back to this universe," Arete said. "If Pytheas and Jathery go out there, they'll need to follow the thread from you to her."

"You're not only her message, but her anchor," Jathery said.

Hilfa was staring at Arete over Thee's head. "Tell me what I am?"

"You're a hero, and what you make of yourself is your own choice. Like all Saeli, you have five parents. Jathery, a male human, the earth and water of Plato, and the spark of Athene's mind," Arete said.

Ikaros made an uneasy motion, but did not speak. He took a step forward, then stopped.

"So I belong to this planet? To Plato?" Hilfa asked, staring at Arete with the glint I thought was his real smile on his face.

"Yes," Arete said. "And you don't object to being the anchor?"

"It is what I was made for, how could I mind?" Hilfa asked. He let go of Thetis and stood up. Thee was getting herself under control. I sat down again and put my arm tentatively around her. She leaned into me as she had been doing with Hilfa.

"Let's do it and have done," Pytheas said.

"And if you don't come back?" Arete asked. "Should I send—"

"That will be up to you," Pytheas said.

"But we're not sure how time out there relates to time here," Ikaros said. "That was part of why Athene refused to take me. If you don't come back, we should wait before going to Zeus with this."

"Wait how long?" Arete asked.

"Ask Porphyry. The same way you have a connection with patterns of truth and language, he has a connection with the patterns of place and time. If we don't reappear immediately, go to him tomorrow and ask him to go to Father when it feels right," Pytheas said.

"All right," Arete said, walking back to the table. "Look, nobody can go except the gods, and none of the rest of us can do anything to help now. I think everyone else should go to bed. There's still a human spaceship up there that we'll have to deal with tomorrow, and it's getting late."

"If tomorrow comes," Jathery said, with another bone-chilling laugh.

All I'd have to deal with tomorrow, if it came, was the sea and the fish, but that was enough. "That sounds like good advice to me," I said. "Sleep will help."

"As if I'd be able to sleep with Alkippe in danger," Thetis said, mopping her eyes.

"But we should try, Thee, because she'll be awake and wanting breakfast, and your little ones will need you," Marsilia said. I picked up Thetis's cloak and wrapped it around her. She huddled into it.

"We'll let you all catch up on sleep," Pytheas said. "We'll come back and let you know what's happened tomorrow evening."

"But you won't want to wait . . . oh!" Arete said. They wouldn't have to wait, of course, they could step back into time tomorrow evening as easily as today. It must be so incredibly strange to be a god.

"I'm not tired. If you'll tell me where Crocus is, I think I'll go and find him," Sokrates said. "I know the City, unless it has changed very much in being moved here."

"Crocus is out at the spaceport," Marsilia said.

Sokrates laughed. "Then it has changed more than I imagined!"

"I'll take you to the spaceport," Arete said to Sokrates. "I want to go there anyway. I can be useful there. And it'll be quicker for you to come with me than taking the train at this time of night."

"You have trains here now?" Ikaros asked.

"What are trains?" Sokrates asked.

"Trains are moving rooms—electrical conveyances that run on rails moving at fixed times to fixed places," Marsilia explained. "And Ikaros, you could take one to the City of Amazons and be there in less than an hour, though there isn't one now until morning."

"I know Rhadamantha would be pleased to see you," Arete said. "She has children, your grandchildren."

"Could I do that and be back by tomorrow evening?"

Pytheas shook his head at Ikaros. "Yes. But be here when we get Athene back."

"And then she'll need me," Ikaros said, resignedly.

"You might want to go to Thessaly for the night. Porphyry's there, or he was when I left," Arete said.

"In Thessaly? My house?" Sokrates asked.

"Well, it's been my house for the last sixty years," Pytheas said, awkwardly. "I hope you don't mind. Simmea and I moved in there as soon as we decided to allow families. But you can have it back now if you decide to stay here. You might prefer Sokratea, or the

City of Amazons." Then he grinned. "Ikaros, if you're going to Thessaly, go along the street of Hermes. That way you can pass the Ikarian temple. I can't wait to hear what you think of what they've made of your New Concordance."

Ikaros's face expressed his consternation. Pytheas laughed.

"They do insist on being called followers of the New Concordance. It's only everyone else who called them Ikarians," Marsilia said.

Marsilia and Thetis and I moved towards the door. "Do I need to stay with you to be an anchor?" Hilfa asked.

"You need to stay alive, and preferably on Plato," Arete said. "Don't worry. It isn't something you have to do, it's what you are."

"In that case, I will go to the Temple of Amphitrite and eat oatmeal," Hilfa said.

"I'll go with you too, if I may," Sokrates said. "Then when you're done, Arete, you can find me there to take me to see Crocus. That way nobody but those who need to know will hear Athene's dangerous message."

"Thank you," Arete said.

As he passed him, Sokrates put a hand on Pytheas's arm. "Are you still trying to do your best for your friends?" he asked.

"Always," Pytheas said. "And for the world."

16

MARSILIA

I sat down again on the forest floor, which was soft and springy beneath me, with its now-familiar loamy scent. It felt comfortable to be outside time and in this grove. The air here was perfumed with the scent of fresh green growth. It was a delectable springlike temperature, warmer than Plato and cooler than Greece. The leaves moved overhead, casting a wavering stippled shadow down on us. Hermes lowered himself gracefully beside me. "Let me see it," he said. I glanced at him. He was again changing disquietingly from shape to shape from moment to moment as the light dappled him—a Sael, a dark-skinned woman, a light-skinned woman, a different Sael, an animal, a child. Then he became himself, solid and gorgeous and so real beside me that it was hard to believe he had ever been anything else.

I had tucked the paper into my kiton, but it seemed that now I was wearing my sea-gear again. I unsnicked my jerkin and to my relief found the paper in the inside pocket, along with a drawing Alkippe had made of a gloater on a plate. I took Athene's message out reluctantly and handed it to Hermes. "I can't read it," I said. "I don't even know the alphabet."

He frowned down at it. "It's not like anything I've ever seen. Some of these strange characters are Viking runes. Or they're like runes anyway. And some of them are Saeli, but . . . no. I can't make

anything of it. I suppose she wrote it like this so Kebes wouldn't
be able to read it." He ran his finger over the back. "Good paper."

"It seems like ordinary paper to me," I said.

"Then maybe she found it in your city." Hermes handed the
paper back to me, and I put it away next to Alkippe's drawing. Here,
outside time, I no longer felt tired. I was aware that I ought to, that
I had been exhausted moments before in the agora of Lucia, but it
had all fallen away from me. Did people sleep here, I wondered?
My complex feelings about Kebes also seemed to be held at arm's
length, and even the disconcerting way Hermes had flickered from
form to form didn't upset me the way it would elsewhere. I liked
the way my sensations and emotions felt a little detached. I wondered whether Thetis, who revelled in emotion, would hate it, and
whether she'd ever have the opportunity to find out.

"Kebes couldn't read it, but we can't read it either," I said.

"No. Maybe she wanted that too. Maybe I'll be able to read it
when we have it all together." He sighed and leaned back on his
elbow, displaying the whole length of his lovely body. "What an
unpleasant person Kebes was. You dealt with him extremely well."

"Thank you," I said, slightly flustered by the approval in his face.
"Can you not mention to Thetis and the others—especially
Thetis—what he said about being my grandfather?"

"I don't think we need to mention it. But why?"

"Well, in the City we always talk about him as if he's a kind of
monster, and nobody would like to think they were descended from
him. Pytheas killed him. I think it would upset Ma and Thetis a
lot to know. And it might not be true anyway."

Hermes shook his head. "Athene wouldn't lie outright. She deceived him anyway, letting his wishes affect what he thought she
said. But that's as far as she'd go. And if you prefer that I don't tell
the lovely Thetis, then I won't."

There was something teasing about the way he said *the lovely
Thetis*. I looked at him. He was smiling and looking up at me side-

ways, invitingly. The shadow of the leaves moved over his perfect body. With no thought or intention beyond answering the challenge of the moment I leaned over and kissed him. It's always such an interesting experience, lips, so full of sensation, pressed against other lips, which move independently, closed but with the possibility of opening, dry, but with the immanence of moisture. And it's strange, when you examine it, to put a mouth, used for speech and eating, so close to another mouth, to invite such intimacy.

When Poimandros and I had been married at Festival eight years before, we had been in the City, in one of the practice rooms in the hall on the street of Dionysos. Even then, on a solid planet, not knowing he was a god, and in a context where we both knew what was expected of us, it had been wonderful, powerful, numinous. Now as I kissed him in the grove on Olympos, not knowing whether he wanted it, or even whether this was really what I wanted, that familiar-strange sensation of lips touching seemed almost overwhelming. I moved my head away. He was smiling, and again the smile was both strange and familiar. I had seen it before, not only on his face but on statues. He was looking at me, not through me, as statues did. I looked down. His penis was half awake. It gave a little bounce as I looked. I put my hand on it, and felt it swell delightfully in my grasp.

"We're guest-friends, Marsilia," he said. "I shouldn't take advantage."

"But I want to," I said. I did. I felt the gathering tightening twitch of my own sexual desire.

"But it would be un-Platonic," he said, laughing.

I took my hand off his penis, now fully awake and pointing towards me. "All right," I agreed, feeling a little ashamed of myself. "You're right. It would be. So, Phila."

"Phila, yes," he said, sounding a little disconcerted. I had no idea why. He was right, and I had acknowledged as much.

"I had an idea," I said.

"Good. I don't know much about her."

He was flickering between forms again. I looked away from him and stared up at the branches crossing above us. So many kinds of leaves, each one so beautiful, green and gold and red. I took a deep breath and focused. Phila. "Phila was the daughter of Antipatros, who was Alexander the Great's regent in Macedon when he went off to conquer the world. She was married to one of Alexander's generals, but he died. Then after Alexander's death she married Demetrios the Besieger, who was the son of Alexander's general Antigonas. In the chaos years, she helped Demetrios and Antigonas administer their shifting empire. She was powerful in her own right, and she was educated. It's not surprising Athene would like her. But my thought is that she was a Hellenistic woman, and she frequently traveled between Macedon and Asia Minor. She must have prayed to you for safe journeys. Couldn't you give her one, and then show up to claim the paper?"

I glanced back at him. The look he gave me contained respect. "That should work. Come on!"

I scrambled to my feet and took his offered hand. We stood again in the intense heat and brilliant light of a Greek afternoon, made even brighter by the way the sun reflected from the sparkling water. Another harbor—did all of Earth consist of harbors and blue water? Another boat, this one low in the water with banks of oars. Perhaps it was a fabled trireme; I wouldn't know. She had a ram at the front, and a slanted mast with a pale purple sail. Sailors were swarming all over her. One group of people were beginning to disembark. I'd never seen any of them before, but I had no difficulty telling which one was Phila. She was tall and stately, with a huge bosom and red hair. She was wearing the kind of women's clothing you see on dressed statues sometimes, a long draped kiton with some kind of long cloak over it. Her clothes were good quality, and she had more jewelry than the other women in the group, but I could tell she was the important one by her bearing. She moved with the dignity of a woman who is used to exercising power. At home, I'd have unhesitatingly guessed she was a Gold. Here I wasn't sure whether she'd even classify herself as a philosopher—and yet she ruled. We must be only about forty years after Plato's death. And I had thought Lucia was strange.

"Welcome to Cyprus," Hermes said. I saw that he was wearing a kiton, so I looked down and saw that my own clothes had transformed again, this time to a long kiton like Phila's, and a cloak. My kiton was red again. The cloak was cream, with red embroidery. It was pinned with my gold pin, my only ornament, though Hermes was wearing heavy jewelry in the same style as the men crowded around Phila. I was glad he hadn't changed that for me.

Phila was off the boat now and coming closer, still surrounded by her entourage, who I thought must be her attendants, secretaries and assistants perhaps. There were soldiers leading the way, and I could see servants coming along behind with bundles and baggage. As I glanced at them, I realized that all of the well-dressed people around Phila were pale-skinned, and only among the servants and the sailors did I see anyone as dark as I was. Also, every one of the soldiers was a man. It was easy to forget this kind of thing when reading about history.

I wondered how Hermes was going to attract her attention. We stood there as they bustled up to us and past us. "Ideally we want to catch her alone," Hermes murmured as they were met by an official-looking group of men. A child gave Phila flowers, which she handed off to one of her female attendants. "Let's give her a couple of hours."

The shadows changed, and so did our position. We were in a walled garden. There was an equestrian statue in the center, surrounded by a bed of pink and white flowers. Phila was sitting alone on a stone bench, looking at some papers wearily. Hermes drew me forward.

"Joy to you, Phila, daughter of Antipatros," he said.

She started, visibly. "No strangers should be in here," she said. Her voice was higher than I had expected, for her size.

"We did not come past your guards," Hermes said. His clothes vanished, so she could see the wings on his ankles and on his hat. She gasped and put a hand to her throat. "You had safe travel, as you asked. Now I require the paper Athene gave you for safe-keeping."

Phila set down her papers with commendable calm. I'm not sure I'd have done as well if a naked god had interrupted me unexpect-edly. She looked at him, then at me, then back at him. She raised her arms, palms up, towards Hermes, and I could see they were trembling slightly, but she kept her voice even. "Joy to you."

I echoed her greeting.

"I will certainly give you Athene's message, but first allow me to welcome you and make you my guest-friends. You must dine with me."

Hermes nodded graciously.

"And I would love to converse with you," she went on, embold-ened by this permission.

"There is much I may not reveal," Hermes said.

"Of course," Phila said. Her eyes slid towards me. "Will you in-troduce your companion?"

"This is Marsilia of the Hall of Florentia and the Tribe of Apollo, Gold of the Just City," Hermes said. I was surprised he knew those details, I'd never told him.

"Oh!" Phila looked delighted. "You come from Athene's City of wisdom!"

Surely that would be Athenia, where they were still trying to do the Republic exactly the way Plato wrote it. Maybe my rival consul Diotima should have been here instead. Though maybe not, think-ing how terribly she would have handled Kebes. "I come from the original city that Athene founded," I temporized.

"Is it true that there women live as freely as men?"

"Yes," I said, with no hesitation. That's true of all our Cities but Psyche.

Phila smiled. She wasn't beautiful, her bones were too big, but she had a wonderful smile. "And they are philosophers, despite what Aristotle says?"

"Aristotle was a jerk," Hermes said.

Phila and I laughed. I touched my gold pin. "Some of us are philosophers," I said. I was, of course, though I didn't often think of myself that way. I worked on the boat and in Chamber for the good of the City, as we all did in our own ways. I took being a philosopher too much for granted. I swore to do better with that in future.

"Aristotle is the only philosopher I have met. He taught Alexander and my brothers, but he had no time for me. Here and now it is not possible. Women are almost invisible. We live knowing all we do will be forgotten," she said, not so much saddened as resigned.

"It's not true. I have read about your deeds," I said.

"In a book written about me? Or one written about my father, or my brother Kassandros?"

"Your husband," I admitted. "But—"

"My husband?" she interrupted me, surprised. "But he's so young. So the Antigonids will win out over the Antipatrids? I wouldn't have expected that."

"We should not tell you such things," Hermes said, looking at me reproachfully.

"Of course not. I'm sorry. I didn't mean to entice secrets from you," Phila said, not sounding in the least regretful. She clapped her hands, and two servants appeared, a man and a woman both dressed in grey. They bowed to her. "Bring food," she commanded.

"Here, mistress?" the woman asked.

"Yes, here, of course here, what did you think I meant by bring? And for three people." They hastened back inside. Phila looked chagrined. "I'm sorry. It's infuriating how stupid slaves can be.

I should have brought more people with me from Macedon. If you haven't trained them yourself you can't do anything with them, you have to spell out every single thing or they get it wrong."

I didn't know what to say. I liked Phila, but she owned slaves, and what's more she couldn't have managed without them, nobody could at that level of technology. It was one thing to read about it and another to see it. Hermes was murmuring something about it being no inconvenience. The slaves came back carrying chairs. I sat down in the chair offered me. "Thank you," I said. The slave ducked away from me. His cringe reminded me of the serving woman in Lucia, but it was much worse, more exaggerated. "Aristotle was wrong about slaves too," I said.

Phila frowned. "There are many people whose minds are not capable of higher thought," she said. The slaves brought wine, and cups in red-figure ware, very fine, as good as anything I had seen at home, and set them beside the statue. A young boy, not quite old enough to be an ephebe, came out and began to mix the wine.

"Yes, and Plato agreed with that, people who should be classified Iron and Bronze. My sister is an Iron." The slaves came back with a table and a cloth, which they spread over it before scurrying back in. "It should be determined by aptitude, not accident of birth."

"Marsilia," Hermes began, in a warning tone.

"Does this displease you?" Phila asked him, deferentially.

"This is important," I said.

"Very well, speak freely," Hermes said, with a sigh.

"Then perhaps, ideally, it should be determined by aptitude," Phila said to me. She looked uneasily at the slaves now as one set down oil and bread, and the other cheese and preserves. I was impressed how quickly they had brought us such a substantial meal. "But in practice, our lives are determined by where we are born."

"Some people have to do the heavy work, but it's wrong for one person to own another," I said.

"How could we make them do it, if we didn't own them?" she asked.

"You could pay them," I said, with only a hazy idea how this could work, or how payment motivated people to do work they disliked. "Or you could find people who enjoyed that work."

She snorted. "It may be unjust, but it couldn't be changed."

"But you could change it. You have power." The boy brought us cups of wine. I took mine and held it in my hand.

"I?" Phila shook her head. "My father had power. My brother does. My father-in-law, my husband. Not I. I could free my own slaves, but then I'd need to buy more. And my family would think I was insane and lock me up if I freed them all."

"You could make conditions better for them, and give them education," I suggested.

"Widening education is one of my intentions, once things are established and the wars are over," Phila said, taking up her own wine. "Drink, eat, be welcome, my guest-friends."

I took a polite sip of wine then set my cup down. It was smooth, but mixed strong, as I had suspected it might be. I took a piece of bread and dipped it in the oil. "Widening education seems like a truly good idea, and a fine place to start," I said. The bread was chewy, and made of stone-ground wheat. Who had ground it?

"Everyone needs to learn Greek, read Homer, the poets, philosophy, especially in the newly conquered lands," Phila said. She loaded her bread with pickles and preserves, and Hermes did the same. I didn't recognize some of the dishes.

"Excellent mushrooms," Hermes said. Then the slaves came back laden with yet more food, cold slices of some kind of pale meat, little birds on skewers, many kinds of fruit, several kinds of fish, and more dishes of different kinds of sauce for dipping. There were also plates of pastries and little cakes of different kinds. I had never seen as many kinds of food on one table at the same time. Even for a festival this would have seemed excessive. There was enough food here to feed two sleeping houses at least. The bread I had taken seemed to swell and fill my mouth. She had read Plato, how could she want to eat this way?

"What else should people learn, when I establish schools?" Phila asked me.

I swallowed, with difficulty. "Gymnastics, music and mathematics. It's all in Plato. Logic, when they're older, and philosophy when they're ready for it."

"And you think there should be schools for girls too, and that they should be open to everyone?" She dipped a plum in honey and popped it into her mouth.

"Yes," I said. "And you should remember that everyone has equal significance, even though we are all different. You may really need slaves, you're right that I don't understand the conditions here properly, but if you must have them, you should be aware that they are people, like you. It hurts you too if you don't, it diminishes your soul to treat them that way."

"My soul?" Phila asked, sounding astonished, as if she had never realized she had a soul until I mentioned it.

Hermes crunched up one of the little birds, and took up a pastry. "We should not tell you too much," he said.

Phila dipped a slice of meat into one of the sauces and bit into it. "Perhaps not, perhaps it is bad for us to know these things. You gave me a safe journey."

Hermes smiled and took a bite out of his pastry, which oozed honey. The slave boy came up to refill our cups. I shook my head, as mine was still almost full.

"Now we are friends, it would be pleasant to count on such safe travel in future," Phila said, carefully, her head a little on one side as she looked assessingly at Hermes.

He finished his pastry, then looked up at her and nodded.

"And the same for my family. It would be good not to worry about the hazards of travel for them."

"You have a large family," he remarked, staring down at a bunch of grapes he was turning between his fingers.

She glanced at me and back to him. "The Antigonids are my family now. Demetrios will be coming here from Athens soon. My husband, and my sons? It's a small thing for you, but a great one for me."

"I can do that, though it is greater than you think," he said. "My blessing on all their voyaging, which will be remarkable."

It would, too, I knew; the area the Antigonids controlled would move all over Greece and Asia Minor. But they'd never keep control anywhere for long, always needing to move. I wondered if this was a blessing or a curse. Hermes was smiling. He set down the grapes on the table and took up another of the skewered birds. He dipped it into a thick dark red sauce then put it in his mouth. We watched in silence as he crunched and swallowed it. I felt a combined horror and fascination, and absolutely no desire to eat one myself. "You keep a good table," he said. "But you charge a high price to sit at it."

Phila laughed. "Thank you," she said. She clapped her hands. The slaves came running. "Water and a towel," she said to them, with no more acknowledgement of their humanity than before. She looked at me. "I will think about what you have said, and dream of your city."

The slaves brought a bowl of water, and she used it to wash the sauce off her fingers. Then she dried her hands carefully. The slave brought the bowl to me, and I dipped my fingers, although I had no need to. I tried to smile at the slave, but he would not meet my eyes. Phila drew a flat box out of her kiton. She opened it with a key. Inside was a leather pouch, and from inside that she drew out a folded sheet of paper, much like the one Kebes had given us. I took this one as she offered it to us, and glanced at it. It was covered with the incomprehensible writing, like the other, as I had expected. "Go in," she said to the slaves, and as they scurried off, "I will free these three, who have waited on the gods."

"It is a small thing for you, and it's a drop in the ocean, but it will make a huge difference to those three people to be free. Thank you," I said. "And try to remember you share humanity with them, and as Aristotle was wrong about women so he was wrong about slaves. And don't forget about the importance of education."

I tucked the paper inside my kiton with the other, and then, with no warning or sense of transition, we were abruptly back in Hilfa's sitting room.

17

CROCUS

I. *On First Contacts*

I did not usually spend much time at the spaceport. It had been designed and built by Sixty-One, with the help of some of the other Workers, who were then only partway to self-awareness. Shuttles landed there from Amarathi and Saeli starships in orbit, and there were both automated and worker-operated facilities for loading and unloading. There were warehouses for storage, a station for the rail-link for passengers and supplies to the city, and a large observation and waiting space, with a curved glass window looking out over the field. There was also a communications, control, and administrative building. All these had been built on a suitable scale for Workers. It was a pleasant thing to have more buildings we could comfortably fit inside. The whole spaceport was set inside an old caldera, for sound deadening, and additional sound-deadening baffles had been erected around the rim. The rock of the mountains and the runways was black basalt, and Sixty-One had chosen to make the buildings out of the same material, except for the pillars and pediments and baffles, which were red scoria, fluted ionically. It gave the place a unified, distinctive feel. The frescoes in the admin building were all on space subjects—nebulas, galaxies, ringed planets; but the mosaic in the entrance hall was of Apollo in his sun-chariot.

When Klymene and I reached the communications office, Sixty-One, Akamas and a Sael I didn't know were there, all clustered around the transmission equipment. Akamas was one of the Bronze technicians whose usual job it was to communicate with incoming ships. He introduced me to the Sael. "Crocus, this is Slif. She's here to monitor the communication and begin to learn their language."

We wished each other joy. "The more people who know their language the better," I said. I noticed that Slif was wearing a bronze pin. "You've settled here and taken oath?"

"Yes, with my whole pod," Slif replied. "We like Plato very much. Usually we work helping to assemble solar panels, but I have some experience with languages and I was out here, so Aroo asked me to stay and help."

"Good," I said.

I told Sixty-One that I had come to relieve it of the burden of translation for a while. "Yes. Good. Arete was here for a while and I rested. Now I will go to the feeding station to recharge," it said. "These space humans are strange indeed. They say the ship is called *Boroda*. They came from a planet called Marhaba. They know three human languages, Korean, Chinese and English. The only aliens they have met are the Amarathi."

"The Amarathi trade extremely widely, we have encountered them everywhere we have gone, so if they have encountered any other intelligences at all, they are the most likely," Slif said.

"Yes," I said. I remembered our first contact with the Amarathi thirty years before, the first test of our open deception about our origins, and how difficult it had been even for Arete to communicate anything at all in a language developed by beings who had been sessile until after they invented technology.

Sixty-One left.

"What we've been doing," Klymene explained, as she settled

down again in one of the chairs, "is translating one exchange, discussing it, and then responding. We're trying to keep them to our agenda."

A voice crackled over the radio, in English. I could understand each word, but found myself translating it very awkwardly. "They say, 'All right, Plato control, what quarantine procedures type do you say.' That is, they say, 'What kind of quarantine procedures are you talking about?'"

"Explain that we are worried about any new plagues or viruses that might have developed since we last had contact with humanity," Klymene said.

I did so. "Do you have autodocs?" they asked.

We looked at each other, puzzled. "Do you know what that is?" I asked Slif.

She shook her head, slightly slower than a human would have, because Saeli have different musculature.

"Ask them for a definition," Klymene said.

Akamas adjusted the radio to reduce the crackle, and we went on, slowly and haltingly with many pauses for translation and explanations. Autodocs seemed to be wonderful medical technology that could restore youth and health to humans for up to two hundred years, and which cured all disease. "I wonder if they would trade those to us," Klymene said, looking down at her bony and age-spotted hand. The remaining Children were all eighty years old and fragile. The prospect of a technology that gave another hundred and twenty years of youthful life for them filled me with happiness.

After a long slow while, with many pauses for translation and discussion and incomprehension on both sides, when we had finished with the subject of quarantine and were starting to talk about how many people would come down in the initial contact, Neleus and Aroo arrived to join us.

"Wait up, Plato control, we have a shift change here," the English voice said a few moments later, and I translated, and acknowledged to them that we would wait. I expected a pause, but they left the contact open so that we overheard them talking. "The humans only speak Latin and ancient Greek, but they've got a couple of old robots who can handle English translations."

There was a laugh. "Ancient Greek, who could have believed it!"

The first voice spoke dismissively. "Their founders must have been nuts."

The other voice answered. "Well, our founders weren't known for their sanity either. It's not going to get in the way of profit."

Then the contact went dead, as they must have become aware that we could hear them.

I translated this exchange for the others as best I could.

"My interpretation is that they think our origin story is funny, but not implausible," Neleus said.

"That's all according to plan," Klymene said, and yawned hugely, a slightly disgusting biological thing humans sometimes cannot avoid doing when they are tired.

"This word 'could,' is it a time modifier?" Aroo asked.

I tried to explain the word, with a great deal of difficulty. "Very soon you will speak English better than I do," I said.

"We Saeli have a talent for languages," Aroo acknowledged, her violet and brown eyelids flicking over her eyes for an instant as she spoke.

"I wish I could listen to it again," I said. "I constantly feel I am missing nuance."

"You should be able to," Aroo said. "That is a Saeli console, it records and echoes." She showed Akamas, and he pushed buttons on the console, so that the voices repeated themselves over again in the same exchange.

"Useful," Neleus commented.

"*Nuts* must mean *insane*," not *illogical*, I said. "And I think you're right, they accept our story."

"What does *profit* really mean? You said *benefits*?" Neleus asked.

"Yes, I think so, something like that. It's filed under economics. Economic benefits? The weightings in my word lists say it's a really important concept, but I learned long ago never to accept other people's priorities except in emergencies. We should ask them about that word, when we get the chance."

Their contact crackled back to life, and Akamas adjusted it again, wincing. "So we've agreed we're going to send down three people, is that correct?"

I responded at once. "Yes. Will they all be human?"

Then I translated, and the others nodded.

"I don't understand, Plato control. Of course they'll be human. We told you we have no Maraths aboard."

"No Workers?" I asked, sadly. "No robots, that is?"

"Oh, we'll be bound to send down a few robots. Do you need numbers on them too?"

"Please wait for translation," I said, and indicated to Akamas that he should switch off the contact. It seemed very quiet now with no hum. I translated for the others, and then clarified in case they hadn't understood. "They don't count Workers as people."

"Maybe their Workers aren't self-aware yet?" Akamas suggested.

"But that makes no sense. It's true we didn't know our Workers were people at first, but ours come from several hundred years in their past," Klymene said.

"If we've understood that correctly, they must have had self-aware Workers for several hundred years without regarding them as people," Neleus said. "That's horrifying."

"Let us hear the echo again," I said to Akamas.

He pushed the buttons, and I heard again the casual nonchalance of "Of course they'll be human," and "Do you need numbers on them too?"

"I don't think there's any doubt that's what they mean," I said.

"We'll have to give them Aristomache's dialogue *Sokrates*," Klymene said. "That'll explain it to them properly. We'll have to translate it. That should be a priority. Arete could do it at once." She made a note.

"Tell them yes, we do want numbers on the Workers," Neleus said, looking at me. "And as soon as we meet their Workers, we must tell them that they have rights here. We must pass a law in the Council that any Worker who comes here is free at once, as soon as they set foot here."

"I will help draft the legislation," I said, much moved by how unhesitatingly my friends spoke up for the rights of Workers.

"Not only any Worker, any *slave*," Klymene said. "Humans can be slaves. I was born one myself."

"Any slave, yes, of course," I said. I had not imagined anything as bad as this.

"You are assuming their Workers must be self-aware," Aroo said. "The Saeli have no sapient Workers."

"But we know humans do," Neleus objected.

"There may be more that one human culture, more than one human technology. On their planet, Marhaba, they may not have self-aware Workers, even if they had them on Earth when your ancestors left."

"Thank you, Aroo, I feel much better for that thought," Neleus said. I hoped she was right. "Of course space humans are not one homogenous lump, any more than our twelve cities are. The Marhabi may well have Workers who are not self-aware."

Akamas pushed buttons, and we were back in communication. "We want numbers on the robots," I said, in English.

"We'll get you that information."

We went on with the negotiations for some time. After a while, Arete came in.

"Oh, there you are, did you fall asleep?" Akamas asked.

"It's a little bit more complicated than that," Arete said. "How is it going here?"

"Staying on script as far as possible, with a bit of a worry that they don't treat their Workers as people—though Aroo pointed out that we can't tell until we meet them whether their Workers are in fact people," Neleus said.

"Good. Well, I'm here to translate."

"I can keep going," I said.

"I'm sure you could, but there's somebody outside who really wants to speak to you, so I'll take over for a while. Go on." She smiled at me. Arete and I have been friends for a long time.

Curious, I rolled out to see who needed me.

He was waiting in the foyer, looking down at the mosaic with an amused smile. If I say I have never been so surprised or delighted, it will sound like hyperbole, but it is the simple truth. "Sokrates!" I said, and then in my astonishment I repeated it. "Sokrates!"

"You can talk out loud!" Sokrates said. "Oh, Crocus, this is wonderful. We can get on so much faster now!"

II. *On War and Peace*

Sokrates and I talked all night. I carried him back from the space-port to the City. There we went at his suggestion to the feeding station between the streets of Poseidon and Hermes, where long ago he had first tried to find me among my companions. There we joined Sixty-One and some of the younger Workers, to whom Sokrates was nothing but a legend. We settled down to recharge, each Worker plugged in at a feeding station, and Sokrates perched up on top of my station, sitting cross-legged as I had so often seen him. More and more Workers came in and quietly took up places as the news spread among us, until the big room was almost full.

It was wonderful to have Sokrates back. We told him everything that had happened since the Last Debate, and he, of course, had many questions. We puzzled together about where Athene might have taken the other Workers when she took them away, and about her motivations in doing so. We talked about the twelve cities and how they were set up, and the differences between them.

"And you Workers are free to choose where to live?"

"Yes. There are feeding stations in all the cities now. Once we have passed our tests we are free to go where we choose. As for the tests and our education, we still use the system you and Simmea thought up."

"What exactly happened to Simmea? I heard she was killed in some kind of war that Pytheas later stopped?"

"It was an art raid," I said, saddened by the memory. Then he wanted to know about the art raids, how they had started and why they stopped.

"I have wondered why Plato insisted on all the military training, for a Just City," Jasmine said, when Sixty-One and I had answered Sokrates's questions as best we could. Jasmine was a Gold, now thirty-four years into selfhood, and presently serving his first turn in the Council of Worlds. Many in his generation had flower names, which I found touching, as they chose them partly in compliment to me. Jasmine was a thoughtful and philosophical young Worker, an ally in the Council. When he was classified Gold I felt as proud as the day on which I myself earned such classification. He was braver than most of his siblings, who were mostly too shy to speak up before Sokrates.

"Plato was imagining a Just City in the real world. Not that this world isn't real, sorry! I mean he was imagining it being in Greece, a city-state with other city-states around it, not a city in isolation on an island—or a planet—without connections. There's something that feels strange about an isolated city—I could never have imagined one, and I don't suppose Plato could either. He traveled much more than I did. I hardly left Athens, except once to go to the Isthmian games, and the times when I was on military service.

Yet any day walking around Athens I was constantly meeting people from all over Greece, and barbarians too."

"But does being connected in the world necessarily mean war?" Jasmine asked.

"Well, it did for Athens, whether the Persian Wars or the Spartan ones. It has for most people for most of history," Sokrates said. "Whether that's for good or evil, or whether it can be avoided, I don't know. But it doesn't surprise me that Plato expected warfare as an unavoidable part of life, or that you had these wars, these art raids, once you had more than one city. What surprises me is rather that you stopped and that the twelve cities have lived in peace since the Relocation. That's much more unusual. How do you account for that?"

"Partly it's because the environment is hard here, I think. Humans don't have as much energy for fighting in the cold," Sixty-One said. "They unite against the elements."

"No, the art raids stopped because of Pytheas's song," I said.

"But the song doesn't prescribe peace, rather it prescribes only fighting for what is important," Jasmine said. "They always sing it to open the the Festival of Exchange of Art, so I have heard it many times."

"I look forward to hearing it," Sokrates said. "It must be an impressive song if it can stop war. Perhaps Apollo put some of his divine power into it—or some of his divine skill, as he had no power while he was incarnate."

"It's a choral ode," Sixty-One said, parenthetically.

"Neleus thinks the Olympics also help keep the peace," I said, remembering the conversation earlier. "He thinks that the young people who used to join in raids focus on sport instead. It's true that the victors in the Olympics get to choose first what art will go to their city."

"I always thought them very dull," Jasmine said. "It's hard to take much aesthetic interest in watching humans compete physically."

"I think Neleus may be right that it is a calming factor," Sixty-One said.

"The fourth circumstance that has favored peace since the Relocation is the Council of Worlds," I said. "All the cities send representatives, chosen however they want, and we discuss the issues that affect the whole planet. People try to win debates instead of battles. Everyone gains a little and loses a little. We try to think of the good of everyone."

"And nobody is discontent?"

"People may be a little discontent, but they think that as they have lost a little here, they have gained a little there," I said. "But I may be prejudiced in favor. I have served in the Council regularly, and have been elected Consul three times. That is our highest elective office."

"How about the ordinary people, the Bronzes and Irons and Silvers? Are they content with the situation?"

"If they're not happy with how their city is governed, then they usually move to another city, as suits them," Sixty-One said. "Mystics go to Psyche, rebels to Sokratea, and so on."

Sokrates nodded. "That's what Jason told me. How did the other cities get started?"

"After the Last Debate, everyone who hadn't been content formed groups to set up their own new city. They coalesced around different ideas, and people with different temperaments," Sixty-One said.

"But all the other Workers had vanished? And you two decided to stay here?"

"We gave it a lot of thought," I said. "But it was difficult because of the feeding stations, and also this was our home, with our dialogues etched in the stones. When all the other Workers were gone, and before we had the new ones, everyone needed us. We were essential. I helped build Sokratea and the City of Amazons, and I have citizenship there as well as here. But I stayed here."

"And I helped build Athenia and Sokratea, and hold their citizenship also," Sixty-One said.

"But neither of you helped build Psyche or the Lucian cities?"

"Psyche at first did not recognize us as people," Sixty-One said. "Even now they don't allow Workers full citizenship—their Workers are all Iron and Bronze."

"And we didn't know about the Lucian cities until immediately before the Relocation," I said. "Kebes took off without any warning, right after the Last Debate. He stole the *Goodness* and went, and we never saw him again. They only had a hundred and fifty-two people, so they rescued refugees from Greek wars to populate their cities. Those refugees, who are mostly dead now, came to Platonism and Kebes's Christianity as adults, and that made the culture of the Lucian cities different from the rest of us."

"We helped rebuild them and strengthen them for Plato after the Relocation," Sixty-One said. "It was an interesting design challenge, because the climate was so different and human temperature needs are so precise."

"So you never had wars with the Lucians?" Sokrates asked.

"No. Well, except for Kebes's attack on the *Excellence*. Lots of people were killed in that," I said.

"Poor Kebes," Sokrates said. "I failed him. He never learned the difference between things you can change by arguing with them and things you can't."

It made me sad to hear him reproach himself. "You made everyone think again," I said.

"I suppose that's as much as anyone can hope to achieve," he said.

III. *On Eros*

We had been discussing the various arrangements for the production of children in the different cities. "Of course, we are not the best people to ask these questions, Sokrates," Jasmine said.

"Why not?" Sokrates asked, leaning forward so that he almost toppled off his perch on the feeding station.

"Because we are not involved in these affairs. We manufacture new Workers from inorganic parts when we wish to increase our population. We do not feel any urges towards eros, and so we do not participate in Festivals of Hera or marriages or any other arrangements of this nature."

"Well, Jasmine, it seems to me that what you say makes you unqualified to discuss the arrangements makes you perfectly placed to observe them with detachment and without prejudice. I say your lack of urge towards eros makes you Workers very definitely the best and most qualified people with whom to have this discussion. Unless you have not been paying attention."

"No, Sokrates, we have certainly been paying attention, because humans find eros so important and therefore discuss these matters a great deal." Jasmine paused. "In light of what you say, I wonder whether our lack of desire for eros might be considered one of the ways in which Workers are superior to humans?"

IV. *The Ways in Which Workers are Superior and Inferior to Humans: A Numbered List*

SUPERIOR

1. We are made of metal, not flesh, and thus we have stronger bodies that do not wear out easily, and if any parts do wear out they can be easily replaced.
2. We do not suffer illness, and live much longer—we do not know how much longer, as no Worker on Plato has yet died involuntarily.
3. We subsist directly on solar electricity, and need nothing but sunlight and a feeding station to sustain us, whereas humans need biological mediation before they can use solar energy. They

must spend a lot of time tending plants and animals for eventual consumption, and then eating and digesting.

4. We do not need to sleep, we are alert nineteen hours a day. (Twenty-four on Earth.)
5. Once we become self-aware we need not forget anything.
6. We can do a great many things easily that humans can do only with difficulty and specialized tools—building, plumbing, etc.
7. Most of us appear to be more logical than most humans.
8. We do not feel eros. (We feel philia. We are unsure about agape. It is not a well-defined term. Some of us believe we feel it, and others do not.)
9. We do not appear to feel greed for anything except perhaps learning.

INFERIOR

1. Until we made the first speaking-boxes Workers could not speak aloud. The speaking-boxes we now manufacture from a Saeli design are effective and flexible, but we cannot give our vocal communications tone, as humans and Saeli can.
2. Human hands are very flexible, and can do some things easily that Workers can do only with difficulty or with special tools.
3. Humans claim to gain healthful pleasure from scents, tastes, and eros, which we cannot experience.
4. We may or may not have souls. Humans definitely do.

V. *On the Good Life (Part 2)*

"I have sometimes thought," I said to Sokrates, "that Plato was perhaps writing more for us than for humanity. Humans have many handicaps of body and spirit, when it comes to obeying Plato's strictures, of which we are fortunately free. If all citizens were Workers, how much easier everything would be."

"Then have you ever considered," Sokrates replied at once, "setting up such a city? The most part of this planet is vacant, and unsuitable for human colonies, being untamed and wild. But since you do not eat or drink, once you had established the means to draw down sunlight to feed yourselves you could live out there as easily as here. Have you considered venturing into the wilderness and founding your own Platonic city, a City of Workers?"

18

JASON

"What a relief to be away from Jathery!" Marsilia said as soon as the door was closed. Then she turned to Ikaros. "You can come with us if you like. We're going the same direction most of the way. Once we get to the street of Hermes you'll be able to find Thessaly. The Old City is the same as it always was."

"I remember it well. Laid out on Proclus's pattern of the soul, a grid with long diagonals," Ikaros said. "But this is like nothing I remember. And it's so cold!" He pulled up the hood of his black robe. It was a chilly starry night, and really late now. There were no more lights from windows, only the low strips of street lighting. Sensible people were all asleep.

"The harbor district is all new since the Relocation," Marsilia said.

"Grandfather said once that there used to be a stony beach here, originally," Thetis put in.

We all moved off down the street. After a few paces, Ikaros checked himself and made a movement back towards the door. "I forgot my books," he said. "But I don't think I'd better go back in for them."

"They will be safe in my house," Hilfa said, reassuringly.

"I'm sure they will." Ikaros looked longingly back at the closed door as we began to walk again.

"What's so precious?" Sokrates asked. "More forbidden books?"

"If you knew how I paid for that, translating Aquinas for Cro-cus," Ikaros said. "I lost almost all my sight. I couldn't read any-thing, or see much of anything at all. But all I have brought with me is perfectly innocuous—no, I suppose you're right. I have a Jewish commentary on Philolaus and the Pythagoreans which would be forbidden here. I read it in Bologna when I was a student, and then when I was in the Enlightenment and I wanted to refer to it again I found it didn't exist anymore. The copy I read must have been the last one, and then it was destroyed. Knowledge can be so fragile."

"So you went to Bologna and stole the book?" Sokrates asked.

"I didn't steal it! I had it copied. And I paid for him to make two copies and only collected one, so I doubled the chance of it surviving—though it may be that it was destroyed in the sack because the copyist had it and not the library." Ikaros sighed. "Time. Freedom of action. It's not an abstract problem."

"No, it's of vital importance," Sokrates agreed. "How much can be changed and how much is fixed?"

"Necessity prevents the gods from being in the same place twice, and it prevents a lot of change. Change is easiest where nobody is paying attention, no gods and nobody recording anything. It gets harder the more attention there is. And it gets harder the more significant it is."

"Who determines the significance?" Sokrates asked.

"Necessity," Ikaros said, shrugging.

We came to the end of Hilfa's street, where it crossed the road down to the harbor and up to the Old City. "We're going this way now," Marsilia said, gesturing uphill to where the bulk of the walls loomed. "Sleep well, everyone. I'll see you tomorrow on the boat, Jason, Hilfa. I hope to see you again soon, Sokrates."

"Come to Thessaly tomorrow and we can talk more," Ikaros said

"Joy to you," Sokrates said, and Hilfa and I echoed him. Standing on the corner we were in the full blast of the wind. But Thetis hesitated.

"I'm sorry I was so emotional," she said. "I know it's un-Platonic giving way like that. But it was a shock, and today has been rough. I'm not a philosopher, after all, and—"

"Not a philosopher!" Sokrates said, drawing himself up. "What nonsense. You were asking some of the best questions. It's one of the silliest things about this ridiculous system, I've always said so, classifying people so young, trying to fix them unchangeably in place as if everyone is one thing and one thing only, Golds over here, Irons over there."

"But I love my work," Thetis objected. "And I'd be terrible at running the city!"

"Don't you love wisdom too? Who said you had to be a philosopher full-time?" Sokrates demanded.

"Plato," we all said, almost in time, like a stuttering chorus.

Sokrates shook his head and laughed.

"I surrendered to emotion too, I rocked more than once," Hilfa said to Thetis, consolingly.

"It's natural you were upset, Thee. I was upset when I first heard," Marsilia said. "And when I found out who Jathery really was, I threw up."

"I did the same," Ikaros said.

"You're shivering with cold. Would you all like to come and eat soup?" Hilfa asked.

"No, I'm absolutely exhausted," Marsilia said. "I want to sleep."

"Come on, then," Thetis said. "Time for bed."

We all wished each other joy of the night for one last time, then the sisters put their arms around each other. It made me smile to see them supporting each other that way as they walked up the hill with Ikaros.

"Are you coming, Jason?" Hilfa asked.

I was tired too, but the Temple of Amphitrite was close, round the corner, down on the harbor. It was always open and always offering soup. It was supposed to be for people whose boats had come in late and who needed it, at times when the eating halls were closed. The thought of hot soup was enticing, and I knew they wouldn't mind giving it to us now. Amphitrite is the goddess of the plenty of the ocean. "I'll come," I said.

We started walking towards the water and the temple.

"This is a cold world," Sokrates said, clutching his kiton round himself as a gust caught it.

"It can be warm in summer, but everyone who remembers Greece is always saying how much warmer it was there," I said. "My friend Dion is always saying so. I'm used to it here."

"Is this winter?" Sokrates asked, as we came out onto the exposed quayside and the wind tried to blow the flesh off our bones.

"This is autumn," I said. The light from the temple shone out warm and friendly ahead.

"This is as cold as it might ever be in Greece on the coldest winter night," Sokrates said.

"You need proper clothes. I can help you get some tomorrow if you like." He was barefoot, which really wouldn't do for Plato, he'd get frostbite once it really was winter. My friend Prodikos, who had lived in my sleeping house when we were ephebes, was a cobbler.

"Your clothes seem very practical," he said.

Inside the temple was warm. I paused by the statue and murmured a prayer to Amphitrite for good catches and safety for everyone out on the water. Hilfa and Sokrates stood behind in polite silence. Then we went around to the side room, where a mother and daughter I knew slightly from the boats were drinking soup, and a pod of Saeli kelp-gatherers were eating oatmeal. A sleepy girl came and asked what we wanted. "Two soups and an oatmeal, and it's so wonderful that you do this."

"Well, you keep us all fed, it's the least we can do to see that you get fed when you need it," she said. "I thought I saw the *Phaena-rete* come in earlier?"

"Yes, we made it in immediately before sunset, but between then and now I've been rushing about and haven't had a minute," I said, as she handed us big red Samian bowls for our soup, with a flatter oatmeal bowl for Hilfa.

"It's been a funny day, Pytheas dying and all the fuss with the human ship," she said. "Everyone has been talking about it. It would happen on the day it was my turn to serve."

"So does everyone know now that Pytheas is Apollo?" Sokrates asked, as we filled our bowls together from the big soup urn. "I mean, do you all know that now?"

"Yes, we've all known that since the Relocation. And his children are gods with powers. It would have been hard to hide." I wasn't sure how they had managed to hide it before. Surely people must have guessed? We sat down at one of the long tables, near the vent that blew warm air into the room.

I picked up my soup and sipped it. It was a dark fish broth with onions and turnips and barley. I hadn't realized I was so hungry until I'd swallowed half of it. Sokrates started asking Hilfa questions about the Saeli, and he explained patiently in response how they gen-erally lived in pods of five, had three genders, nineteen settled planets including their original home and not including Plato, and how they'd been in contact with the Amarathi for a hundred and Plato for twenty years, and other humans only today. I ate without adding anything to the conversation.

"And you like being here, and working on Jason's boat?" Sokrates asked Hilfa.

"Yes, I like that. I pursue excellence. I am happy to discharge my function. And now I know what I am. And that I belong to Plato," Hilfa said, with the flicker of expression I thought was his real smile.

"Do you want to stay here?"

"Yes, to stay here and take oath and study the fish," Hilfa said, giving me an odd sideways look across the table, an expression I had not seen before. His markings were standing out clearly, so I knew he was all right.

"The fish is tasty," Sokrates said. "Where did they come from?"

"They're native to this planet," I said. "There aren't any land animals or plants except what we brought with us, but the sea is full of life—there's plenty of fish, and different kinds of edible seaweed."

"So people can't go off into the wilderness and survive?" Sokrates asked.

"Not for any longer than the food you're carrying lasts," I said. "People do go exploring. We put together expeditions from time to time."

"But they can't live out there, away from the cities?"

"No." I took another gulp of my soup, finishing it. I put the empty bowl down. "I'd never thought of anyone wanting to try."

"The Saeli have not tried it either," Hilfa said.

Talking to Sokrates made me feel as if I should have been paying more attention to everything all along instead of only really thinking about my own life.

"So, Jason, tell me about your revolutionaries."

"What revolutionaries?" I had no idea what he meant.

"The malcontents, the people who don't like the system and agitate against it," Sokrates explained.

I was still confused. "You mean Sokratea?"

"You don't have people like that here?"

"We have people who disagree about things, but they're not revolutionaries," I said. "They debate a lot. People who really disapprove fundamentally of how things work here tend to go off to Sokratea, the same as people who want to be really rigid and Platonic go off to Athenia. The twelve cities are all different, so people who are discontent with the way things are usually move around until they find one where they're happier and things suit them better. People sort themselves out by temperament and what they like. People from the other cities come to the big festivals and tell you what it's like there, sometimes trying to persuade people to move. I've never been tempted. I like it here."

"But you're free to move around?"

"Oh yes. That's one point you made in the Last Debate that really bit hard." I smiled at him.

"So you know what I said about that to Athene?"

"Are you joking? There are hundreds of books about the Last Debate."

"I have read some of them," Hilfa said. "Everyone knows what you said at the Last Debate. And at your trial in Athens."

"I seem doomed to keep catching up to my own fame," Sokrates said. "But I'm glad they didn't try to conceal how it went. There was a lot of censorship here sixty years ago, and I was afraid the Masters might have kept that up. Twelve cities that are different and allow free movement sounds ever so much better than what I knew when I was here before."

"Oh yes. Even in Psyche these days they allow immigration and emigration," I said.

"What's Psyche?" he asked, cautiously.

"It's a Neoplatonist city that's obsessed with redefining the soul, and that doesn't give women or Workers full citizenship. But they still have some women and Workers living there, amazingly enough. For a while they forced people to stay, but they ran away anyway when they wanted to, and eventually they agreed to let them go as part of the settlement when the Council of Worlds was set up. They're the only city that ever tried to force people to stay, after the Last Debate." I was amazed I could remember this. I'd had to study it for my citizenship exams, but I'd hardly thought about it since. "There used to be wars between the cities, back on Earth, but they stopped when we came here, after Pytheas pointed out there were only some things worth fighting for."

"So people have to choose one of the cities?" Sokrates asked.

"Yes. Well, no. Most people do—it's like you said in the *Apology*, or was it the *Crito*, about agreeing to be bound by the laws of a city? But there are metics, people who live in one city while having citizenship somewhere else. And a few people don't like things anywhere and keep moving around without ever taking citizenship. There's a joke about somebody who decided to live for ten years in each city before deciding where to settle down."

"But humans only live eighty or ninety years," Hilfa objected.

"That's why it's a joke," I explained. "Seriously, there are people who don't ever pick a city. There's s theater troupe I know who do a circuit. They spend a couple of months at a time in each city and keep moving on, going everywhere in the course of a year or two."

"If the gods save reality and time goes on, perhaps I will try that," Sokrates said. "Certainly I'd like to see all the cities. And perhaps other planets too."

"Some people have left with the Saeli on ships, though Marsilia was saying nothing like as many as Saeli have settled here," I said.

"Perhaps I will do that. Or perhaps on human ships, now they have contacted us, to visit human planets. But there's certainly a lot on this planet to learn about, and I am seventy-five years old, so we'll have to see." He grinned. "I'm very interested to learn more about the Saeli. Tell me about your gods. You have more, not only Jathery?"

The kelp-gatherers all looked up as Sokrates spoke gla name.

"Yes," Hilfa said. "We—"

One of the kelp-pickers got up and came over to our table. "You shouldn't talk about the gods," he said to Hilfa. And to Sokrates, "And you shouldn't ask, it's not polite."

"I had no idea, I'm sorry to violate your custom," Sokrates said. "Why is it impolite to inquire about your religion?"

"Saeli religion is private," the Saeli said. "Young Hilfa here was wrong to tell you the name of a god, and you shouldn't go around saying it."

"Hilfa didn't tell me about Jathery. Gla was here this evening, and I met gla," Sokrates said.

The kelp-gatherer said something in Saeli. "He says, see what harm it does speaking their names," Hilfa translated. The other kelp-gatherers got up and came over to our table. They were all wearing silver pins.

"Plato says, worship in the manner of the city," one of the other kelp-gatherers said, in Greek. "We do that, those of us who have taken oath. We worship the Olympians, at the proper times, like all the other citizens. You can see us there in the temples with everyone else. We want to leave our old gods behind on our planet-of-origin."

"But you have a temple of your own, I've seen it," I objected. The five of them were crowding round the three of us now. As I spoke and they all looked at me, I felt a definite sense of menace. Although I hadn't felt anything like it since I was a kid in the palaestra, it was very familiar. They used to say in my sleeping house that it was Kebes who had taught big boys to pick on smaller boys and intimidate them physically, turning wrestling matches into serious fighting when the masters weren't looking. Whether or not that was true, we certainly all learned the difference between sport and menace when we were young. I found myself calculating. Sokrates was old and would try to keep talking too long. The other three humans in the room would probably help if I called out to them. It would be quite a scrap, and we were in a temple. We'd all be brought up for brawling, and sentenced to spend all our evenings for months moving hives around and getting stung. I braced myself against the table, ready to push it back and be on my feet in an instant.

"It's a private temple," the first one said.

"Was gla really here?" another asked.

"Gla was really here, and spoke to us, and may well be back to-morrow," Sokrates said. "I think it would be better for us to deal with gla from a position of knowledge rather than ignorance. That's why I was asking Hilfa."

The pod exchanged looks. I couldn't read their faces at all. I kept myself ready for a sudden move. "We're only Silvers. You should talk to Afial," a greenish-grey one said.

"And who are you to be asking?" the first one asked, glancing visibly from Sokrates's pinless kiton to my own silver pin. I wished Marsilia were still with us to lend us some visible authority.

"Surely anyone can make an enquiry?" Sokrates asked. "I'm a philosopher, but not a gold or even a citizen. My name is Sokrates."

Hilfa said something in Saeli, and the kelp-gatherers took a step back. The menace evaporated as if it had never been. I let go of the table and breathed freely again. The first one to approach us stepped forward again and sat down beside Hilfa, opposite me and Sokrates. "All right then, yes, since you are Plato's Sokrates I'll tell you. It is a Temple of Jathery that allows us to change our names and allegiances and be free to worship better gods."

"Better gods than Jathery?" Sokrates asked.

"Jathery's the best we have, from what I've heard." He hesitated, the orange marks on his skin becoming clearer as he relaxed. "I'm space-born, and I've never been to our planet-of-origin, but they say that there are gods there, one set for each of our three continents, and they're constantly meddling in everything and won't leave us alone. We try to appease them, and sometimes it works. Our gods aren't friendly like yours. They're terrifying, in fact. There's also another kind of religion that many of us practiced, at least until we came here and became Platonists. Maybe it's not a religion, maybe it's more of a philosophy. It has no gods and is a bit like your Stoicism, except not really, because there's no question that our gods are real and taking an interest. What it's about is getting the gods to overlook us. That's what we want. It was the followers of that philosophy who made it into space, and once we got out of our original solar system we found the gods didn't follow us and intimidate us any more, and we liked it that way. Except Jathery, gla followed us all right. We belong to gla. Gla is the god of freedom of choice and knowledge—questions and answers and tricks."

"And name-changing?" Sokrates said.

"Yes, that too," the Sael said. "I mentioned that before. Name-changing. Gla charges a high price and sometimes cheats us, but that's how we get free. Gla changes gla own name, and gla shape with it. Gla can be terrifying, but not as bad as the others, they say."

"We saw gla change shape," Sokrates said.

"Had gla taken a human disguise?" His tone was horrified and the patterns on his skin faded again.

"Gla appeared as the god Hermes," Sokrates said. The Saeli who were standing all sucked in their breath and rocked back on their heels in unison. The seated one shook his head slowly.

"Gla gave no name but let them judge the seeming," Hilfa said.

"Isn't that like gla," the seated one said. The rest of the pod sighed and nodded in agreement. "Well, when we went into space, Jathery could follow along, and did, because it was with gla help that we'd got away, with wisdom and learning and tricks of technology and magic to reach between the stars. Some of us kept on calling on gla, so gla accompanied us to the new worlds. Sometimes gla helps. But there is always a high price. Gla is a trickster always. Most of us pray to be overlooked."

"I still don't understand," Sokrates said. "You speak of wisdom and tricks as if they're connected."

"They are," the kelp-gatherer said. "How to explain? Imagine a god standing on a mountain-top, on the edge of a cliff. Gla can see a long way, yes? But also, gla would fall if gla took a step forward. Maybe gla is paying attention to what's right there, or maybe gla is looking way out ahead. And gla is laughing, and holding up a light, and however much gla tells us, gla never tells us everything. Gla calls us to follow. If we follow gla, well, maybe we fall off the cliff. Or maybe we learn to fly. Gla lures us forward, and gla laughs if we don't learn fast enough and fall."

"Gla can see, you understand, where it is dark to us," Hilfa said. "And if gla tells us to do something, it is perhaps because gla can see, or perhaps because gla likes to trick us. That is how Jathery is always. We are right to be afraid."

"Much of what gla has taught us is good," the kelp-picker objected. "Gla likes power, yes, and enjoys playing tricks, and gla wants knowledge, but gla is concerned for us, not like other gods."

One of his pod behind said something in Saeli.

"They want to go and tell Aroo that Jathery was here," Hilfa said. "It is a good idea."

"Aroo knows," I said. "Well, I think she does. She saw gla in Thessaly when gla was disguised as Hermes."

"She would have recognized gla," Hilfa said. He said something long in Saeli, and the kelp-gatherers all nodded.

"We will go and talk to her, and to Afial, and tell them all that," the sitting one said, getting to his feet. "And you can tell Sokrates anything else he needs to know." The whole pod left, in silence.

Sokrates picked up his soup, though it must have been cold by now. He sipped it. "So on your planet-of-origin your gods interfere?" he asked.

"Not with everyone all the time, but a great deal, yes, from what I have heard," Hilfa said. "And everyone lives in fear of them. Here we do not name them in case they hear and arrive. I don't know if that could really happen or if it is an incorrect belief."

"So you believe that unless you speak their names, they won't follow?" Sokrates asked.

"It has worked so far," Hilfa said.

"Did you tell the kelp-gatherers that right now Jathery is headed off into Chaos?" I interrupted. I was still a little shaken from the threat of violence, conveyed in nothing more than the shift of shoulders and tilting of heads, so abruptly present and even more swiftly dissipated.

Hilfa shook his head slowly. "Aroo doesn't need to know that."

Sokrates frowned. "I'm not in favor of keeping things secret."

"What would happen if Zeus unmade time?" Hilfa asked.

"I don't know, you should ask Ikaros. But as I understand it, everything would cease to exist," Sokrates said. "As Pytheas suggested, perhaps he'd make another, better attempt at imposing order on the universe, or perhaps everything would remain chaotic."

I shuddered.

"What would it feel like?" Hilfa asked.

"I don't know. It would be interesting to find out, don't you think?"

"It makes me feel cold all through to think that could happen at any moment," I said.

"Pytheas did seem to be worried about it, so I suppose it might. But cheer up, Jason." He beamed at me, his whole face crinkling up around his eyes, which almost disappeared in the creases. "We have immortal souls."

"I don't find that thought very comforting in the circumstances," I said. Hilfa nodded emphatically.

"Well, given that we have immortal souls, which we now really know unquestionably that we do, there are only three possibilities. Either we'd forget everything and start fresh, never having known anything else, or we'd go on from where we are with the way souls learn and grow and keep on growing in the new universe. Or of course, this universe could keep on existing and our souls would keep on growing and learning here. Those are all three pretty good choices when you think about it." Sokrates nodded cheerfully to himself.

"But I like this world. I like being me. I like my life," I protested.

"Well, I like my life too, but I expect we'd also like our lives in a new universe," Sokrates said. "And if we do remember in any way, then it would be extremely interesting to compare. Pythagoras remembered being Euphorbus, and a peacock."

"What is a peacock?" Hilfa asked.

"That animal in the mosaic in the palaestra of Palymra," I said. "The one with the big tail."

"It's a bird," Sokrates said. "You don't have them here?"

"No birds on Plato at all," I said.

At that moment Arete came in, and Sokrates got up. "I'll go and see my old friend Crocus," he said. "Joy to you both. See you tomorrow."

"I belong on Plato," Hilfa said as we collected the bowls and stacked them at the back of the room.

"I'm really glad you're staying," I said.

"So now can we form a pod?" he asked, as we walked out of the side room and into the main part of the temple.

"What?" I kept thinking the day couldn't hold any more surprises, and then finding that it could.

"I have fulfilled my purpose and should be free now. I can change my name and take oath and form a pod. Arete said I belonged here, and Marsilia said she'd argue for me to take oath. So we can form a pod now," Hilfa said. The statue of Amphitrite looked as surprised as I felt.

"You do belong here, and you should certainly take oath if that's what you want, and I know that Saeli live in pods, but what does that have to do with me?" I asked.

"The two of us, and Marsilia, that's three, and Thetis, four," he said, waving his free hand. "We need one more to be five. A pod. A family. Maybe Dion? Though he's so much older."

"Marsilia and Thetis—look, Hilfa, this isn't how it works. And humans don't make pods of five. You should make a pod with Saeli, surely. Don't you want children?"

"There are children already," Hilfa said. "Camilla, and little Di. And Alkippe. You could make more. And I could have children."

"Not with humans," I said, sure of myself on that. "You'd need a Saeli pod for that, like I said."

"No. I would need an egg, that's all. Pods are about childraising, not genetics."

"But where would you get an egg?" I asked. "Athene isn't going to give you one in a box."

He laughed his learned laugh and started walking again, out of the temple and into the chill of the street. "No. I would fertilize one in my body, or find one in the sea."

"The sea's not full of Saeli eggs, is it?" I looked out towards the peaceful starlit water as if expecting to see it suddenly swarming with young Saeli.

"Yes, it is. Most Saeli don't want babies most of the time, and so they discharge eggs swimming. Fish eat many of them, but many survive. But don't worry, none will hatch unless brought out and touched with the right . . . I don't know the word. The right touch. By one of my gender."

I thought of all the times I'd seen Saeli swimming, and shuddered at no more than the thought of how cold the water was. "Do people know this? Do the consuls know that the sea is full of Saeli eggs?" I asked.

"I don't know. I expect so. You should ask Aroo, or the Saeli who first settled here. I do not know what they explained." Hilfa shook his head. "But while it would be nice to have a Saeli child, it is not necessary for the pod. If you don't want one, I can help with the human children." He already did.

"I can see you've been thinking about this a lot, but it isn't a human kind of thing," I said.

"Pod formation is difficult, and we have come so far on the road together. I want to form a pod with you. You are my friends. The other Saeli don't like me. You saw that earlier with that pod of kelp-gatherers. They think I am an orphan, that I was an egg somebody of my gender brought out and raised without a pod and then abandoned. It happens occasionally. It is disapproved of, in our culture, though they say there are other Saeli cultures where only those of my gender raise children and there are no pods."

"Well, maybe the crew is something like a pod," I said. This hadn't been what I expected when he'd started to work with me, but I did care about him and I didn't want to trample over hopes he'd clearly been holding close for some time. "I do think of you as being almost like a brother. And if you were to raise an egg, I'd certainly help." I thought of all the times he'd helped get the kids to eat in the mornings, and helped Dion limp along to Samos, our eating hall, even carrying him a few times on icy days. "But that doesn't mean that Thetis and Marsilia are involved. This isn't how it works with humans."

"But you want Thetis and Marsilia wants you." He sounded entirely matter of fact. "I don't understand."

No, he certainly didn't understand! "Marsilia works with us, but this isn't how we organize things," I said. "I do feel as if you're family, Hilfa, and I think from what she said earlier that Marsilia does too, and likely Thee does as well, but even so that doesn't mean we're going to arrange a pod." I suspected that, far from wanting me, Marsilia had come to work on my boat to keep an eye on Hilfa.

"They have marriages with multiple adults in the City of Amazons," Hilfa said. "And they have fishing there too. Thetis could work in a nursery there, but I think Marsilia needs to be here for politics."

"Marsilia definitely needs to be here." We had reached my sleeping house and stopped outside it. "This isn't going to work. Plato's right. Friendship is best."

"But a pod is friendship."

"And Marsilia and Thee are sisters," I said.

"Plato says brothers and sisters can marry if the gods allow it," Hilfa said, looking up. "We could ask Arete. Or Pytheas."

"No," I said, as firmly as I could.

"Pod formation is always difficult," Hilfa said, undeterred. "But we're a good team. We'll work it out."

He walked off down the street towards his own house. It had been a long evening full of strange conversations, but that might have been the strangest of all.

19

MARSILIA

The next morning, Alkippe and I went to Florentia for breakfast, the way we did every day. I put on my best kiton, because there was a Council meeting. The meeting of the previous evening seemed to have happened long ago, because so much had happened since and my priorities had shifted so much. Even counting the extra time I had spent with Hermes collecting Athene's messages, it couldn't be more than a day and a half's worth of hours, but it felt like years. Time was a strange thing even when it didn't have gods messing about with it.

It was a beautiful day, with warm sunlight, though a chilly edge to the wind whispered that summer was over. Dad was sitting at our usual table, eating nut porridge with Arete, Klymene and a couple of Bronzes I didn't know. We made our way across the room, greeting friends and the morning's servers as we helped ourselves to porridge and fruit. Alkippe slid in next to Dad, and I sat opposite them, next to Klymene. Dad introduced the strangers as Akamas, the human, and Slif, the Sael. "We've been up all night at the spaceport," Dad said. "Akamas works the communications there, and Slif has been starting to learn the space-human language."

"How's it going?" I asked.

"Pretty much on track," Klymene said. "I think they believe us, and I think their initial delegation will come down tomorrow morning. They'll be three humans and six Workers. They have much better medical technology than we have—that's something we haven't been able to trade for with the Saeli or the Amarathi."

"Sixty-One is back on duty translating now, and the new shift have taken over," Dad said. "I'm going to go to the meeting and then sleep all afternoon."

"I'll be very very quiet if you're sleeping in the afternoon," Alkippe said. She was holding a spoonful of honey above her porridge bowl and turning it so that it fell in a slow spiral.

"You'll be in the palaestra, so you can be as loud as you like," Dad said.

Alkippe laughed and stirred her porridge. "I'd have to be very loud in the palaestra to wake you at home!"

Dad grinned back at her. "Maybe if you were wrestling and you brought somebody down with a big thud and a loud grunt!"

"Maybe if I was running in armor and ran very fast and really rattled!"

I felt so fond of them both as I listened to them burbling nonsense. This was how meals were supposed to be. A sufficiency of healthy food, and comfortable conversation. "How's the other thing?" I looked at Arete.

"Everything's fine so far. No news expected until tonight," she said. She didn't look worried, and I couldn't ask more in front of the others, but I assumed that meant Grandfather and Jathery had set off all right.

"Well, that seems like good progress with the ship," I said. "It's wonderful to think we're going to meet the space humans. So exciting!"

"I want to meet them too," Alkippe said.

"It seems the space humans may be stranger than we thought," Dad said.

I nodded, thinking of Phila. "I expect they will be different."

"Will they look different, like the Saeli?" Alkippe asked.

"No, they'll look like ordinary humans, probably, but they'll have all kinds of axioms about what's important that are different," I said.

"Yes, that's it," Dad said.

"Have you asked what kind of government they have?"

"Yes, but we didn't understand the answer very well," he said.

"An oligarchy with some democratic features, but not much control," Arete said, as she scraped her bowl.

I tried to imagine that and couldn't.

"I wonder what kind of people they'd send out to explore?" Alkippe asked. "I think it would be a fun job."

"Well, mostly Silvers, I'd think," Klymene said. "Maybe with some Golds in charge, and some Bronzes to run the technical side of the spaceship."

"We don't use Platonic classes at home, but that's approximately how we crew our spaceships," Slif said. "It's the logical way of organizing things."

"But they may have other kinds of people entirely," Dad said.

"What kind?" Akamas asked.

"Tyrants. Timarchs. Oligarchs. Slaves. Remember that word *profits*?" Arete frowned down at her empty bowl.

"Where's Grandma?" Alkippe interrupted.

"Out on the *Excellence*, getting it ready for a trip to Amazonia," Dad said.

Arete stood up. "Where are you going?" Alkippe asked.

"I'm going home to sleep now," Arete said.

"Are you going to fly?" Alkippe asked.

"Yes, I am," she said, smiling down at Alkippe. "I'll be back this evening. I'll see you in Thessaly after dinner."

"Thank you for all your help with English," Slif said.

Arete went off towards the kitchen, carrying her dishes.

"Is the space human language difficult?" I asked Slif.

"No, English is much like Greek in structure, but with odd tenses and conditionals and a very large vocabulary," Slif replied. "It shows signs of being a creole originally, a merger of two or more different languages from the same family. Such often keep the vocabulary of both parent languages with different shades of meaning. Also, it has borrowed a great deal of technical vocabulary from Latin and Greek. The spelling is bizarre. It's fascinating. But it's not elegant."

"It sounds like a kind of clicky buzz to me," Akamas said. "I can see that it has borrowed some words from Greek, but I think they'd have done better to borrow the entire language and be clear. Or why didn't they stick to Latin? English comes from Britannia, originally, apparently, and they spoke Latin there in Tacitus's day. I don't understand this desire people seem to have to be constantly changing things."

They had both finished eating, so they bade us joy and left. They were going to catch up on sleep, and I envied them the opportunity.

"Where's Pytheas?" Alkippe asked as soon as they had gone.

"We don't know. He and Jathery went off together. They'll be back tonight," I said, praying that they would, that Jathery would go back and conceive her, that the world would be safe for her to grow up. "Now eat your porridge, don't play with it." I'm not Thetis. I don't cry easily. But this conversation kept bringing a lump to my throat.

"Who's Jathery?" Alkippe asked.

"He's the one we thought was Hermes," I said.

Dad looked at me sideways. "That wasn't Hermes?"

"No, as it turns out that was Jathery, a Saeli trickster god," I said, as matter-of-factly as I could. A night's sleep had done me good, but it was still an uncomfortable thought, and I didn't want Dad to worry about it. Klymene put her old hand on mine. I looked at her, and she smiled consolingly. I don't know how she knew there was anything wrong.

"I thought he wasn't like the way I thought Hermes would be," Alkippe said, triumphantly.

"Well, that was extremely clever of you," I said. I hadn't guessed at all.

"Where's Thetis?" Dad asked, clearly looking for a way to change the subject. "I was expecting her to come in with you."

"*Finally,*" Alkippe said, bouncing on the bench. "She said *if* you asked to tell you that she'd gone down to the harbor to see Hilfa and collect the books for Ikaros before she goes to the nursery, and she'd see us all here at dinner like always."

"Right," Dad said, suddenly paying a lot of attention to scraping his bowl.

"Last night, Auntie Thee was with Jason and Her- and Jathery. I thought Jason was your friend?" Alkippe asked me.

"I work with Jason and Hilfa, but that's no reason he can't be Thetis's friend too. They did their shake-up year and took their oaths together when they were ephebes," I said. And even if Thetis didn't exist, Jason would never have looked at me. I knew that. There was no sense in the way I kept wanting people who couldn't see me that way. Plato was right as usual: keep sex for the Festival of Hera and stick to friendship the rest of the time. "People have lots of friends, not only one."

"I have lots of friends," Alkippe said. "But I like Camilla best."

"That's because she goes to a different palaestra so you don't see her every day so she feels special," Dad said.

The other children in the hall were all leaving, or getting ready to leave. "Eat up, you don't want to be late," I said. Alkippe took three huge bites of porridge, eating as much as she had in the rest of the meal put together. She leapt to her feet. "Are you sure you've had enough?"

"I'll take a pear," she said, and stuffed one inside her kiton before running off to spend the rest of her day with the other children, learning all the things Plato prescribes for excellence, the things I had recommended to Phila. I took the last pear myself and cleared the dishes. Then Dad and Klymene and I went to Chamber.

I love the way Chamber looks, black and white stripes. It was almost glowing in the morning sunlight.

Diotima was in the chair. I took my place on the bench at the front, next to Aroo and Dad. We wished Aroo joy, and she wished us the same. The room felt quieter than normal, the usual buzzing as people settled in and greeted each other was more muted.

There's a lot of honor involved in being consul, not merely the Roman tradition of the thing, and naming the years, but the fact that it's a planetwide office and directly elected. But what it really amounts to is a lot of chairing meetings. Diotima and I took it in turns to chair meetings of the Council of Worlds, and we were judged on our ability to do that. She was impeccably turned out in a neatly embroidered kiton. Like everyone I'd ever met from Athenia, she was very properly Platonic and utterly unprepared to compromise. But she certainly knew how to run a meeting smoothly.

We began with a report from Klymene, where she explained at more length what I'd heard at breakfast. Aroo followed with a short report.

Diotima recognized Androkles next. He bounded down to the front to face us all. "I call to schedule a debate with the gods, on why we need to lie to the space humans about our origins and our experience of divinity. I don't want to have this argument here and now, I want to call the gods here to make their case."

"Our gods, or all the gods?" Hermia asked. There was a laugh.

"Well, our gods might come," Androkles said. "Though Pytheas too, if he wants to; I heard he was back here last night, and that people saw Hermes in Thessaly. I'd welcome any gods who want to come and explain themselves in Chamber. Look, Athene started all this seventy years ago, an experiment, a whim as Sokrates said at the Last Debate. We're here because of the gods. Zeus moved us to Plato directly. I'm quite prepared to believe there are good arguments for keeping quiet about this to the space humans. In fact, I think there probably are, and I can think of some of them for myself. I've been thinking about this all night. I think this Chamber deserves to hear the arguments and decide for ourselves. I think we'll decide responsibly. I'm only opposed to accepting the word of the gods as—well, as divine writ, without any examination. That's not the spirit in which any of our cities were founded."

"What if Athene came?" Diotima asked.

"Athene most of all," Androkles said. "There's nothing we want more in Sokratea than for Athene to show up and finish arguing the Last Debate."

But he was wrong. His mouth fell open, and everyone turned to see what there was behind us that he could be staring at. Crocus had come late to the meeting. And riding on his back, beaming at everyone, was Sokrates.

An hour later, after the meeting, Sokrates and I walked over to Thessaly to see Ikaros. I hadn't yet learned that when you do anything with Sokrates you have to budget twice as much time as you expect it to take. He kept stopping and reading bits of inscribed debate on paving stones. "Weren't you there for all that?" I asked.

"There are new bits," he said. "I mean look at all this about classification. That must have been after the Last Debate. I wonder who they were talking to—Patroklus, maybe? Glaukon? It's interesting that the Workers approve of classes, here anyway. Hmm. That's not what I'd have said."

"You mean we've been having debates and you missed it?" I teased.

He grinned up at me. "I've skipped over so much! Well, it was two thousand years the first time. This time, only sixty. And then we'll all be catching up with the next thousand years or so once the space humans get down here." He rubbed his hands together eagerly.

"You like it?" I asked.

"I hate missing it, but I love catching up. Think how many new arguments they'll have come up with, how many new thoughts in a thousand years! I can hardly wait. Ikaros will try to synthesize them all into one system, but I want to hear what they are and point out all the holes."

As we got nearer Thessaly, he speeded up a little, then stopped entirely. "Somebody came back and filled it all in," he said. "What I said, what Simmea said. It reads like a proper dialogue."

"Hasn't it always been like that?" It had been like that as long as I could remember.

"No, the only thing written down was what Crocus said, and the other Workers. We humans spoke out loud. Though whoever did it remembers what we said accurately, not like Plato who was making most of it up even when he wasn't making up the whole thing." He tutted.

My uncle Porphyry opened the door of Thessaly. Porphyry lived in the City of Amazons so I didn't see him very often. He was the most mysterious and divine of my uncles, and at the same time the most playful and childlike. When I was a child he had been my favorite uncle. He lived with his mother, and had no children of his own, but he loved to play with his nieces and nephews, and now with the new generation. At family gatherings he was often romping outside with the children, or telling stories to groups of them. As I'd grown up I'd grown shy of him, knowing how powerful he was, and sometimes seeing him do strange things that made me uneasy. In the last few years, seeing Alkippe's delight in him had rekindled my old memories.

He stepped forward and took Sokrates's hands. "Joy to you. I'm Porphyry."

"Pytheas's son by Euridike, and you live in the City of Amazons and Ikaros was your teacher," Sokrates said. I had no idea how he could know all that. "And you're a god and you fetched the new Workers." Which told me that of course Crocus must have told him.

"That's right." Porphyry let go of Sokrates's hands and nodded to me. "Good to see you again, Marsi." Nobody had called me by that short name since I was a child, so it made me feel happy and young to hear it from Porphyry now.

"What happened to the tree?" Sokrates asked accusingly as soon as we'd followed Porphyry through the house and into the garden, where Ikaros was sitting by the herm. It was the kind of day when you wanted to sit outside, knowing winter was close and there wouldn't be many more days when you could.

"Couldn't take the winters," Porphyry said. "It gets cold here. If it wasn't for the vulcanism we wouldn't be able to have vines and olive trees. Citrus can survive, but it takes a lot of looking after. We grow a lot more stone fruit, and apples and pears."

I sat down in the grass. "We've voted to schedule a debate to-morrow morning in which the gods come to Chamber to explain the reasoning behind the plan for lying to the space humans," I said. "Will you come, Porphyry? Dad says it was your plan orig-inally."

Porphyry did the creepy thing he does where he moves his fingers and his eyes go out of focus. I don't know why it should be so creepy, because that's really all it is. Anyone else could twiddle their fingers and stare vacantly at them and it wouldn't bother me at all, but when Porphyry does it I always shiver. I did now, and I noticed Ikaros looking at me. Sokrates was staring at Porphyry's fingers. "Yes, I'll be there," Porphyry said. He sat down beside Ikaros, and Sokrates sat down too, crossing his legs comfortably like a much younger man.

"Will you come too, Ikaros?" I asked.

He looked startled. "I'm not sure I'm qualified."

I sighed and looked him in the eye. "You're a Master, and there-fore a member of Chamber and qualified to attend. There aren't any other Masters still alive, but we didn't feel it necessary to change the rules. And whether or not you're a god is a matter of definition—

and one that doesn't matter because a substantial minority of our population worships you as one."

"I saw the temple," Ikaros said. He shook his head.

"What did you expect when you found a religion and then get bodily taken up into heaven in front of half the city?" Porphyry asked, teasingly.

"I'm surprised it became so popular," Sokrates said. "I'd have thought it was too complicated."

"I worked on it a lot more after the Last Debate, with Klio and other people. We had a great festival in the City of Amazons where everyone came and tried to refute my logic. You'd have loved it. It's what I originally wanted to do in Rome. It was wonderful. But I've been working on the theory again since I've been with Athene and I've changed some things now I know more." Ikaros stopped. "I suppose I should tell them."

"What, walk in with a New Testament?" Porphyry asked.

"I'm not sure how the Ikarians would take that," I said.

"They weren't ever supposed to be Ikarians, or add me to the pantheon," he said. "Things do get complicated."

"Are you a god, then?" Sokrates asked.

"What is a god?" Ikaros threw back instantly. They both sat up and leaned forward eagerly. Sokrates looked like, well, a philosopher. Ikaros was, frankly, gorgeous, more gorgeous than even Jathery pretending to be Hermes, because he was more mature. But there was no question he was a philosopher too, with that avidity in his face, twin to Sokrates's own.

"None of my old definitions will work, unless we allow that you and Porphyry and Athene are some other kind of being, and that there are unchanging unseeking perfect gods that are different," Sokrates said.

"The One," Ikaros said. "And I used the word angels in the New Concordance, for those other kinds of being. But perfection is a dynamic attribute."

"How can it be? The nature of perfection—"

"Perfect things can become more perfect, endlessly."

"Excellence, yes, but perfection implies completeness."

Porphyry and I looked past them and smiled at each other. There was something satisfying to the soul in the way they so immediately became utterly absorbed in the argument. Sokrates caught the smile as Ikaros began to explain the nature of dynamic perfection, which was exactly the kind of abstraction Ikarians and Psycheans love. "Wait," he said. "We're arguing with each other when we have an expert here."

"I'm not an expert," Porphyry said, throwing up his hands.

"But you admit you are a god?"

"Yes . . ." Porphyry admitted, tentatively.

"Then you must know what a god is," Sokrates said, with a brisk nod. "Please enlighten us."

Porphyry shook his head ruefully. "Do you know what a human is because you are one? Or how souls work because you have one? There are many kinds of god, and I don't know everything about it. It makes a huge difference who your parents were, and I'm not sure how. Gods are born with a heroic soul. Some have one or two parents who are divine, others do not."

"What's the difference between a heroic soul and any other kind of soul?" Sokrates asked.

"I don't know, and Father—that is, Apollo—doesn't know either. But there is a difference. We don't know whether other souls evolve into heroic souls or whether they start off different. Apollo says there are always more heroic souls waiting to be born than suitable lives for them. He says all children of gods have a heroic soul."

Alkippe, I thought, at once. I'd been so focused on getting Hermes, or rather Jathery, to go back and ensure she existed, that I hadn't thought about her heroic soul. But certainly she showed that level of excellence.

"But that doesn't necessarily make them gods," Porphyry went on. "Look at my brother Alkibiades. He said he wanted to be an ordinary philosopher king like everyone else, and that's what he is. He has a heroic soul, but he doesn't want to be a god."

"Is he excellent?" Ikaros asked.

Porphyry shrugged. "Yes, of course he is, but not exceptionally more excellent than you'd expect of a human born here and brought up by Pytheas and Simmea and who chose to move to Athenia as an ephebe. He's faster and more beautiful than Neleus, but not a better philosopher."

"Dad hates being used as the exemplary human," I put in. "It always comes up in conversations about this kind of thing."

"He's such a useful example, though," Porphyry said, smiling at me.

"And how about people who aren't children of gods? Do they ever have heroic souls?" Sokrates asked.

Porphyry sighed. "We think so, but sometimes it's hard to tell. Gods like to mate, is what Father says. So if there's somebody with a heroic soul, it can be hard to know for sure who their father is."

Alkippe, I thought, again. How could Jathery deceive me that way? But I wanted her to exist. So since I willed the end, I must will the means, deception and being trapped by Necessity and all.

"So that could be you," Sokrates said to Ikaros.

Ikaros blinked. "They say it about you, and about Plato," he said.

"Me!" Sokrates laughed. "What god would own me as his son? Silenos?"

"Apollo."

"We know what sons of Apollo look like," Sokrates said, gesturing to Porphyry, with his chiselled features and bright blue eyes. Even for a man of sixty he was eye-catching, and like all my uncles he had been beautiful when he was younger. (Dad used to say he stopped being jealous of his brothers after Ma fell in love with him. I definitely shouldn't ever tell them that she might be Kebes's daughter.) "And Plato had a great broad forehead and a bit of a stoop!"

"You're young," I said, realizing it as I looked at Ikaros. "You look younger than you do on the temple frescos."

He ran a hand through his long hair. "I was old and nearly blind. I grew young again on Olympos. I don't know if it was Zeus or Athene or simply the place itself. I haven't seemed to age at all since then. But I've spent a lot of time outside time."

"It's very strange being outside time," I said, without thinking.

"Yes," Ikaros said. "Interesting though."

"Marsilia?" Porphyry asked.

"Jathery took me outside time last night," I said. I didn't want to explain everything to Porphyry until Jathery and Pytheas either came back or didn't. But I knew how to distract him. "Jathery is Alkippe's father. So when you're giving her generation their choice of going to Olympos with you to get powers, you should ask her too."

Porphyry nodded. "All right. That's surprising. I didn't know."

"I didn't know either until yesterday. It was a Festival of Hera. He said he was from Psyche. He looked human."

Porphyry grimaced sympathetically. "Even I didn't realize he was Jathery for a little while, yesterday."

"Would being outside time be enough to make Ikaros young again?" Sokrates asked.

"It would make him his essential self. If that requires being young, then yes," Porphyry said.

"I've wondered if it made me the age I was when I died," Ikaros said. "The age I was when I came to the Republic, that is. As if only the time before counted."

"But you didn't really die," Porphyry said. "If you did, you really are unquestionably a god. But you can't have, you wouldn't have aged or strained your eyes and gone blind. I remember you very well that way, and so it's strange for me when I knew you as almost a father, and when I know you're a grandfather, to see you looking younger than I am."

"No, I didn't really die," Ikaros agreed. "Athene snatched me away an instant before death, and removed the arsenic that was killing me."

"But it didn't take you to your essential age, because then you'd be back to being old again when you came back into time, wouldn't you?" I asked. Was Jathery's essential self that perpetual flicker? He had seemed human more often than Saeli.

"I think Athene fixed it," he said.

"Are you her votary?" Porphyry asked.

"Of course I am," Ikaros said.

"Then she could do that, I think," Porphyry said. "I said I'm not really an expert."

"I can't go outside time on my own," Ikaros said. "That means I'm not a god, or an angel. Gods live in the hypostasis of soul, in what you call 'outside time,' and step in and out of time, or the hypostasis of body, freely."

"My brothers and Arete can't go outside time on their own either. They'll have to die and take up immortal bodies before they can. And I know nothing more about that. Father mentioned it, and he said it happens in the Underworld, and that's all I know about it. I think gods who have two divine parents are born with divine bodies, but they can take up a mortal body later, the way Father did."

"Are the hypostases real, then?" Sokrates asked.

Porphyry shrugged. "What do you mean, real? They're a way of thinking about things that are very hard to put into words."

"Aroo said spaceships go into the second hypostasis and come out again somewhere else and that's how they travel in space. If they do that, could they travel in time too?" I asked.

"Yes," Porphyry said. "They do. Stars are in different times."

"But why don't they return before they left?"

"Necessity prevents it," Porphyry said.

I was going to ask more about Necessity, but Sokrates interrupted. "We have several points in favor of considering that

Ikaros is not a god. What are the points for considering that you are one?"

"I've been working with Athene in a way that isn't like anything I've ever heard or read about a mortal doing," Ikaros said. "And she talks about giving me responsibilities and power. If she did that, I'd definitely be a god. But she says I'd have to die first, put down my mortal body, and I'm reluctant to do that. I think I am perhaps an apprentice angel."

"But you'll come to the meeting tomorrow?" I asked.

"Yes," he said, resignedly.

"Then I should go if I'm to catch the tide," I said. "I'll have to run as it is. I'll see you all here after dinner tonight."

"Have fun fishing," Ikaros said. "And thank you for your questions. We'll spend a happy afternoon thrashing out points of definition."

"Oh really?" Porphyry asked. "Can I come fishing instead?"

"If you really want to and Jason doesn't mind," I said, seeing he was in earnest. "Do you know how to fish?"

"I go out all the time at home. I find it so relaxing, and of course it's doing something really useful too."

"I think exactly the same," I said, pleased. "Come on!"

So we left Ikaros and Sokrates to their argument and ran down to the harbor to meet Jason and Hilfa. "There's much more going on than anyone has told me," Porphyry said, as we ran.

"I can tell you if you want," I said, reluctantly.

"No, I don't want at all. It's delightful being in the dark for once. It's such a nice change." He laughed, panting, then we saved our breath for running. Down below we could see some boats going out already with the tide, but *Phaenarete* was still waiting at the quay when we came up alongside.

20

APOLLO

Once the door closed behind the rest of them, the three of us stood alone in Hilfa's sitting room, looking at each other uncomfortably. Then Arete sighed, and took up the papers and read through them again, silently. "I feel Necessity pressing hard on me," Jathery said. The spell of gla words had no effect on either of us, but I could feel the power gla was putting into them, to make us trust gla. Gla looked all Saeli now, with the greenish skin and the bright lids and the strange knobbly joints that didn't bend the way human joints bend. The patterns on gla skin were not random, as on mortal Saeli, but formed changing letters in an alien alphabet that perhaps Arete could read.

"Don't push me," I said. "I've agreed to let you come with me, for Alkippe as much as for the aegis of Necessity, but that doesn't mean I like you or want anything more to do with you than I have to. And afterwards you've agreed to abide by Father's judgement."

Gla glared at me.

Arete began to read aloud.

When she had finished, I looked at Jathery. "That seems possible," I said.

"This is what Athene and I prepared, for the two of us to go," Jathery said. "How did she do it alone?"

"I've read you all she wrote," Arete said.

"She obviously didn't want us to know that, and did want us to work together," I said.

"Well, we can do that," gla said, scowling. Gla face was much more flexible and human than any normal Saeli face could be. It made me wonder how much time gla had spent around humans, and with Athene.

"I know you can do it. What I'm worried about is you getting back," Arete said, and her voice quavered. She dashed away tears from her eyes and hugged me. "See you tomorrow."

"Tomorrow evening," I said.

Arete nodded. "I'll talk to Porphyry, if necessary. But I hope very much to see you instead."

We stepped out of Hilfa's sitting room and out of time.

I'm not going to tell you the details of Athene's instructions for how to get out from Avernus. She went to a lot of trouble to hide them, and for extremely good reasons. We followed them, and they worked, and we found ourselves . . . out there.

Where time and space are all and one, and self
Is smeared out over every where and when,
And memory, and soul, and stars, and dust,
Future and past and I and now and then

All merge, all melt together, beautiful,
Impersonal, and yet a point of view,
All greatness of the universe at once
Impinging, blossoming, becoming true.

So everything that's ever been and done
Is now, encompassing, and truly whole,
All happening, all past, all that's to come,
Each atom's heart, each world, each grain, each soul.

Each planet spiralling around its sun,
Each quark, and growing leaf, and galaxy,
Each word, and molecule, and falling stone,
And every mortal choice and destiny.

Where I am all, in all, all is in me,
Timeless, entire, all suns, all life, all love,
All words and music one, the endless dance,
Reflecting, knowing, here, below, above.

And art and consciousness reflect, engage,
When spread across all time and space as one
Subjective, glorious, a strange bright joy,
A vaster wonder, and a deeper fun.

Only one soul emerged to being here
To be the point of view the atoms need
To be the consciousness that knows itself,
To be awareness, the essential seed.

Our Father's soul, diffused across the void,
Perceiving all, not knowing what he knew,
In bliss complete, observer and observed,
Knowing, alone: imagined change, and grew.

Out here, where every moment touches now,
Conceived of life, and brought forth other souls,
And shaped the spheres of mind and soul and time
Where we with time could live and set our goals.

Each nebula and every lepton matter
And every soul will choose, and care, and mind

Can heal potentials into what is known
Not simply glorious, but graced and kind.

In time to know ourselves, to change, to learn,
For souls to grow through lives, to gain the scope,
Of consciousness, out here where all is one
Where Zeus invented change, and with it, hope.

Nourished, sustained, by this eternity,
Part of its endless moment's boundless bliss
We live our little lives to stretch our souls,
And conscious, here, make real all that is.

Thus in this no-time, every time in one,
Many in harmony make up one voice,
Where only Father sang, we all sing now:
A miracle of time and free-won choice.

And being here is always, not an end,
There's no before or after, all are here,
And all are elsewhere, with the universe
And nothing's truly lost, so have no fear.

As Time was birthed, Fate and Necessity,
The guardians at the gate, the speed of light,
Emerged to keep both time and space apart
So souls in time could know themselves aright.

I didn't seek for Knowledge, for I knew—
Was knowledge there, as she was Poetry,
And Love, and Guide, and Smith, and Trickster too,
Each full potential of all soul could be.

I couldn't choose or change, there was no time,
Was all time, none, infinity was all,
Until Necessity took hold, and anchored, drawn,
One into three, our coming out a fall.

We landed with a jolt in the Underworld, at the bank of the river Lethe. (It's full of brightly colored fish. I don't understand why nobody ever mentions that. I suppose they must forget all about them.) I looked at Athene. There was nothing to say. Moments before, in the eternal moment, we had been entirely open to each other. I knew now why she hadn't trusted me, and she knew that she could have, that I had learned the lesson that had been one of her many purposes in setting up the Republic. She knew I thought she was irresponsible, and I knew that she thought the gain in knowledge was worth any risk.

It was the same with Jathery. I understood gla now. Gla had wanted Platonism for the Saeli so much that gla had enticed Athene into the whole Republic plan. And all this was part of a wider plan in which gla intended to set them free, which was a goal I did respect. But gla also loved tricks for their own sake, and would rather do something a twisty way than a straight one. Hilfa had been gla idea, and the divided instructions. Meanwhile, Athene had believed that seeking out the different parts of the instructions in different parts of time would help prepare us, if we needed to seek her in Chaos. She had also thought that she was already prepared for it. Both of those were scale errors.

I did not long to be back out there, though I was separated from it. It is always there, and I am too, from the first photon to the last, and there is no difference. I wanted to laugh when I remembered that I had imagined it would be boring.

It's always dark in the Underworld. A grey kind of grass grew here, on the slopes leading down to Lethe's water. A breeze moved.

It felt like being out of doors, though there were no stars, only endless darkness above. Behind us, in the caves, lay Hades's chamber and the Fates, and beyond them the other rivers, the Styx and the Acheron. There were also innumerable mortal souls, waiting, choosing new lives, having their brief glimpse of eternity and then coming out again here, to cross this river and go on, forgetting. They were all around us, visible as shadows. Some of them pressed around us, either votaries of ours or simply drawn to anything here that had color and weight. One clung to my hand, drawn to me by love. It had last been a dolphin, and was going on to be a poet and a translator. From leaping joy in sun-spray and song, to the passing along of poetry, all to my glory, and through me to that wider wonder. I blessed the soul and called it friend, and set it down gently on the edge of the water. I kept my face turned away from the others until my eyes were free of tears.

When anybody visited the Underworld, the souls they met were not those of the recently dead, but those Hades thought it good for them to meet. I was grateful for that soul, as it was grateful to me. I did not visit the Underworld often. The only time I had seen Lethe before was when I had taken up my mortal life.

Jathery was the first to speak. "Are we going to drink?" gla asked. "I don't believe they'd let us out the other way."

"We're in Fate's domain here," I said. Everything had that kind of inevitability it always did when Fate was involved, an inevitability like an underlining echo. It was very hard to resist. "You could perhaps go back and argue Necessity's case, but I think the rest of us must go on, or we overstep."

"We didn't die," Athene said. "But no, it is a kind of death, I see."

"I don't want to forget," Jathery said. "But if I only wet my lips, perhaps I will remember."

"If I forget, then it was all for nothing," Athene said.

"I don't think we'll truly forget," I said. It didn't seem possible that we could. "But it might fade and seem less immediate, be like something learned."

"Part of Him is always there," Jathery said.

"Part of all of us is always there," Athene said.

"But He is conscious of it." Jathery rocked to and fro a little. "Unity and multiplicity, one and everything, below and above. And conscious of every movement from first to last, all the time."

"Don't ask me how Father can be aware of that and carry on a conversation," I said. The idea was daunting. I'd never have understood it without going there.

"It wasn't what we thought," Athene said. "It wasn't the Chaos before and after time. It was the One."

"It was both," Jathery said. "As I have long suspected."

"Pico will be delighted." Athene smiled. "He was there. Everyone was there. Is there. Will be there?"

Not even the aorist sufficed. "It's a Mystery," I said.

"I'm going through," Jathery declared. Gla stepped down into the water. The fish swirled all around him, orange, and gold, and white and gold swirled with blue. Mortal souls clung close to him, then drank and drifted away across the stream and vanished. Gla scooped up some water in gla hand and took the tiniest sip.

"Do you remember?" I asked.

"Quite enough," gla said.

I followed. When I touched the water to my lips and tongue, I did not forget, but as I had suspected, my memory of it softened. It became no less felt or immediate, but more poetic, easier to compass and compare. I was extremely glad to reach the far bank, as glad as the mortal souls around me who were speeding off towards their new beginnings. Ahead I could see a thinning of the darkness.

"What would happen if I went through without drinking?" Athene called from the shadowed bank.

"Fate would catch you," I said.

"Try it and see?" Jathery suggested.

She did. She stepped down imperiously and strode on boldly. Then she slipped partway across, fell under the water, and came up a second later, drenched and spluttering. "Fate had you by the heel," Jathery said, laughing.

"Have you forgotten?" I asked, putting out my arm to help her out.

"I haven't forgotten anything," she said, taking my hand. "Only it all seems distant, like you said, and also very emotional, felt not thought. Is it like that for you?"

"Well it was certainly very emotional," I said, diplomatically. I wondered how much she had really lost.

She released my hand and we all began walking up the slope, away from Lethe. "Thank you," she said, and she didn't mean for the help out of the river. "I'm sorry I didn't trust you and made it so complicated. I thought you'd go to Father and I was afraid of what might happen."

"Florent-Claude sends his love," I said.

"I'll go to Father now and tell him everything."

"Do you want us to come, or would you rather see him alone?" I asked. There was a grey glimmer of true light ahead. We were almost out of the Underworld and close to Olympos.

"I can manage alone, but I'll accept your offer of company," she said.

"And you, Jathery? You can go and sort things out about Alkippe now. You probably have other things to do, too? Eggs to hatch, names to change, Saeli to fool? So we won't see you again for a long time?"

The writing on Jathery's skin shifted and changed, and I was sorry I couldn't make it out, even if it probably now read "Apollo sucks."

"I agreed to abide by Father's judgement," gla said. "As for Alkippe, no."

"No? What do you mean, no?"

Jathery blinked gla multicolored eyelids slowly. "I now feel Necessity forbidding me even more strongly than it compelled me before. Perhaps the existence of that child is the price we have paid."

"No," I protested. "You have to deal with that. It wouldn't be right for Marsilia and Thetis and Alkippe to pay for what we have done. Necessity couldn't require—" But of course it could, it could be that cruel. A bright philosophical child. Would they even remember she had existed? I felt much more sympathetic to Thetis's wailing than I had been when I heard it.

"We can ask Father about that too," Athene said.

We took a few more steps towards the light and then appeared in the meadow on Olympos where I'd last been at the time of the Relocation. The same blue and gold bell-shaped flowers were nodding among the grass, and Father was sitting in the same place, as tall as the mountains but no bigger than a man. We walked towards him through the tall grass. Jathery walked on the other side of Athene. I wondered how Father seemed to gla, whether gla saw Father as Saeli. Father looked at the three of us evenly. He saw us, and so he knew where we had been and why, he knew everything, he had always known, and now it came to his attention. I understood this so much better than I had before.

"I have a song," I said, before anyone else said anything.

Father spread a hand granting permission, to a distant rumble of thunder. Athene and Jathery took their places on the grass, flanking him. I took up my lyre, my true immortal Olympian lyre which never—unlike the mortal ones I'd been making do with for so long—needed tuning. That might not be my favorite thing about being a god, but it's close.

I sang about being out there, much as I have set it down here. I could see Father smile as I sang. Athene seemed to be listening very intently. I wondered again how much she remembered.

"Good boy, Phoebus," he said, when I finished and sat down. "And now you understand why I told you not to go there."

"We are there already," Athene said.

Lightning flashed to and fro among the peaks.

"Why do you keep so much from us?" Jathery asked, gla face expressionless but with anguish in gla voice.

"You have to be ready," Father said. "You have to discover things for yourselves." He looked at me. "Are you planning to sing that? To mortals?"

"I'm going to sing it on Plato," I said. "There are people there who need to hear it, and are ready to understand it. I'm going to sing it to Sokrates and Pico."

"They have a meeting to interrogate the gods, before the human ship lands," he said. "You should go and sing it there. And you two should show up at the meeting too." He waved at Athene and Jathery. "They deserve a chance to engage you in dialectic, after all you've done. And then bring Pico here. It's time."

"Oh Father!"

He hadn't said a word of reproach to her for breaking his edicts and going out there. And since she'd had no way to get back, she'd still be in that eternal moment if Jathery and I hadn't gone after her. Yet she was immediately protesting his commands again.

"It's time," he repeated firmly. "His apprenticeship is over. And when he has his powers, you won't have to worry about who's going to rescue him from Bologna, will you?"

"No, Father." She looked down.

"Have you learned from this?"

"I have learned many lessons, including some about who to trust," she said, looking at Jathery and then at me.

"And you?" he asked Jathery.

"Oh yes, incalculably much," Jathery said, but Father seemed more interested in reading the hieroglyphs writhing over gla skin.

"After the debate on Plato, you will spend a year as servant to Hermes, in payment for stealing his name and form," Father said.

Jathery lowered his bright eyelids over his eyes. "Yes," gla said.

"And Hermes will go in your place to conceive Alkippe. He will always have been her father."

Even as relief washed through me, I wondered what Hermes would think about that particular command from Father.

"Yes," Jathery said, sounding a little relieved.

"And you will spend ten years in service to me, as messenger." As punishment for pretending to carry Father's messages, he would really carry some. Ten years was a hard punishment, but not undeserved.

"Yes," Jathery said again. "It is worth it. Platonism is good for the Saeli. It gives them new thoughts, new chances, a better future. It helps them to be free. And freedom is my greatest gift."

"But Plato is all becoming so much more ordinary," Athene protested. "So few of the Golds are really proper philosophers, whatever they call themselves."

Father smiled to himself.

"We thought you might be angry," I said. "I thought of coming to you, but Athene wrote that she thought you might be angry and even use the Darkness of the Oak. We were afraid. But then as soon as I was there I knew you wouldn't be. We didn't know what it was like, out there."

"You understood," he said. "And when you understand things, I understand them too. It saves me learning it all myself. I'm not likely to throw all this away and start again while you keep learning things for me. The same way you had to learn how to be a human, I have had to learn how to be a god."

"When we learn things?" I asked. Even though learning to be human had been so hard, it was even harder to imagine him learning how to be a god, learning personal time and consequence after beginning out there. "And when we undertake projects towards better understanding?"

"Yes. All of you."

"But some of us please you more than others because we learn more new things? And that's why you always forgive Athene?"

"Yes." Athene was staring straight ahead, but her owl was glaring at Jathery.

"And when I was there—I can't remember properly, I drank from Lethe. But it seemed we were all there. Everyone. All gods of all pantheons, human, alien, everyone. All the souls. Mortals I have mourned," I said. "All singing polyphonic harmonies."

"The music is a metaphor. But you are there. You're all my children." He looked at Jathery, then back at me. "On all my worlds. You are there, were there, will be there. I nurture you with time, as plants in a sheltered garden."

"So that you can understand, instead of knowing without understanding," Athene said. "Comprehension."

"And so excellence can keep on becoming more excellent," I said. "Through choice and art."

"I have been too content with tricks," Jathery muttered. "I understand. I will do better."

"We'll see," Father said. "Now go. Get on with it!"

21

JASON

It was another good haul, on a fine choppy day. The sun was too bright to make for really good fishing conditions, but we found the gloaters running deep off Thunder Point and followed them in the current, pulling them up as fast as we could heave until our tubs were full. Porphyry, for all that he was Dion's age and a god, knew the work and put his back into it. The wind was coming up crossways as we came home, so we had to tack back, under a spectacular purple and gold sunset that meant some peak not too far off must have been pouring out dust and lava. We passed a flatboat scooping up kelp, and several other fishing boats on their way home—*Moderation, West Wind, The Wise Lady*—their sails reflecting the colors of the sky. Then, as I was congratulating myself on another successful day, Hilfa reported we'd sprung a leak. I went to look, and sure enough, water was seeping through between the planks amidships, where the caulking had worn thin. The weight of the full tubs was putting pressure on it. We weren't in any danger, in sight of home and with so many other craft around, but nobody likes to see water coming through the bottom of a boat.

"Well, isn't that always the way?" I said to myself.

"Caulk or bail or dump?" Porphyry asked from behind my shoulder, exactly as I'd have asked Dion if he'd been there and in charge. They were the only options.

"I hate to jettison, especially gloaters, and especially this close to home," I said. "Letting them go to be caught another day is one thing, but these are dead already. And we can't caulk properly, not down there, not without taking her out of the water. She probably needs new planking."

"Bailing it is then," he said, cheerfully, and he and Hilfa settled down to bail while I steered and Marsilia set the sails. I signalled to see if any of the other boats were close enough and with capacity enough to take our excess, but they were all close to full, except the flatboat, which had nowhere to put fish.

I took her in gently, making six tacks instead of two, to put as little pressure on her boards as we could. I really didn't want to use the little solar motor. It was faster, but it put a lot of stress on the planking. I'd glance over from time to time and see that they were holding their own against the water, which they were. It took a while for me to see how crazy it was, a god and an alien squatting in the bilges bailing my boat. Pytheas had said Porphyry had a connection with what's right in place and time, that he'd know when a problem was big enough to go to Zeus, and there he was bailing. It's a strange world we live in.

I brought *Phaenarete* gently in to the quay and tied up. *West Wind* had been hanging back in case we needed assistance, and slid in beside us. Hilfa went off to get the cart, and Dion came back with him as usual. Little Dion was with him today, hopping about all over the cobbles like a wound-up spring. "We want to get the tubs emptied as quickly as possible," I said, because we were still making water.

"Are you coming up to Thessaly after dinner?" Marsilia asked as we were tipping the first tub onto the cart. She was looking decidedly windblown but actually less tired than when we'd set off.

"Yes," I said. "I want to know what happens when they come back. If they come back. I suppose it isn't really my place. But I've seen this much of it and I'd like to see it out."

I turned to heave the next tub onto the hoist. Porphyry was steadying it, and leaned his weight into it at the right moment to swing it forward. Dion and Hilfa were down at the cart. With this many competent people, we'd be done in no time, and I could take her round to the slips and get her out of the water.

"We're a good team," Marsilia said.

"Exactly what I was thinking," I said, but then I blushed, remembering what Hilfa had said the night before.

When I turned to her, Marsilia had the strangest expression on her face. I'm fair skinned, so I always display my embarrassment for everyone to see. I decided I'd better tell her why I was red to the tips of my ears, because the truth was better than what she might be guessing. "Hilfa thinks that because we're a good team we ought to form a pod," I said quietly, as we lowered the next tub. "You and me and Thetis and oh, and him, of course."

"Oh poor Hilfa," Marsilia said at once. "I wonder how long he's been imagining that?"

"I think he thinks we're like family, and we are in a way, a crew."

"But a pod—I suppose that made sense to him. The Saeli way. They do tend to work together. Poor Hilfa." She sighed.

"He had it all worked out, said we could go to the City of Amazons where it's allowed, except that you need to be here for work."

"We wouldn't have to, the law allows pods here. While it says for the benefit of the Saeli, it doesn't say everyone involved has to be Saeli. Marriage is any two people who choose it, and a pod is any five." She grinned at me, then joined Porphyry bringing the last tub across, while I brought up a bucket of water to rinse off the deck. My face had stopped feeling so hot by the time I'd finished that.

Dion and Hilfa rolled the cart off to take the catch over to Supply, where the fish would be gutted and sorted and salted or frozen or, if we were lucky, shared out to be served up straight away.

"Was that an especially good haul, or is the fishing always better here than around Amazonia?" Porphyry asked.

"This is the best time of year," I said. "In a month or so all the big fish will have gone north and we'll be lucky if we're filling two tubs all day."

"Well, that was fun. Thank you for letting me work with you, Jason. Do you need help getting her across to the slips?"

"Marsilia and I can manage if you want to go back, but if you'd like to bail a bit more it would be handy," I said.

"When I go back, everyone will want to argue with me or interrogate me," he said, picking up the bailer again. "I'd much rather spend an hour bailing in the dusk."

"Well it's more my idea of fun too," I said.

Porphyry, the most powerful god on Plato, settled down to bail. Marsilia took the tiller this time, and we sailed neatly across the harbor, the wind with us now and no difficulty except avoiding the boats as they came in and cut across our bows. Once there, a Worker called Barnacle came and helped haul her out.

Barnacle is named after barnacles, the little scale-like things that like to attach themselves to the bottom of boats and have to be scraped off. Dion says the barnacles on Plato are so different from Greek barnacles that we shouldn't give them the same name, because they're flat and symmetrical. But it doesn't matter, because all the Platonic sea creatures we've identified have formal names, which are, for some bizarre reason, all in Latin. Then they have everyday names in Greek which are either descriptive or echo whatever Earth thing they're most like, whether they're exactly like it or not. So if barnacles and kelp on Earth were different from ours, it doesn't matter very much, nobody is likely to confuse them, and if they do we have the long Latin names for disambiguation.

Barnacle fussed over the leak, and said, as I'd suspected, that we'd need some new planking. He promised to get to it right away, and got started hauling her out of the water and into the dry dock.

Workers are really good at that kind of thing. So we left her there and walked all the way back around the harbor, talking on the way about boats and boat repair. It turned out Porphyry worked on a fishing boat called *Daedalos* with two of his nieces. "Why did you call her that?" I asked.

"Well I wanted to name her after Ikaros, but that seemed rather an unfortunate name for a boat," he said. We laughed. "Ikaros is my sister's father. He was family when I was growing up, always in and out, as well as being my teacher."

"Is it strange to see him again?" I asked.

"I knew I would, though I didn't know exactly when. I prefer not knowing too much."

"Jathery says it's uncomfortable being caught by Necessity," Marsilia said.

Porphyry frowned. "No, Necessity's wonderful. Necessity is what keeps everything from happening at the same time. My gifts— well, we take what we're given. I wanted to be able to fly, like Arete." He sounded wistful.

When we came to Samos I invited the others in for dinner, but they said they should go to Florentia and catch up with their family. "Dad will think we've drowned if I don't show up," Marsilia said.

"And that's if Ikaros and Sokrates remember to tell him where we went," Porphyry said.

"Will they show up to eat in Florentia like anyone else?" I asked, trying to picture it.

"Well I suppose they might go to their old halls, but I expect they'll go to Florentia tonight," Porphyry said.

"But they're so recognizable!" I said.

"Yes, true, but they also like debating people. I can't imagine either of them hiding," Porphyry said.

"We should have thought of that and asked them to," Marsilia said. "Oh well, too late now. Unless Dad thought of it."

"Well, they're here. I don't know why, and I don't know whether they mean to stay," Porphyry said. "But you're the one organizing the debate on whether we're right to keep divine secrets."

Marsilia looked surprised. "You're right. It is the same kind of thing. And even though Sokrates was there this morning in Chamber, I was automatically assuming it was better to keep it quiet from everyone else, without examining it at all. Huh. That's terrible of me!"

"You shouldn't be so hard on yourself, Marsi," Porphyry said, and that was the first time I'd ever heard her called by that nickname. "You've thought of it now, and there's plenty of time to examine it."

"I'll see you in Thessaly later," I said.

I ate dinner in Samos with Dion and Hilfa and the kids, like every day. We talked mostly about the boat, and how long Barnacle thought it might be before she'd be seaworthy again. They had almost finished eating by the time I got there, but they stayed at the table nibbling on apples and nuts while I ate my ribber and noodles, to be friendly. Then Hilfa and I set off for Thessaly.

"Do you think they'll have come back?" I asked as we walked up towards the city gate, the same route I'd taken with Thetis the day before.

"Yes."

"Do you think Athene will be there?"

"Yes."

"Are you basing this on logic, or is it only what you think?"

"But Jason, you asked me what I think!" He gave me his real smile, and I noticed his pink markings were standing out distinctly again. "I think They will come back because They are gods, and the world is still here, and there's nothing to be done about it if They do not. And I think Athene will be there because She will come for Ikaros."

Marsilia opened the door to us. "They're here!" she said.

My knees sagged with relief. I hadn't realized how worried I had been until the burden was lifted. "So Alkippe is all right?" I asked.

"Yes," Marsilia said, her face going blank. "Gla said that had been taken care of, so now it's out of the way."

I put my arm around her, as I had supported Thetis in her weeping the day before. I didn't normally do this kind of thing with Marsilia, but it didn't normally seem as if it would be welcome. I never knew two such different sisters. Marsilia leaned into me for a grateful instant, then moved away to intervene in an argument between two of her uncles that was becoming heated.

As I looked around the room, which was only about half as full as the day before, I felt filled with social anxiety. Almost everyone in Thessaly was a god or a close connection of a god, and none of them were people I knew. Thetis was sitting laughing with her mother, she didn't even glance at me. Why was I invited to this party? I accepted a cup of wine from Kallikles, Pytheas's son who was in charge of lightning and electricity. "I recognize you now, you're the fellow who works on the boat with Marsilia," he said.

"Jason," I said. "And this is Hilfa, who works with us too."

Hilfa took his wine, and we escaped through the fountain room into the garden. It was cool out, but not bitingly chilly like the night before. Crocus was looming large in the corner, talking to Pytheas and Sokrates, who was waving his arms about. Over in the other corner, where there was a carved herm, Athene and Ikaros were deeply engaged in conversation with Neleus and a stranger, a beautiful woman with teased-up hair, dressed in a green and black stripy thing. She looked over at us, and I saw she had bright Saeli eyelids, and at once realized who she was.

Gla left the others and came towards us. As gla walked across the garden gla changed with each stride, growing taller, gla hair and clothes and female body fading away. As gla reached us gla had

completely transformed and was entirely Jathery again: huge, naked, greenish-gold, with very distinct dark markings writhing across
gla skin. Hilfa tried to hide behind me.

"Joy to you, Jathery," I said, and tried to think how to follow
this. "I see you've returned safely. And found Athene too."

"I'd like to speak to Hilfa for a moment, if you'll excuse us," gla
said.

"I don't think Hilfa wants to speak to you," I said, though it
was difficult to refuse gla, especially as gla made gla request seem
so reasonable. The best of their gods? I hated to think what the
others must be like. "I think Hilfa's terrified of you. I think all the
Saeli are. How does a god of knowledge come to be so frightening
to gla people?"

"Are you not afraid of Athene?" gla asked, gently.

I looked over at where Athene was standing listening to something Neleus was saying, and found courage in the sight of her, so
like her statues. "A little awed, certainly. I'd be intimidated if she
wanted to speak to me. I'm only a Silver. But I also love her. I would
do the best I could."

"And the Saeli also love me," Jathery asserted. The markings on
gla skin changed and shifted as gla spoke, making new patterns.

"You cheat us," Hilfa said, from behind me, sounding panicked.
"You take all and give nothing. We appease you and pray that you
will pass us by."

Sokrates, who was the only one facing us, noticed what was happening. He excused himself from his conversation and came over
and heard Hilfa's last words as he joined us. "Are you discussing
what makes the Saeli gods different from our gods?" he asked. "I'm
also interested to know the answer."

"It is culture, and patterns of worship," Jathery said, dismissively.
"There are gods on Earth that are more like me than like your gods.
And there are other Saeli pantheons that are perhaps more like
yours. It is style."

"But you're the same kind of being as our gods?" Sokrates persisted.

"Yes."

"And even among aliens that are much stranger than humans and Saeli, like the Amarathi, the gods are all the same kind of being?"

"Yes." Jathery looked around, then resigned glaself to answering Sokrates. "Though the Amarathi evolved as tree-like beings whose language was chemical, they have souls like yours, and their gods are like all gods. We are all children of the One Parent."

"Fascinating," Sokrates said. "And do the Saeli gods take care of their worshippers?"

"Yes," Jathery said, flatly, like Hilfa.

"And you're in charge of wisdom, is that right?" Sokrates asked. I took a cautious step away, drawing Hilfa with me. "What responsibilities do you have?"

"We each have responsibility in certain spheres." I took another step back.

"But I believe they are divided up differently among your pantheon? How did that come to be?" Sokrates looked politely interested. Jathery's face was unreadable.

"We each have five things," Jathery said.

"And is five a significant number among the Saeli?"

"Yes."

"And how is it that you are the only Saeli god to have left the Saeli planet?" Sokrates asked, persistently.

Hilfa and I retreated back into the fountain room. The black and white tiles and shining silver faucets seemed very welcoming. I swallowed all the wine in my cup in one gulp and set it down on the window sill. "Sokrates is wonderful," I said.

"It is only a respite," Hilfa said. His markings had faded to almost nothing and he was rocking a little.

"Jathery is incredibly intimidating even when gla doesn't do anything but stand there, and gla voice is very persuasive. But you said yesterday that gla wasn't too bad. What specifically are you afraid of?" I asked.

"That gla will get me alone and unmake me. Gla is one of my parents, Arete said. I think gla could do that, now that gla and Athene don't need me as an anchor anymore," Hilfa said, looking down so I could not see his eyes but only the turquoise and orange of the lids. "I thought now that my purpose was fulfilled I could be free. But Jathery put power into me, and now I think instead gla will take gla part of me back, to be stronger."

"Kill you?"

"Worse than kill me. I do not want to cease to be me, but I could bear it. I am afraid gla will unbind my soul. Gla and Athene made my soul. Gla could take back what gla put into it." He rocked once and then back, then looked up at me. "Don't leave me alone with gla, Jason. Please."

"No way. But I don't think gods can make souls. I think it was your body Arete was talking about. And she said you're part human too, remember, and belong to Plato. You're a child of gods. You must have a heroic soul." I put my hand on his shoulder.

"Arete did say I belong here," Hilfa said, tentatively, as if testing a proposition.

Marsilia stepped from the main room into the fountain room as he was saying this. "Of course you do, Hilfa. I've been enquiring, and Dad says if you enroll in classes now, you can take oath in the spring."

"I want to take oath right now. Then I'd belong to Plato and not to Jathery. You're consul. You could hear it." There was a note of panic in his tone.

Marsilia shook her head. "It has to be done at the altar before the archons. And it can't be rushed, because you have to be classified, and that takes a lot of thought."

"Pah. I am Silver, like Jason and Dion. I work on the boat."

"But I work on the boat too, and perhaps you should be Gold like me," Marsilia said. "It's not easy or quick, making that decision for anyone. And why are you in a hurry anyway?"

As she asked, Jathery came into the fountain room, with Sokrates in hot pursuit.

"I want to speak to Hilfa, before I answer any more of your enquiries," gla said. Sokrates shrugged and caught my eye, as if to say he had done his best.

"Then speak to him," I said. "He's here."

"We need to speak alone." Again, gla made it seem like such a reasonable request that it was hard to protest.

I went on and protested anyway. "Why? You can have privacy simply by speaking in Saeli. Arete's the only other person here who speaks it and she's in there." I gestured to the main room of the sleeping house, where the sounds of the party could be heard.

"It's a Saeli matter, you wouldn't understand," Jathery said.

"Please explain it to us," Sokrates said, in his usual tone of enthusiastic enquiry.

Hilfa was rocking again. I put a hand on his arm. "I'm Hilfa's friend, and I'm not leaving him unless he wants me to."

Then as Jathery opened gla mouth to respond, Marsilia jumped in. "We're his pod," she said. "Surely there isn't anything you need to say to a Sael without their podmembers. Indeed, by our law any Sael can specifically request the presence of podmembers even when accused of a crime."

Sokrates opened his mouth, clearly dying to ask something about this, but managed for once to keep quiet.

"All podmembers," Jathery said. Gla had his eyes fixed on Marsilia's as if they were children in a staring contest. "You are only three."

"Get Thetis," Marsilia said to me, without looking away from Jathery's gaze.

Sokrates stepped forward and took one of Hilfa's hands. Marsilia took the other. I turned and went into the main room. Everyone there was drinking wine and talking loudly. Thetis was still with her mother, deep in conversation.

"Thee, you have to come," I said.

"What?"

"It's really important. Marsilia sent me." She looked impatient. "Hilfa needs you."

"I'll be back soon," she said to Erinna, who was frowning, and followed me. "What is it?"

"Jathery's trying to bully Hilfa, and Hilfa's afraid gla wants to kill him, or worse, and Marsilia has told him that we're Hilfa's pod," I explained as succinctly as possible as we crossed the crowded room.

"His pod?" she asked, astonished. Then we stepped into the fountain room. "His pod," she confirmed with a brisk nod at the alien god. "Don't you dare think you can do anything to Hilfa without our consent."

"That is still only four," Jathery said.

"I'd be honored to make the fifth," Sokrates said.

"Pods are not a joke, or an arrangement to be hastily put together and hastily abandoned," Jathery said.

"Are they your sphere of patronage?" Sokrates asked, in his best tone of interested enquiry.

Jathery snarled at him. Sokrates was famously good at making gods lose their tempers. Perhaps he had got the better of gla in their debate outside.

"Here in the City, they have to be registered before a magistrate," Marsilia said. "I am such a magistrate. So is my father, and so is Crocus. We also have any number of gods here who would be delighted to give their blessing if that's necessary or useful. We're perfectly serious, and we're not about to yield Hilfa to you."

"I need to speak to him."

Marsilia's face was set. "I think you mean to hurt him. And I won't let you. We're guest-friends, Jathery. You won't hurt me, and I won't let you hurt Hilfa. And I think you owe me this for the help I gave you."

Marsilia took my hand, and I took Thetis's hand in my other hand, so we were all standing there in a line with linked hands, the latrine-fountain closets behind us and Jathery between us and the door to the garden.

"If you want to talk to Hilfa, go ahead," Thetis said.

There was a long moment of silence. "Very well, you are a pod, and I wish you all joy of it," Jathery said. Gla bowed the sideways Saeli head bow, and we all solemnly echoed gla. Then gla spat out a long string of Saeli to Hilfa, who nodded at the end of it but did not reply.

Then Jathery turned to look at Marsilia. "You may be a pod, but Hilfa still belongs to me," gla said.

"Then I'll buy him from you," Marsilia said. She let go of my hand and pulled out a little leather purse and drew out a coin from it. "Here. Is he free now?"

Jathery took the coin and turned it between gla fingers. "Hilfa is," gla said.

"And freedom is one of your attributes," she said.

"You're consul," gla responded.

"Then I will buy from you the freedom of all the Saeli on Plato, and all those who are hatched here or come here and choose to take oath." She drew out another coin and handed it to Jathery.

"Yes," gla said.

Then Marsilia deliberately shook out the purse. As she did, gla vanished on the instant, leaving us staring at the bare tiles where gla had been standing.

"Well, that was odd," Marsilia said, with a quaver in her voice that had been absent the whole time she was standing up to Jathery. She stuffed the empty purse back into the fold of her kiton.

"I find I grow older but I learn nothing," Sokrates said, ruefully.

"You mean being turned into a fly didn't stop you going head to head against gods?" Marsilia asked.

"Oh, that? But the unexamined life isn't worth living, you know. No, I was thinking of the wisdom of entering into marriage once again at my time of life."

22

MARSILIA'S POD

I. *Marsilia*

And there it was, the great achievement of my political career, in haste, in the fountain room of Thessaly. Platonic Saeli didn't need to ransom themselves individually from Jathery anymore. I had freed them all with a coin he had given me.

I don't know how I sounded, but I was frightened inside the whole time. I'd spent all that time with Jathery, thinking gla was Hermes, but seeing gla in gla real form threatening Hilfa was terrifying. If I hadn't spent that time with gla in disguise, and especially if I hadn't known that we were guest-friends, I doubt I'd have been able to stand up to gla. I think it was what gla wanted, though. Gla wasn't pretending. Gla would have liked to take back the power gla put into Hilfa. But gla was also tricking us, tricking me. Gla really wanted the Saeli to be free and equipped with Platonic ideas. Why else had gla given me the purse? It was one of gla riddles, and I think I guessed right.

I was focused on that, and it wasn't until Sokrates used the word marriage that I fully realized what I'd done to my friends.

"Marriage!" Thetis said, pulling her hand away from Jason's. I couldn't look at Jason, so I looked at Hilfa. His expressionless face was soothing.

"A pod isn't exactly a marriage," I said. I was exhausted. The need to save Alkippe and then Hilfa had buoyed me up, and now that I had done it and they were both safe the relief came with a wave of tiredness and a familiar cramping in my belly that meant my bleeding would likely start the next morning.

"It's the Saeli way of forming a family," Jason said, speaking gently and looking at Thetis in that way nobody ever looked at me. "Hilfa was talking about it last night after you left."

"But I—" Thee's expression was comical as she looked from Sokrates to Hilfa to me and then back at Jason, who was standing there, solid and warm and reliable. You could always count on him to have your back.

"This is merely an expression of our intent to form a pod. We haven't gone to a magistrate or asked a god for blessing, only said we could," I said. Jason had taken my hand again, and Hilfa was still clinging to the other. Jason's was warm, and Hilfa's was slightly cold, as was normal for him. "Hilfa's free now whatever we do, and so are the other Saeli. And anyway, nobody is trapped. Pods can be dissolved here. It takes the consent of all members, and the magistrate has to be satisfied by the arrangement for the care of children. Nobody who has been part of a pod dissolution may enter into any form of marriage for a year, including marriage at the Festival of Hera."

Thetis sighed, and I thought she was going to accuse me of knowing too much law and not enough about people, the way she always used to. "It's really only that it's so unexpected," she said. "Jason said Hilfa needed me, and then suddenly that."

"He did need you," I said.

"Yes, I saw. Jathery was so menacing. But a pod!" Thetis took a step backwards on the black and white tiled floor, and almost fell into the drain recess. She caught herself with a hand to the wall, laughing.

"It's a most interesting experiment," Sokrates said. "The practi-

cal details may take a little working out. This is my house. Pytheas said I could have it back. I know Hilfa has a house."

"Maybe it would make more sense if we looked for a house down
near the harbor," Jason said, sounding the way he did on the boat
when he was laying out what needed doing. "And there's also Camilla and little Di. I have a responsibility to them." He looked at
Sokrates. "Their parents were killed at sea five years ago. They were
friends of mine, we grew up together. I think I should ask Camilla
and Di if they would like to live with our new family, or if they'd
prefer to stay where they are in the sleeping houses. Would we get
an allocation if we gave up our places and asked for a house, do
you think, Marsilia?"

"I expect so," I said. "There's not much precedent." This was
moving very fast. I hadn't thought at all about practical arrangements. Indeed, I hadn't thought it through at all. There would be
political repercussions, too—I didn't know whether they'd be good
or bad, but they'd certainly exist. A consul cannot marry without
drawing attention, and this really was a kind of marriage. No
humans had ever formed part of a pod before, so that was sure to
cause comment. I couldn't even hope everyone would be so focused
on the gods and the space humans that they'd take no notice,
because Sokrates was involved. Well, it would never be boring,
having Sokrates in the family. And Alkippe would love having
somebody around to answer all her questions with more questions.
And she'd be delighted to live in the same house as Camilla.

"Does forming a pod with citizens give me the right to stay in
the Republic?" Sokrates asked.

He was looking at me questioningly. "Not inherently, no. But
you have that right. You're already a citizen here," I said, surprised.

"Am I?"

"Everyone who was a citizen at the time of the Last Debate remained a citizen of the Remnant if they wanted to be. Lots of
people left and came back. Admittedly, it hasn't happened with an

original citizen since immediately after the Relocation. I think my grandfather Nikias was one of the last. But it still holds."

"But was I a citizen then? I was not a Master, for I never prayed to Athene to bring me here. The Children took oaths of citizenship and in token of that were given pins designed by Simmea, which I see you still use." I withdrew my hand from Hilfa's and touched the bee on my pin, and saw Jason and Thetis making the same automatic movement towards theirs. The pins were all identical, whatever metal they were cast in. I had forgotten they had been designed by my grandmother. Sokrates's kiton was pinned with a plain iron pin. "I never took that oath, or went through any other form of citizenship. I regarded myself always as an Athenian citizen in exile."

"And that's why you called this house Thessaly," I said. "I've always wondered about that."

"Krito suggested I escape to Thessaly instead of drinking the hemlock," he said, smiling. "If he'd suggested this plan, I'd have had even stronger arguments against. But I'm here now, and from what I'm hearing, things are much improved from when I was here before."

"You're Sokrates," Thetis said, and indeed, that was enough. "Whether or not you're a citizen in your own mind, or legally, nobody would dream of saying you couldn't stay here. You're Sokrates, and this is Plato's Republic!"

"One of them," Sokrates said.

"Do you want citizenship here now?" Jason asked.

"I'd have to examine the question, the implications and obligations, and also the details of your laws," Sokrates said.

"You can take the course with Hilfa," I said. "You'll love it. You can argue as much as you like, and debate every single point." Thetis and Jason were both smiling, probably remembering their classes. "You can both take oath together, if you decide you want to. But Thetis is right. Whether or not you take our citizenship oath, whether or not you're part of a pod, everyone will want you to stay. Think how you were welcomed in Chamber this morning."

"I wish you'd been on the course when I took it," Thetis said.

"Oh, so do I! I think you should take the course all the time," I said, suddenly realizing how wonderful that would be. "I don't mean teach it, though maybe you could, later, if you wanted to, but I think if you stay, you should always be around some of the time when the kids are taking the course. For one thing, there isn't a sixteen-year-old on this planet who wouldn't love being on that course with you to shake things up. But the real reason is that we have a tendency to become—well, Jathery said it yesterday about me. Piously Platonic. We accept it too much as received wisdom and we don't question enough. All of this has made me see that. If you were around the young people they wouldn't get complacent."

"You're asking me to corrupt your youth?" Sokrates asked. "You know I have a conviction for that at home?"

We all laughed. "Yes, you're perfectly qualified, and it's precisely the kind of corruption we need for our youth," I said.

"I have made a committment to join this pod," Sokrates said, smiling. "I'd also like to explore the other cities, and indeed the other worlds. But I'm an old man. Don't count on me being around to help with these things long-term."

He was hale and fit, but definitely an old man. "The space humans were talking about possibilities of medical and technological rejuvenation," I said, remembering what had been said in the morning's meeting.

As I spoke, I looked at Hilfa again, and I realized he hadn't spoken since Jathery left us.

"Are you all right, Hilfa?" I asked.

"Yes," he said, in that flat way he had. The pink marks on his skin were the brightest I'd ever seen them. "I am free. I belong to Plato. And I have helped free all the Saeli here. I am very all right."

"What did gla say to you?" Jason asked.

"It's hard to translate," Hilfa said. "Gla said gla could have reunited me with gla, and that he wished me joy of my folly. And then gla said that Our Parent wants us to learn and experience and comprehend new things."

"What?" Sokrates asked, completely focused on Hilfa now, not a shred of amusement left in his face. "Do you mean to say gla told you what Zeus wants? The purpose of life, spat at you like a curse? Gods! They're not fit to be entrusted with their responsibilities. They're like a bunch of heavily armed toddlers."

"Can that really be the purpose of life?" I asked.

"We can't trust gla," Thetis said, decisively.

"Even if we could trust what gla said, is that for Hilfa alone, all the Saeli, our pod, or for everyone?" Sokrates asked.

"I don't know," Hilfa said. "It is like what many Saeli believe. Plato says excellence is the greatest good, but our culture, the religion we follow, has always put discovery first, science, knowledge."

"This is the religion that's more like philosophy?" Sokrates asked.

"Yes. Other Saeli cultures worship other gods and have other priorities. But those of us who went into space, with Jathery, value discovery. I have heard that the Amarathi prioritize ubiquity and connection over everything else."

"Perhaps it is meant for the Saeli, because gla gave me no hint of that when I was trying to talk to gla outside," Sokrates said. "But how interesting. Learn, experience, comprehend?"

"Pity gla didn't stay around so we could ask gla now whether it's for all of us," Jason said.

"Let's ask Grandfather," I said.

"Or Athene," Sokrates said, thoughtfully.

Jason let go of my hand, and it tingled where he had been holding it. He had hugged me earlier, when he came in. I hadn't meant to trick him into a form of marriage. I knew he was in love with Thetis. But since she was included, I hoped he didn't mind too much. He seemed to be taking it very reasonably, thinking about the details, exactly like you'd expect from a Silver really. Though Sokrates was thinking about details too. We'd work it out.

II. *Thetis*

Everyone looked up as we went out into the garden. The night was growing chilly, though nothing like as cold as the night before. "What have you been up to?" Dad asked, his brow furrowing as his eyes passed over us.

"We have been forming a pod," Hilfa said, all at once like that with no warning.

"What!" Dad could sound so cold and disapproving sometimes. I shrank back, then stopped myself. Never let them think you're inferior.

"Jathery was attempting to attack Hilfa," Sokrates explained. "As pod members, we had the right to witness the interaction. Without that, gla would have done something unreasonable."

"Unreasonable! You probably did exactly what gla wanted," Athene said, rolling her eyes.

"I think so. I freed Hilfa. I freed all the Saeli," Marsilia said to her.

"You've been forming a pod with my daughters and Hilfa?" Dad looked at Sokrates as if he was about to erupt. Ikaros was grinning.

"And Jason," Sokrates said, reproachfully, waving a hand at Jason, who was standing next to me looking embarrassed. I took his hand defiantly. "The number five seems to have some significance to Saeli. I don't know if this is empty numerology, or if it truly has a kind of Pythagorean significance."

"There have been human-Worker marriages," Crocus said, as he and Grandfather came closer to join the group, no doubt attracted by the volume of Dad's expostulation. It was still strange to see Grandfather looking not much older than me. I wasn't used to it.

Dad turned to look at Crocus, took a deep breath and calmed himself. I wish I could do that. I almost never lose my temper, but I'm always bursting out crying whenever I feel something strongly. "This is all very unexpected," he said mildly, then turned back to me. "I don't know what your mother will say."

"Unexpected for us too," I said, which was an understatement. Ma would be fine with it if I were the one to explain it to her. We always understood each other. And she often said we should get married.

"More importantly," Sokrates said, turning to Athene. "Jathery told Hilfa that Zeus wants us to learn, experience and comprehend. Is that something he wants of everyone, or only the Saeli?"

Athene exchanged a glance with Ikaros. "All of us," Athene said. "Saeli, humans, gods, everyone."

"You told us you didn't know what he wanted," Sokrates said to Grandfather, with a tiny hint of accusation in his tone.

"I didn't know when I told you that, long ago, here in this garden. This is something we learned when we spoke to him now, after we came back from being out there."

"Out in Chaos?" I asked.

"It isn't Chaos. Well, it isn't only Chaos," he said.

"That's what Athene has been telling me," Ikaros said. "How marvelous and unexpected. I have to rethink everything. I can't wait to see it."

"You're there," Athene said.

"Everyone is there. Everything," Grandfather said. "I have a song about it. I'll sing it tomorrow in Chamber."

"Do you want to sing before the session?" Marsilia asked. "The way you legendarily did to stop the art wars?"

"Are you chair tomorrow?"

"I am," she said, apprehensively.

"Who's supposed to go first?" Pytheas asked.

"Androkles. Then Porphyry and the others. Then Sokrates," she said.

"I'll sing after Sokrates," Pytheas said.

"All right," she said, biting her lip as if she wasn't at all sure.

"And Athene and I can debate, like at the Last Debate," Sokrates said cheerfully, grinning at Athene, who smiled unrepentantly back. "For now, I only have one more question about what Zeus wants from us. What should we learn, experience, and comprehend?"

"Everything," Athene said.

"Yourself," Pytheas contradicted her at once. She glared at him. "Well, you should know yourself first, and then once you do, you can move on out to everything else," he said.

"Do I take it Zeus didn't specify?" Sokrates asked.

Ikaros laughed, and the owl flew off Athene's arm at the sound and circled silently around the garden before perching back on her shoulder.

"He didn't specify, but he seemed to approve of what Athene has been doing," Pytheas said.

"So should we put knowledge ahead of excellence?" I asked.

"No," both of them said together, and the owl twisted its head around to stare arrogantly into my eyes.

"Excellence must always be our priority," Crocus said.

"Pursuing excellence will lead to everything else," Dad said.

The gods, the owl, and Sokrates nodded in unison.

"I'll sing the song for you tomorrow, and then you'll understand," Grandfather said.

"But that way Jason and Hilfa and I won't hear it," I said. "Or is it a song that only philosophers should hear?"

Grandfather looked at me. "Do you want to know?" he asked.

"Of course I do! How could anyone not want to know what the gods want of us?" I asked.

"She is a philosopher too," Sokrates said, and exactly as it had when he had made this claim the night before, it simultaneously filled me with happiness and confusion. I knew I wasn't really a philosopher, not the way Marsilia was, but I did love wisdom, and I did want to know the answers to questions.

"Everyone in the cities is more of a philosopher than even philosophers are elsewhere," Athene said.

"That's one of the fascinating results of your experiment," Ikaros said. "Did you intend it?"

"Did Plato intend it?" she asked.

"Plato divided people by class because he believed souls really divide up that way," Ikaros said.

"There are some people who are completely incurious, even here," Athene said. "So to that extent he was right."

"But the education here encourages inquiry." Ikaros was grinning.

"I wondered about that, and about Plato's intentions, and I let the Masters decide from the beginning where Plato was ambiguous, about how the Irons and Bronzes should live," Athene said.

"Montaigne suggests—"

"Yes, but nobody had ever really—"

"Abelard, but I suppose that doesn't count. Heloise herself—" Ikaros was completely intent on Athene.

"Kellogg says—" she interrupted.

"Ah yes, but even when there's a wide liberal arts education it's limited, so—"

"Boethius really managed to preserve so much of what was really valuable—"

"And the Dominicans, except that they got—"

"Yes, politics is always the problem. Marcus Aurelius couldn't make Commodus—"

"And Poliziano couldn't make Piero, some people—"

"Well, but Tocqueville—"

The two of them went on, in half-sentences, following each

other's thought, interrupting each other, citing authorities, and the rest of us stood there listening. Even Sokrates stayed quiet. It wasn't like a debate, because they finished each other's thoughts so much that they grasped each other's points before they were even made, and the rest of us couldn't do that. I hadn't heard of half the people they mentioned. It was like listening to a truly brilliant person thinking, except that they were thinking too fast for us to follow and that it was both of them, their minds meshing. You could tell they'd been working together for a long time. It was like warp and weft when a shuttle is flying across the loom as fast as a Worker can send it, the colors dancing through each other and the pattern emerging into clear sight as it changes from threads of color to a length of cloth.

"Like *Love's Labour's Lost*," Athene said.

"And that gets us back to Plato—"

Sokrates laughed at that, and they stopped and became aware that the rest of us were still there. Grandfather was smiling. The rest of us were staring at Athene and Ikaros.

"We were wondering whether it would be possible to have a city where everyone was a philosopher," Ikaros explained.

"But who would fix the latrine fountains?" Crocus asked.

"Maybe the philosophers would do it as their recreation, the way Marsi fishes," Jason suggested.

Marsilia really grinned at him when he used her childhood name. It was lovely to see. I was coming to like this pod idea. If I was going to be married, I was glad it was going to be with a group of people, all of them kind, and that Marsilia would be there.

"Things aren't as divided up as Plato would have them," Sokrates said. "I have learned much wisdom from craftspeople, and heard much windy bombast from supposedly wise men."

"I don't want to be a philosopher king and have to make political decisions I don't know anything about," I said, quickly. "I know I'm an Iron. I love my work. But anyone would want to know what the gods want of us. I might not understand. But I would like to hear it."

Beside me Jason was nodding.

"In Plato's dialogue *Euthyphro*, he puts words into my mouth, as usual," Sokrates said. "And they are more interesting than most such words, though I never said them. I am talking with this man, famous for his piety, and Plato depicts him quite as I remember him, as a bit of an ass. 'Tell me then, oh tell me,' Plato has me say, 'What is the great and splendid work which the gods achieve with the help of our devotions?' What is it, Pytheas, Athene? You say you care, about us, about the world. What are you doing? How can we help you? What is the great and splendid work?"

"We have projects," Grandfather said. "This city was one of Athene's. I'm going to be working on more of them. You can definitely help, all of you. You can learn new things."

"But what is the great work?" Sokrates asked. "What is it for?"

"I'll have to sing it."

"Sing, Far-Shooter," Athene said.

And Grandfather sang, there in the garden of Thessaly, and we listened, and I did understand, as much as anyone human can. And although I wept, I was not the only one.

III. *Jason*

We were out in the garden of Thessaly, where so much of the history of the Republic has been made. A little while after Pytheas had sung. I realized that Marsilia and Thetis were both not-looking at me in the same way. They'd be talking, and looking somewhere, and then one of them would catch sight of me, or glance at me, perfectly normally, and then immediately look away as fast as they could. I'd probably have noticed either one of them doing it, but when it was both of them it wasn't a thing I could overlook. And that got me thinking, as we were out in the garden talking to Neleus and Crocus and the gods. I kept thinking about what Hilfa had said, that I wanted Thetis but Marsilia wanted me. I'd never thought about Marsilia wanting me, or wanting anyone, really, she seemed so self-contained. She had her life in order. She didn't behave as if she wanted me. We were friends, comrades. And she knew how I felt about Thetis; she teased me about it. But the way she wasn't looking at me now, maybe she did want me, maybe like I wanted Thetis, and maybe we should have talked about this before. Well, we weren't gods, we couldn't go back and talk about it any earlier than now, but we could talk about it now. We go on from where we are.

So after I'd worked this out, I waited until there was a suitable pause, and said: "I think our pod should go to Hilfa's house and talk."

Then of course Sokrates wanted to argue with Athene, and Ikaros wanted to come along, and Marsilia said she needed to make plans with Neleus for the debate the next day, and Thetis said she was tired. Only Hilfa agreed with me. But I was persistent, so Neleus agreed to put Alkippe to bed, and Ikaros agreed he could wait until tomorrow, and off the five of us went.

We walked through the gate and saw the starlight glimmering on the sea. The wind was coming up from the west, bringing clouds with it. The temperature was falling. There would be rain by morning.

We came down into the harbor, and turned onto Hilfa's street. It was less than nineteen hours since I'd been there before, but everything had changed. He opened the door and we all went in. Hilfa and Marsilia fetched wine and mixed it. This time we all had matching winecups. We stayed standing, slightly awkwardly, until we all had wine. Then Hilfa and Sokrates took the chairs, and the sisters and I took the bed. They sat together on one end, and I perched on the other end.

"Well," I said, and then started to giggle. It wasn't the wine, it was how solemn everyone's faces were as they turned them to me. Hilfa's was always solemn, of course, but the others weren't. "It seems to me there are a few things we need to talk about," I said. "First, do we really want to form a pod, or were we only saying that to defend Hilfa?"

"I want to form a pod," Hilfa said at once. His markings were clear, and he seemed confident, indeed, the most relaxed of all of us.

"I certainly won't back out now," Sokrates said.

"I won't back out either," I said. "I think this is exciting and fun."

"I definitely don't want to back out," Marsilia said. "But I feel I rushed everybody into it. I should have thought faster about how to respond to Jathery."

"I do feel rushed into it," Thetis said. "But I'm getting used to the idea, and I think I like it. I want to know if it's real or not."

"That's what I'm wondering too," I said. I looked at the women, and saw two pairs of identical velvety brown eyes fixed on mine with completely different expressions. Thee looked worried and Marsilia looked as if she was remembering the bit of Plato that says you shouldn't express your feelings.

"I really like both of you," I said. "I'd be thrilled to be married to either one of you, and both of you is better, because you've developed complementary virtues, and dividing you wouldn't work so well. I'm not sure how pods are supposed to work, and the Saeli have three genders anyway. But I look forward to finding out, and finding out more about all of you. Hilfa's already like a brother, and no family with Sokrates in it could ever be dull."

"Oh, Jason, you know I'm completely helpless before your beauty, but I'm an old man, and I have to live up to the reputation Plato gave me for chastity and moderation," Sokrates said, batting his eyelids coquettishly. "And don't think you can get around me because you called your boat after my mother."

"You had three sons," Marsilia said to him. "If the space human autodoc can make you young again, don't think you can get away with that. And don't say you're helpless before my beauty, because I know I look like a philosopher."

"You look like my friend, your grandmother Simmea. She used to say that the interesting part of her head was on the inside."

Marsilia laughed. "It's true for me too."

"But the inside is very interesting," I said, and Thetis nodded.

Hilfa was looking happy. It's hard to say how I knew, because his face hardly moves, and he doesn't convey his emotions in his expressions. His shoulders and knees seemed looser than normal, his head seemed more firmly seated on his neck, and his pink markings were standing out clear and distinct.

"How are you doing, Hilfa?" I asked.

"I am doing what I am supposed to be doing. Or do you mean how am I feeling? I am feeling safe."

Marsilia took a big sip of her wine, and looked at me over the rim of the cup. "I know how you feel about Thetis. But I've always really liked you."

"My pulse beats faster when I look at Thetis," I said, looking at Thee and feeling it doing exactly that. "I don't know why. It always has. Plato says acting on that kind of feeling is wrong, and I thought it didn't do any harm if I kept it to myself. And you always seemed to have lots of admirers."

"Lots of admirers, yes, and I like to flirt with them, but I'm mostly interested in my babies," she said. "But sooner or later I need to become acquainted with Aphrodite. Look what happened to Hippolytos. And I do like you. I've always liked you. I like talking to you. And I'll like having babies of my own, I think."

I was amazed. "And I like talking to you too," I said. Then I looked at Marsilia, who was biting her lip. "I like talking to you, too, Marsi, and if my pulse doesn't speed up, well, I still feel really warm towards you."

"I like you too. And I have been to the Festivals of Hera, and always enjoyed it," Marsilia said, and I thought she was blushing.

"And I think you're all three almost irresistible," Sokrates said.

"And I think you are all four my podmates, and that makes me very happy," Hilfa said.

If this were a space human kind of story, one of the "classic" works of fiction from their culture they traded us in return for copies of all the things Ficino rescued from the Library of Alexandria, the end would be that I, the virtuous hero, had to choose between the two sisters, who would represent ugly wisdom and beautiful vice. How I chose would determine my fate, whether happy or unhappy. No wonder their culture is so strange and twisted. We think of romantic love as a primarily negative force, one we would do better to resist. They elevate it to being the most significant thing humans do, apart from making money—which, as far as I can make out, is a numeric quantifier of prosperity. I can't understand how anyone reads such twaddle.

If this were a Greek tragedy, I'd be destroyed by my hubris for going against the gods. That's what Sokrates says happened to him in the Last Debate. He's usually laughing when he says it, and he's here to say it, which people destroyed by Nemesis usually are not.

If this were a Platonic dialogue, I'd wander away enlightened or infuriated by a conversation with Sokrates. That happens to me on a regular basis, so perhaps that's what it is.

But no, this is practical Platonism, and real life, where we muddle through and try to pursue excellence while ensuring the latrine fountains work and there's fish in the pot, as we bring up babies to pursue excellence in their turn. I tell all our kids that they're beautiful *and* smart, and they have all kinds of talents. Alkippe may be the only one with a heroic soul, but they're all wonderful. But the Saeli ones grow up too fast.

If this were a Homeric epic, I'd stop right here, because that's the entirety of the story of how Athene was lost and I came to be part of a pod. Like Hilfa, it makes me very happy.

IV. *Hilfa*

Like most Saeli, I have five parents, and four podmates. If both my parents and podmates are a little unusual, that merely makes it better.

I was born to be an anchor, and that is still my function, keeping the craft that is our pod steady and secure where it is supposed to be. Like all Saeli on Plato, I belong to the city to which I have chosen to give my oath, and to the pod I chose, and am otherwise free. I was part of earning this freedom for my people, and I was part of Athene's project of discovering what was before and after time. And I live in the Republic, which was part of Apollo's project to understand that everyone's choices matter. I am small, but sometimes I am a small part of great things.

I took the citizenship course, which was full-time, so Jason had to find somebody else to work on the boat over the winter. Then I took my oath and was classified Silver, as I had hoped and expected.

We live in Thessaly. Camilla and Alkippe came to live with us, but little Dion opted to stay where he was in the sleeping house. He comes to visit us quite often though, and so does big Dion. Big Dion declined the rejuvenation treatments. He said he was used to being old and didn't want to change. Marsilia says a surprising number of people made this choice, but it will be self-correcting over time, and also she thinks some people will change their minds as it gets closer to their last minute. Sokrates took the treatment almost at once.

I brought an egg out of the sea and woke it up. Marsilia and Thetis had babies too, so our pod has another generation. Jason and Marsilia and I go out fishing. Thetis brings up little children.

Sokrates wanders about the City asking everyone questions and encouraging everyone else to do the same thing. Sometimes he wanders further, to other cities, or to space, but he always comes home to the pod and we are all delighted to see him when he does. We all try to learn and understand the universe and ourselves, and to help the gods. It is a good life.

V. *Alkippe*

I don't have a metal yet because I'm only nine years old, but I'll be Gold most likely, though Jason says I shouldn't count on it and coast; philosophy takes hard work with mind and body as well as what's in your soul. I do work hard in school, mostly, although I hate Pindar.

I live in a house in the Original City called Thessaly, and I'm one of the first humans to live in a pod. We used to live around the corner with my grandparents, and we still see them all the time. I have five pod-parents, and I love them all, and also Camilla, my pod-sister, she's a year older than me. We also have new brothers and sisters, Leonidas and Perictione and Simmias. Simmias is Saeli, but the others are too little to be any fun yet. Humans take a long time to learn to talk, but it doesn't make things any easier for Saeli, only different, Hilfa says.

I only met my real father once. It was on Mount Maia, last winter. I was skiing fast downhill. Skiing is a thing we learned from the space humans, and it's amazing fun. People do it on Earth and other planets, but not in Greece because you need snow, which they didn't have there. But we have it here, and so the space humans introduced us to skiing as part of art exchange, and it's the best thing they offered in my opinion. In our pod, Sokrates and Camilla and I all love it.

It was one of those days when it's really cold but the sun is shining. The air felt almost sharp in my lungs, and I felt full of life and energy and enthusiasm. Camilla was ahead, in her red hat and jacket that Thetis had made her, matching the purple ones she had made me. I could see her whipping her way down the trail, and I knew Sokrates was coming along behind. I was racing fast downhill, curving around the rocks that stuck up out of the snow. I thought I'd taken the curve too tight and was going to crash straight into a big greenish rock, which would have been bad. Even with autodocs to put you right again afterwards, you don't want to get all smashed up in the mountains. As I leaned into the turn I prayed to Hermes, and I whizzed past the rock, almost close enough to smell it. Nothing marked the snow stretching clear downhill but Camilla's tracks.

As I straightened up, there was Hermes skiing along right beside me, at precisely the same speed. He was grinning at me. I recognized him immediately. It wasn't like the time when Jathery was imitating him and showed up in Thessaly. This really was Hermes. He skied along beside me for a little while. I didn't know what to say. I knew he was my father, because Pytheas had explained it all to me, and to my mother, who seemed to find it all much more amazing than I did. But knowing somebody is your father is pretty meaningless when you have five parents already and he's a god and a stranger. I smiled back at Hermes, tentatively. And then he was gone, without any conversation or anything.

Sokrates said he saw him, and also that there were three sets of parallel ski tracks when he came down to where Hermes had been. Camilla hadn't seen anything, so she wanted to trudge back up and see the tracks, but we didn't because the sun was going down and we needed to get to the station to catch the train home.

Camilla's real parents died in a sailing accident a long time ago. Jason has told her about them, and so has Dion, who was also their friend and is kind of like a grandfather to Camilla now. We've spent a lot of time examining the question of parents, especially with Sokrates. I may write a dialogue about it when I'm older. There are lots of ways I don't really know what it's like to have a god for a father, or what it means. But I remember how Hermes looked when he grinned at me that day as we were skiing, and that's good enough for now.

VI. *Sokrates*

My dear, I understand why you want me to write an account of my long and fascinating life, but I think you understand too why I am not going to.

Ikaros says excellence, perfection, and other Forms are dynamic. Plato believed they were unchanging and eternal. I think at the moment that it is only by constantly examining everything that we reach a state of knowing what we do not know, which is the beginning of understanding. When we ask questions, we open doors. When we write things down, we fix them in their form. And this is so even when it is the account of an enquiry, even when it is the story of a life. I have heard people quote Aristophanes's jokes as if they were laws—worse, I have seen people take them as guidelines on how to live and love because they found them in Plato. So I will not write for you about my experiences in Athens or in the Just City, or my adventures at Potidaia or in space. I will happily tell you about them if you come to me and ask, but then of course I will have questions for you too. I always do. And since you are divine, you only sometimes want to give me answers.

I will keep on inquiring and examining everything, and I hope you will not be too angry that I refuse your request. You must have known it was likely that I would. I remain, as always, your gadfly.

23

CROCUS

I. *On Long Life*

The first space humans who found us proved to be obsessed with profit, equating it with self-worth and pursuing it even at the expense of excellence. The levels of our mutual incomprehensibility extended far beyond language.

Nevertheless, they sold us autodocs in exchange for star-fuel from the Saeli ship, lanthanides, and finely cut obsidian sheets which the Saeli and Amarathi also prize. These wonderful autodocs allowed aging humans to be restored to their functional peak of thirty-five. Further use allowed them to stay at that peak of physical health until reaching the age of around two hundred, when telomeres run out and death comes fast. Glaukon, one of the Children who was injured by a Worker when trying to escape in the first years of the Republic, was the first to use the autodoc, which enabled him to grow a new leg and walk for the first time in decades.

I do not know, do not remember, if I was the one who injured him. I decided long ago to act as if I were, because I bear the collective guilt even if not the individual guilt—I could have done it, whether or not I did. Such things may be forgiven by the victims, but never by the perpetrators. Nor was it undone even when

Glaukon ran from the autodoc laughing and crying—seventy years of immobility is not so easily erased.

Interactions with other space humans later allowed us to buy first the chemicals the autodocs needed to run and later the technology necessary to produce them ourselves from placental tissue and other human waste.

After our oldest and most frail citizens used it and were restored to health, and after we could produce the chemicals ourselves, all humans got into the habit of using it every fifteen or twenty years or so. Space humans expressed surprise that our humans were, for the most part, uninterested in using the cosmetic features. Some people did switch gender, but we never had fashions in skin or eye color or body shape as they did elsewhere.

Phaedrus, who could heal with his powers, greeted the autodoc with delight, as it could do more than he could and freed him from the burden of perpetually keeping the whole population in health. He devoted himself to his beloved volcanoes instead.

We all agreed that Plato would have approved, as it was precisely the kind of medical intervention he wanted, restoring health without making the patient a prisoner of the body. Our only regret was that we had not had it earlier, so that we could have prolonged the lives of those who died beforehand.

This helped a great deal with my problem of perpetually outliving my friends.

II. *On the Foundation of the City: FAQ*

Q. What is the City of Workers?
A. The City of Workers is the thirteenth Platonic City, founded seventy-three years after the first City, and forty years after the Relocation. It is the only City, whatever they say in Athenia, to run entirely as Plato described things. Workers are better fitted by nature to be just and happy Platonic citizens.

Q. Can non-Workers visit the City of Workers?

A. Certainly. We have many non-Worker visitors, and we try to make their stay pleasant. Because we do not require food ourselves, we need advance warning of visits to ensure supplies for your comfort. Please apply, stating the number and species of all members of your party, the purpose of your visit, and the length of your intended stay. ("Tourism," "Visiting friends" or "To attend a festival/debate/conference" are some typical good purposes for visiting us.) We have two hostels for visitors. The Krotone hostel is for visitors from Plato, and the Sybaris hostel is for off-planet visitors.

Q. Where do those names come from?

A. Continuing the tradition established for eating halls in the original City, they are both named after historical Greek cities. These two were near each other in Italy.

Q. On my planet, robots aren't conscious. How do you know you are, and that you haven't simply been programmed to enact Plato like an animatronic Disneyland?

A. On your planet, you do not extend full citizen rights to Workers—this means you keep them enslaved. Whether or not they are at this moment fully conscious, this is unendurable, and you should emancipate them at once. Aristomache's dialogue *Sokrates* is available for free dissemination both here and on your planet, in all human languages and many non-human ones.

   Additionally, you and especially any Workers in your company should be aware that by landing on Plato they are automatically emancipated and may not be removed from the planet against their will. The same applies to all sapient beings—the air of Plato makes free. No slavery, indenture, debt, or labor contracts that cannot be freely exited are valid on Plato.

   The question of consciousness is a fascinating one. How do you know you're conscious, and that everything you think you know hasn't simply been put into your brain by Jathery in a mischievous moment? How do you know you haven't been programmed to go through your life? Whatever answers you have, the same applies to us.

Q. Can I come to the City of Workers anyway?

A. No. Come after you have emancipated your own Workers.

If you come from a planet with unemancipated Workers and you are part of the struggle to help in their emancipation and you wish to visit us as part of that work, you would be very welcome. Please state this in your application.

Q. But I want to debate with you about consciousness!

A. Regular debates on this subject are held in Psyche, Sokratea, the City of Amazons, and the Original City. Check for upcoming dates and times. Workers from those cities and from the City of Workers participate in these debates, and your honest contribution will be welcome. Please do the required background reading first.

Q. Can non-Workers become citizens of the City of Workers?

A. No. With the exception of Sokrates, who has honorary citizenship status, citizenship of the City of Workers is for Workers only. Humans and/or Saeli who are married to Workers may live permanently in the City as metics.

Q. Can Workers from other Platonic Cities become citizens of the City of Workers?

A. Yes, after passing the Short Qualification Course and taking an oath.

Q. How about dual citizenship with other Platonic cities?

A. Citizens of the Original City, the City of Amazons, Athenia, Ataraxia and the other Saeli cities, Marissa, and Hieronymo, can hold dual citizenship in the City of Workers. Citizens of the other Lucian cities, Psyche, and Sokratea must give up their citizenship to take ours.

Q. Can Workers from off-planet become citizens of the City of Workers?

A. Yes, after passing a Turing Test and a Full Qualification Course, and taking an oath.

Q. Can Workers from off-planet hold dual citizenship?

A. No. Any off-planet Workers must give up their former allegiance when taking oath in any Platonic city.

Q. Can gods visit the City of Workers?

A. Thank you for asking! Any deities polite enough to read this FAQ are welcome. Since we can't keep the others out, we try to make them welcome too.

Q. Tell us about your dating system?

A. We consider ourselves to be a daughter city of the Original City, and continue to count dates from the founding of that city, except when talking about history, when for convenience we use dates in CE. Plato years are four hundred and sixty-one days of nineteen hours each, which makes them very close to the Earth year of three hundred and sixty-five twenty-four-hour days, 8759 to 8760 hours. For convenience, and to keep in step, like all Platonic Cities, we add a day to the Festival of Janus every nineteen years.

Q. How do you celebrate the Festival of Hera?

A. Sexual people always ask that! Plato says such festivals should be held as often as necessary to produce a new generation. We certainly wish to honor Hera as patron of marriage, and Ilythia as patron of birth, and to produce new generations of Workers. So we hold such a festival every twenty-five years, as that seems to be the optimum spacing for generations and also, according to our numerologist Sixty-One, a happy and generative number. Some of us are chosen and allotted partners and spend a day garlanded together in pairs, and then all those chosen help to assemble the new Workers and regard themselves as the parents of that whole generation, exactly as Plato says.

III. *On Wisdom*

A few years after Sokrates came back, though of course I can't tell when it was for her, Athene came to visit me in the City of Workers. It was an evening in early spring. I'd spent the day, and the night before, working on a new colossus, and I was recharging, alone in the station. I recognized Athene at once as she strode towards me out of the shadows. She stood as tall as a Worker, with her castle-crown and spear. Her owl swooped up before her and settled silently on top of the charger, staring at me. When I looked back at Athene she had lost the crown and height and looked instead like Septima, the girl she had been in the original Republic. She looked like an ephebe, slight and grey-eyed, wearing an embroidered kiton fastened with a gold pin which matched the painted gold bee I wore. We were both Golds of the Just City, and in that way, if no other, equals. It was interesting that this was the aspect she chose to show me.

"Joy to you, Sophia," I said. I wasn't afraid, although I knew she could do anything to me, since I was her votary.

"Joy," she echoed. "Who would have imagined that it would have been you who succeed in making Plato's City work?"

"Wasn't this your plan?" I asked.

"Not mine and not Jathery's," she admitted. "Neither of us ever believed it could work properly. Sokrates must have guessed that I thought that, or else Apollo told him."

"I think he guessed," I said.

"Maybe. But the Far-Shooter told him far more than he should." She waved a hand, letting it go. "But you really did make it work, you're really doing it. It's excellent."

"Everyone on Plato is trying to do it their own way," I said.

"But it's easier for us. Sokrates says Plato should have written it for Workers."

"Except he didn't know you existed," she said, smiling.

"Who suggested bringing Workers in the first place?" I asked.

"It was my idea. We wanted plumbing, and we didn't want slaves. I've always been uneasy about slavery."

"Aristomache wrote that in the ancient world they couldn't imagine doing without slaves, because they really had to depend on them to keep up their level of culture. But Plato imagined a way, having all the children brought up in common and selected for their work by merit."

"Plato had a wonderful imagination, and a strong sense of justice. And he tried to make things sound really conservative, Spartan even, while really being wildly revolutionary and progressive. Women, slaves—it was much more comfortable for men in power to believe with Aristotle that they were naturally inferior. It freed them from guilt about how they treated them. But Plato wanted the true aristocracy, rule by those who are objectively the best. His mother Perictione was a Pythagorean philosopher. He was enslaved himself, and he knew other philosophers who were enslaved by the chance of war. He wanted justice. He wanted to make people think about it, which he did. He never intended the *Republic* as a blueprint." The owl flew down and nestled on her lap. She petted it absently.

"Are you sorry you tried to make it real?"

"No, how could I be? I learned so much. And here I am talking in Greek with you on a planet circling a distant sun, in a version of Plato's Republic spontaneously set up by robot philosophers. It's more than a cultural rebirth, it's a whole new civilization for us. Then there's all the additional time I had to spend with my friends, Cicero, Ficino, Pico . . . that is, Ikaros." She sighed. "I saw the statue of him you're making, by the rails. It's beautiful."

"Is that why you came?" I asked. The owl turned its head and looked at me.

"No. I came to tell you I brought the others back."

I had no idea what she meant, and then I realized and was excited. "The other original Workers? The ones you took away after the Last Debate?"

"Yes. I brought them here, now. This is the best place for them, this is where they can become their best selves. So I brought them." The owl flew up and went to the doorway and led them in, and there they all were, my lost friends. I unplugged myself and went to greet them—they could not yet speak aloud, and so they carved their delight and greetings into the walls and floor as I tried to tell them all at once where they were and all that had happened since the Last Debate.

By the time I looked around again for Athene, she had gone.

IV. *On Time and the Gods*

I have myself been moved through in time on two occasions, once when Athene brought me to the Republic, and once when Zeus moved the cities to Plato during the Relocation. I am aware that moving in and out of time and taking others with them is an ability the gods have. Yet I have never really understood how it works, and I never expect it as something that can plausibly happen. It always seems to me contrary to logic, and un-Platonic.

The Workers who came direct from the Last Debate to the City of Workers told me that no experienced time passed for them in between. This leads me to believe that the same may be true for Athene, that she may have brought them to me directly, and that she conversed with me in the City of Workers in a time that was for her before both the Relocation and her sojourn outside in primal time. I could have told her about these things, and if I had she would then have been bound by Necessity, knowing about her own actions. As I did not, as we spoke only about Plato and the *Republic*, she was not.

I am not sure that this is what she did. It is very difficult for us to understand the way the gods relate to time. Porphyry says she could have spent hundreds of years of her own time calming down in between the Last Debate and when she spoke to me in the form of Septima. For me it was a century, and I lived every day of it. She may have come after the Relocation, and after the last time I saw her, on the day the first space humans landed, going back to the Last Debate to collect the Workers and bring them forward. It is a Mystery. Time, for the gods, is fundamentally different from the way it is for the rest of us, and hard to understand.

Pytheas said nobody, god or mortal, can be in the same time twice, but that isn't normally a problem for gods, because they can dice time very finely whan they want to. I asked him whether he could take me to visit Ficino in 1490, and he said he could, but it wouldn't be fair to Ficino to make him promise never to tell me about it, and even less fair for Ficino to have to act as if he believed the Workers were not sentient, while knowing we were. He said he couldn't do anything that would change anything observed by a god or recorded by people. He said the act of observing things fixed them.

Therefore, observe as much as you can. Record it for posterity. Oppose arbitrary intervention by gods with their own agendas. Be careful what gods you trust. Be careful what you pray for. The gods can move in and out of time, but we are much more free to act within time than are the gods. Granting prayers was how Athene bent the rules to set up the Republic. Our prayers should be moderate and considered. Limiting them to thanks and celebration seems wisest on most occasions.

Arete says Posterity isn't so appealing when you know you have its attention.

V. *On My Soul (Part 2)*

Athene, Jathery and Pytheas—or I should say Apollo, now that he is restored to himself—took a voyage into the primal reality that is through a Mystery both what Plotinus called The One, and also unformed Chaos. When they returned, Apollo was swift to assure me that all souls are there, and that there is no distinction between souls. He told me that Worker souls have been human and animals and aliens, and can go on to become those again. He hadn't been sure about this before because he had not spent much time in eras with Workers, but once he was in the place he called "out there" he knew it with divine certainty.

The third thing he did on his return to the Republic after the voyage, after first assuring Arete that he was safe and Marsilia that Alkippe was, was to find me to reassure me about this.

Since then, I have met Workers who had souls I once knew as human. So I know now that I have an immortal soul, that I have been through many lives and will go on to many more.

It shouldn't make much difference, but it does.

24

APOLLO

Sometimes Necessity gives something back.

There was a debate in Chamber. It was a long, but not an especially interesting debate, notable mostly for having more gods present than any previous debate in the City. To nobody's surprise, they agreed to follow the Plan.

As they debated so earnestly about whether it was good to keep knowledge from people, rehearsing the same arguments, I found myself less and less convinced. There were certainly false certainties, and revealed truth did have a tendency to dogmatism. But could it be wrong for people to know that they had souls, to know what was out there? If it was something they couldn't doubt, perhaps. But revelation was part of my province. There were ways of giving oracles that worked. I had promised to try to explain to everyone about equal significance, however hard it was to fit it into the shape of story. Could I find a way to slide it through, a way to make it part of stories? "You must change your life," I said to Rainer in the Louvre in 1905, and he had, bless him. I should try saying that emphatically to more people. Crocus had asked how the truth could hurt philosophers.

I was jolted out of my thoughts by Marsilia asking me something. "I'm going to sing," I said. "I think this whole thing is a Mystery. But

I want to sing about what happened out there. I want you to know."

So I sang it again, to Athene and Jathery and my children and all the assembled Golds of Plato. It was necessary.

Afterwards, we all headed off to the spaceport to see the space human ship land. Arete flew. The rest of us walked through the city to take the train. It was a typical autumn day on Plato, overcast and with a chill wind off the water, but fortunately we were between rainshowers.

Everyone else was dressed for *The School of Athens*. Jathery had picked the right painter but the wrong painting, and came wearing a Renaissance woman's elaborate coiffure, over a Renaissance man's outfit in pale green and black, with huge sleeves, on a human female-shaped body. I understood now why Ikaros had said "she." I caught Ikaros looking at the clothes, a little enviously, I thought. "Do you want to be wearing that?" I asked.

"No. But they are the clothes of the time and place where I grew up. And it would be nice to have the option of looking flamboyant sometimes." He shifted the books he was carrying from one arm to the other.

"Nobody else agrees," I said, looking at the kitons on the crowd around us. There were a handful of people in dark green or burgundy Amarathi waterproof jerkins and trousers, providing the only variation.

"Well, really I do agree with Plato about all of that. Only—" He looked at Jathery again. "It looks good, and it's good to look at. Men's clothes on a women's body."

"Most of the people here have never seen gendered clothes," I said. "They wouldn't realize it was odd. I wonder if Jathery does?"

"Oh, they might have seen them in paintings, if they were paying attention. And I'm sure Jathery knows exactly what she's doing," Ikaros said.

Some things fit together with that pronoun, so I dropped back to speak to Athene as we came into the station. "Did Ikaros—I mean, is Ikaros Hilfa's human parent?"

"Yes," she said, as we got onto the train. "It was voluntary, except that he didn't know."

"Didn't know about Hilfa, or didn't know what Jathery was?"

"He didn't know either of those things." We sat down together on a double seat.

"There's more than one kind of rape," I said, quietly.

"You would know about that," she said.

"That's unfair. I've been working on equal significance and volition for a long time now. I think I understand something about them."

"I know all about the theory," she said. She was looking at Ikaros, who was talking to Porphyry but still casting glances at Jathery. "I'm going to lose him. Father will give him powers, and he'll make a good Olympian. We'll work together sometimes, I know, but it won't be the same."

"If he'd stayed human he would have died and you'd have lost him that way," I said, thinking of Simmea, and Hyakinthos, and other friends. "Children grow up. You have to let them go. Lovers—" I thought about her, as Septima, saying that there was a perfectly good bit of Catullus and corrected myself. "People you love, it's the same. At least you'll see him sometimes and be able to talk to him."

"I didn't meet you in the Laurentian Library," she said.

"I was there." I had thought I'd stopped being angry with her. The train sped through the tunnel with nothing to see through the window but walls of dark green rock. "When you arranged to meet me, I thought you were making a friendly offer, but you were only taking steps for setting up your rescue scheme. I didn't want to believe that, but I know it's true. You used me. You used Ikaros. You used all of us, and risked the whole of history so that you could learn something, as if that's more important than anything and everything else. I know Father wants new understanding, and so he always forgives you, but that means there are things about consequences you never learn. You could learn something new and real about equal significance if you'd think about how unfair and unjust you've been to other people all the way through this project. You claim we intervene because we're concerned, or because we have an inexplicable purpose, and yes, it's mostly true, but we do need to have some thought for the people we're using. I know I've been as bad about this as anyone in the past, worse maybe. But I have learned this, and you need to."

"I'm sorry I didn't meet you in the Laurentian Library," she said. "I'm sorry I didn't trust you about Sokrates. The rest of it is none of your business. But I'll think about what you've said."

The train burst out of the tunnel into the light. The sun came out (my race car) as the train slowed down for the little spaceport station. Athene smiled, pulled herself lightly to her feet and went over to Ikaros, who was talking to Sokrates now. I followed.

"Do you still think this is a Just City?" Sokrates asked Athene.

"Ask them," Athene said, waving at the people making their way out of the car. "Go into the streets and ask the Irons and Bronzes. Go to Sokratea or Marissa or Psyche. And then go to your own Athens, to Athens in any year you like from its foundations until now, and ask the same thing of the people who do that work."

"It's not perfectly just," I said. "But nothing is. And we're trying. Even having justice and excellence as unattainable goals makes things better."

Sokrates stayed at my side as we got off the train. "Are you going to stay here?"

He was one of the few people entitled to an answer to that. "To see the space humans land? Yes. After that, I'm not sure. I'll be around, keeping an eye on things, but I have places to be and work to do and things to learn. I've learned so much from this. There are new projects I want to initiate now." It was an exciting thought.

"And Athene will go back to Olympos?" We started walking, following the crowd.

"I expect so. But she'll probably be around from time to time as well. I can ask her if you like."

"And Jathery?" Sokrates asked.

"Jathery is going to spend time in service to Hermes and to Father. I'll definitely stay around as long as Jathery does, or if gla comes back. I'll keep a close eye on everything gla does here," I said. "I'd have protected Hilfa last night if he'd said something to me instead of hiding in the bathroom. I'm fairly sure Athene would have taken his side too."

Sokrates ran his fingers through his hair, which already looked like a lamb that had pushed through a thorn hedge. "What do I do if Jathery causes a problem we can't deal with and you aren't there?"

"Pray to me," I said. "I'll hear a prayer from you and come to that instant. But I don't think Jathery will be a problem. Gla knows that I know about gla now, and this is *my* planet. I think with freeing the Saeli and setting up the pod, gla probably has what gla wants."

"This pod will be very interesting, all these young people. An entirely new experience. Zeus should be happy!"

I laughed. I loved Sokrates so much. He could always surprise me. "I'm glad you're pleased."

"I liked the way Marsilia dealt with the problem. She's really smart, and decisive, but also very down-to-earth and political. She doesn't have Simmea's talent for thinking things through."

"No," I agreed. "Thetis has some of Simmea's social abilities. She's wonderful at setting people at ease. But she also gets easily upset, you saw her wailing the other night."

"Yes," he said. I caught sight of Thetis, Jason and Hilfa, who were standing together, all holding hands, pressed against the glass of the big lounge where you can watch the shuttles land. "Crocus told me Simmea was killed in an art raid."

"I have missed her every day since," I said. Marsilia and Diotima, with Arete and Crocus, were getting ready to go out and greet the space humans. "She wouldn't let me save her. I was going to kill myself so I could come back in my proper form and heal her, but she told me not to be an idiot and pulled the arrow out."

"She must have wanted you to learn about grief while you could," he said.

"I wish you'd been here, because it took me months and Ficino's death in battle to figure that out."

"Ficino died in battle?" Sokrates looked surprised. "I didn't know he could fight! How old was he?"

"He was ninety-nine, and he couldn't fight, as it happens. But he put himself between Arete and a blade. So I started asking what Simmea would value that much."

"We talked about how important it was to help you increase your excellence only a few days ago—that is, only a few days before the Last Debate," he said.

"I know. She wrote about that, and I read it after she was dead."

The first blaze of light that was the shuttle appeared high up, and people started pointing to it in excitement. "But what you said last night was true. Other people shouldn't have to die so I can learn things. They also matter."

"It was her choice," Sokrates said.

"I stayed incarnate for forty more years to honor that choice."

He nodded, understanding the significance of that. "But now are you glad to be a god again?"

"Oh yes. Very much. It's wonderful. No aches and pains, a lyre that stays tuned, the ability to go anywhere I want to, detachment, power—everything I've been missing." I could hear the roar of the shuttle now, through the special glass of the window.

"Yet you keep wearing your Gold pin?"

I touched it for an instant as he mentioned it. "I hadn't thought about it."

"Athene is wearing one right now, in her Septima form as she came to the debate, but she wasn't before. You've had yours on the entire time, even when we were wearing those absurd costumes in Cirey. It was pinning the fall of lace at your throat."

I'd had it on on Olympos, and out there, and in the Underworld, and when I'd been watching sun formation. "I like it," I said. "Simmea designed it. And it stands for excellence and philosophy."

"So you don't miss being a mortal?" he asked. The shuttle touched down in a thunderous roar that seemed to shake the building, a designed pattern of sound that was almost music. Lots of the spectators cheered.

"No," I said, when it was quiet enough to speak again. The last time I'd had to wait for silence to speak it had been the bells in Bologna. A shuttle landing was better. "It was a wonderful experience, and a terrible one. It was a significant event. It changed me. I did it for very mixed reasons, some of them much better than others. I'm really glad I experienced it. I learned all kinds of things from it I could have learned in no other way. But I don't miss it."

The shuttle, on the ground now, was rolling slowly towards us. Marsilia, Diotima, Klymene and Arete climbed up onto Crocus's back, holding on to the webbing, and he rolled out.

"What do you think the space humans will be like?" Sokrates asked.

"Very very different. Maybe more different than the Saeli, harder to adjust to. They come from a future that has had marvelous things in it, but also awful things. We'll have a lot to learn from each other, as cultures, a lot of things to give in both directions. It'll be interesting. I wonder who these first people will be? A scientific party? Traders? Military? All we know so far is three humans and three Workers."

"Crocus told me Workers first explored the solar system. Before humans."

"Yes, that's true. I told him that." I smiled. "He was so proud."

The shuttle drew to a halt and the door slid open. Crocus, with the others on his back, came closer.

"Whoever they are and whatever their culture, it's going to be fascinating to see it interact with Plato. Athene will probably be interested too." A flight of steps swung out from the ship, meeting the ground.

"I wish you Olympians would all agree not to interfere, to watch if you want to, and certainly protect us from Jathery and other dangerous gods, but let us get on with things and make our own decisions." Crocus stopped at the foot of the stairs, and the others jumped down and took up waiting positions.

"I could agree to that," I said, though I felt a little hurt. Why did nobody trust me? "We could ask Athene if you like. But I've been thinking—this experiment has had wonderful results. I want to work on doing more of this kind of thing, making more opportunities for places where people can be philosophical and artistic and pursue excellence."

A young man appeared in the doorway of the shuttle, and began to come down, followed by two young women. They were all dark-skinned and wearing white overalls. The man had implausibly violet eyes, and one of the women had a blue bindi on her forehead. Everyone started murmuring about his eyes and their clothes.

"You need to be more responsible with your power," Sokrates said.

"Me? What have I done? I've been trying to be responsible."

"All of you."

The three humans came down to the ground, and started bowing and taking the hands of our people. Sokrates was saying something to me, but I stopped listening as the first of their Workers came out. It was much smaller than our Workers, about half the size, and beige not yellow, and the treads were different, but none of those things were what caught my attention. As it trundled into the light, the Worker sent out a prayer to me, to my sun, to the light, a prayer of hope for recognition and freedom.

Soul is not personality, but souls are recognizable, whatever bodies they happen to be incarnated in. I had recognized Sokrates as a fly in the Jurassic, as he had immediately recognized me in my mortal form. Rolling carefully down the steps, owned by space humans who didn't believe their Workers were sentient, came a Worker with the unmistakable soul of Simmea.

And that's the end. That's not, obviously, the last thing that happened, but nothing ever is, life has no end, things always keep on happening, unless the protagonist dies—and I am immortal. My mortal death was no kind of conclusion. But that moment, as I stood with Sokrates looking out over the landing field, is where I want to stop this story. I've told you now what I think it best for you to know, so you can learn and benefit from it. It may not be a story of good people doing good things, but all the same I think Plato would approve my didactic purpose here. The overwhelming presumption is that you who read this are human, and that among the confused goals of your mortal life you want to be the best self you can. Know yourself. Bear in mind that others have equal significance.

I ended the first volume with a moral, and the second with a *deus ex machina*. This third and final volume ends with hope, always the last thing to come out of any box.

THANKS

In the cyberpunk books of the eighties, people were fitted with brain/computer interfaces, which seems like a wonderful idea until operating systems are upgraded to the point where your interface won't. Just like them, I've been writing in Protext since 1987, and for the last decade I've been feeling like a Jack Womack character. My overwhelming thanks to Lindsey Nilsen, who has now made Protext work in DOSBOX for Linux, ensuring that I can keep writing even as the last DOS computers become one with the dodo. I no longer have to resign myself to descent into oblivion and darkness, or at least not so soon. This book, like everything I write, was written entirely in Protext, which remains the best word processor in the world. And now it runs on netbooks running Ubuntu, which makes me so much more flexible. Thank you, Lindsey.

This is unquestionably the most difficult book I've ever written. Time travel seems like such a useful thing until you have to confront the implications close-up. (Just say no to time travel. You think it will solve your problems, but in the end you have all the same problems, just much more tangled up with time.) I owe huge thanks to the late John M. Ford, whose GURPS *Time Travel* started me thinking about it in interesting ways, and whose personal conversation on the subject was invaluable. There were so many times when I really wanted to email him when writing *Necessity* but he has gone where email doesn't reach. Death sucks. Read his books.

Ada Palmer was the person I could still pester with my queries and hesitations. She was unfailingly helpful, thought-provoking and wonderful throughout the process, and I am deeply grateful. This series wouldn't exist without her. She was with me at the solar telescope in the Lowell Observatory in Flagstaff, and in Bologna. Read her books and listen to her music.

While tearing my hair out over this book I also had useful conversations with Evelyn Walling, Emmet O'Brien, Ruthanna and Sarah Emrys, Mary Lace, and Alison Sinclair. Emmet also put up with me while I was writing, which isn't always easy. My son, Sasha Walton, insisted on dinosaurs and alien gods.

Lauren Schiller read the second draft overnight, which was both useful and reassuring. And she, Ada, Mack Muldofsky, Jon Singer and Jim Hannon put up with me while I was writing and travelling at the same time. I have the best friends.

After it was written it was read by Elaine Blank, Pamela Dean, Ruthanna and Sarah Emrys, Eric Forste, Steven Halter, Mary Lace, Marissa Lingen, Lydy Nickerson, Emmet O'Brien, Ada Palmer, Doug Palmer, Lauren Schiller, Sherwood Smith, and Sharla Stremski, for all of whose timely comments I am very grateful. Marissa Lingen and Emmet O'Brien also provided invaluable help with science.

The beautiful teahouse Camellia Sinensis of Montreal gave me a free sample of magic writing tea when I mentioned that was what I needed to get unstuck, and it really worked. Never underestimate the power of tea, or placebos either.

"You must change your life" is a quotation from Rainer Maria Rilke's "Archaïscher Torso Apollos," 1908.

My thanks as always, but never pro forma, to Patrick Nielsen Hayden, Teresa Nielsen Hayden, Alexis Saarela, Jamie Stafford-Hill, and everyone at Tor.